MARAZANO & LUO YIN

The Dream of the Butterfly

1

Rabbits on the Moon

CUB
HOUSE

Thank you to Studio 9.

Luo Yin

To Thomas Ragon for his encouragement,
always sincere and rewarding.
To Yin for her commitment and kindness from
the other side of the world.

For Rachel, my stubborn little girl
and all the other little girls who are right
to not always listen to their elders...

Richard Marazano

CUB HOUSE

Dream of the Butterfly, published 2017 by The Lion Forge, LLC. First published in France under the Original titles: Le Rêve du Papillon 1 - Lapins sur la Lune
© DARGAUD 2010, by Marazano, Luo, Le Rêve du Papillon 2 - Stupides ! Stupides espions ! © DARGAUD 2011, by Marazano, Luo, www.dargaud.com

ISBN: 978-1-941302-39-2

Library of Congress Control Number: 2017952231

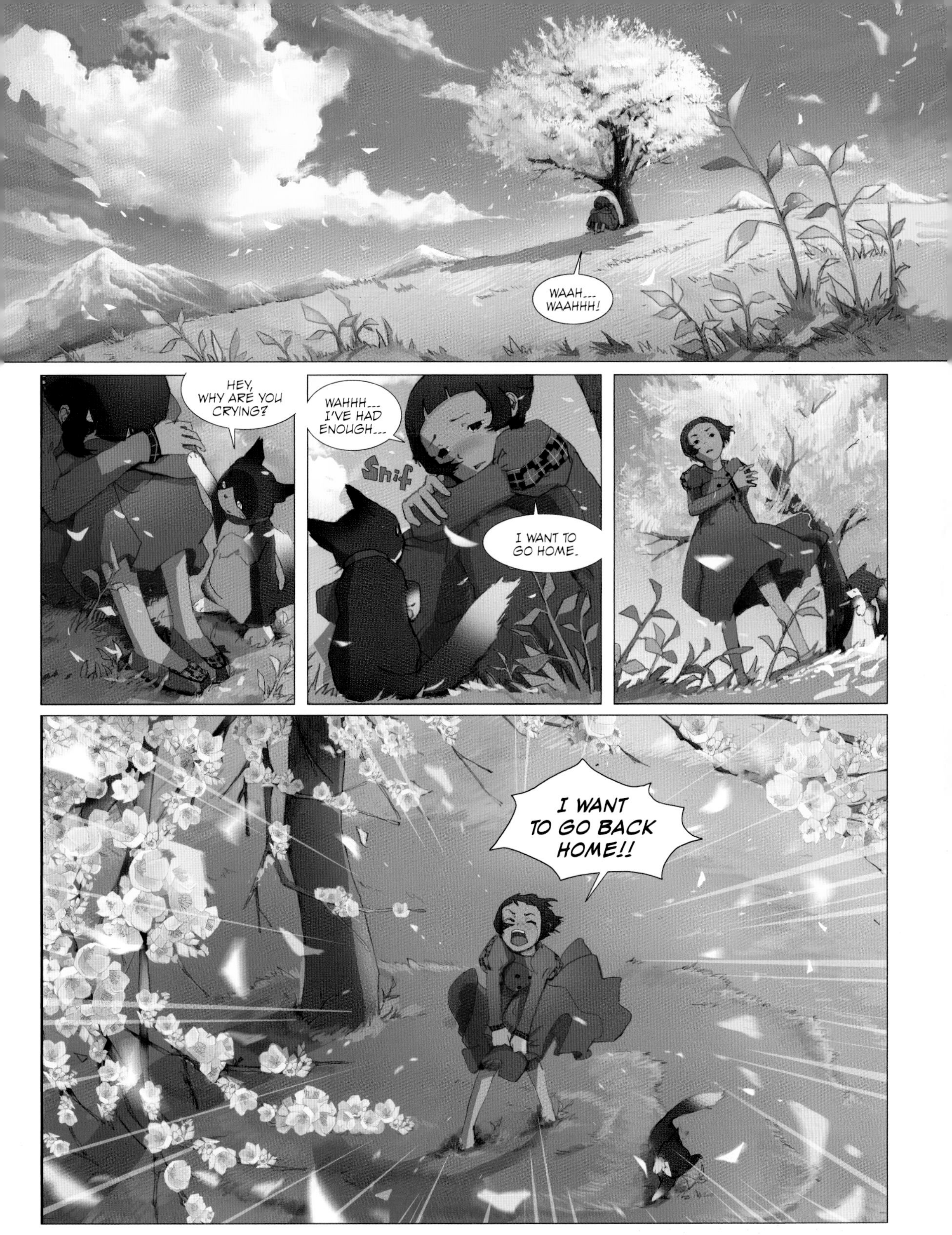
WAAH...
WAAHHH!
HEY, WHY ARE YOU CRYING?
WAHHH... I'VE HAD ENOUGH...
Snif
I WANT TO GO HOME.
I WANT TO GO BACK HOME!!

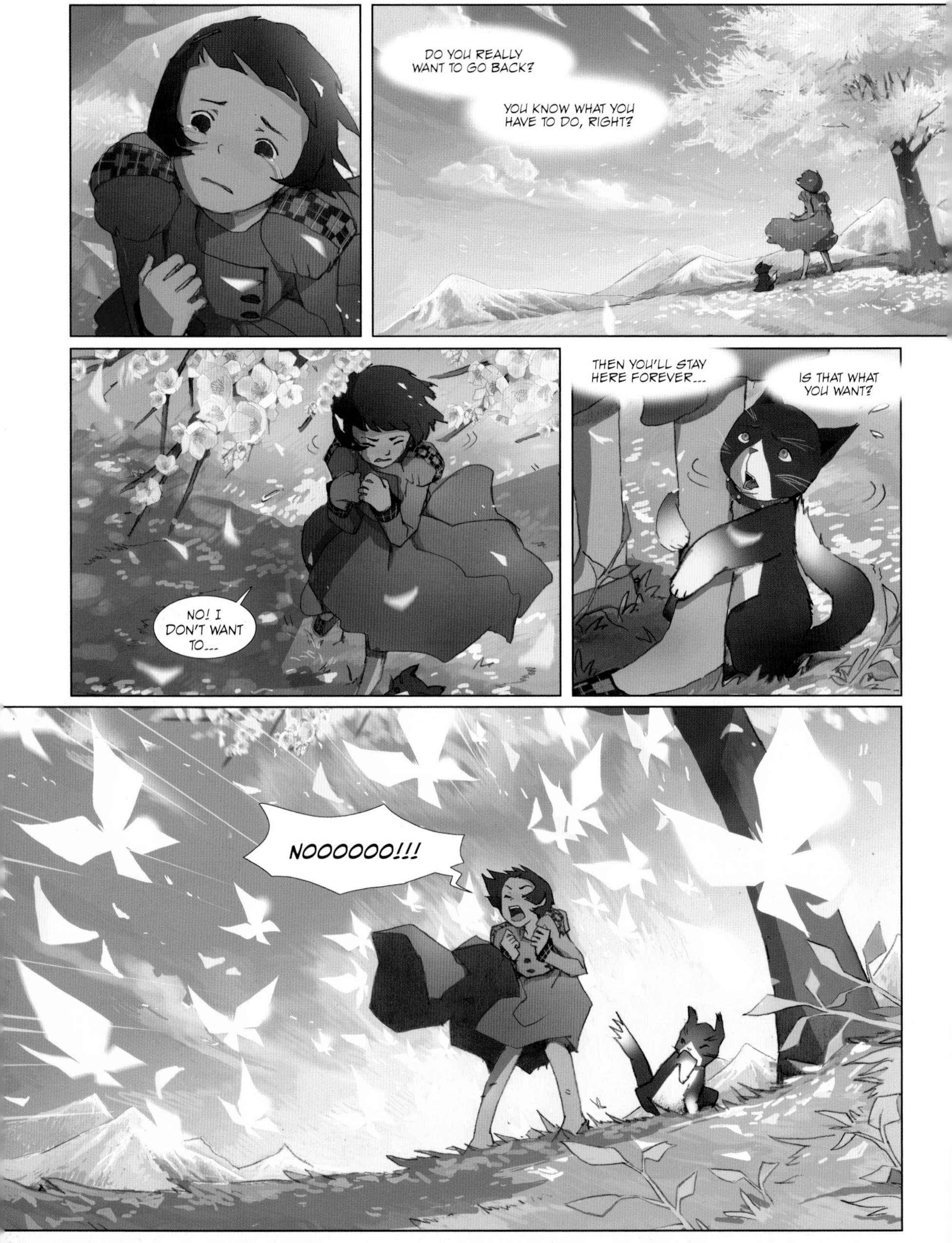
DO YOU REALLY WANT TO GO BACK?
YOU KNOW WHAT YOU HAVE TO DO, RIGHT?
NO! I DON'T WANT TO...
THEN YOU'LL STAY HERE FOREVER...
IS THAT WHAT YOU WANT?
NOOOOOO!!!

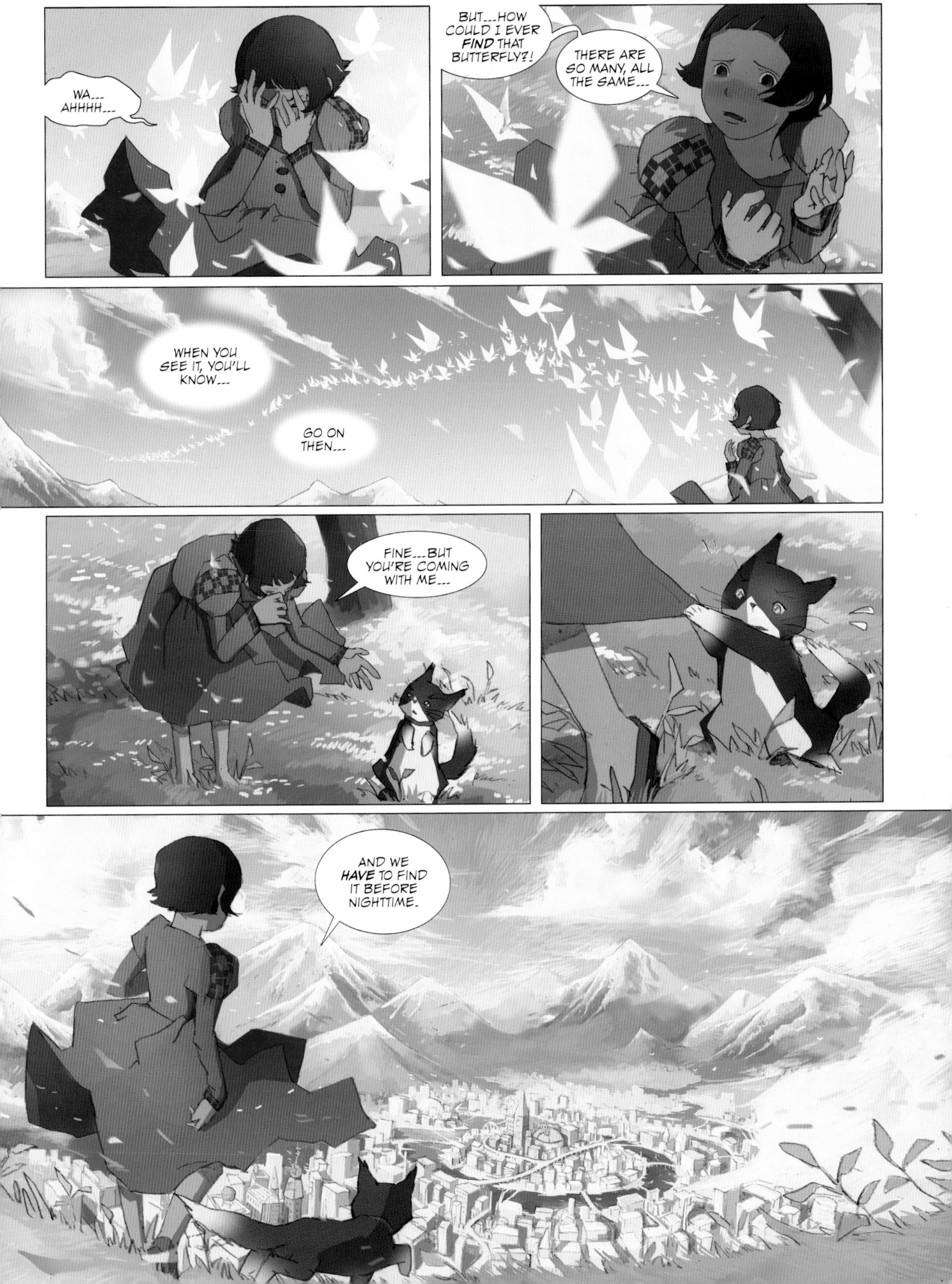
WA... AHHHH...
BUT... HOW COULD I EVER **FIND** THAT BUTTERFLY?!
THERE ARE SO MANY, ALL THE SAME...
WHEN YOU SEE IT, YOU'LL KNOW...
GO ON THEN...
FINE... BUT YOU'RE COMING WITH ME...
AND WE **HAVE** TO FIND IT BEFORE NIGHTTIME.

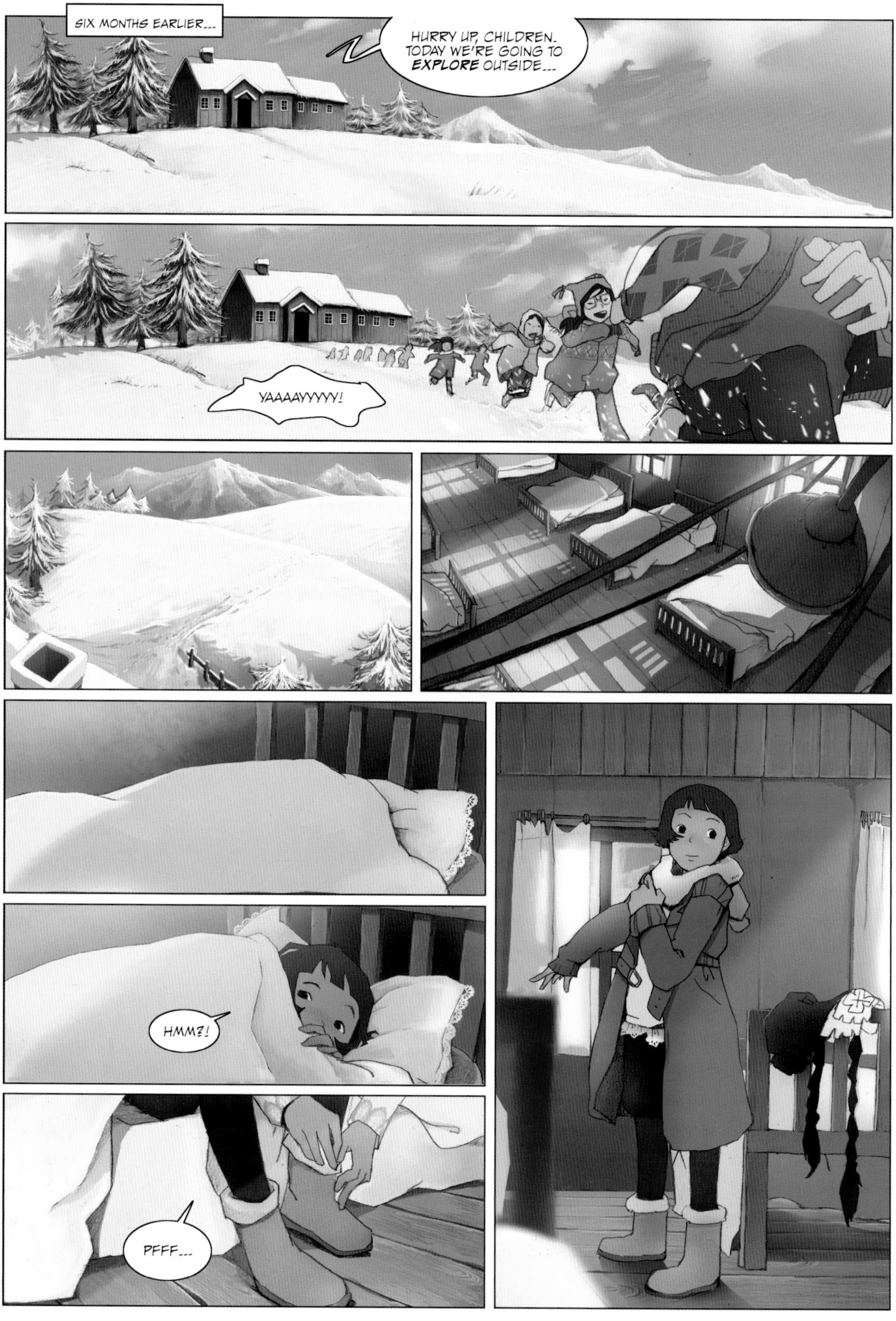
SIX MONTHS EARLIER...
HURRY UP, CHILDREN. TODAY WE'RE GOING TO EXPLORE OUTSIDE...
YAAAAYYYYY!
HMM?!
PFFF...

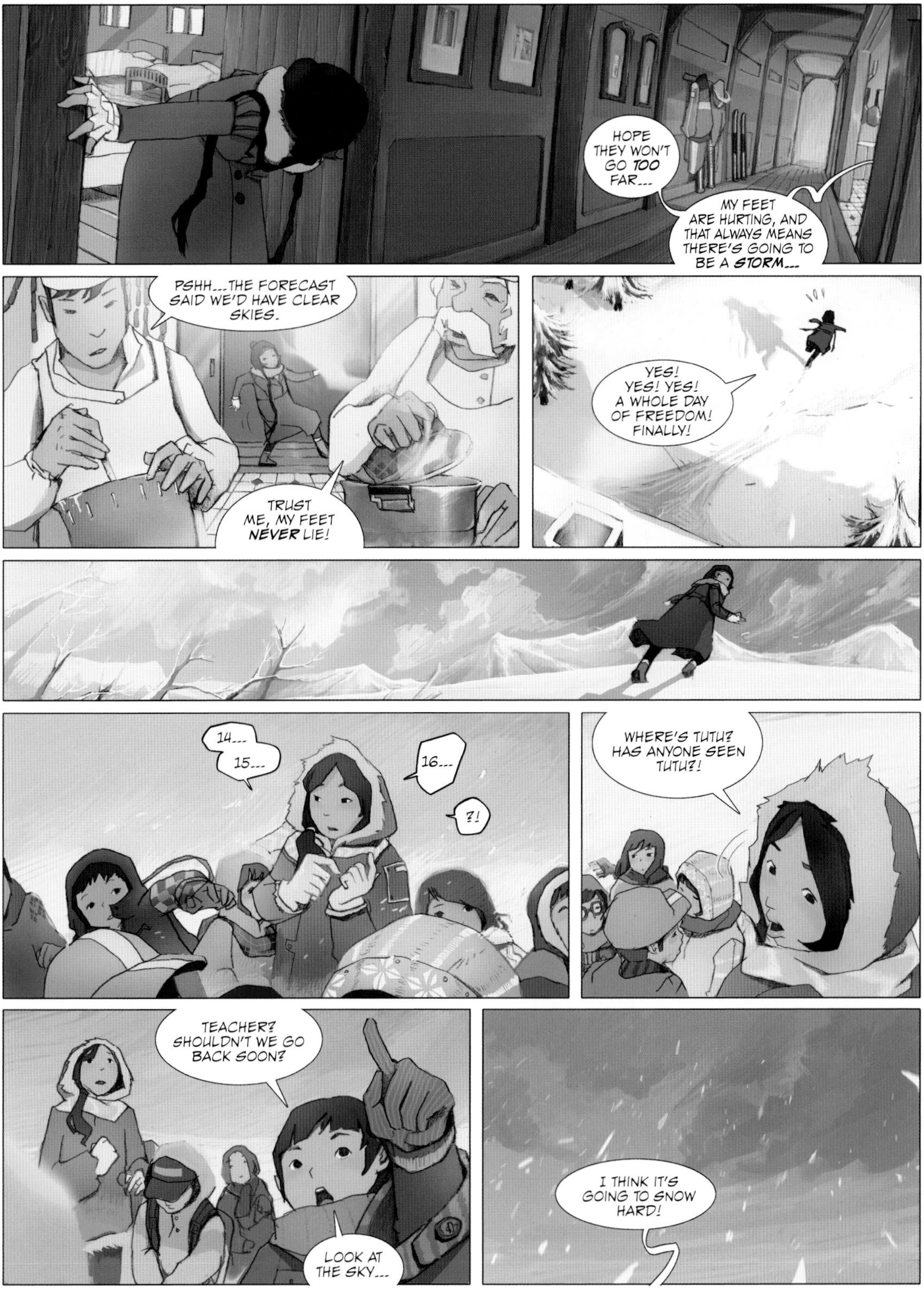
HOPE THEY WON'T GO TOO FAR...
MY FEET ARE HURTING, AND THAT ALWAYS MEANS THERE'S GOING TO BE A STORM...
PSHH...THE FORECAST SAID WE'D HAVE CLEAR SKIES.
TRUST ME, MY FEET NEVER LIE!
YES! YES! YES! A WHOLE DAY OF FREEDOM! FINALLY!
14...
15...
16...
?!
WHERE'S TUTU? HAS ANYONE SEEN TUTU?!
TEACHER? SHOULDN'T WE GO BACK SOON?
LOOK AT THE SKY...
I THINK IT'S GOING TO SNOW HARD!

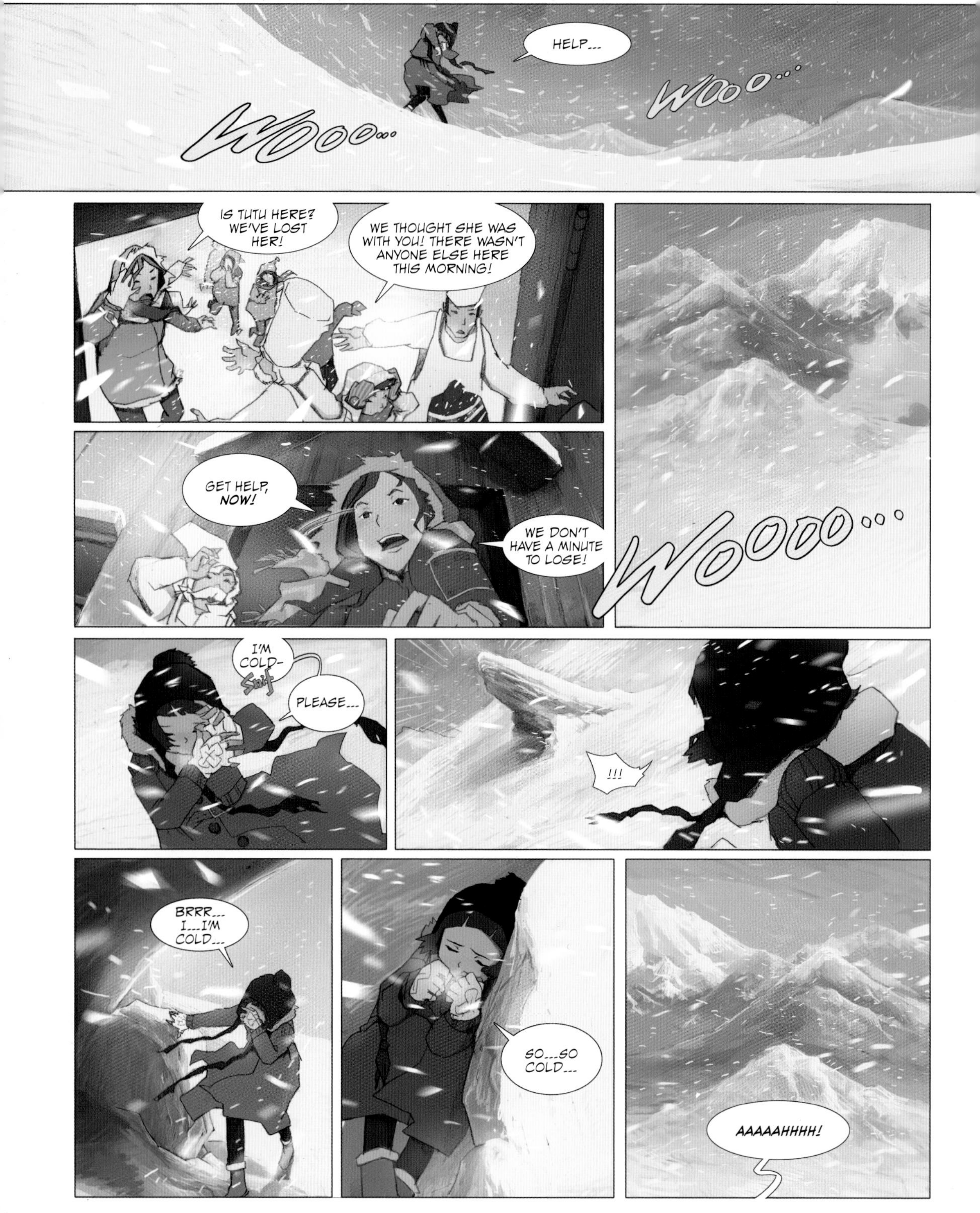
HELP...
WOOO...
WOOO...
IS TUTU HERE? WE'VE LOST HER!
WE THOUGHT SHE WAS WITH YOU! THERE WASN'T ANYONE ELSE HERE THIS MORNING!
GET HELP, NOW!
WE DON'T HAVE A MINUTE TO LOSE!
WOOOO...
I'M COLD-
Snif
PLEASE...
!!!
BRRR... I...I'M COLD...
SO...SO COLD...
AAAAAHHHH!

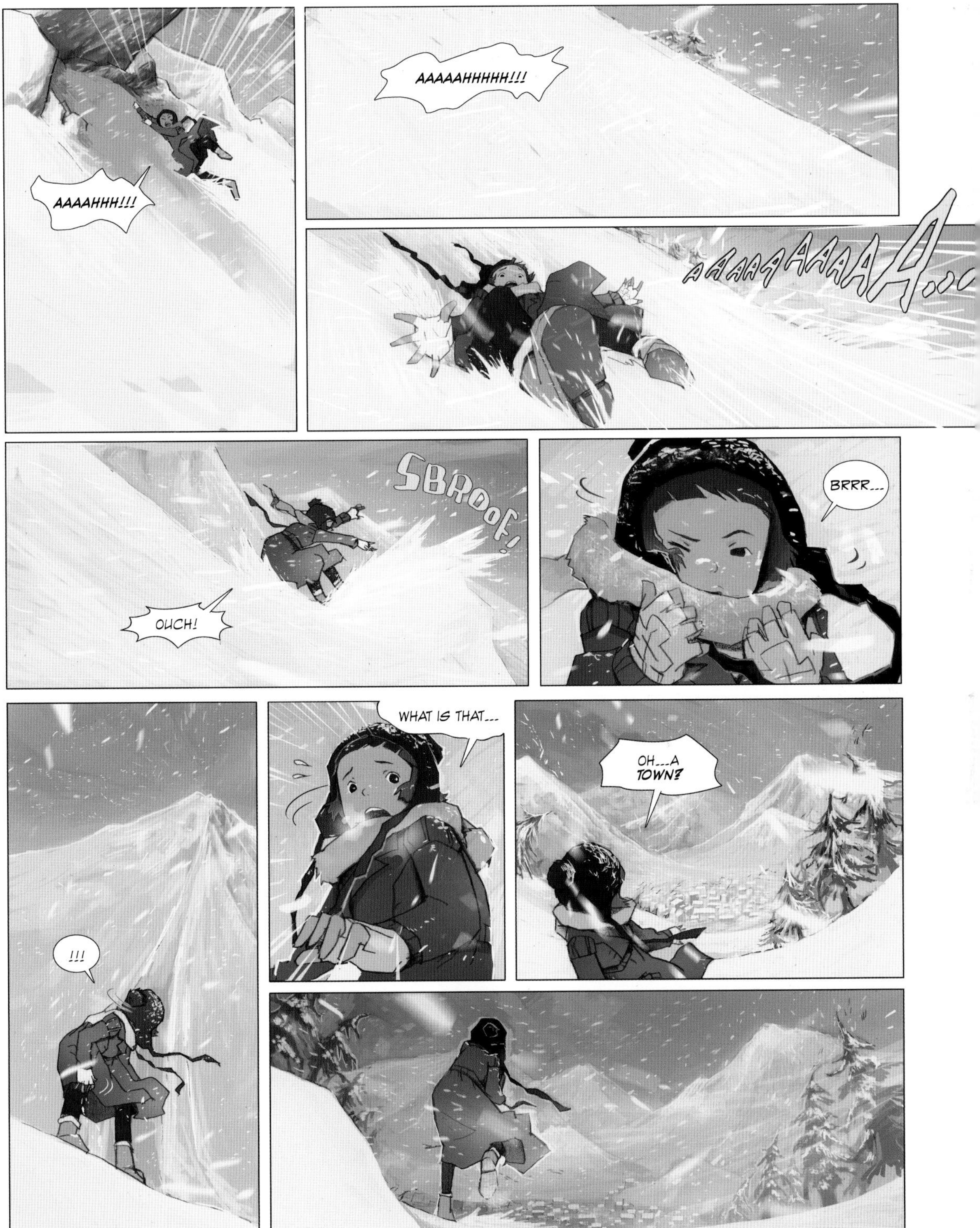
AAAAHHH!!!
AAAAAHHHHH!!!
AAAAAAAAAAA...
SBROOF!
OUCH!
BRRR...
!!!
WHAT IS THAT...
OH...A
TOWN?

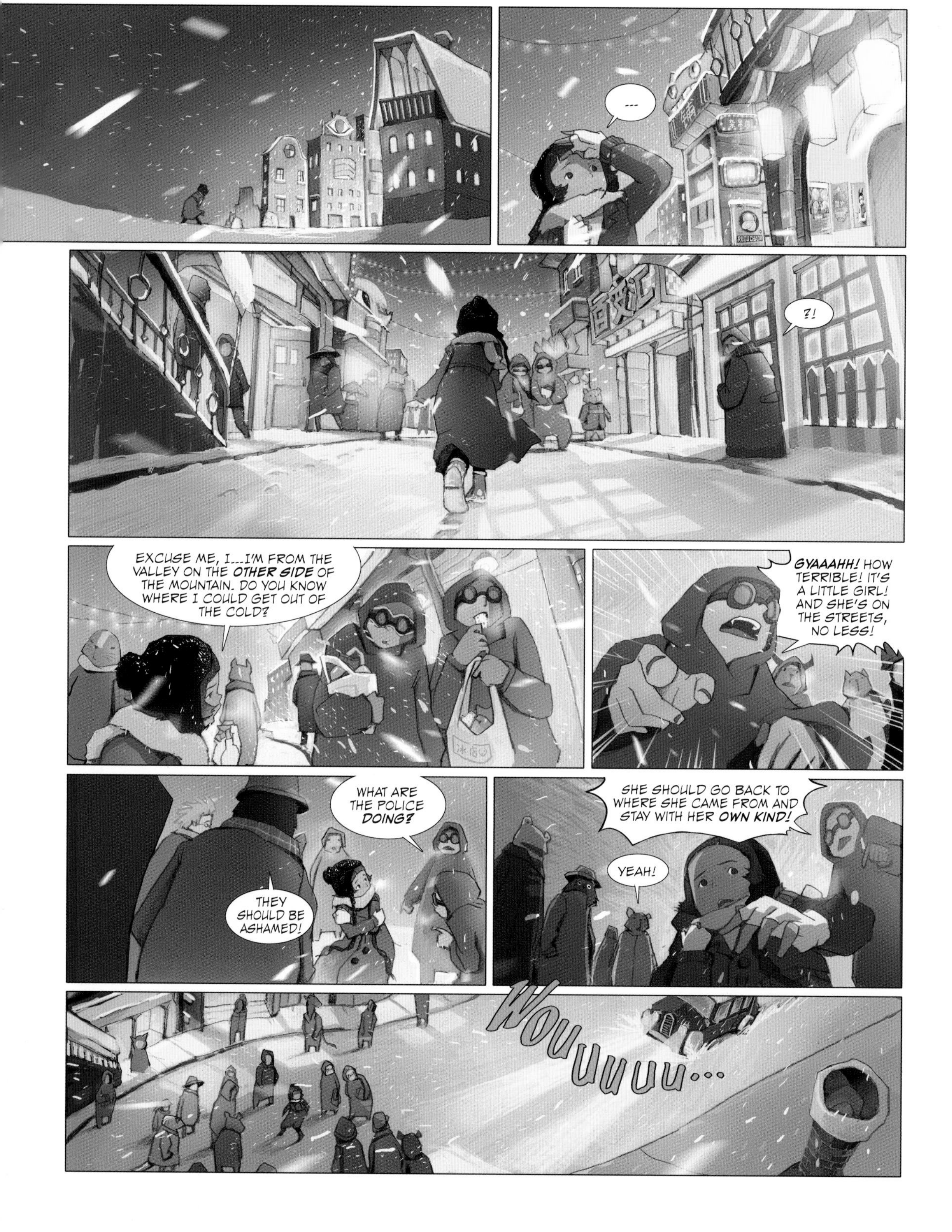
...
?!
EXCUSE ME, I...I'M FROM THE VALLEY ON THE **OTHER SIDE** OF THE MOUNTAIN. DO YOU KNOW WHERE I COULD GET OUT OF THE COLD?
GYAAAHH! HOW TERRIBLE! IT'S A LITTLE GIRL! AND SHE'S ON THE STREETS, NO LESS!
WHAT ARE THE POLICE **DOING?**
THEY SHOULD BE ASHAMED!
SHE SHOULD GO BACK TO WHERE SHE CAME FROM AND STAY WITH HER **OWN KIND!**
YEAH!
WOUUUUUU...

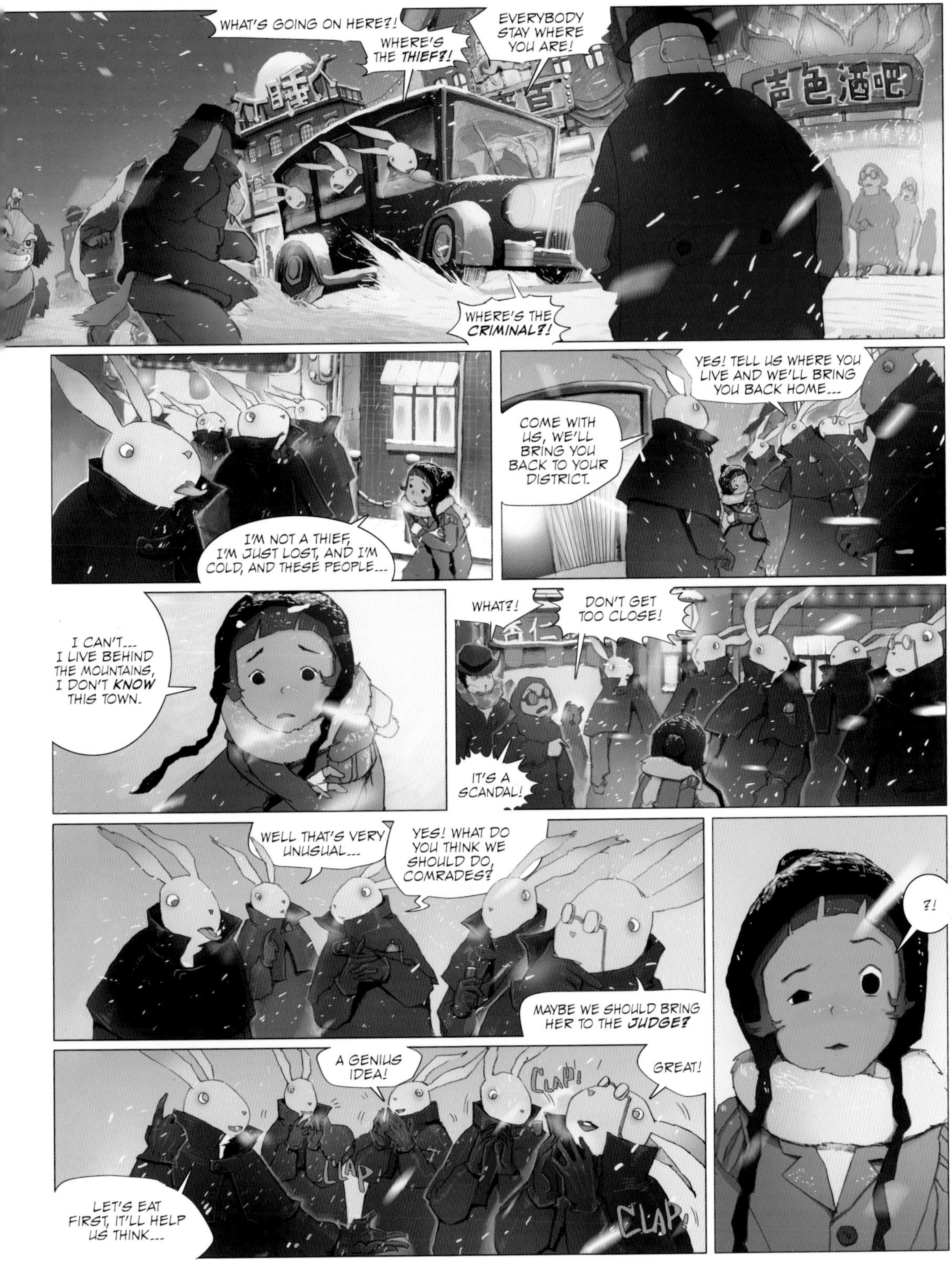
WHAT'S GOING ON HERE?!
WHERE'S THE THIEF?!
EVERYBODY STAY WHERE YOU ARE!
声色酒吧
WHERE'S THE CRIMINAL?!
I'M NOT A THIEF, I'M JUST LOST, AND I'M COLD, AND THESE PEOPLE...
YES! TELL US WHERE YOU LIVE AND WE'LL BRING YOU BACK HOME...
COME WITH US, WE'LL BRING YOU BACK TO YOUR DISTRICT.
I CAN'T... I LIVE BEHIND THE MOUNTAINS, I DON'T KNOW THIS TOWN.
WHAT?!
DON'T GET TOO CLOSE!
IT'S A SCANDAL!
WELL THAT'S VERY UNUSUAL...
YES! WHAT DO YOU THINK WE SHOULD DO, COMRADES?
MAYBE WE SHOULD BRING HER TO THE JUDGE?
?!
A GENIUS IDEA!
CLAP!
GREAT!
CLAP!
CLAP!
LET'S EAT FIRST, IT'LL HELP US THINK...

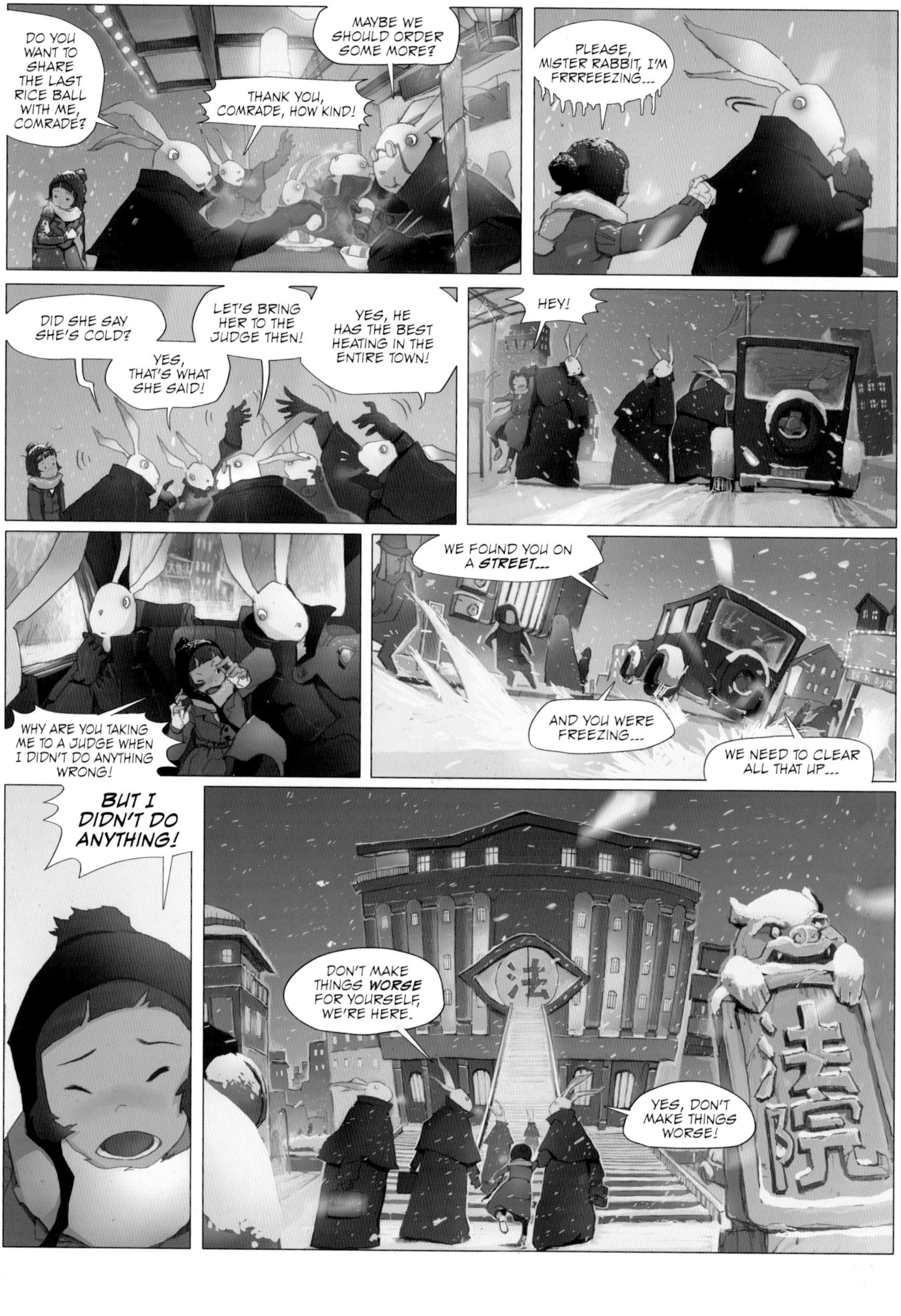
DO YOU WANT TO SHARE THE LAST RICE BALL WITH ME, COMRADE?
MAYBE WE SHOULD ORDER SOME MORE?
THANK YOU, COMRADE, HOW KIND!
PLEASE, MISTER RABBIT, I'M FRRREEEZING...
DID SHE SAY SHE'S COLD?
LET'S BRING HER TO THE JUDGE THEN!
YES, HE HAS THE BEST HEATING IN THE ENTIRE TOWN!
YES, THAT'S WHAT SHE SAID!
HEY!
WHY ARE YOU TAKING ME TO A JUDGE WHEN I DIDN'T DO ANYTHING WRONG!
WE FOUND YOU ON A STREET...
AND YOU WERE FREEZING...
WE NEED TO CLEAR ALL THAT UP...
BUT I DIDN'T DO ANYTHING!
DON'T MAKE THINGS WORSE FOR YOURSELF, WE'RE HERE.
YES, DON'T MAKE THINGS WORSE!
法院

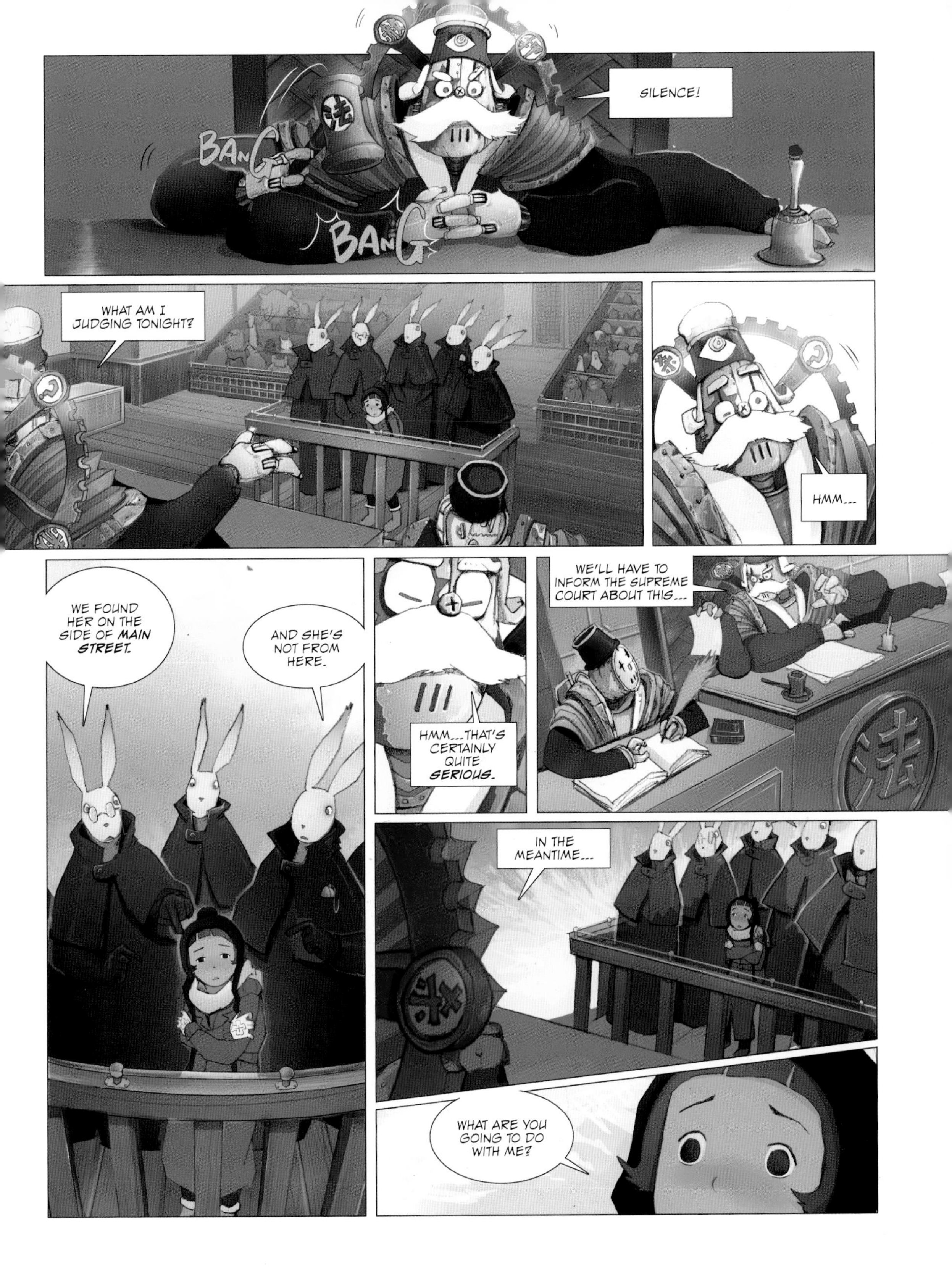
BANG
BANG
SILENCE!
WHAT AM I JUDGING TONIGHT?
HMM...
WE FOUND HER ON THE SIDE OF **MAIN STREET**.
AND SHE'S NOT FROM HERE.
HMM... THAT'S CERTAINLY QUITE **SERIOUS**.
WE'LL HAVE TO INFORM THE SUPREME COURT ABOUT THIS...
IN THE MEANTIME...
WHAT ARE YOU GOING TO DO WITH ME?

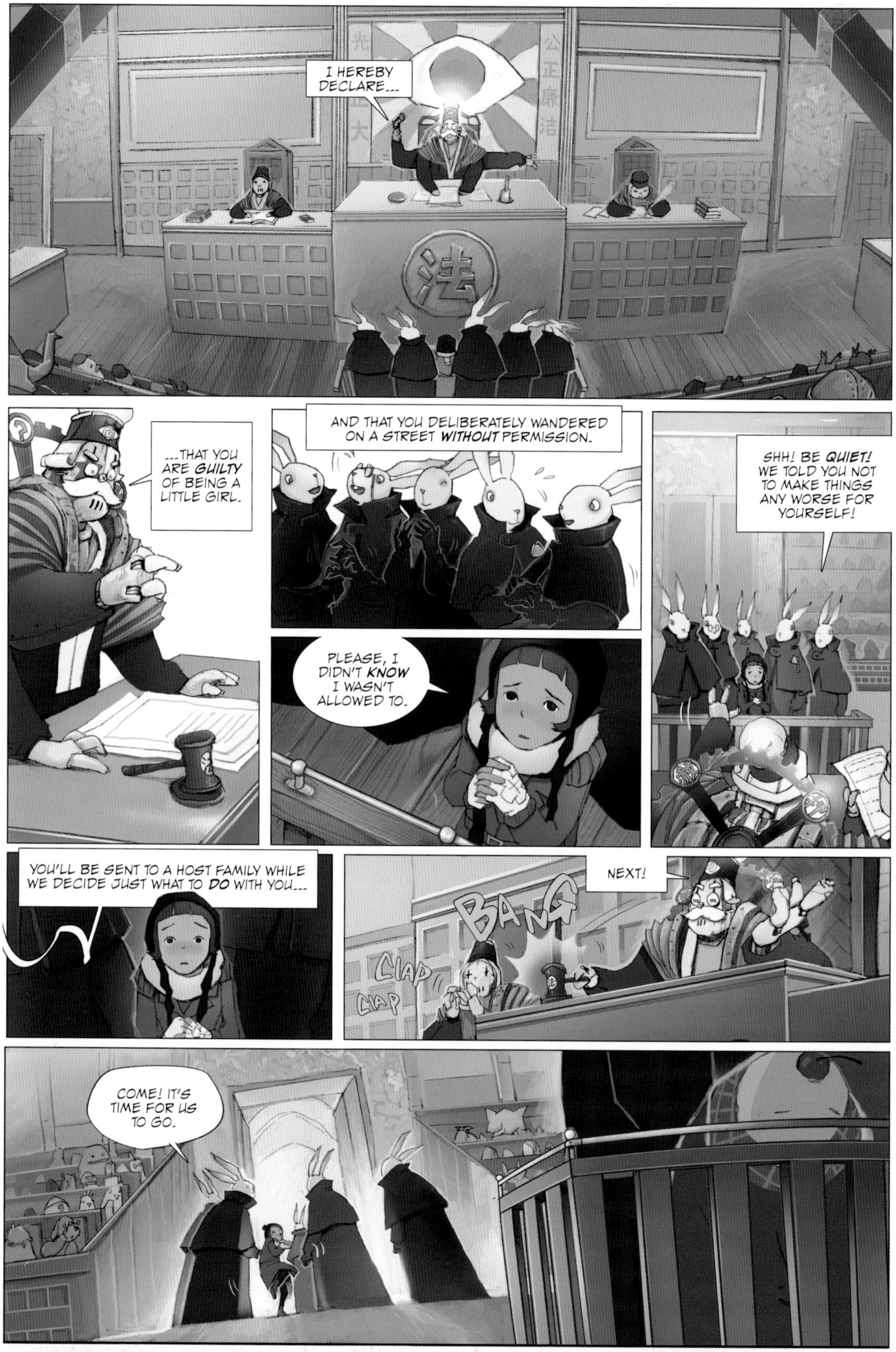

I HEREBY DECLARE...
...THAT YOU ARE GUILTY OF BEING A LITTLE GIRL.
AND THAT YOU DELIBERATELY WANDERED ON A STREET WITHOUT PERMISSION.
PLEASE, I DIDN'T KNOW I WASN'T ALLOWED TO.
SHH! BE QUIET! WE TOLD YOU NOT TO MAKE THINGS ANY WORSE FOR YOURSELF!
YOU'LL BE SENT TO A HOST FAMILY WHILE WE DECIDE JUST WHAT TO DO WITH YOU...
BANG
CLAP
CLAP
NEXT!
COME! IT'S TIME FOR US TO GO.

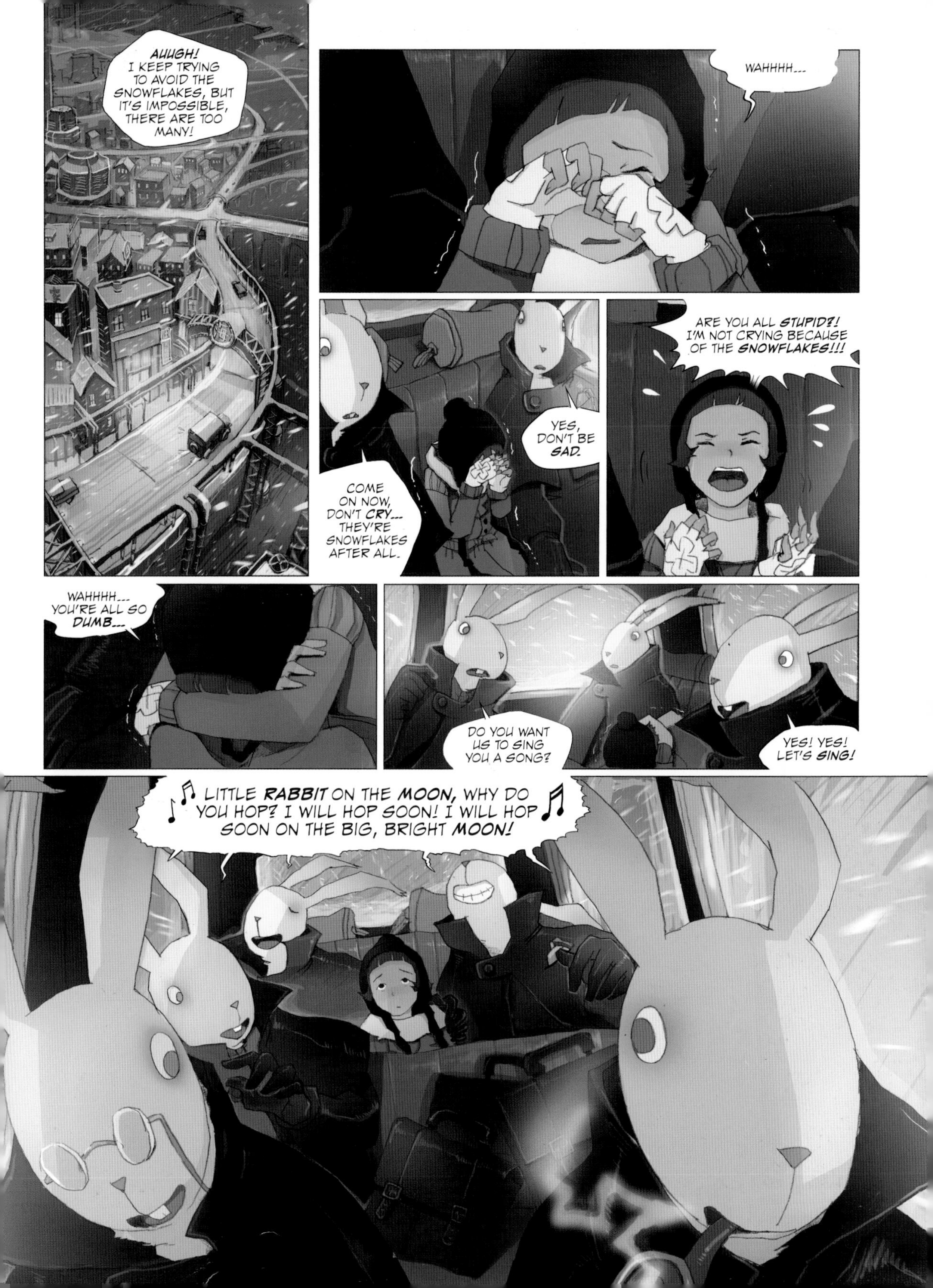
AUUGH! I KEEP TRYING TO AVOID THE SNOWFLAKES, BUT IT'S IMPOSSIBLE, THERE ARE TOO MANY!
WAHHHH...
YES, DON'T BE SAD.
COME ON NOW, DON'T CRY... THEY'RE SNOWFLAKES AFTER ALL.
ARE YOU ALL STUPID?! I'M NOT CRYING BECAUSE OF THE SNOWFLAKES!!!
WAHHHH... YOU'RE ALL SO DUMB...
DO YOU WANT US TO SING YOU A SONG?
YES! YES! LET'S SING!
LITTLE RABBIT ON THE MOON, WHY DO YOU HOP? I WILL HOP SOON! I WILL HOP SOON ON THE BIG, BRIGHT MOON!

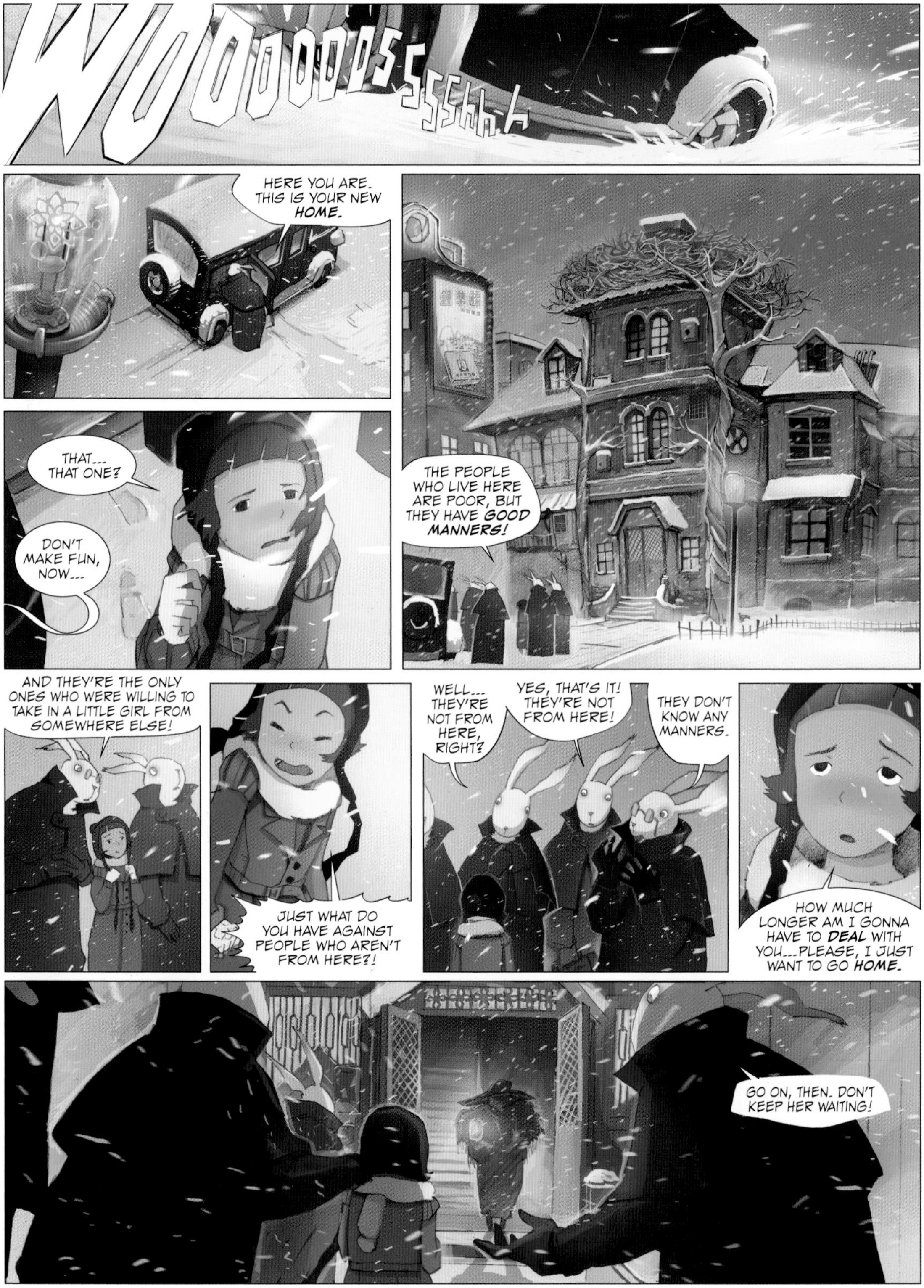
WOOOOOOSSSShhh
HERE YOU ARE. THIS IS YOUR NEW HOME.
THAT... THAT ONE?
DON'T MAKE FUN, NOW...
THE PEOPLE WHO LIVE HERE ARE POOR, BUT THEY HAVE GOOD MANNERS!
AND THEY'RE THE ONLY ONES WHO WERE WILLING TO TAKE IN A LITTLE GIRL FROM SOMEWHERE ELSE!
JUST WHAT DO YOU HAVE AGAINST PEOPLE WHO AREN'T FROM HERE?!
WELL... THEY'RE NOT FROM HERE, RIGHT?
YES, THAT'S IT! THEY'RE NOT FROM HERE!
THEY DON'T KNOW ANY MANNERS.
HOW MUCH LONGER AM I GONNA HAVE TO DEAL WITH YOU...PLEASE, I JUST WANT TO GO HOME.
GO ON, THEN. DON'T KEEP HER WAITING!

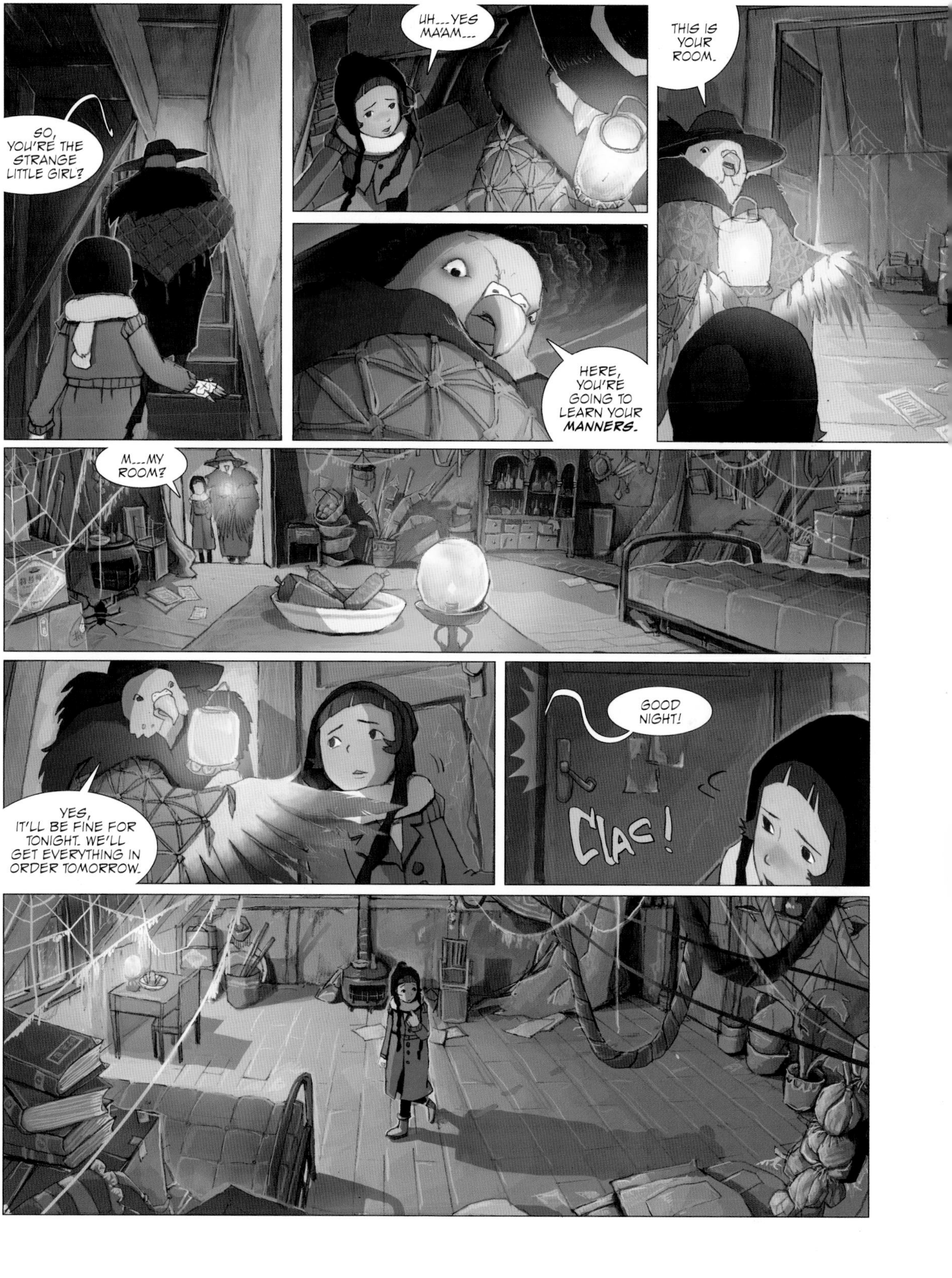

SO, YOU'RE THE STRANGE LITTLE GIRL?
UH... YES MA'AM...
HERE, YOU'RE GOING TO LEARN YOUR MANNERS.
THIS IS YOUR ROOM.
M... MY ROOM?
YES, IT'LL BE FINE FOR TONIGHT. WE'LL GET EVERYTHING IN ORDER TOMORROW.
GOOD NIGHT!
CLAC!

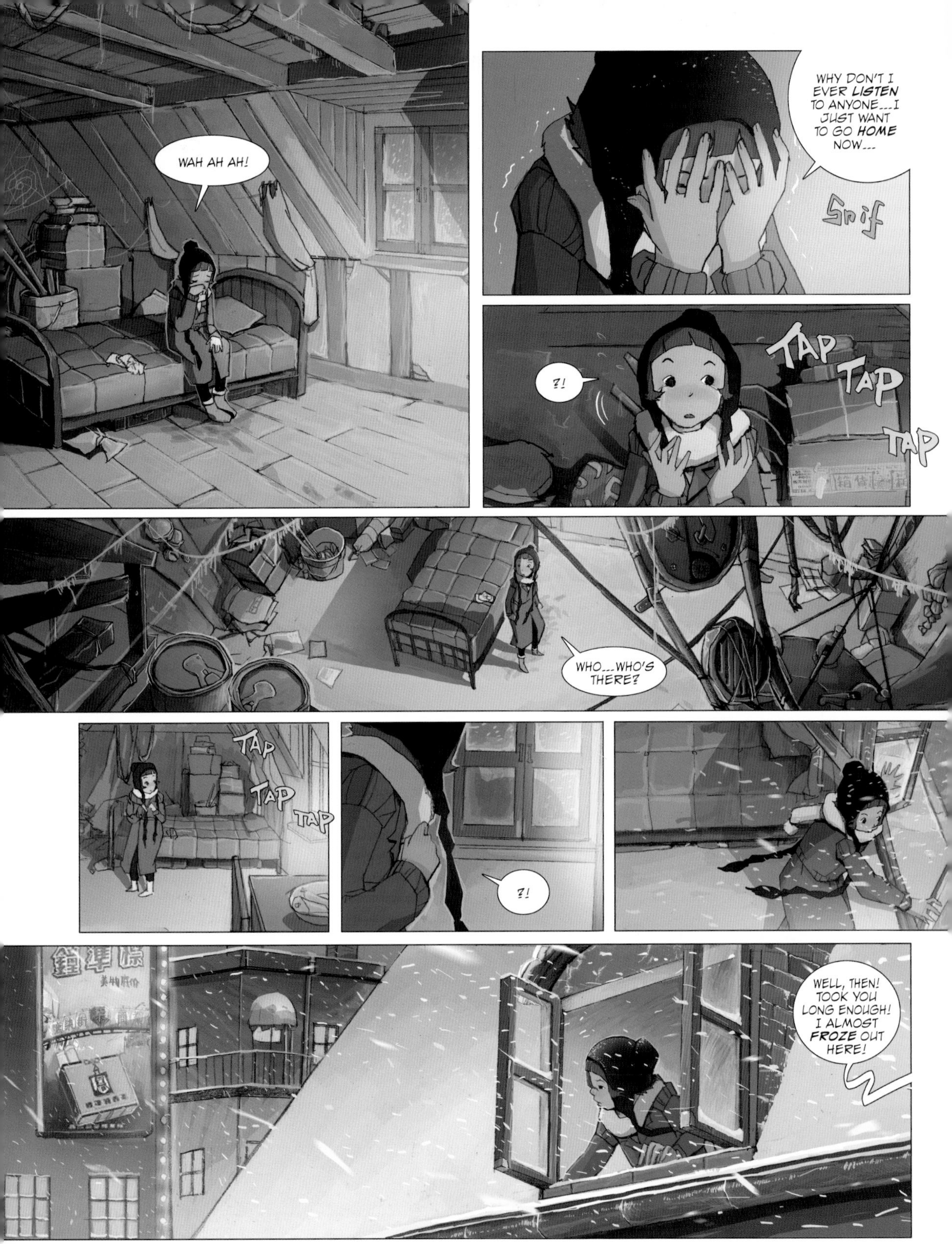

WAH AH AH!
WHY DON'T I EVER LISTEN TO ANYONE... I JUST WANT TO GO HOME NOW...
Snif
?!
TAP TAP TAP
WHO... WHO'S THERE?
TAP TAP TAP
?!
WELL, THEN! TOOK YOU LONG ENOUGH! I ALMOST FROZE OUT HERE!

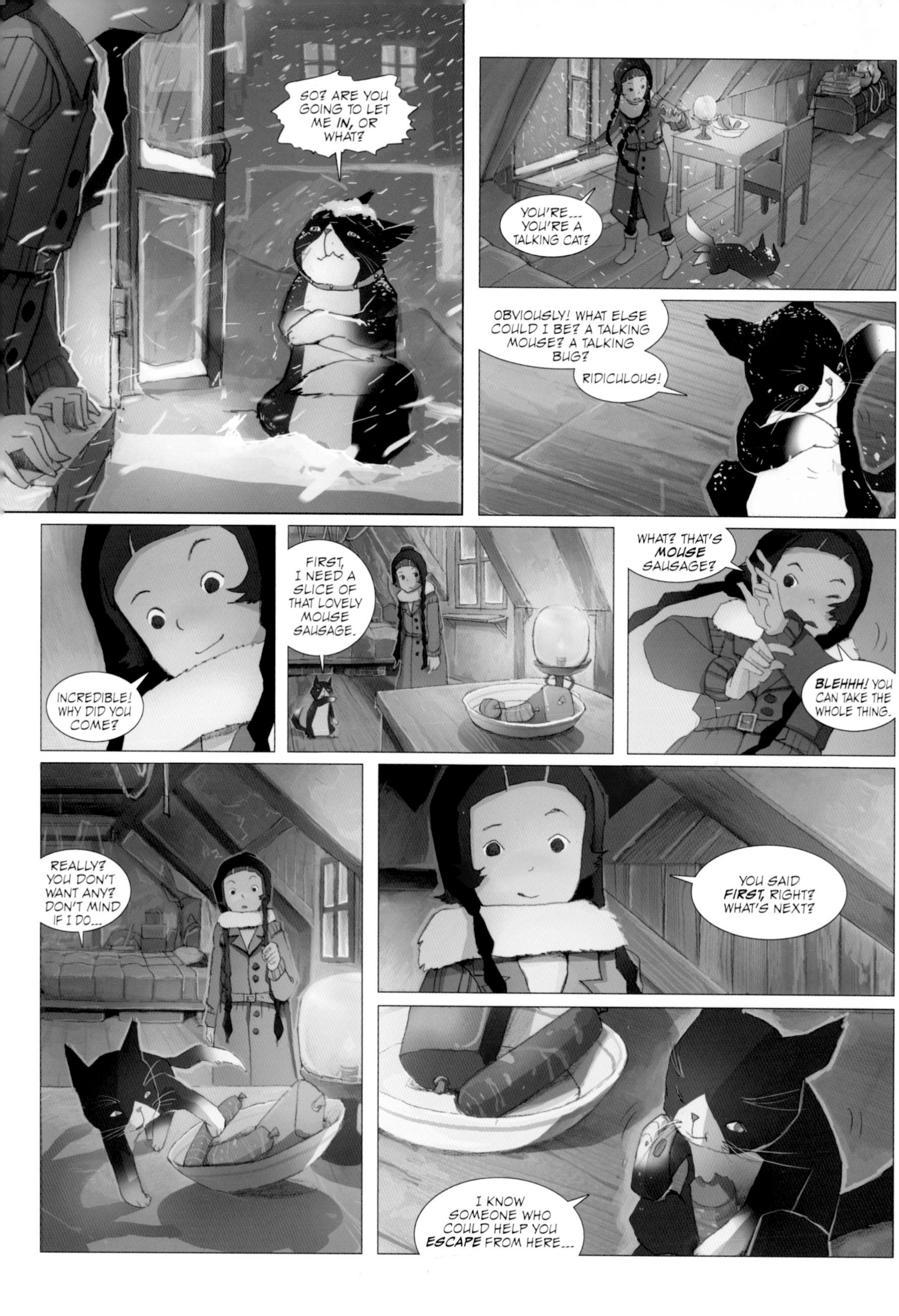
SO? ARE YOU GOING TO LET ME IN, OR WHAT?
YOU'RE... YOU'RE A TALKING CAT?
OBVIOUSLY! WHAT ELSE COULD I BE? A TALKING MOUSE? A TALKING BUG?
RIDICULOUS!
INCREDIBLE! WHY DID YOU COME?
FIRST, I NEED A SLICE OF THAT LOVELY MOUSE SAUSAGE.
WHAT? THAT'S MOUSE SAUSAGE?
BLEHHH! YOU CAN TAKE THE WHOLE THING.
REALLY? YOU DON'T WANT ANY? DON'T MIND IF I DO...
YOU SAID FIRST, RIGHT? WHAT'S NEXT?
I KNOW SOMEONE WHO COULD HELP YOU ESCAPE FROM HERE...

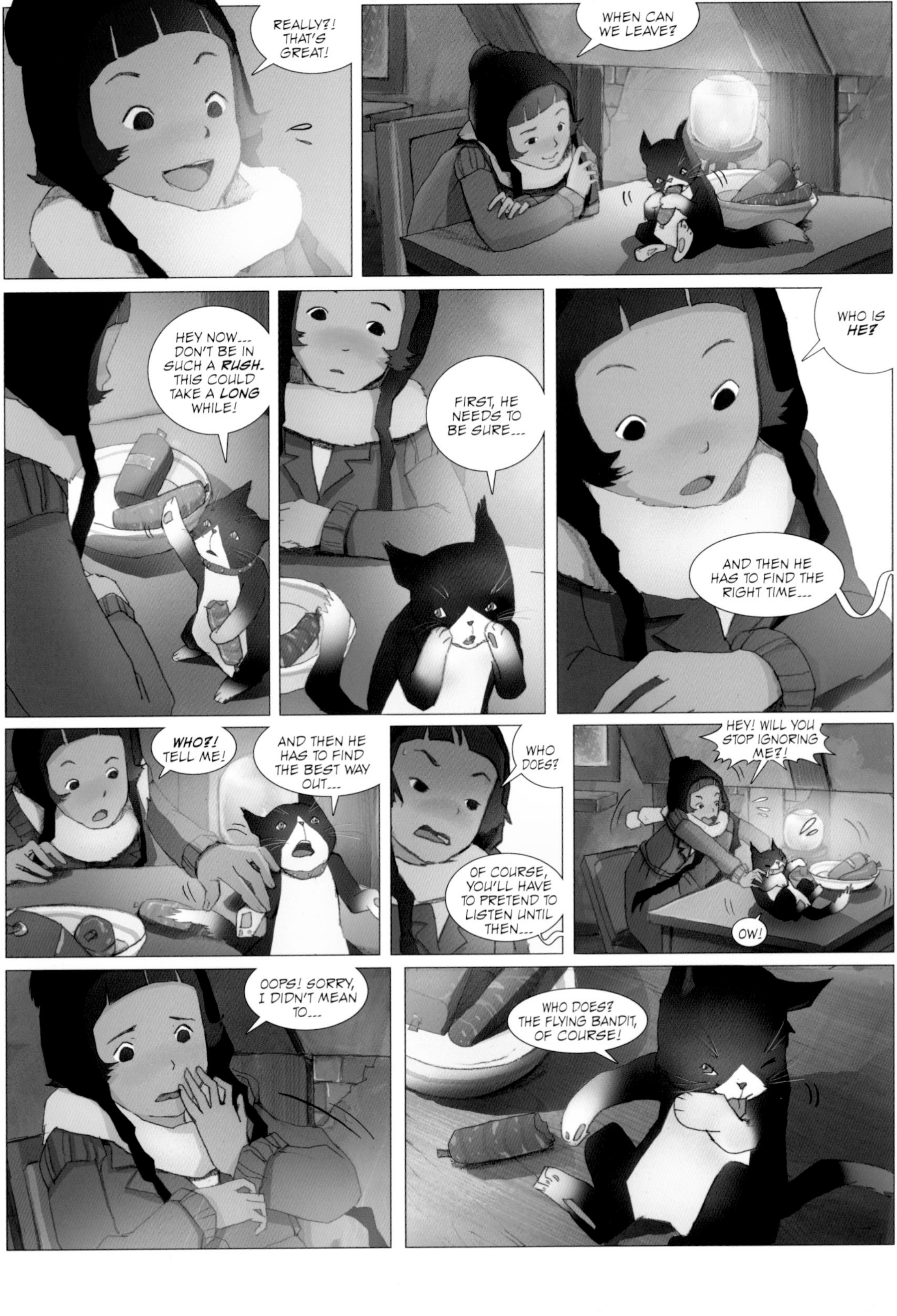
REALLY?! THAT'S GREAT!
WHEN CAN WE LEAVE?
HEY NOW... DON'T BE IN SUCH A **RUSH**. THIS COULD TAKE A **LONG** WHILE!
FIRST, HE NEEDS TO BE SURE...
WHO IS **HE?**
AND THEN HE HAS TO FIND THE RIGHT TIME...
WHO?! TELL ME!
AND THEN HE HAS TO FIND THE BEST WAY OUT...
WHO DOES?
OF COURSE, YOU'LL HAVE TO PRETEND TO LISTEN UNTIL THEN...
HEY! WILL YOU STOP IGNORING ME?!
OW!
OOPS! SORRY, I DIDN'T MEAN TO...
WHO DOES? THE FLYING BANDIT, OF COURSE!

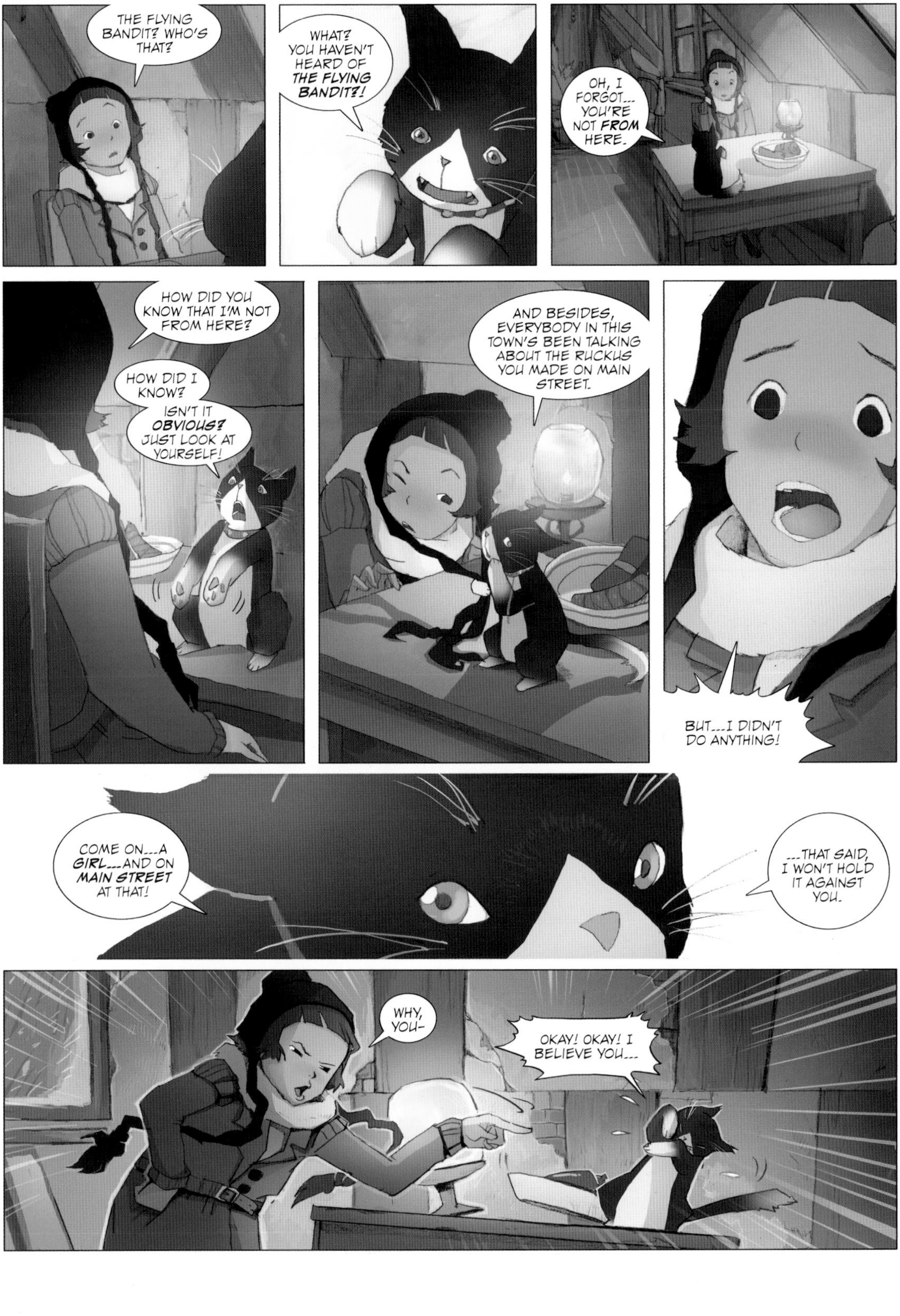

THE FLYING BANDIT? WHO'S THAT?
WHAT? YOU HAVEN'T HEARD OF THE FLYING BANDIT?!
OH, I FORGOT... YOU'RE NOT FROM HERE.
HOW DID YOU KNOW THAT I'M NOT FROM HERE?
HOW DID I KNOW?
ISN'T IT OBVIOUS? JUST LOOK AT YOURSELF!
AND BESIDES, EVERYBODY IN THIS TOWN'S BEEN TALKING ABOUT THE RUCKUS YOU MADE ON MAIN STREET.
BUT... I DIDN'T DO ANYTHING!
COME ON... A GIRL... AND ON MAIN STREET AT THAT!
...THAT SAID, I WON'T HOLD IT AGAINST YOU.
WHY, YOU-
OKAY! OKAY! I BELIEVE YOU...

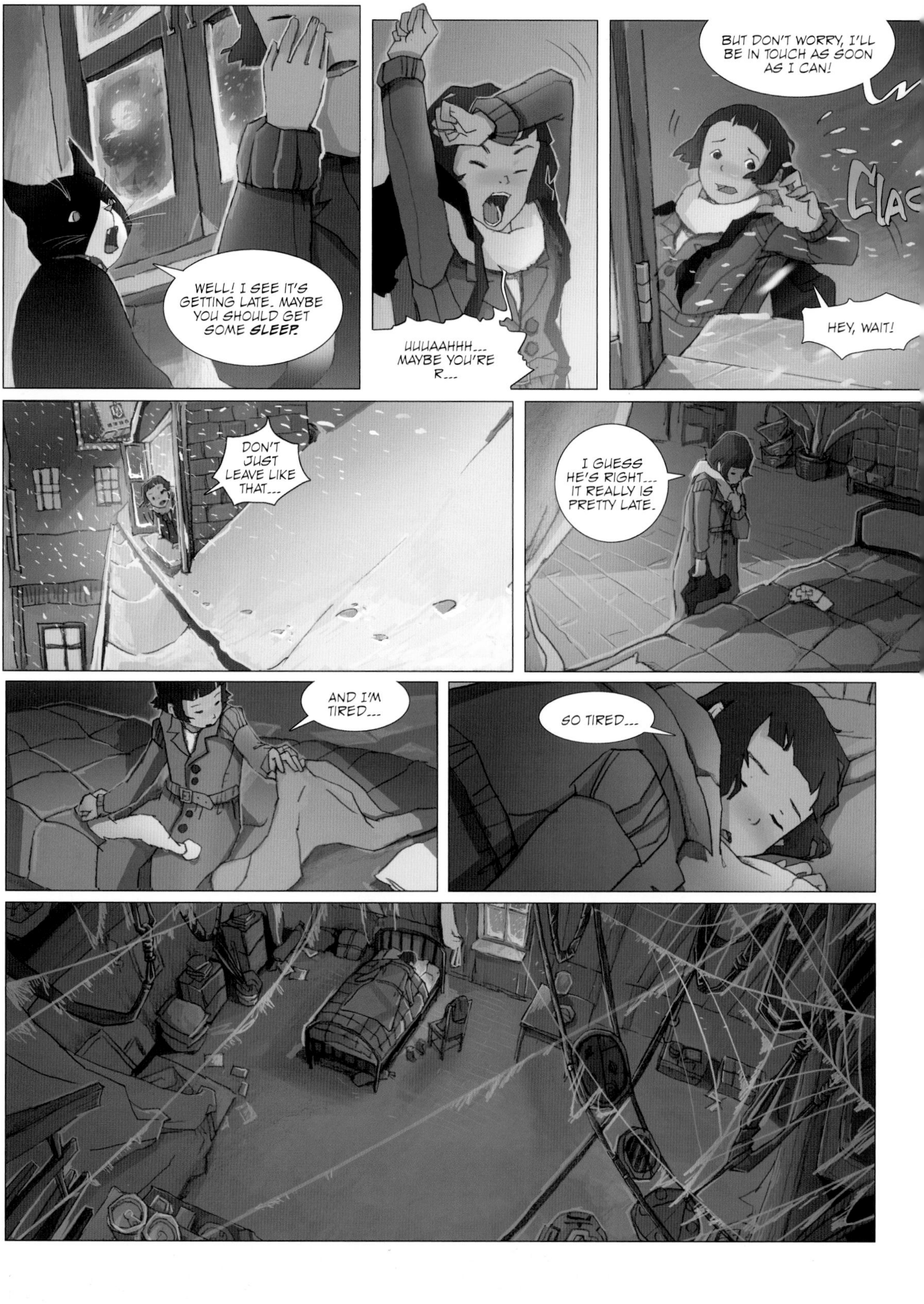
WELL! I SEE IT'S GETTING LATE. MAYBE YOU SHOULD GET SOME **SLEEP**.
UUUAAHHH... MAYBE YOU'RE R...
BUT DON'T WORRY, I'LL BE IN TOUCH AS SOON AS I CAN!
CLAC
HEY, WAIT!
DON'T JUST LEAVE LIKE THAT...
I GUESS HE'S RIGHT... IT REALLY IS PRETTY LATE.
AND I'M TIRED...
SO TIRED...

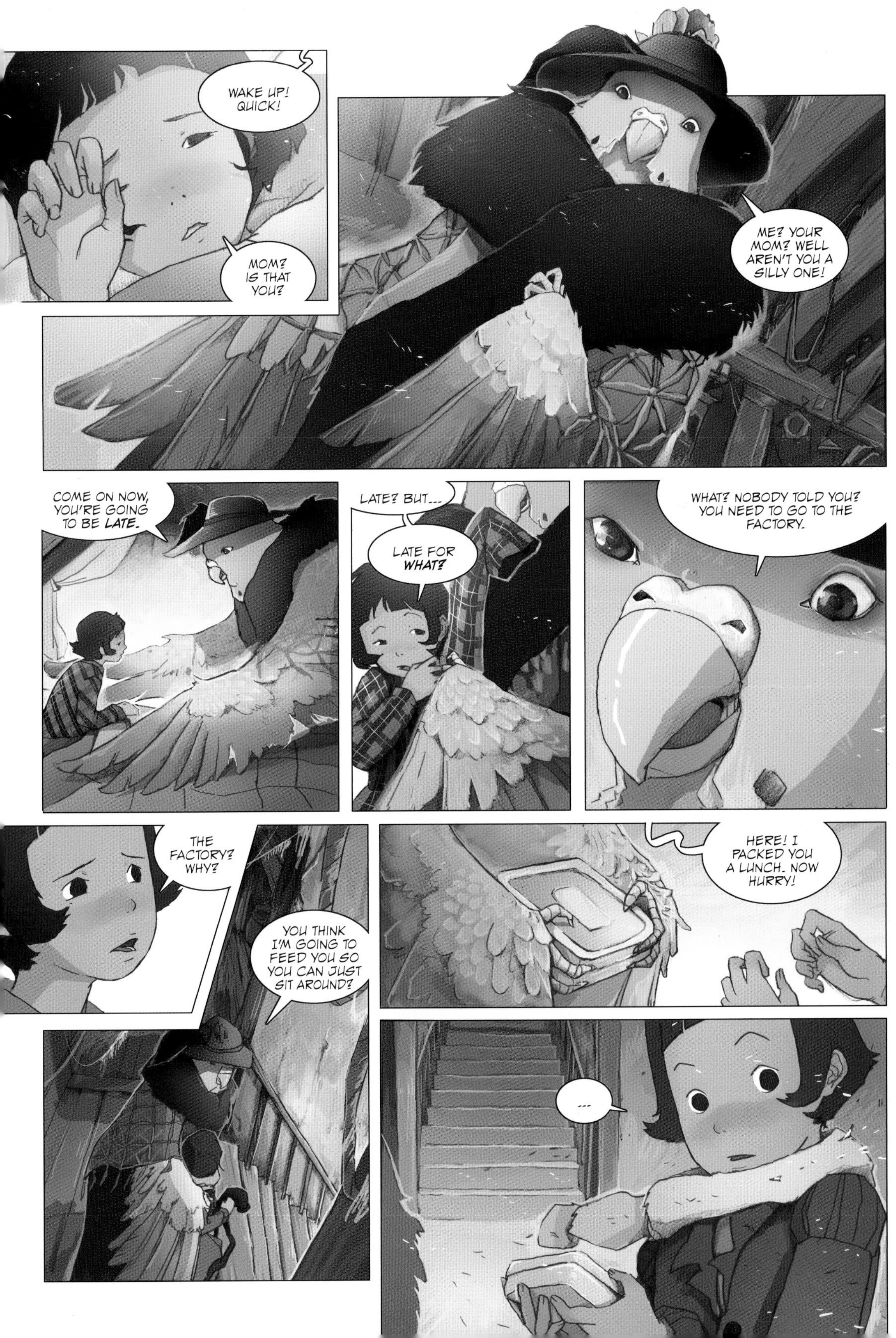
WAKE UP! QUICK!
MOM? IS THAT YOU?
ME? YOUR MOM? WELL AREN'T YOU A SILLY ONE!
COME ON NOW, YOU'RE GOING TO BE LATE.
LATE? BUT...
LATE FOR WHAT?
WHAT? NOBODY TOLD YOU? YOU NEED TO GO TO THE FACTORY.
THE FACTORY? WHY?
YOU THINK I'M GOING TO FEED YOU SO YOU CAN JUST SIT AROUND?
HERE! I PACKED YOU A LUNCH. NOW HURRY!
...

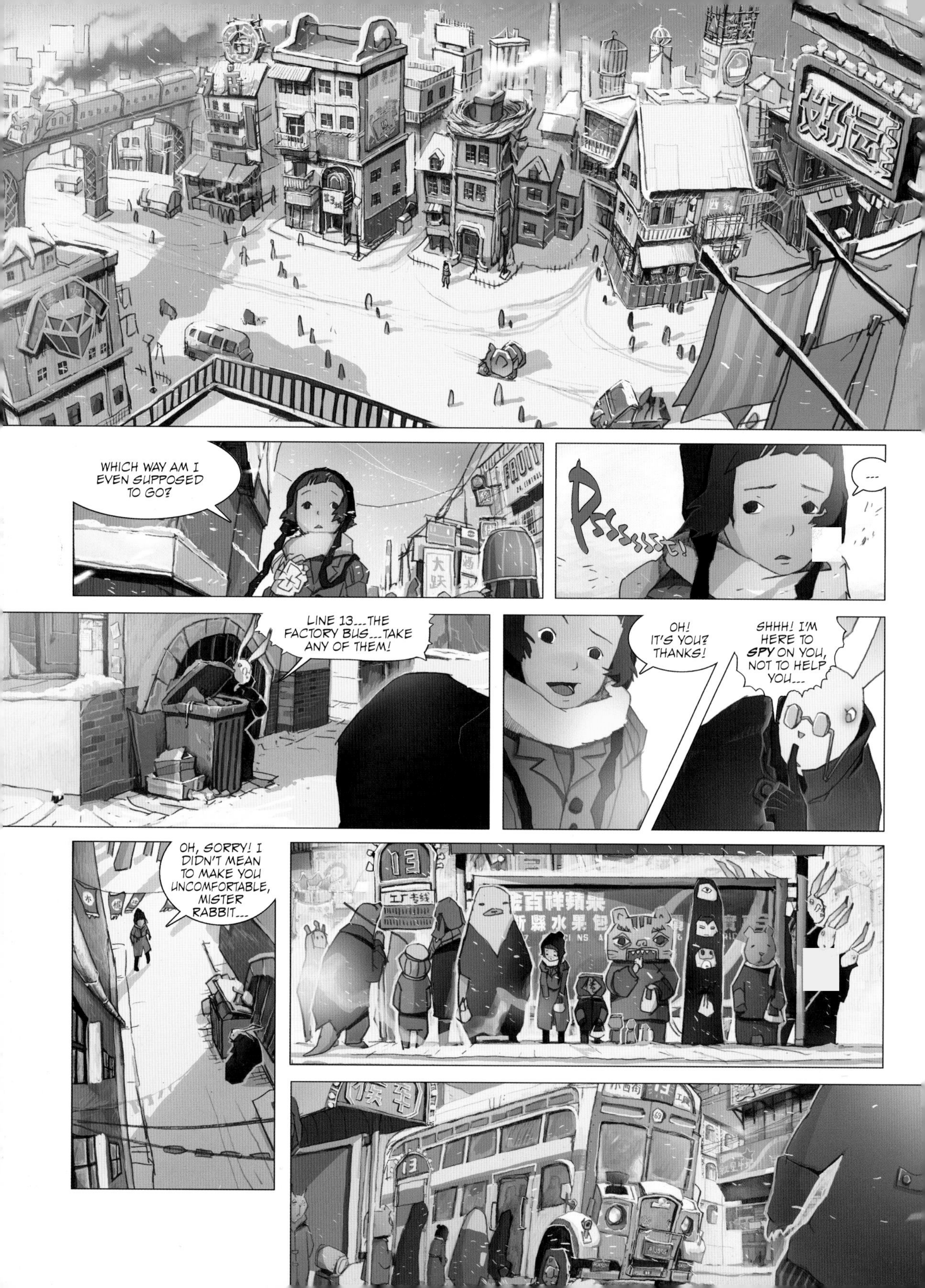
WHICH WAY AM I EVEN SUPPOSED TO GO?
PSSSSSSSST!
...
LINE 13... THE FACTORY BUS... TAKE ANY OF THEM!
OH! IT'S YOU? THANKS!
SHHH! I'M HERE TO **SPY** ON YOU, NOT TO HELP YOU...
OH, SORRY! I DIDN'T MEAN TO MAKE YOU UNCOMFORTABLE, MISTER RABBIT...

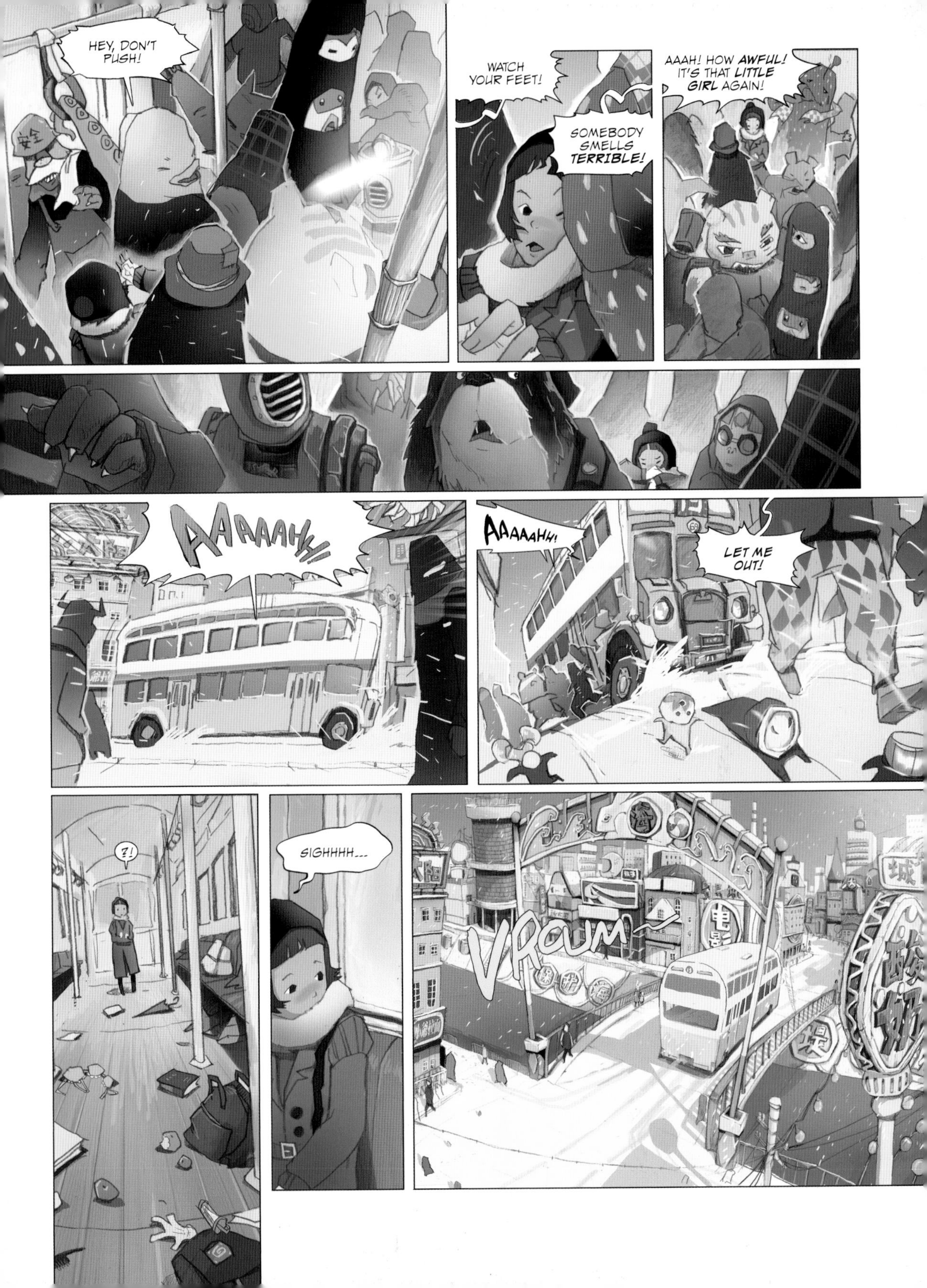
HEY, DON'T PUSH!
WATCH YOUR FEET!
SOMEBODY SMELLS TERRIBLE!
AAAH! HOW AWFUL! IT'S THAT LITTLE GIRL AGAIN!
AAAAAHH!!
AAAAAHH!
LET ME OUT!
?!
SIGHHHH...
VROUM

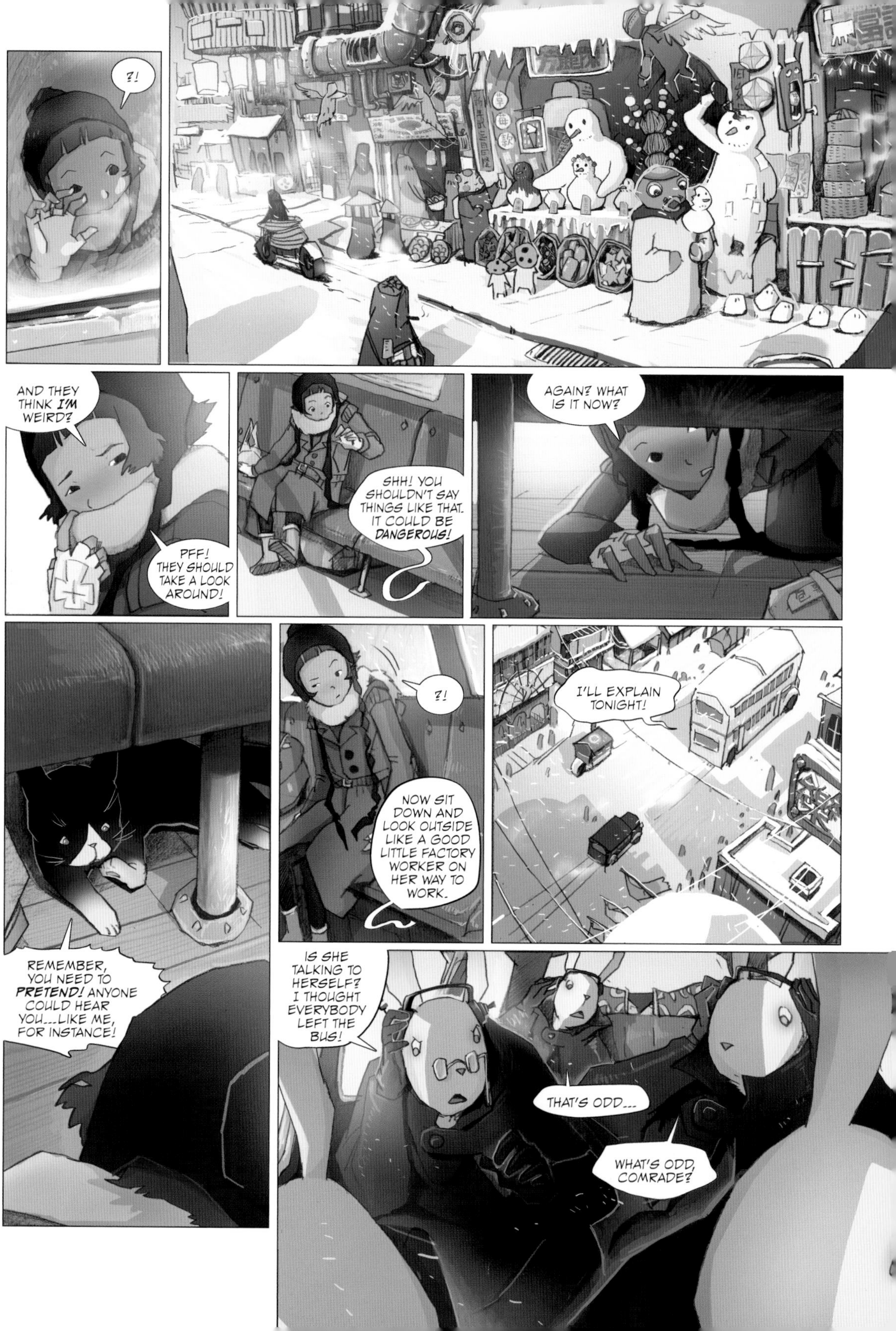

?!
AND THEY THINK I'M WEIRD?
PFF! THEY SHOULD TAKE A LOOK AROUND!
SHH! YOU SHOULDN'T SAY THINGS LIKE THAT. IT COULD BE DANGEROUS!
AGAIN? WHAT IS IT NOW?
?!
NOW SIT DOWN AND LOOK OUTSIDE LIKE A GOOD LITTLE FACTORY WORKER ON HER WAY TO WORK.
I'LL EXPLAIN TONIGHT!
REMEMBER, YOU NEED TO PRETEND! ANYONE COULD HEAR YOU...LIKE ME, FOR INSTANCE!
IS SHE TALKING TO HERSELF? I THOUGHT EVERYBODY LEFT THE BUS!
THAT'S ODD...
WHAT'S ODD, COMRADE?

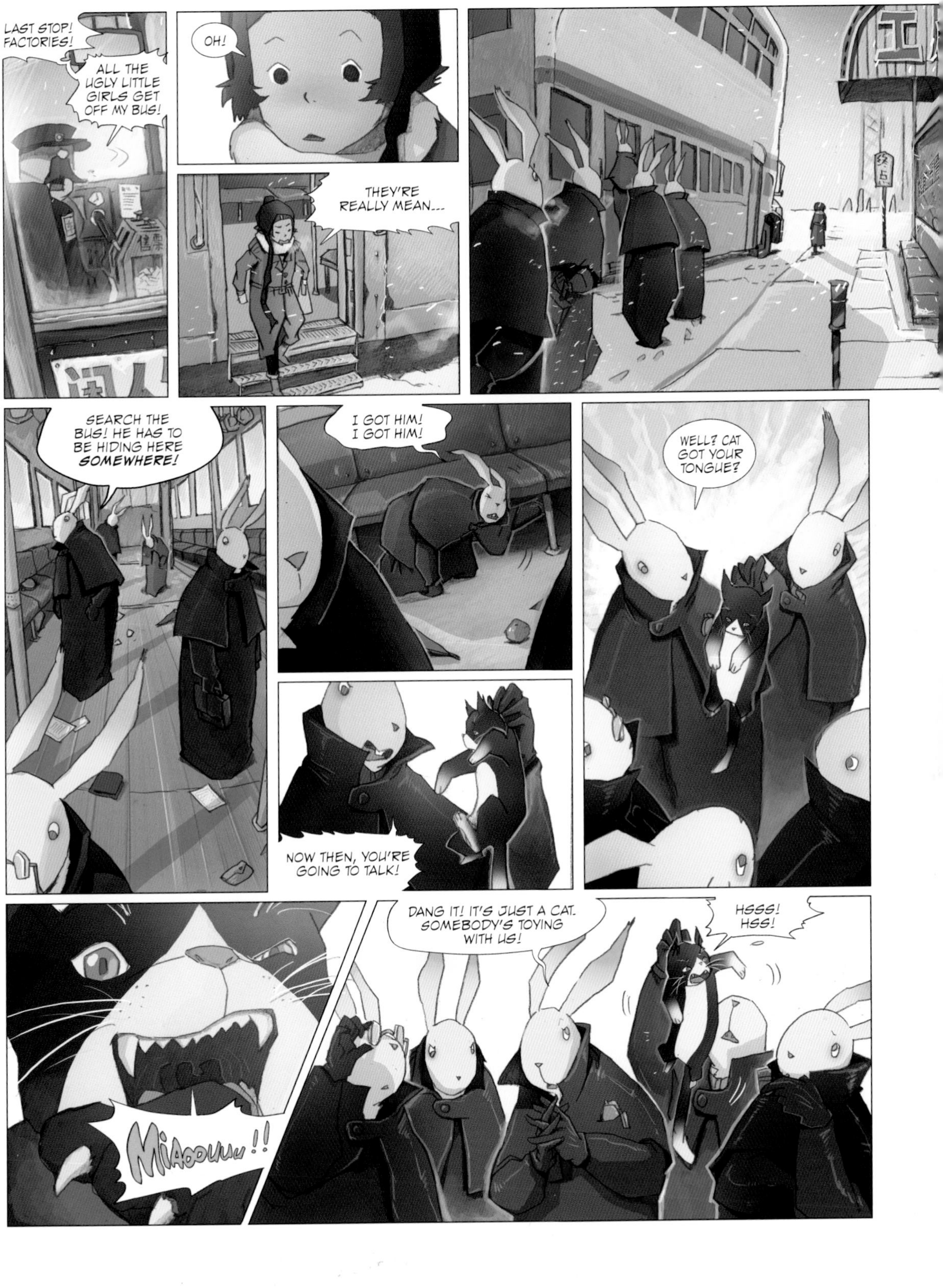
LAST STOP! FACTORIES!
ALL THE UGLY LITTLE GIRLS GET OFF MY BUS!
OH!
THEY'RE REALLY MEAN...
SEARCH THE BUS! HE HAS TO BE HIDING HERE SOMEWHERE!
I GOT HIM! I GOT HIM!
NOW THEN, YOU'RE GOING TO TALK!
WELL? CAT GOT YOUR TONGUE?
MIAOOUUU!!
DANG IT! IT'S JUST A CAT. SOMEBODY'S TOYING WITH US!
HSSS! HSS!

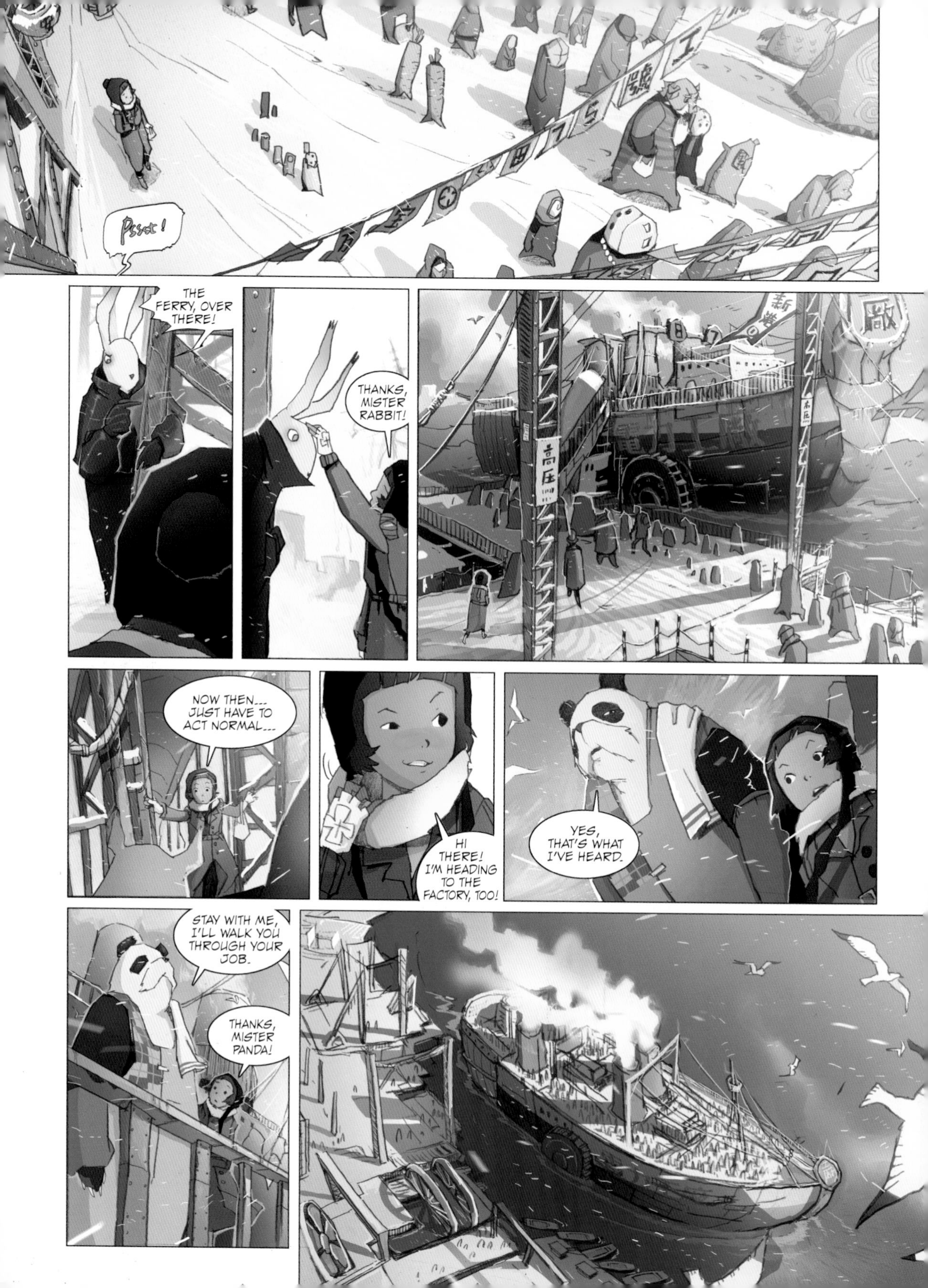
Pssst!
THE FERRY, OVER THERE!
THANKS, MISTER RABBIT!
NOW THEN... JUST HAVE TO ACT NORMAL...
HI THERE! I'M HEADING TO THE FACTORY, TOO!
YES, THAT'S WHAT I'VE HEARD.
STAY WITH ME, I'LL WALK YOU THROUGH YOUR JOB.
THANKS, MISTER PANDA!

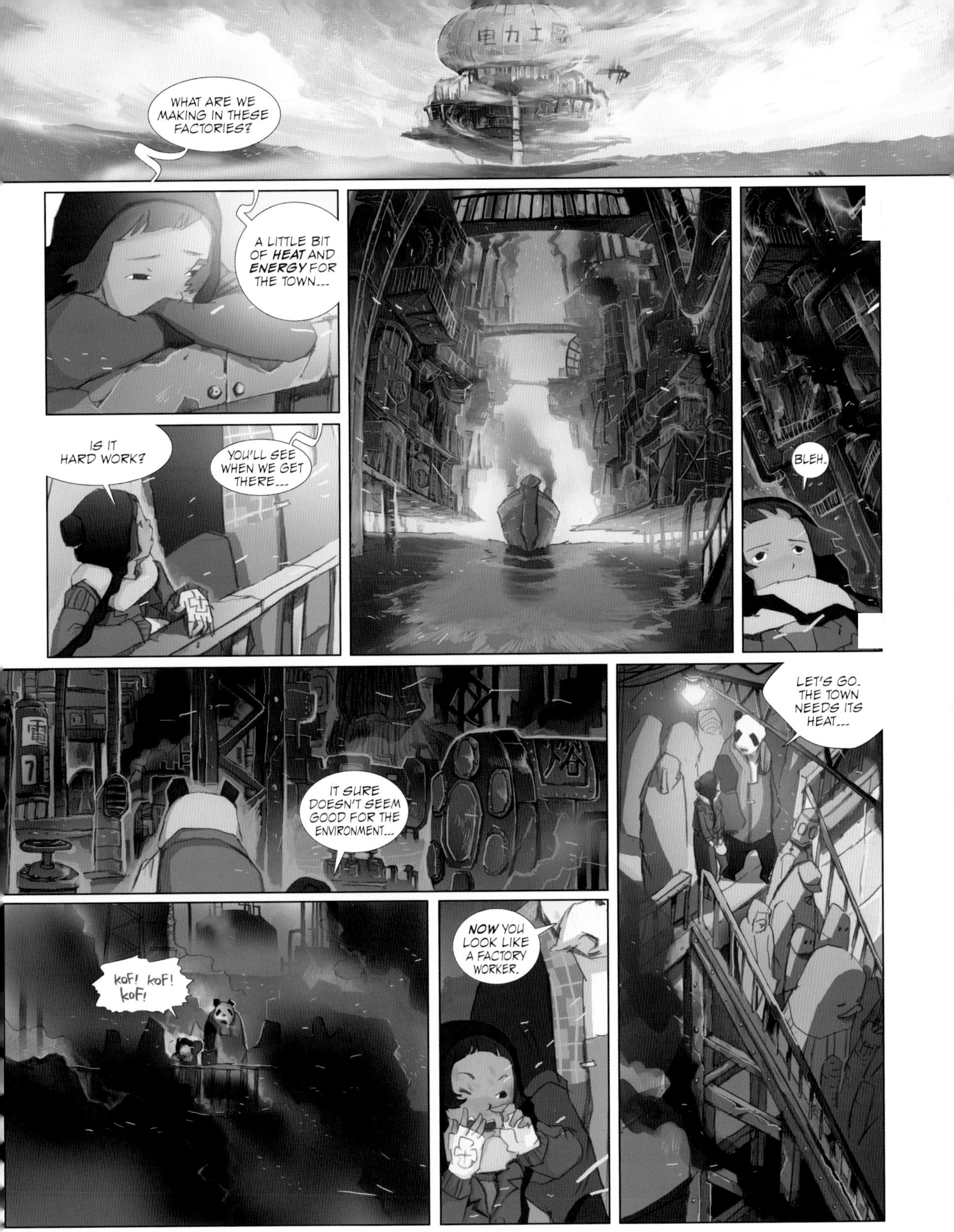

WHAT ARE WE MAKING IN THESE FACTORIES?
A LITTLE BIT OF **HEAT** AND **ENERGY** FOR THE TOWN...
IS IT HARD WORK?
YOU'LL SEE WHEN WE GET THERE...
BLEH.
IT SURE DOESN'T SEEM GOOD FOR THE ENVIRONMENT...
LET'S GO. THE TOWN NEEDS ITS HEAT...
kOF! kOF! kOF!
NOW YOU LOOK LIKE A FACTORY WORKER.

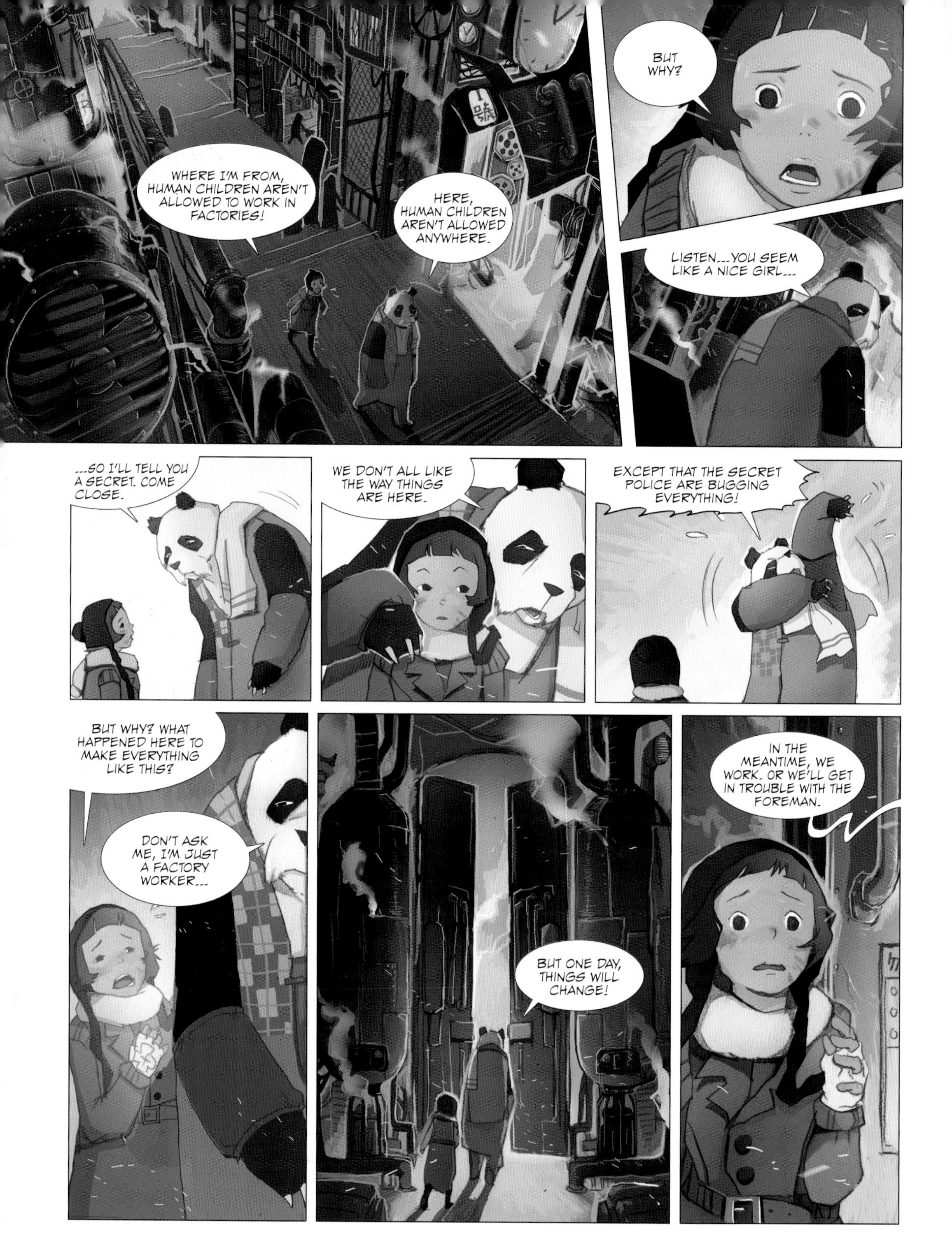
WHERE I'M FROM, HUMAN CHILDREN AREN'T ALLOWED TO WORK IN FACTORIES!
HERE, HUMAN CHILDREN AREN'T ALLOWED ANYWHERE.
BUT WHY?
LISTEN... YOU SEEM LIKE A NICE GIRL...
...SO I'LL TELL YOU A SECRET. COME CLOSE.
WE DON'T ALL LIKE THE WAY THINGS ARE HERE.
EXCEPT THAT THE SECRET POLICE ARE BUGGING EVERYTHING!
BUT WHY? WHAT HAPPENED HERE TO MAKE EVERYTHING LIKE THIS?
DON'T ASK ME, I'M JUST A FACTORY WORKER...
BUT ONE DAY, THINGS WILL CHANGE!
IN THE MEANTIME, WE WORK. OR WE'LL GET IN TROUBLE WITH THE FOREMAN.

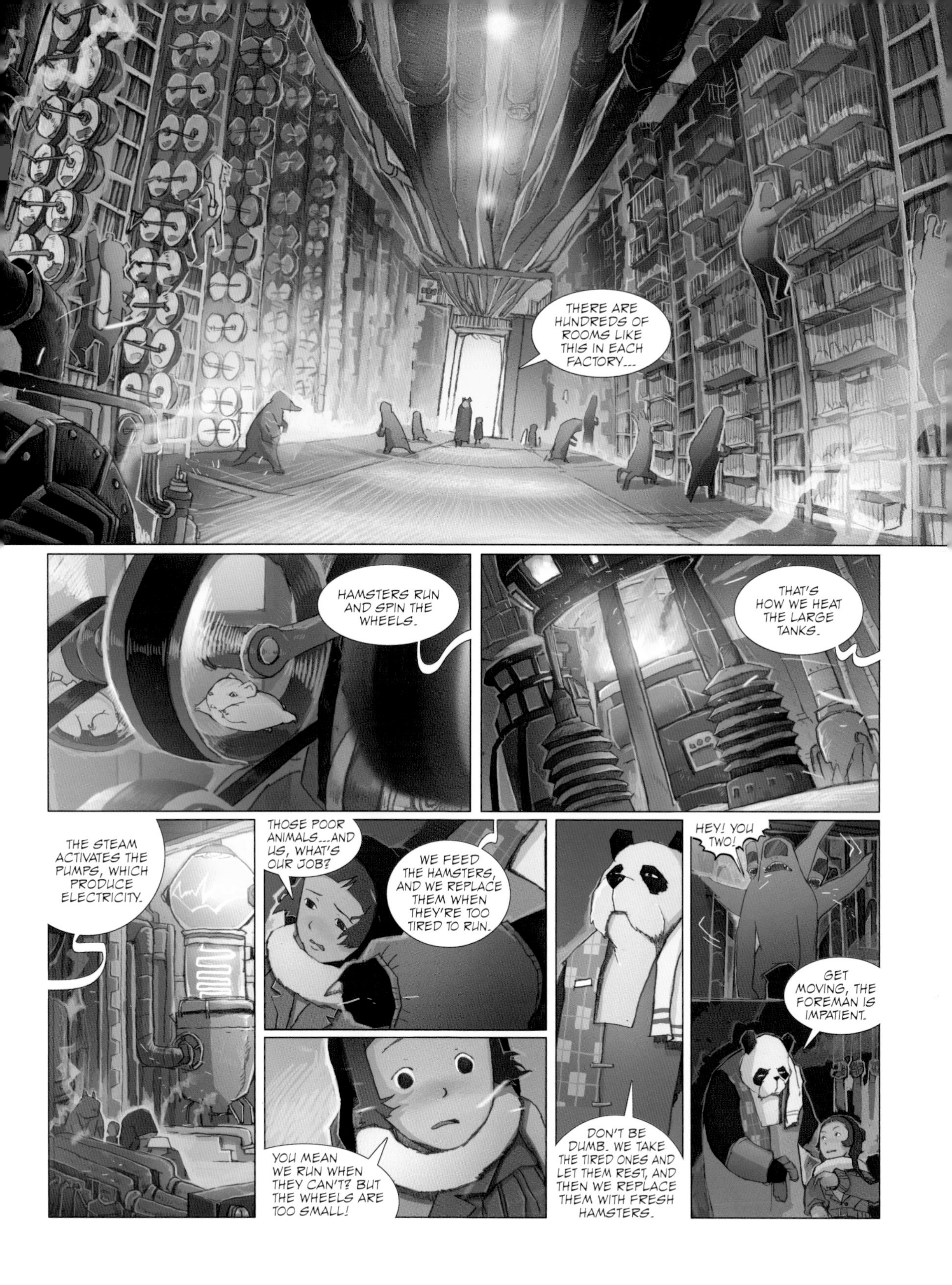
THERE ARE HUNDREDS OF ROOMS LIKE THIS IN EACH FACTORY...
HAMSTERS RUN AND SPIN THE WHEELS.
THAT'S HOW WE HEAT THE LARGE TANKS.
THE STEAM ACTIVATES THE PUMPS, WHICH PRODUCE ELECTRICITY.
THOSE POOR ANIMALS...AND US, WHAT'S OUR JOB?
WE FEED THE HAMSTERS, AND WE REPLACE THEM WHEN THEY'RE TOO TIRED TO RUN.
YOU MEAN WE RUN WHEN THEY CAN'T? BUT THE WHEELS ARE TOO SMALL!
DON'T BE DUMB. WE TAKE THE TIRED ONES AND LET THEM REST, AND THEN WE REPLACE THEM WITH FRESH HAMSTERS.
HEY! YOU TWO!
GET MOVING, THE FOREMAN IS IMPATIENT.

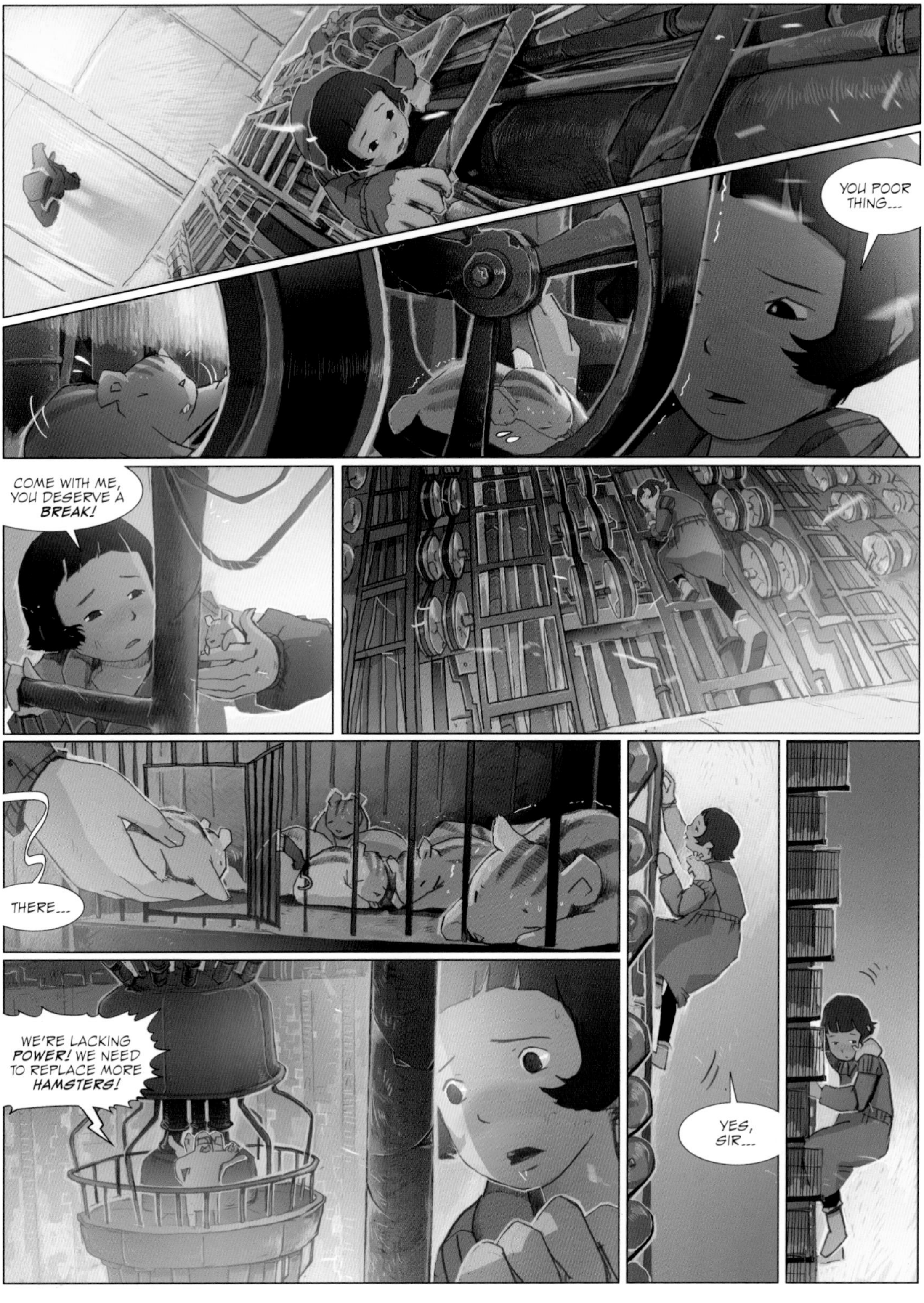
YOU POOR THING...
COME WITH ME, YOU DESERVE A BREAK!
THERE...
WE'RE LACKING POWER! WE NEED TO REPLACE MORE HAMSTERS!
YES, SIR...

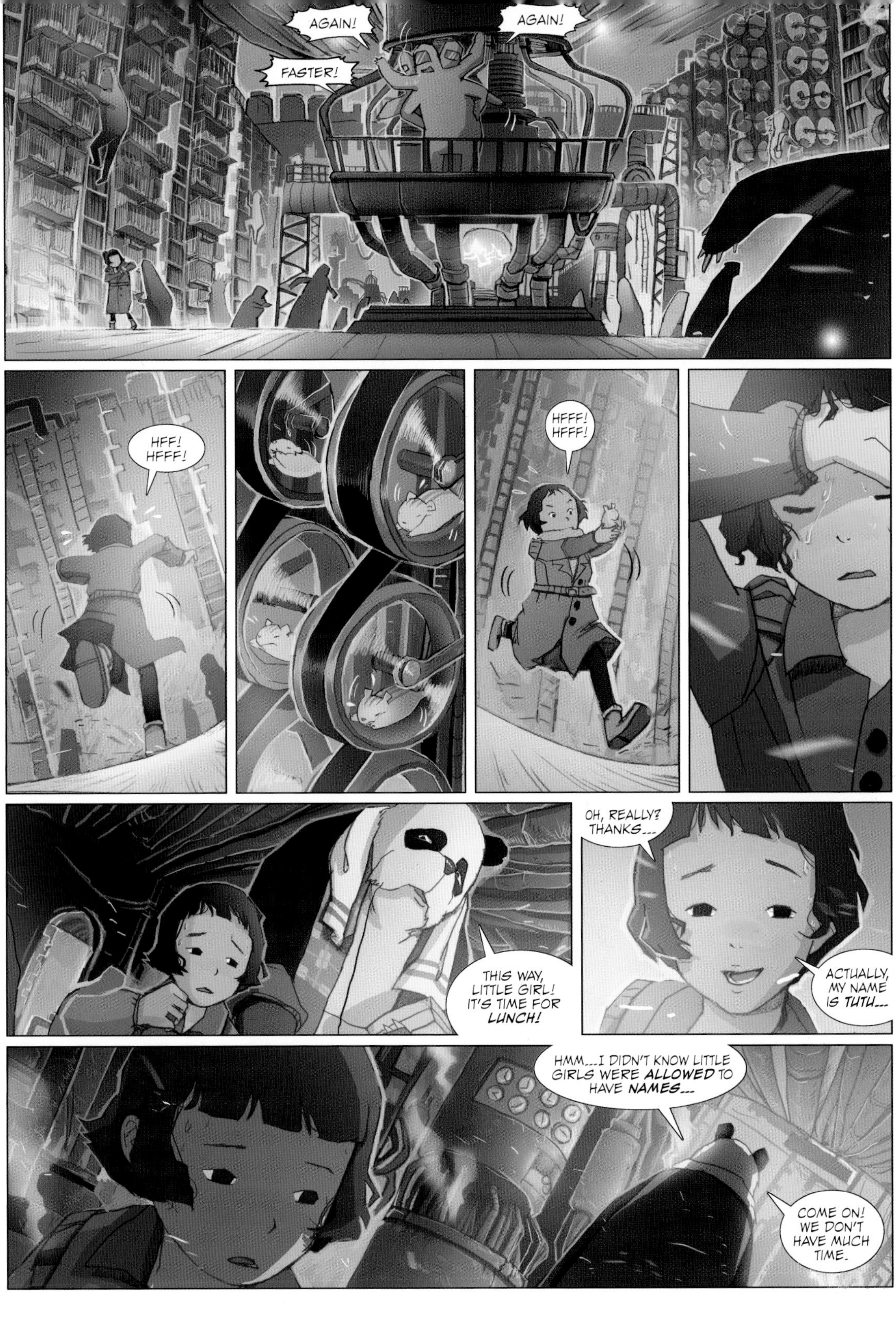
AGAIN!
AGAIN!
FASTER!
HFF! HFFF!
HFFF! HFFF!
THIS WAY, LITTLE GIRL! IT'S TIME FOR **LUNCH!**
OH, REALLY? THANKS...
ACTUALLY, MY NAME IS **TUTU...**
HMM...I DIDN'T KNOW LITTLE GIRLS WERE **ALLOWED** TO HAVE **NAMES...**
COME ON! WE DON'T HAVE MUCH TIME.

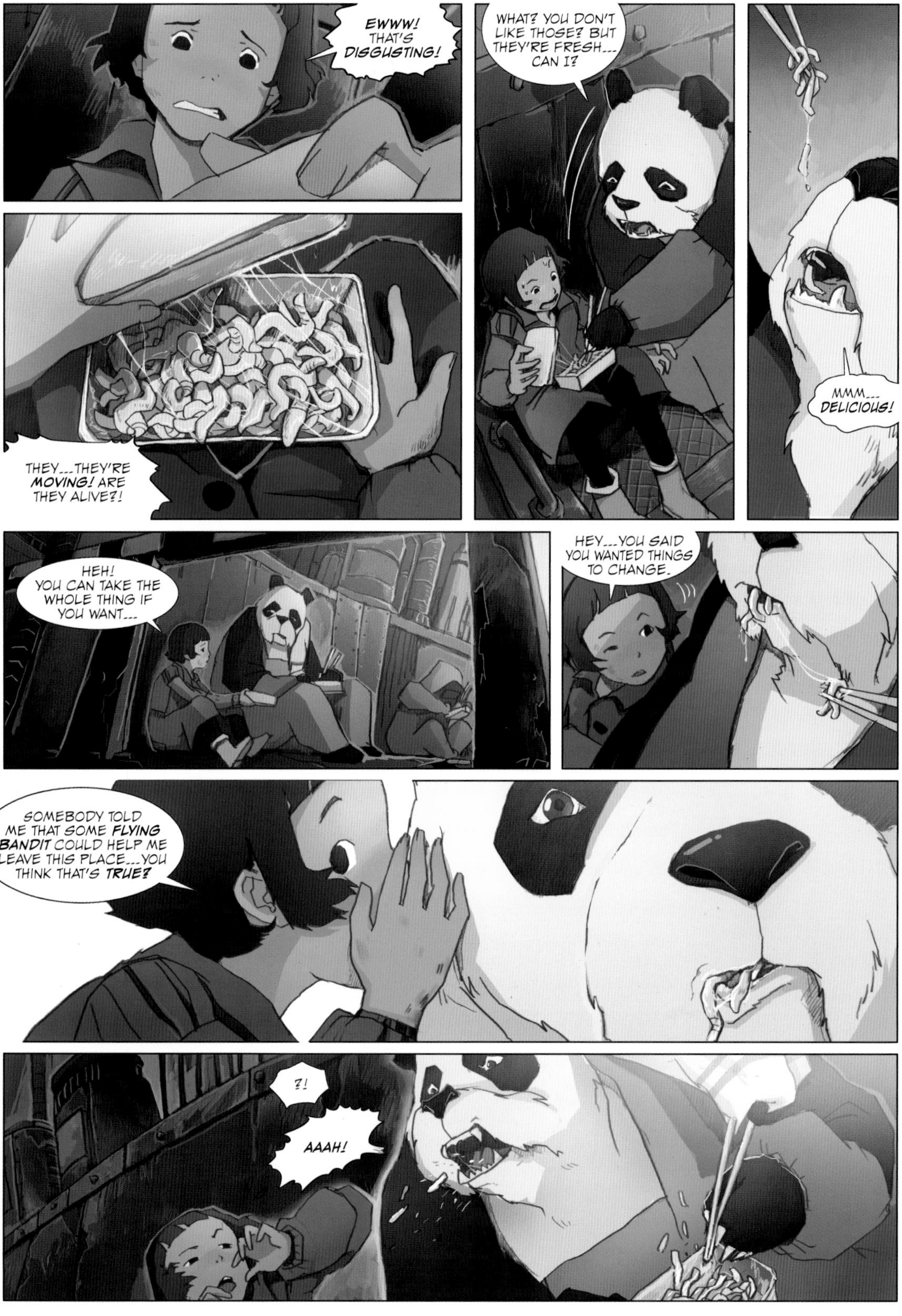
EWWW! THAT'S DISGUSTING!
WHAT? YOU DON'T LIKE THOSE? BUT THEY'RE FRESH... CAN I?
THEY... THEY'RE MOVING! ARE THEY ALIVE?!
MMM... DELICIOUS!
HEH! YOU CAN TAKE THE WHOLE THING IF YOU WANT...
HEY... YOU SAID YOU WANTED THINGS TO CHANGE.
SOMEBODY TOLD ME THAT SOME FLYING BANDIT COULD HELP ME LEAVE THIS PLACE... YOU THINK THAT'S TRUE?
?!
AAAH!

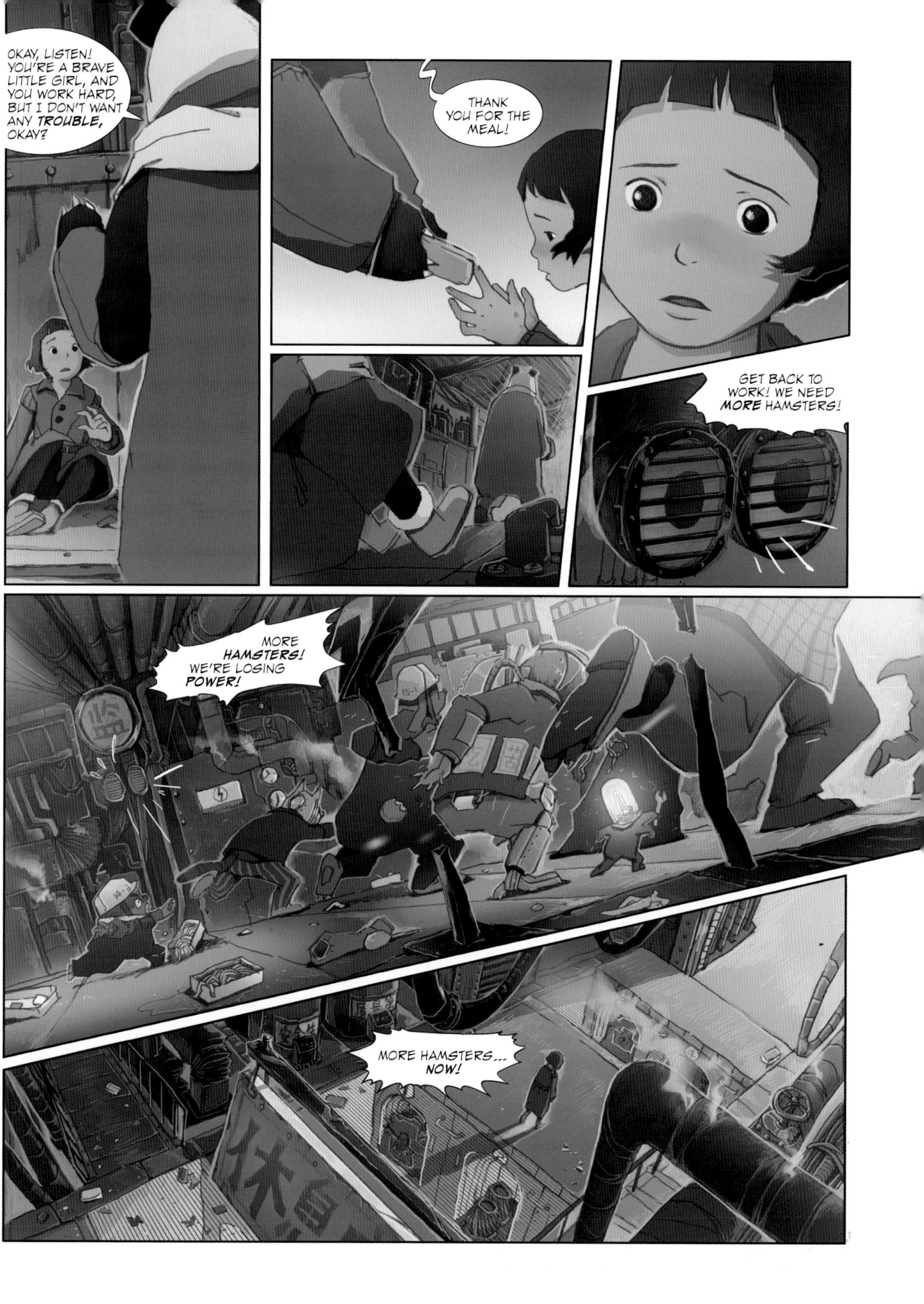
OKAY, LISTEN! YOU'RE A BRAVE LITTLE GIRL, AND YOU WORK HARD, BUT I DON'T WANT ANY **TROUBLE,** OKAY?
THANK YOU FOR THE MEAL!
GET BACK TO WORK! WE NEED **MORE** HAMSTERS!
MORE **HAMSTERS!** WE'RE LOSING **POWER!**
MORE HAMSTERS... **NOW!**

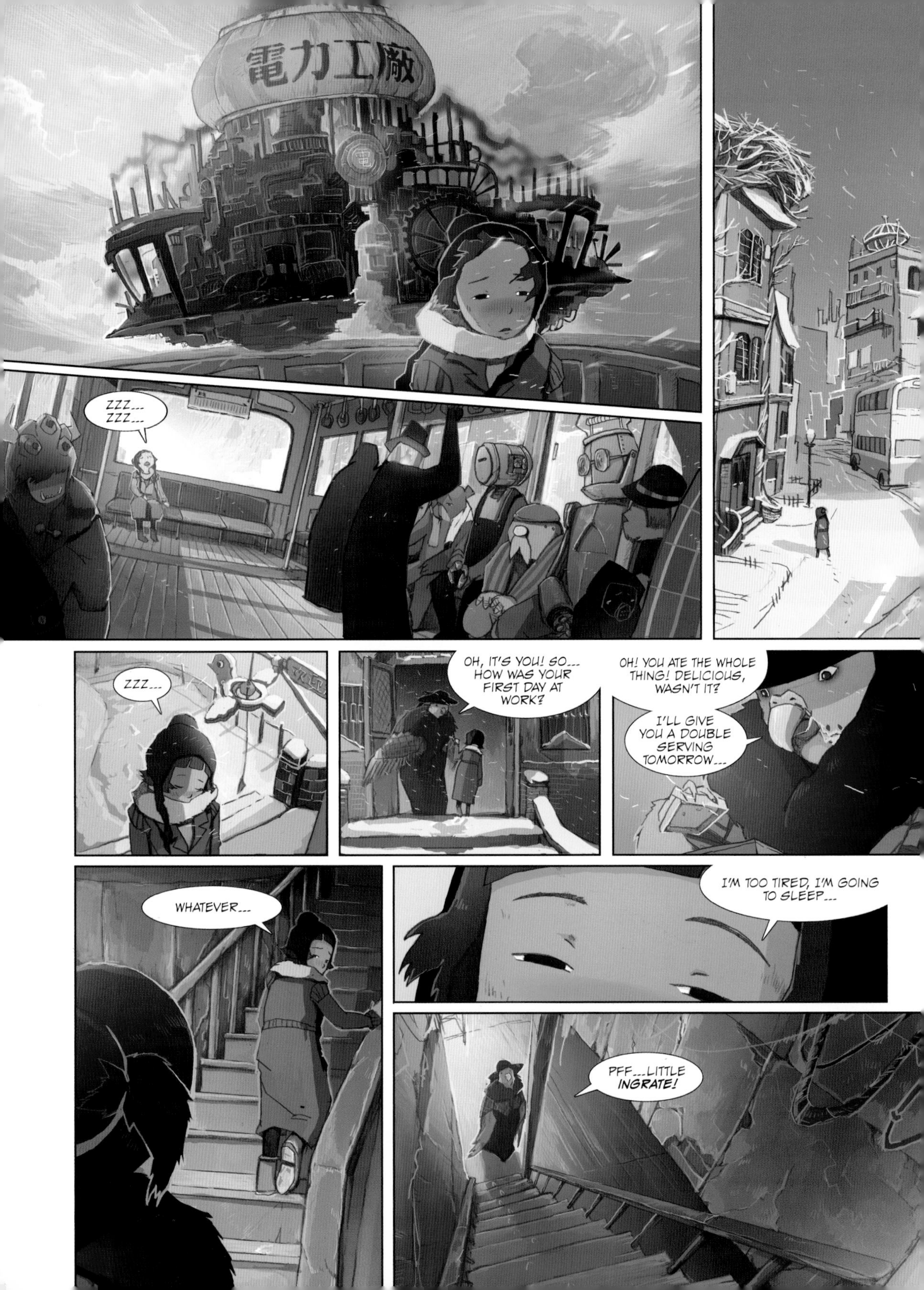

電力工廠
ZZZ...
ZZZ...
ZZZ...
OH, IT'S YOU! SO... HOW WAS YOUR FIRST DAY AT WORK?
OH! YOU ATE THE WHOLE THING! DELICIOUS, WASN'T IT?
I'LL GIVE YOU A DOUBLE SERVING TOMORROW...
WHATEVER...
I'M TOO TIRED, I'M GOING TO SLEEP...
PFF...LITTLE INGRATE!

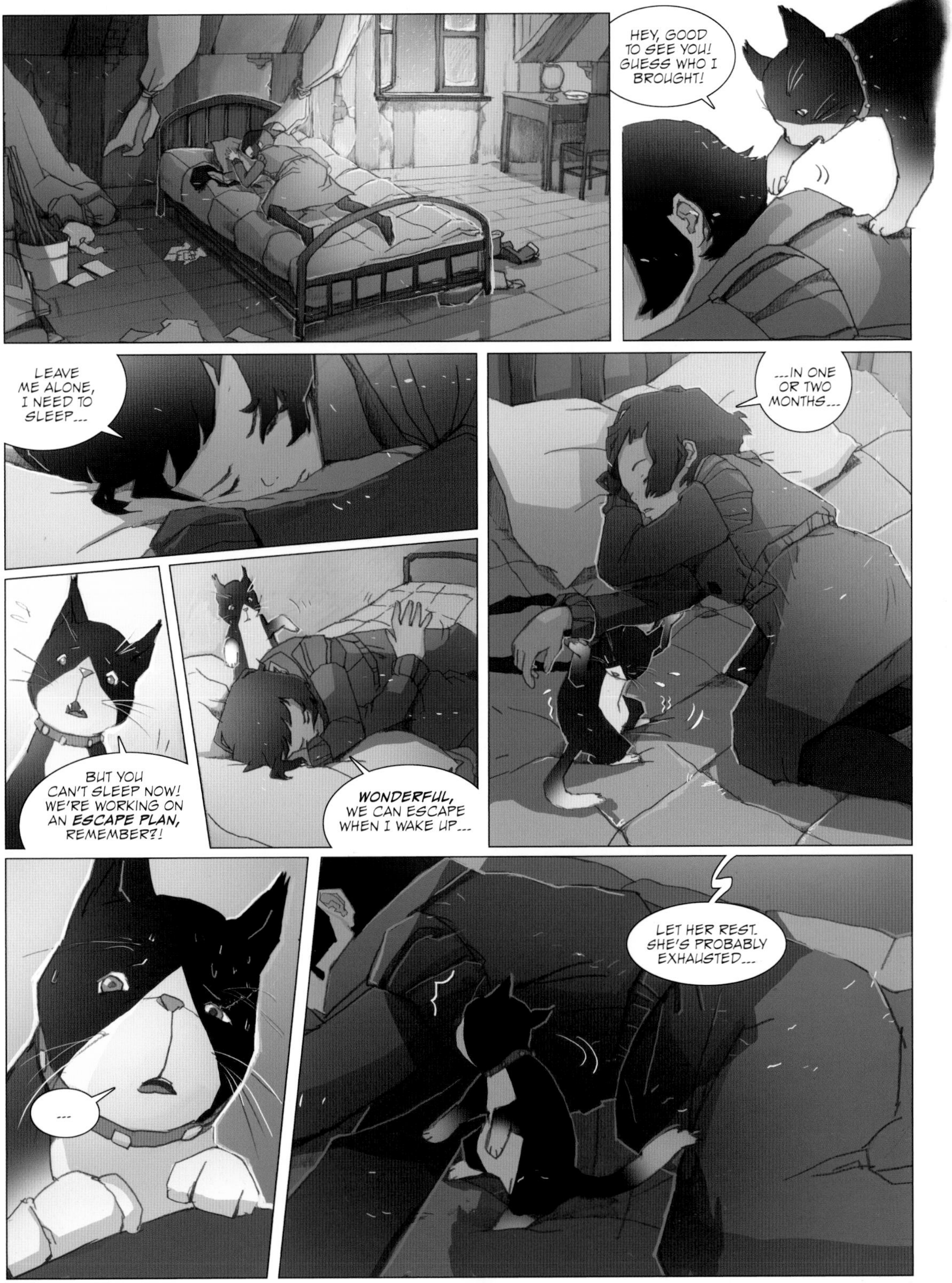
HEY, GOOD TO SEE YOU! GUESS WHO I BROUGHT!
LEAVE ME ALONE, I NEED TO SLEEP...
...IN ONE OR TWO MONTHS...
BUT YOU CAN'T SLEEP NOW! WE'RE WORKING ON AN ESCAPE PLAN, REMEMBER?!
WONDERFUL, WE CAN ESCAPE WHEN I WAKE UP...
...
LET HER REST. SHE'S PROBABLY EXHAUSTED...

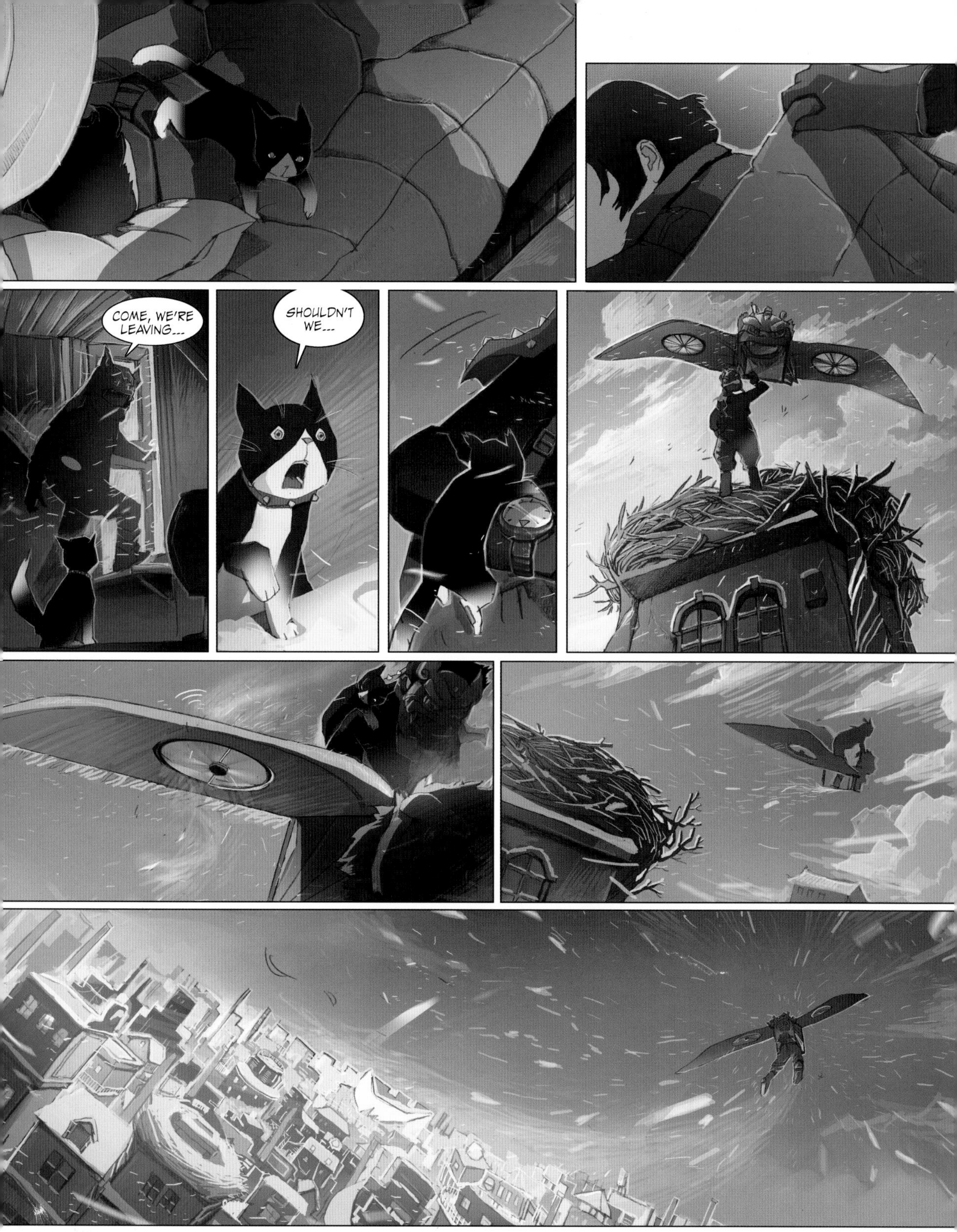
COME, WE'RE LEAVING...
SHOULDN'T WE...

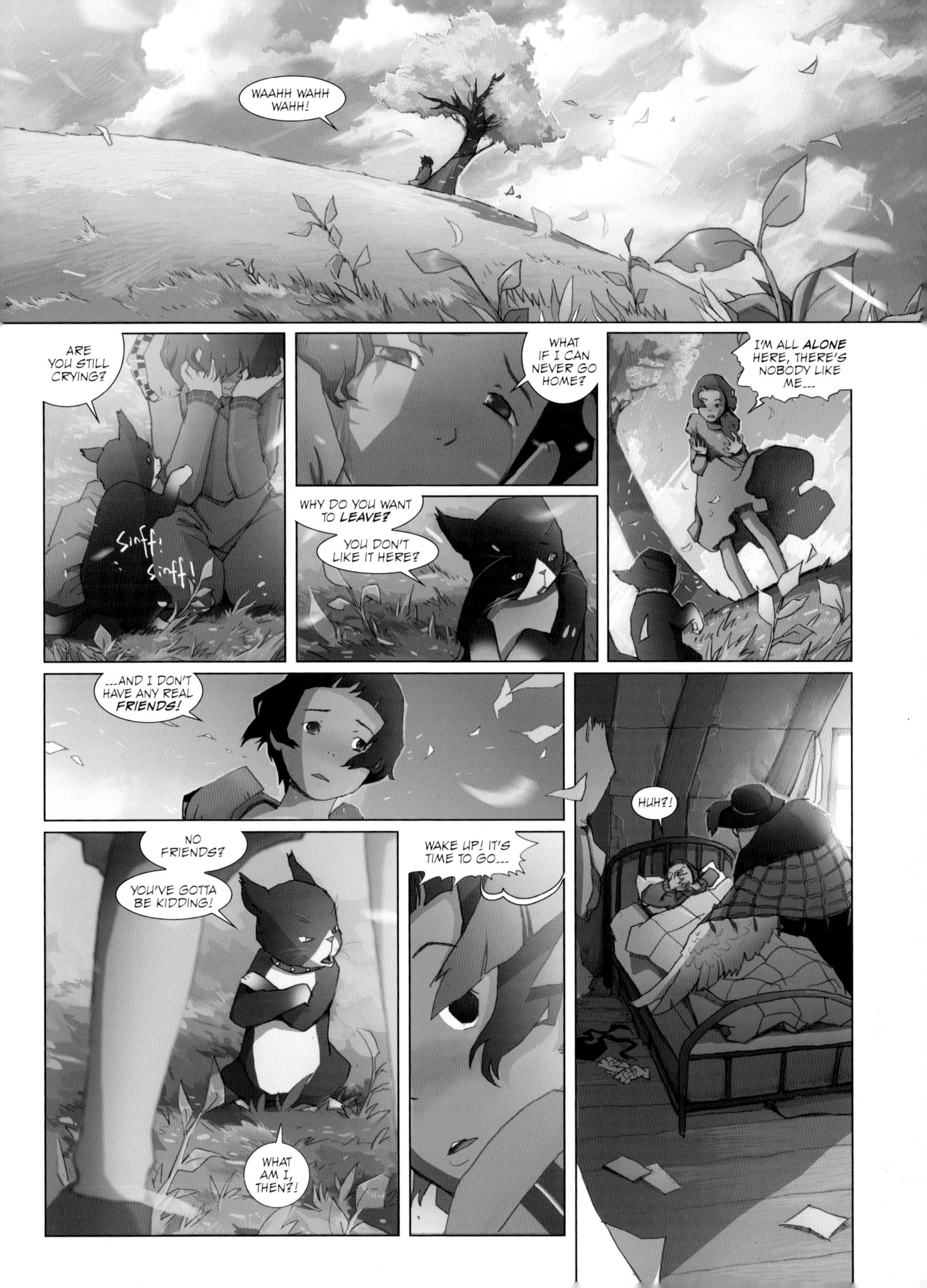
WAAHH WAHH WAHH!
ARE YOU STILL CRYING?
Sniff! Sniff!
WHAT IF I CAN NEVER GO HOME?
WHY DO YOU WANT TO **LEAVE?**
YOU DON'T LIKE IT HERE?
I'M ALL **ALONE** HERE, THERE'S NOBODY LIKE ME...
...AND I DON'T HAVE ANY REAL **FRIENDS!**
NO FRIENDS?
YOU'VE GOTTA BE KIDDING!
WHAT AM I, THEN?!
WAKE UP! IT'S TIME TO GO...
HUH?!

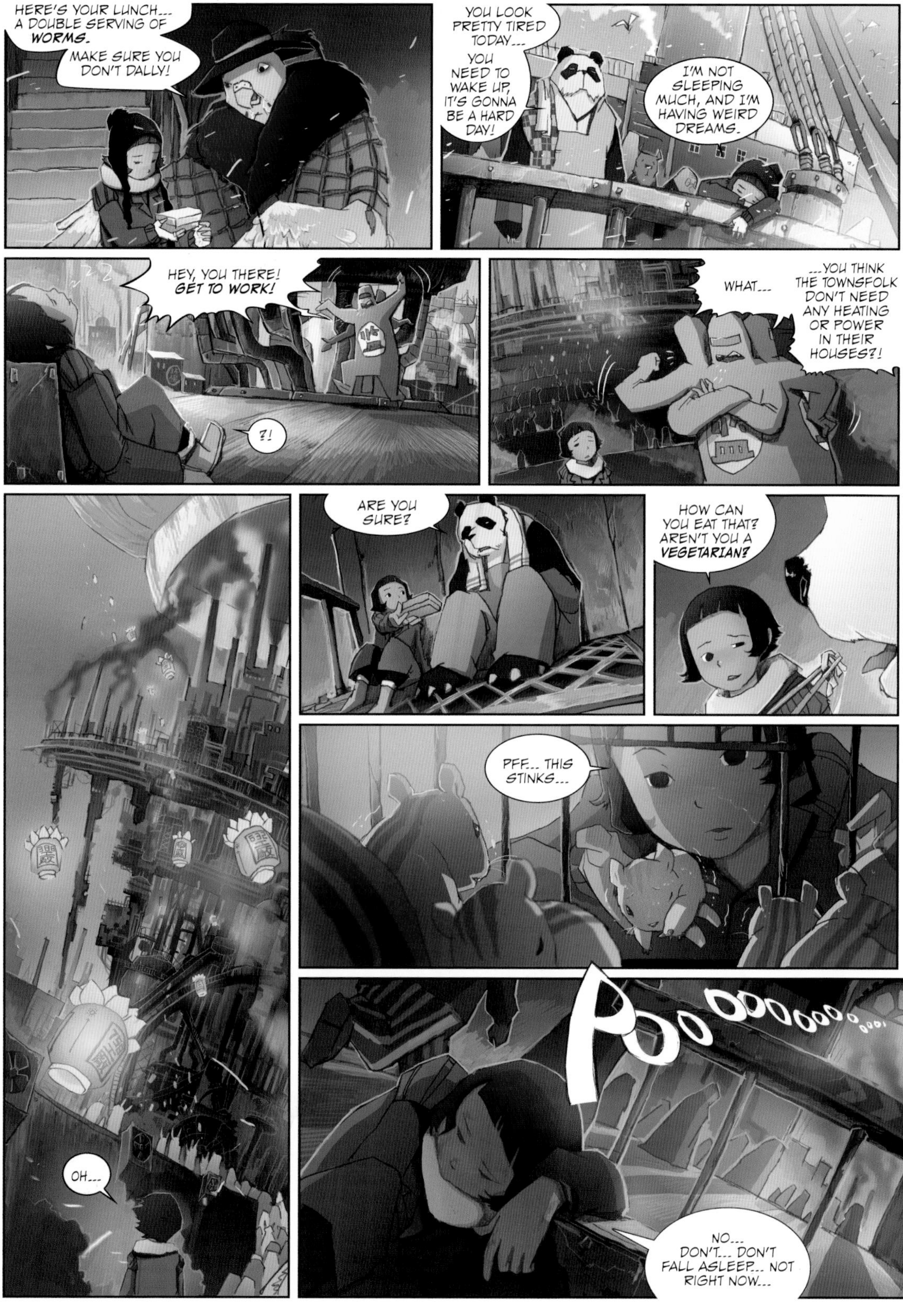
HERE'S YOUR LUNCH... A DOUBLE SERVING OF WORMS.
MAKE SURE YOU DON'T DALLY!
YOU LOOK PRETTY TIRED TODAY...
YOU NEED TO WAKE UP, IT'S GONNA BE A HARD DAY!
I'M NOT SLEEPING MUCH, AND I'M HAVING WEIRD DREAMS.
HEY, YOU THERE! GET TO WORK!
?!
WHAT...
...YOU THINK THE TOWNSFOLK DON'T NEED ANY HEATING OR POWER IN THEIR HOUSES?!
OH...
ARE YOU SURE?
HOW CAN YOU EAT THAT? AREN'T YOU A VEGETARIAN?
PFF... THIS STINKS...
POOOOOOOOO...
NO... DON'T... DON'T FALL ASLEEP... NOT RIGHT NOW...

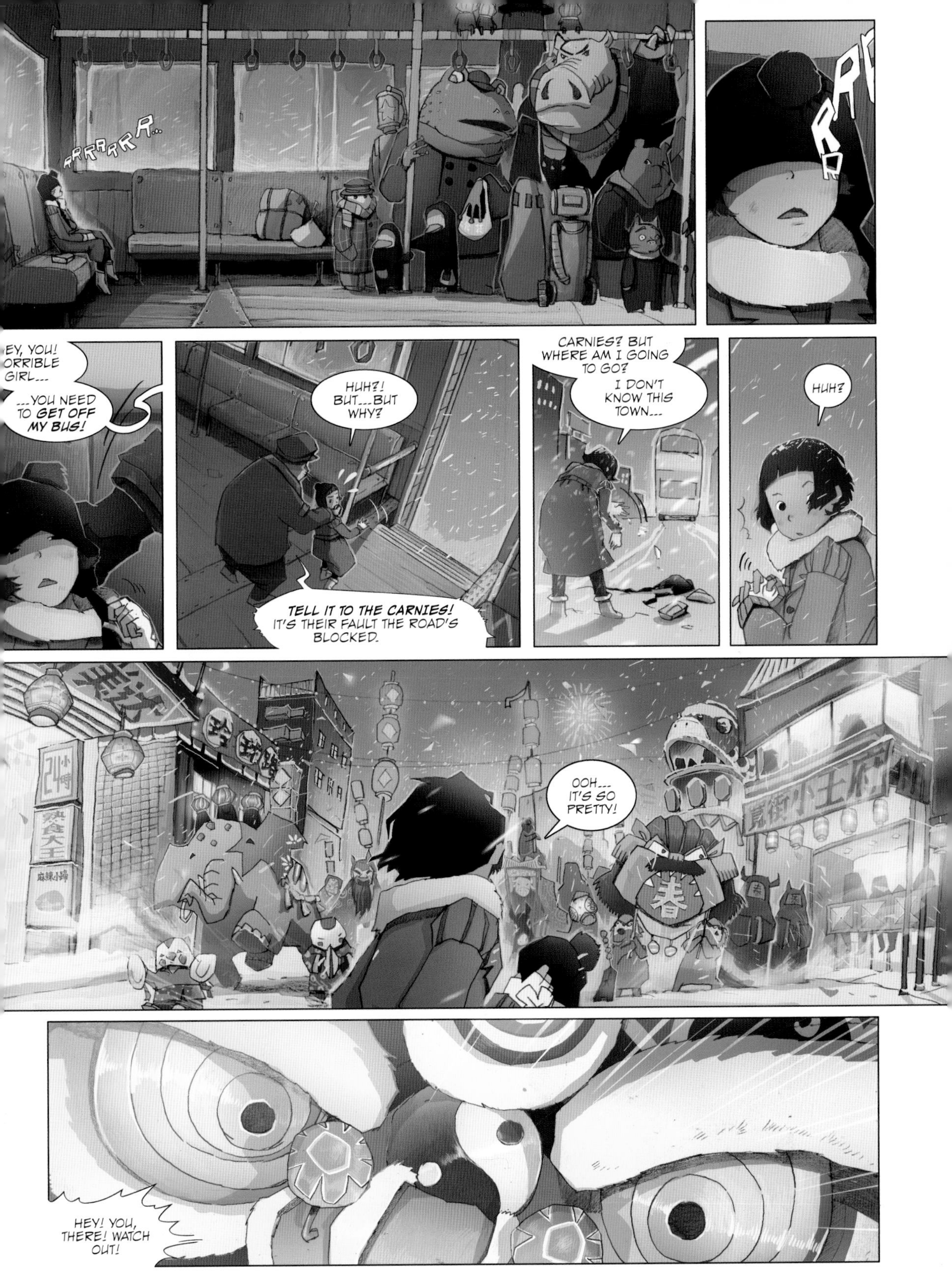
RRRRRRRR...
EY, YOU! ORRIBLE GIRL...
...YOU NEED TO GET OFF MY BUS!
HUH?! BUT... BUT WHY?
TELL IT TO THE CARNIES! IT'S THEIR FAULT THE ROAD'S BLOCKED.
CARNIES? BUT WHERE AM I GOING TO GO?
I DON'T KNOW THIS TOWN...
HUH?
24小時
熟食大王
OOH... IT'S SO PRETTY!
HEY! YOU, THERE! WATCH OUT!

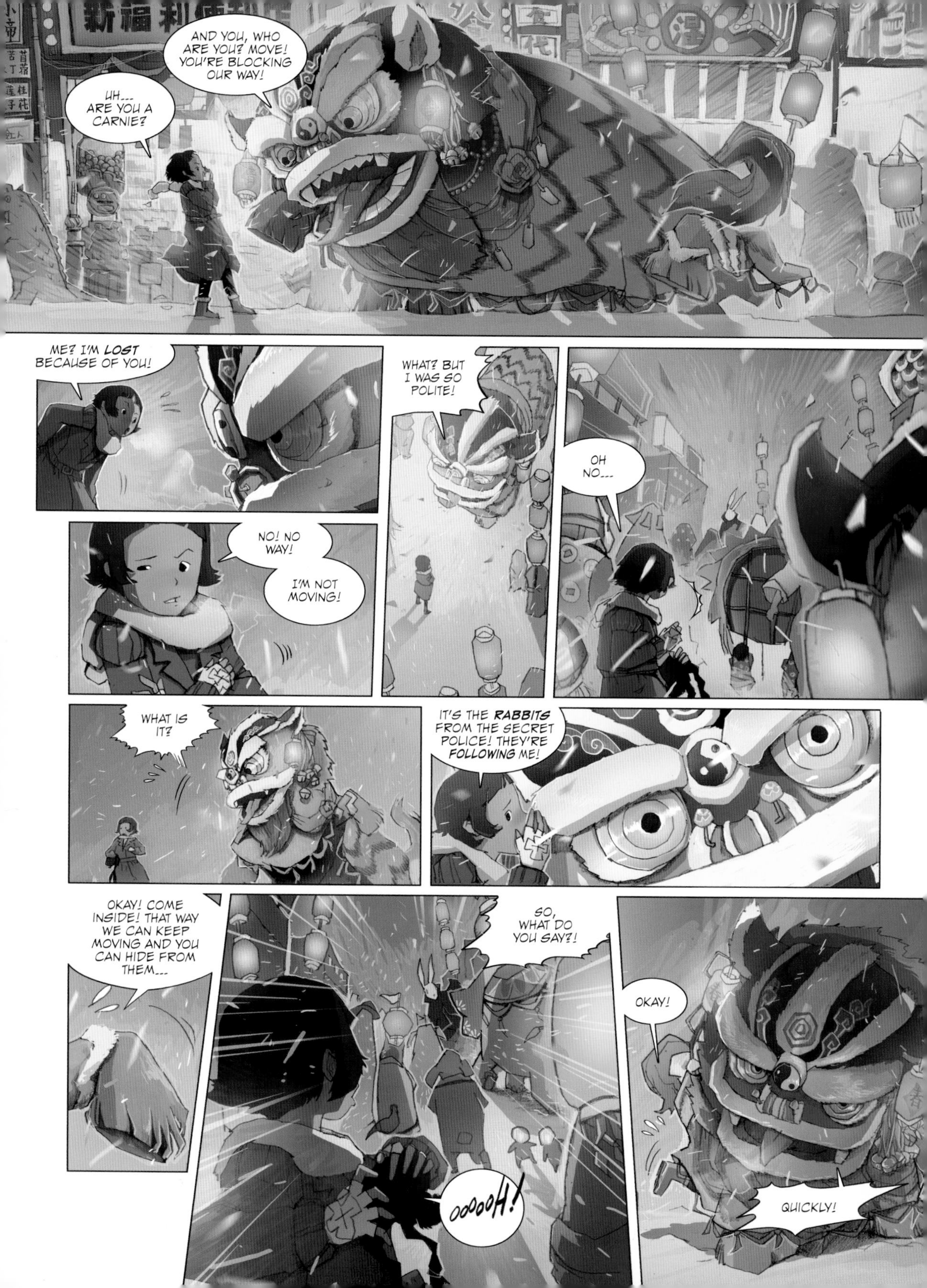

UH... ARE YOU A CARNIE?
AND YOU, WHO ARE YOU? MOVE! YOU'RE BLOCKING OUR WAY!
ME? I'M LOST BECAUSE OF YOU!
WHAT? BUT I WAS SO POLITE!
NO! NO WAY!
I'M NOT MOVING!
OH NO...
WHAT IS IT?
IT'S THE RABBITS FROM THE SECRET POLICE! THEY'RE FOLLOWING ME!
OKAY! COME INSIDE! THAT WAY WE CAN KEEP MOVING AND YOU CAN HIDE FROM THEM...
SO, WHAT DO YOU SAY?!
OOOOOH!
OKAY!
QUICKLY!

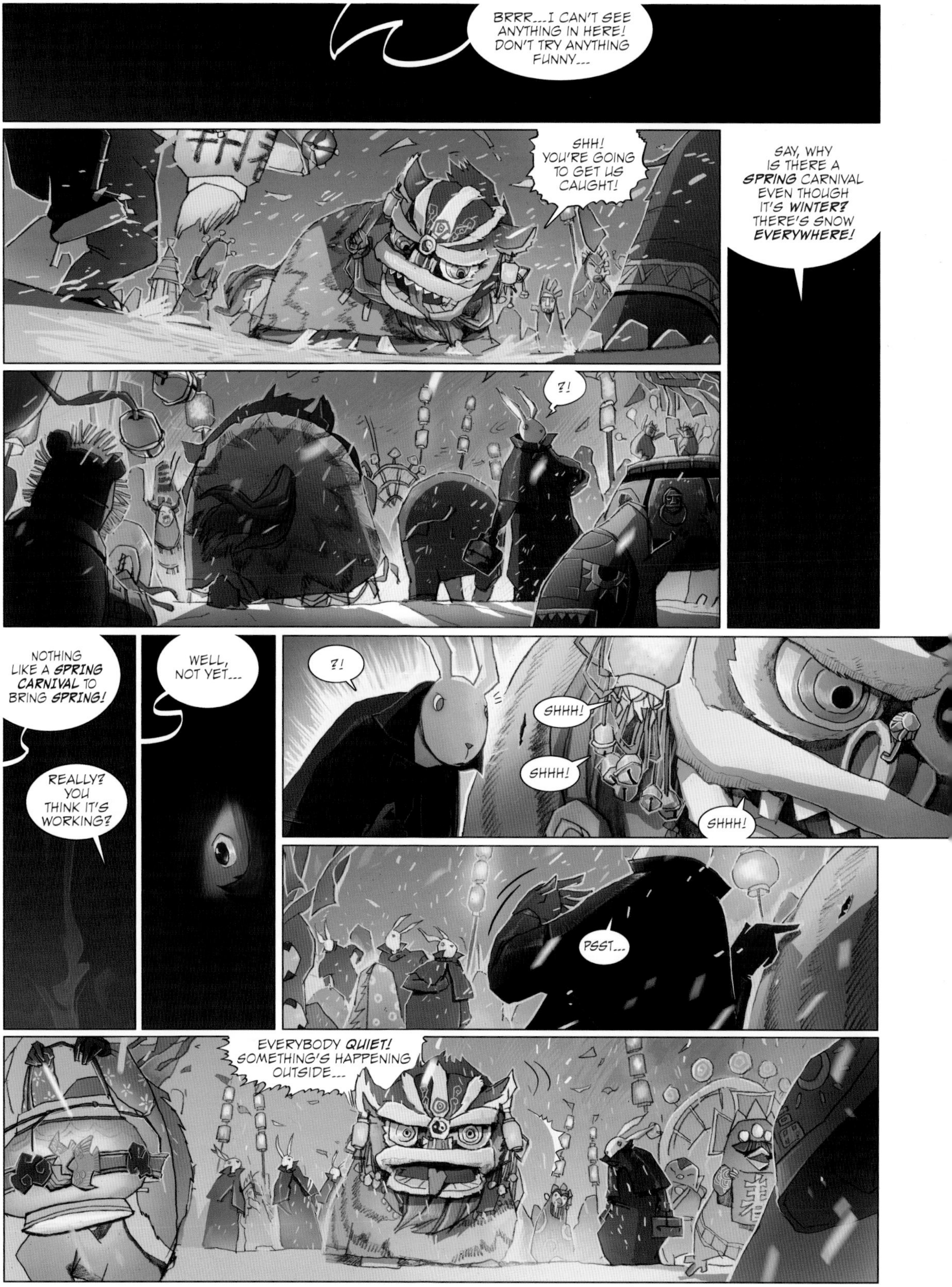
BRRR...I CAN'T SEE ANYTHING IN HERE! DON'T TRY ANYTHING FUNNY...
SHH! YOU'RE GOING TO GET US CAUGHT!
SAY, WHY IS THERE A SPRING CARNIVAL EVEN THOUGH IT'S WINTER? THERE'S SNOW EVERYWHERE!
?!
NOTHING LIKE A SPRING CARNIVAL TO BRING SPRING!
REALLY? YOU THINK IT'S WORKING?
WELL, NOT YET...
?!
SHHH!
SHHH!
SHHH!
PSST...
EVERYBODY QUIET! SOMETHING'S HAPPENING OUTSIDE...

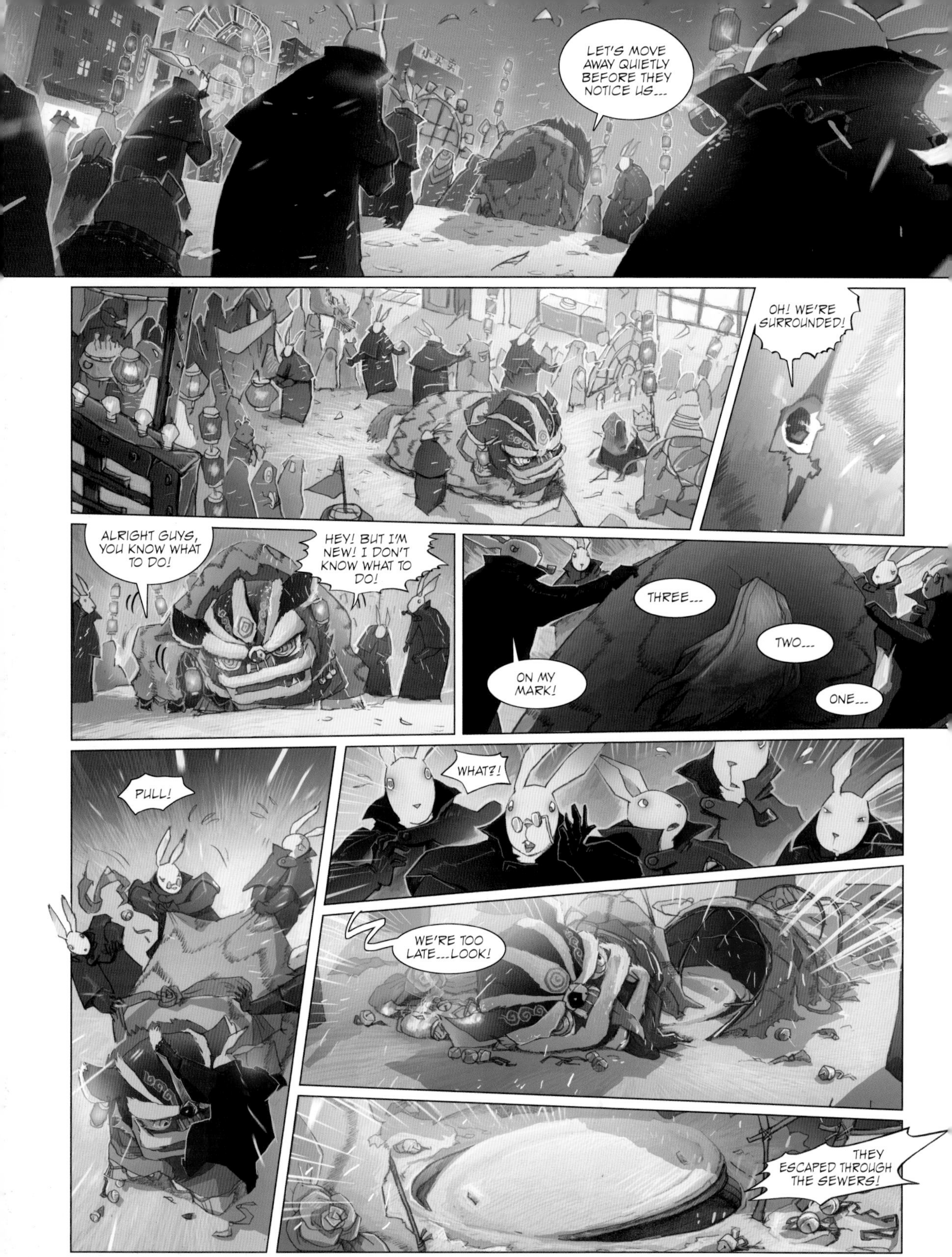
LET'S MOVE AWAY QUIETLY BEFORE THEY NOTICE US...
OH! WE'RE SURROUNDED!
ALRIGHT GUYS, YOU KNOW WHAT TO DO!
HEY! BUT I'M NEW! I DON'T KNOW WHAT TO DO!
THREE...
TWO...
ON MY MARK!
ONE...
PULL!
WHAT?!
WE'RE TOO LATE...LOOK!
THEY ESCAPED THROUGH THE SEWERS!

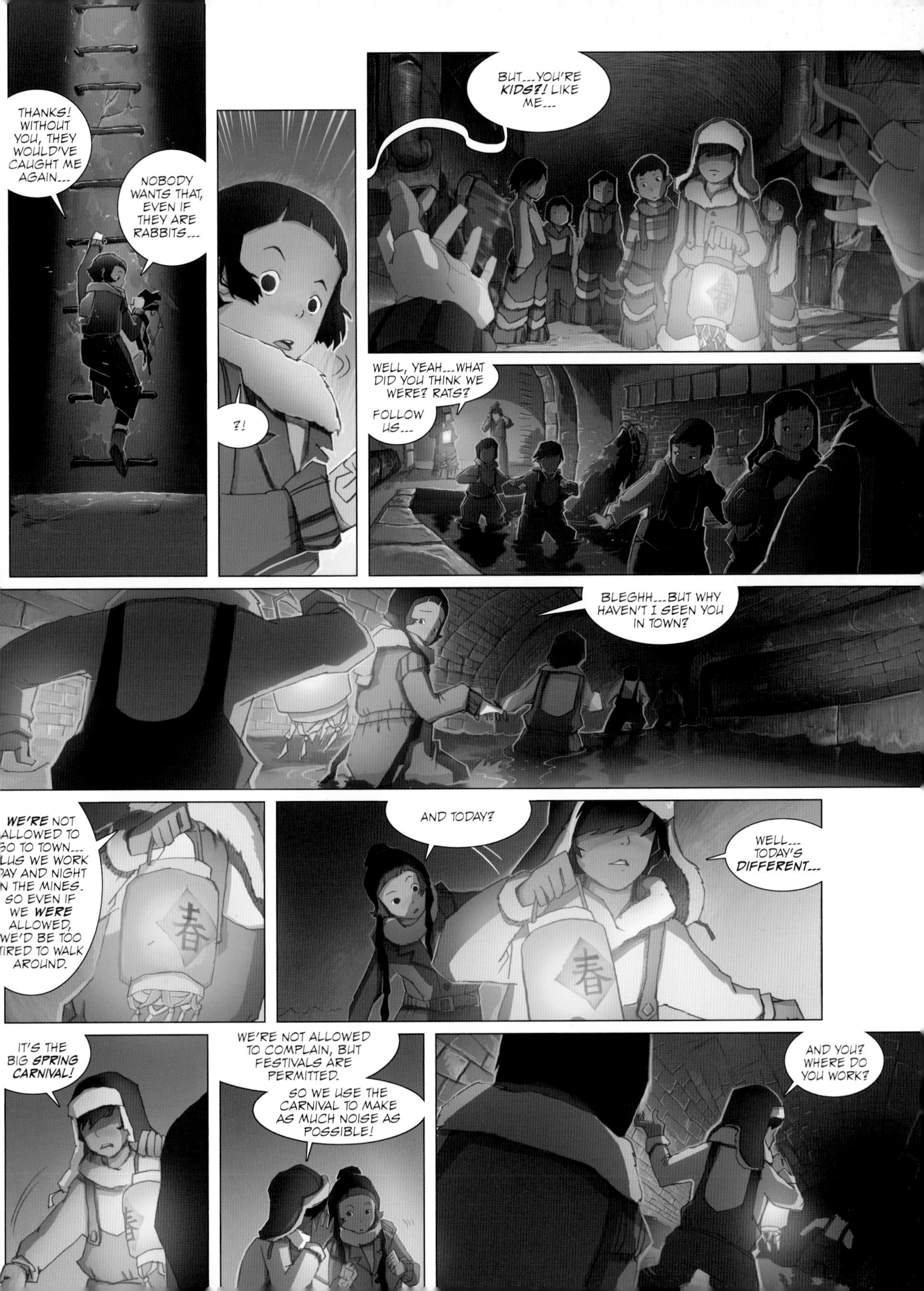

THANKS! WITHOUT YOU, THEY WOULD'VE CAUGHT ME AGAIN...
NOBODY WANTS THAT, EVEN IF THEY ARE RABBITS...
?!
BUT... YOU'RE KIDS?! LIKE ME...
WELL, YEAH... WHAT DID YOU THINK WE WERE? RATS?
FOLLOW US...
BLEGHH... BUT WHY HAVEN'T I SEEN YOU IN TOWN?
WE'RE NOT ALLOWED TO GO TO TOWN... LUS WE WORK AY AND NIGHT N THE MINES. SO EVEN IF WE WERE ALLOWED, WE'D BE TOO IRED TO WALK AROUND.
AND TODAY?
WELL... TODAY'S DIFFERENT...
IT'S THE BIG SPRING CARNIVAL!
WE'RE NOT ALLOWED TO COMPLAIN, BUT FESTIVALS ARE PERMITTED.
SO WE USE THE CARNIVAL TO MAKE AS MUCH NOISE AS POSSIBLE!
AND YOU? WHERE DO YOU WORK?

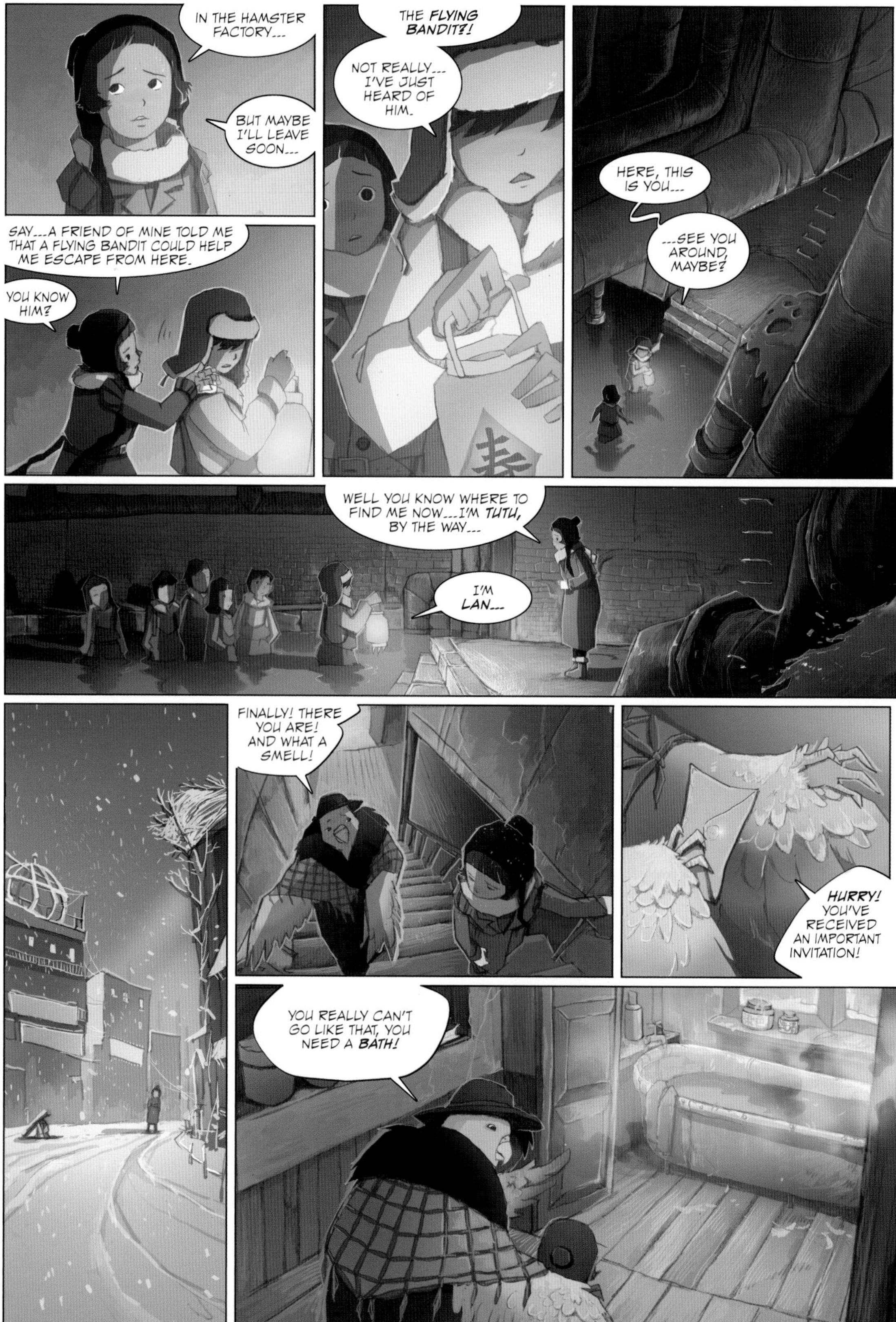

IN THE HAMSTER FACTORY...
BUT MAYBE I'LL LEAVE SOON...
SAY...A FRIEND OF MINE TOLD ME THAT A FLYING BANDIT COULD HELP ME ESCAPE FROM HERE.
YOU KNOW HIM?
THE FLYING BANDIT?!
NOT REALLY... I'VE JUST HEARD OF HIM.
HERE, THIS IS YOU...
...SEE YOU AROUND, MAYBE?
WELL YOU KNOW WHERE TO FIND ME NOW...I'M TUTU, BY THE WAY...
I'M LAN...
FINALLY! THERE YOU ARE! AND WHAT A SMELL!
HURRY! YOU'VE RECEIVED AN IMPORTANT INVITATION!
YOU REALLY CAN'T GO LIKE THAT, YOU NEED A BATH!

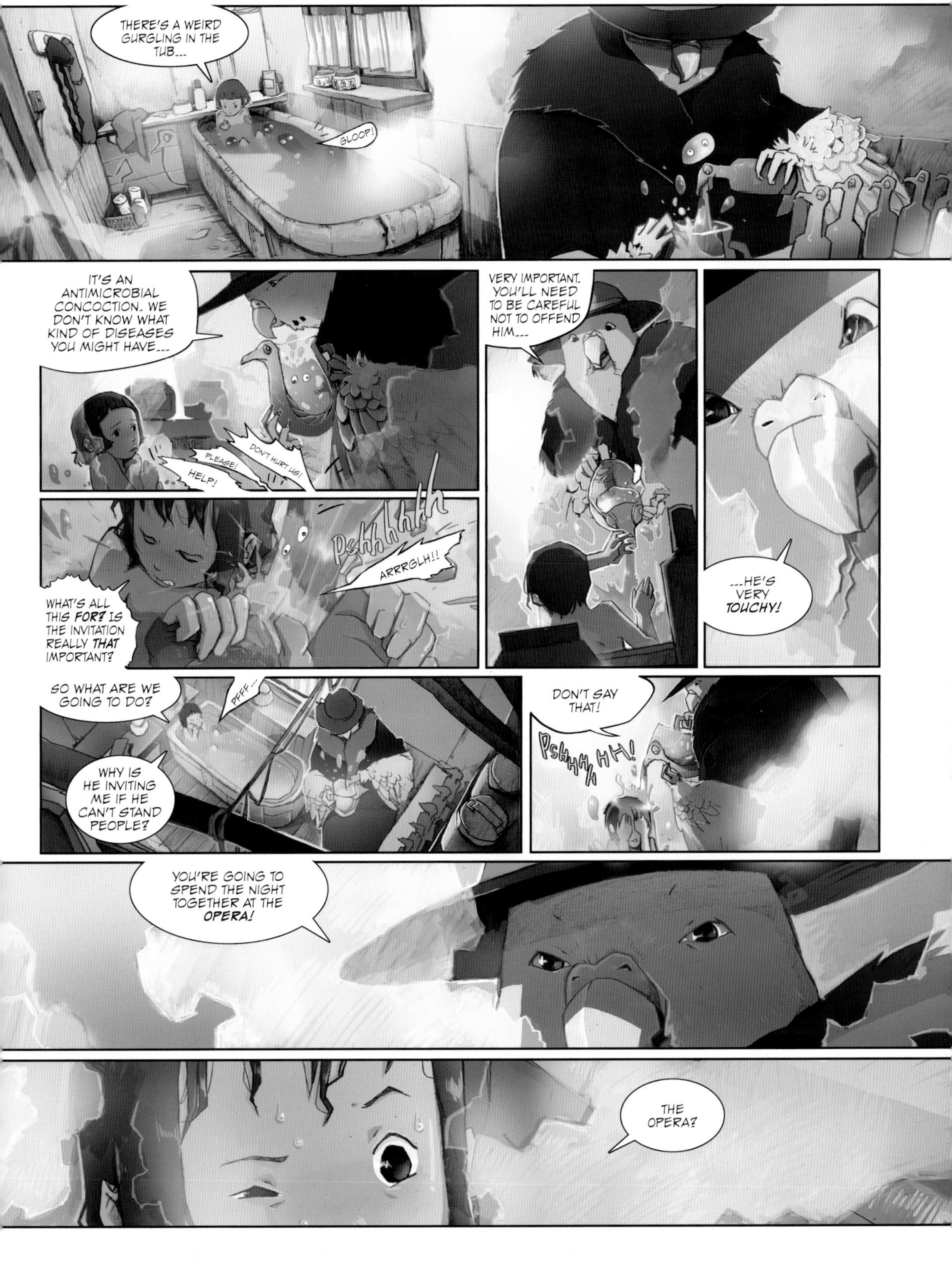

THERE'S A WEIRD GURGLING IN THE TUB...
GLOOP!
IT'S AN ANTIMICROBIAL CONCOCTION. WE DON'T KNOW WHAT KIND OF DISEASES YOU MIGHT HAVE...
DON'T HURT US!
PLEASE!
HELP!
PSHHHHHH
ARRRGLH!!
WHAT'S ALL THIS FOR? IS THE INVITATION REALLY THAT IMPORTANT?
VERY IMPORTANT. YOU'LL NEED TO BE CAREFUL NOT TO OFFEND HIM...
...HE'S VERY TOUCHY!
SO WHAT ARE WE GOING TO DO?
PFFF...
WHY IS HE INVITING ME IF HE CAN'T STAND PEOPLE?
DON'T SAY THAT!
PSHHHHHH!
YOU'RE GOING TO SPEND THE NIGHT TOGETHER AT THE OPERA!
THE OPERA?

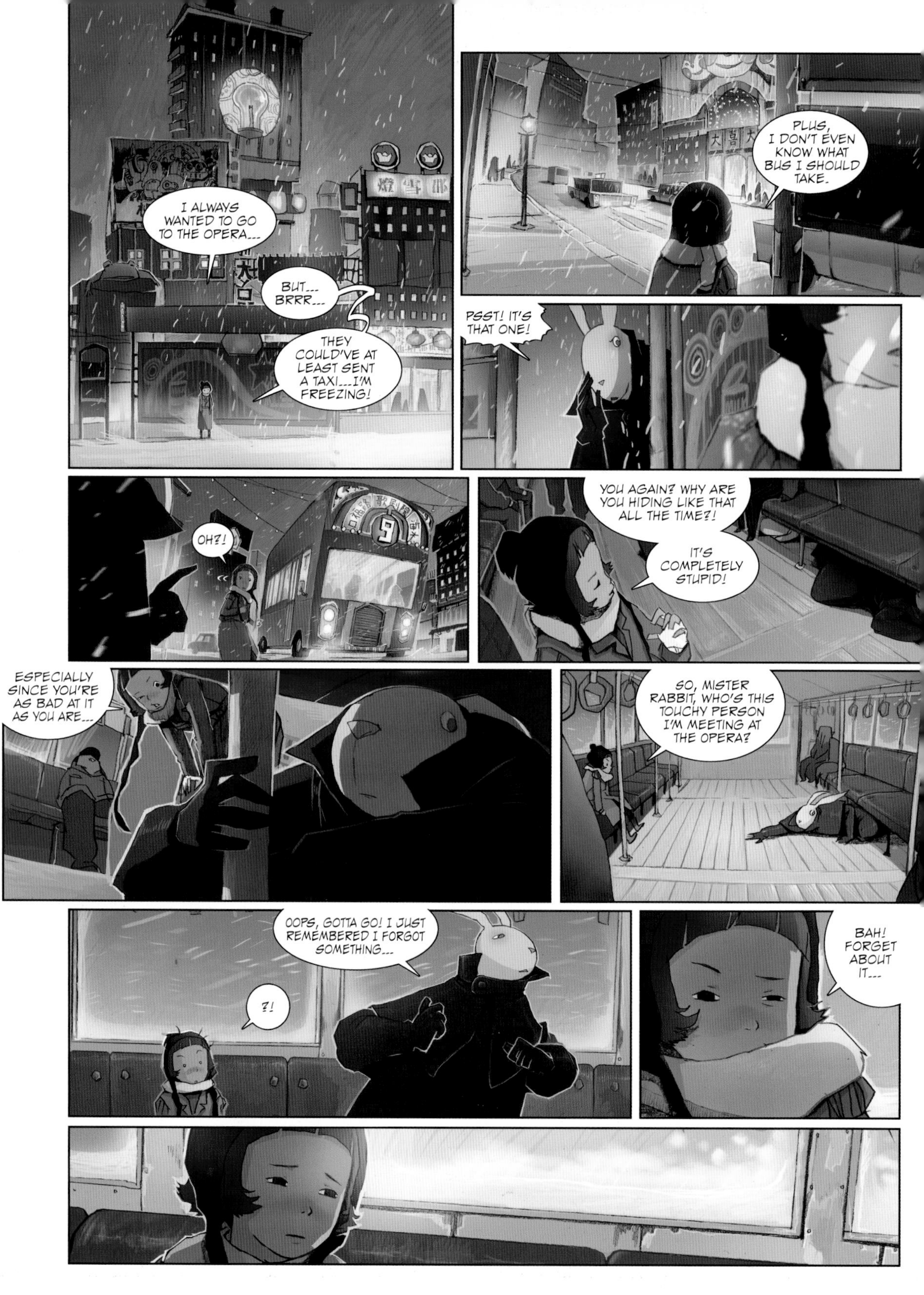
I ALWAYS WANTED TO GO TO THE OPERA...
BUT... BRRR...
THEY COULD'VE AT LEAST SENT A TAXI... I'M FREEZING!
PLUS, I DON'T EVEN KNOW WHAT BUS I SHOULD TAKE.
PSST! IT'S THAT ONE!
OH?!
9
YOU AGAIN? WHY ARE YOU HIDING LIKE THAT ALL THE TIME?!
IT'S COMPLETELY STUPID!
ESPECIALLY SINCE YOU'RE AS BAD AT IT AS YOU ARE...
SO, MISTER RABBIT, WHO'S THIS TOUCHY PERSON I'M MEETING AT THE OPERA?
OOPS, GOTTA GO! I JUST REMEMBERED I FORGOT SOMETHING...
?!
BAH! FORGET ABOUT IT...

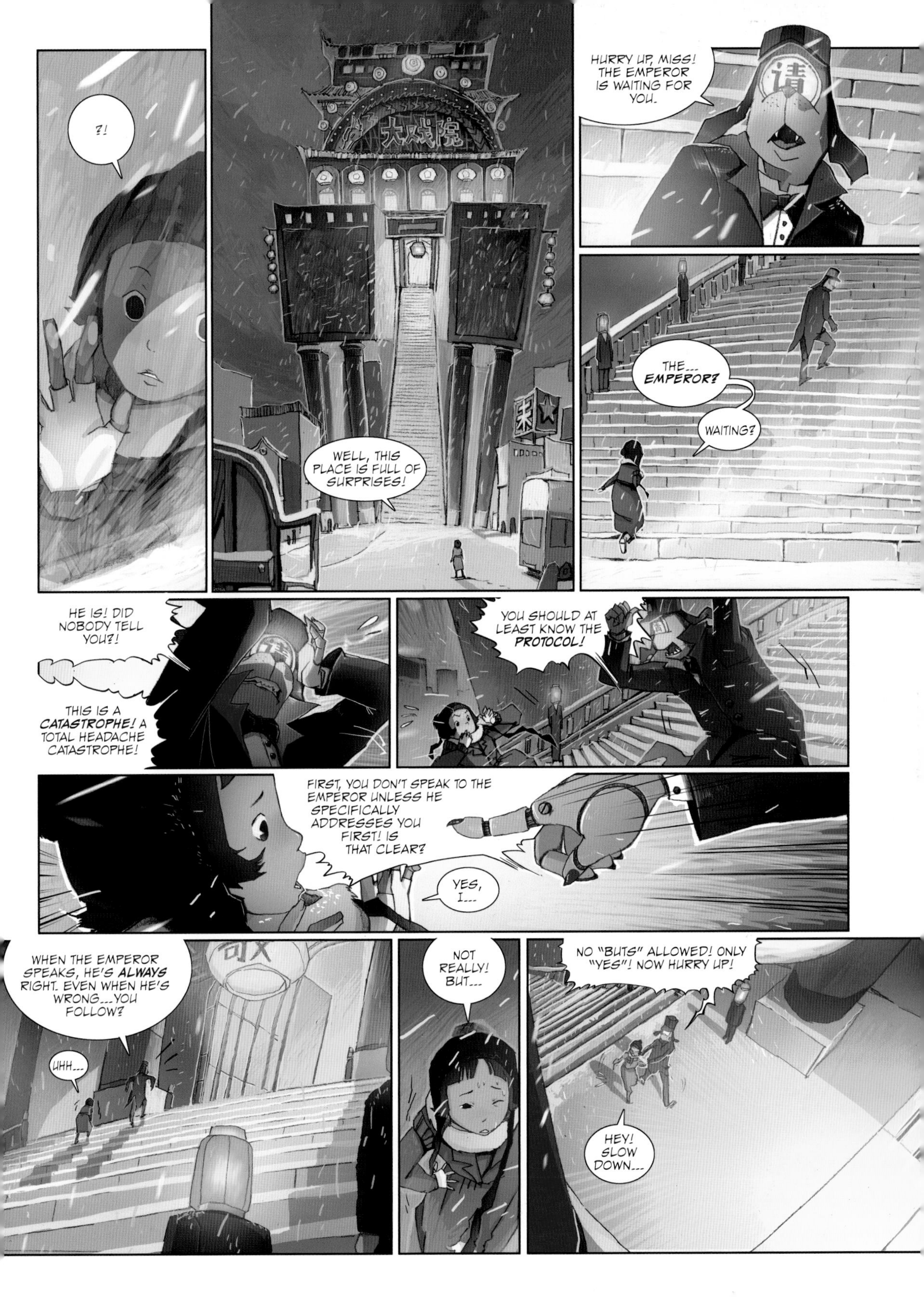

?!
WELL, THIS PLACE IS FULL OF SURPRISES!
HURRY UP, MISS! THE EMPEROR IS WAITING FOR YOU.
THE... EMPEROR?
WAITING?
HE IS! DID NOBODY TELL YOU?!
THIS IS A CATASTROPHE! A TOTAL HEADACHE CATASTROPHE!
YOU SHOULD AT LEAST KNOW THE PROTOCOL!
FIRST, YOU DON'T SPEAK TO THE EMPEROR UNLESS HE SPECIFICALLY ADDRESSES YOU FIRST! IS THAT CLEAR?
YES, I...
WHEN THE EMPEROR SPEAKS, HE'S ALWAYS RIGHT. EVEN WHEN HE'S WRONG...YOU FOLLOW?
UHH...
NOT REALLY! BUT...
NO "BUTS" ALLOWED! ONLY "YES"! NOW HURRY UP!
HEY! SLOW DOWN...

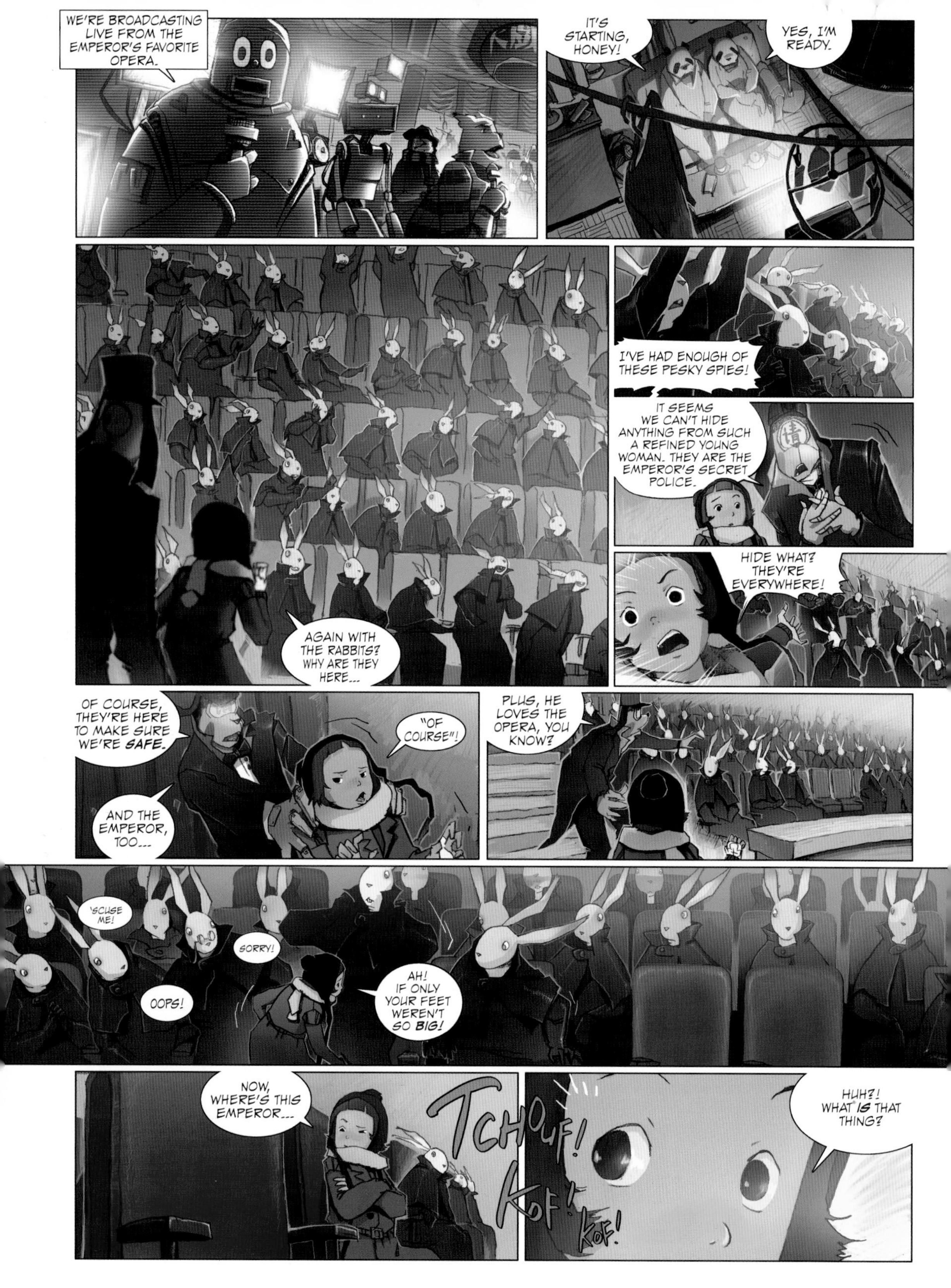
WE'RE BROADCASTING LIVE FROM THE EMPEROR'S FAVORITE OPERA.
IT'S STARTING, HONEY!
YES, I'M READY.
AGAIN WITH THE RABBITS? WHY ARE THEY HERE...
I'VE HAD ENOUGH OF THESE PESKY SPIES!
IT SEEMS WE CAN'T HIDE ANYTHING FROM SUCH A REFINED YOUNG WOMAN. THEY ARE THE EMPEROR'S SECRET POLICE.
HIDE WHAT? THEY'RE EVERYWHERE!
OF COURSE, THEY'RE HERE TO MAKE SURE WE'RE *SAFE*.
"OF COURSE"!
AND THE EMPEROR, TOO...
PLUS, HE LOVES THE OPERA, YOU KNOW?
'SCUSE ME!
SORRY!
OOPS!
AH! IF ONLY YOUR FEET WEREN'T SO *BIG*!
NOW, WHERE'S THIS EMPEROR...
TCHOUF! KOF! KOF!
HUH?! WHAT *IS* THAT THING?

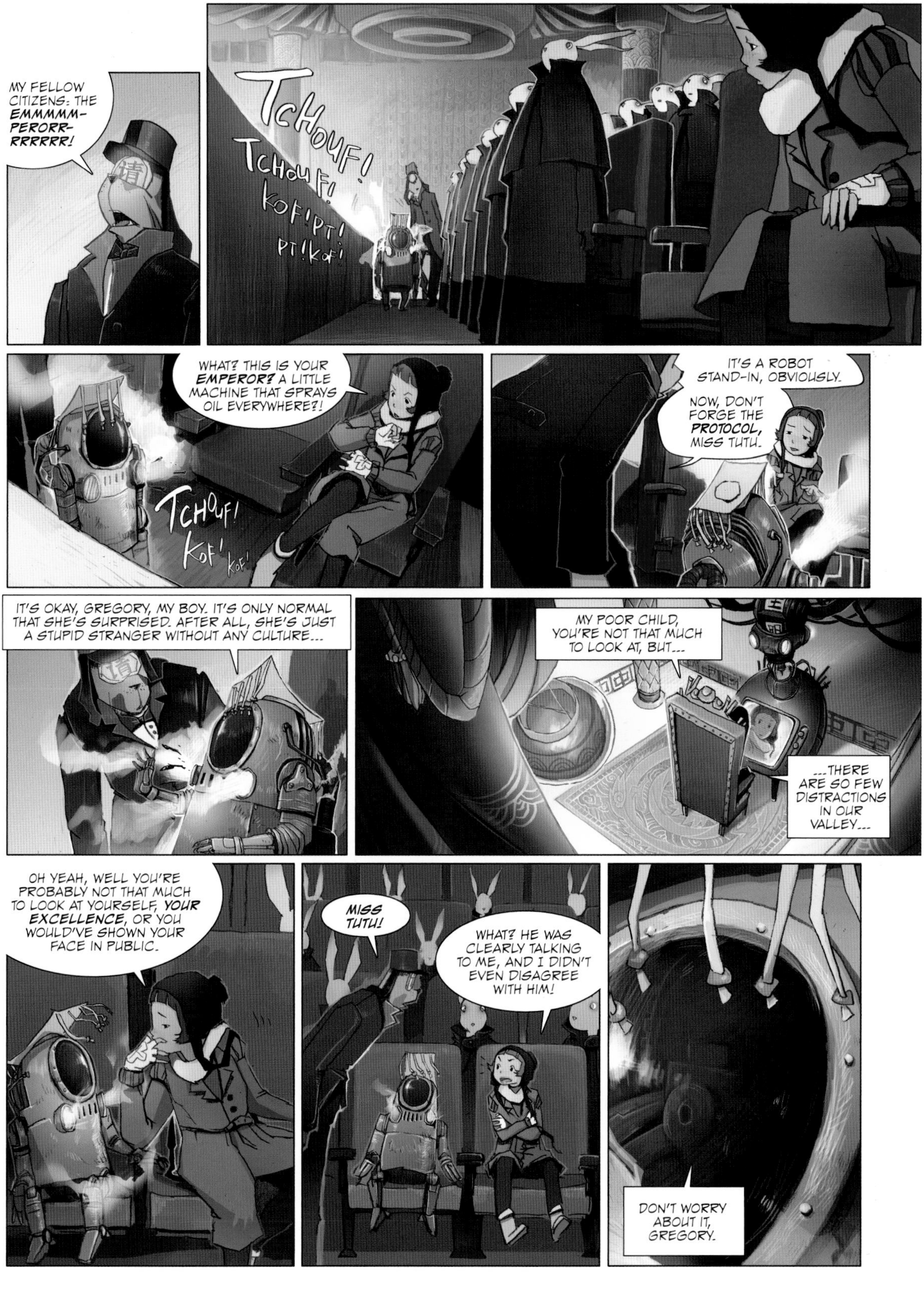
MY FELLOW CITIZENS: THE EMMMMM-PERORR-RRRRRR!
TCHOUF!
TCHOUF!
KOF! PT!
PT! KOF!
WHAT? THIS IS YOUR EMPEROR? A LITTLE MACHINE THAT SPRAYS OIL EVERYWHERE?!
TCHOUF!
KOF! KOF!
IT'S A ROBOT STAND-IN, OBVIOUSLY.
NOW, DON'T FORGE THE PROTOCOL, MISS TUTU.
IT'S OKAY, GREGORY, MY BOY. IT'S ONLY NORMAL THAT SHE'S SURPRISED. AFTER ALL, SHE'S JUST A STUPID STRANGER WITHOUT ANY CULTURE...
MY POOR CHILD, YOU'RE NOT THAT MUCH TO LOOK AT, BUT...
...THERE ARE SO FEW DISTRACTIONS IN OUR VALLEY...
OH YEAH, WELL YOU'RE PROBABLY NOT THAT MUCH TO LOOK AT YOURSELF, YOUR EXCELLENCE, OR YOU WOULD'VE SHOWN YOUR FACE IN PUBLIC.
MISS TUTU!
WHAT? HE WAS CLEARLY TALKING TO ME, AND I DIDN'T EVEN DISAGREE WITH HIM!
DON'T WORRY ABOUT IT, GREGORY.

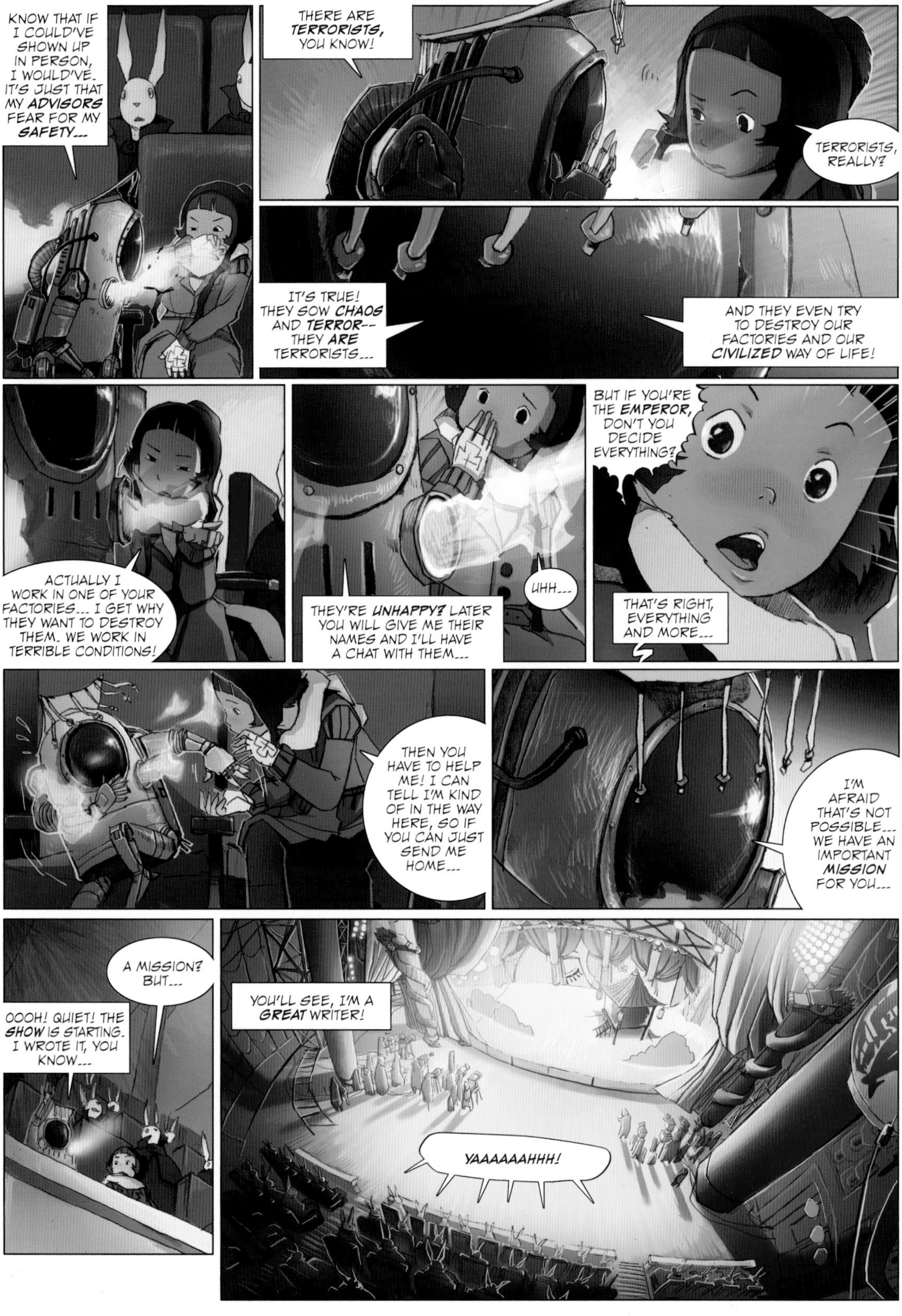

KNOW THAT IF I COULD'VE SHOWN UP IN PERSON, I WOULD'VE. IT'S JUST THAT MY ADVISORS FEAR FOR MY SAFETY...
THERE ARE TERRORISTS, YOU KNOW!
TERRORISTS, REALLY?
IT'S TRUE! THEY SOW CHAOS AND TERROR-- THEY ARE TERRORISTS...
AND THEY EVEN TRY TO DESTROY OUR FACTORIES AND OUR CIVILIZED WAY OF LIFE!
ACTUALLY I WORK IN ONE OF YOUR FACTORIES... I GET WHY THEY WANT TO DESTROY THEM. WE WORK IN TERRIBLE CONDITIONS!
THEY'RE UNHAPPY? LATER YOU WILL GIVE ME THEIR NAMES AND I'LL HAVE A CHAT WITH THEM...
UHH...
BUT IF YOU'RE THE EMPEROR, DON'T YOU DECIDE EVERYTHING?
THAT'S RIGHT, EVERYTHING AND MORE...
THEN YOU HAVE TO HELP ME! I CAN TELL I'M KIND OF IN THE WAY HERE, SO IF YOU CAN JUST SEND ME HOME...
I'M AFRAID THAT'S NOT POSSIBLE... WE HAVE AN IMPORTANT MISSION FOR YOU...
A MISSION? BUT...
OOOH! QUIET! THE SHOW IS STARTING. I WROTE IT, YOU KNOW...
YOU'LL SEE, I'M A GREAT WRITER!
YAAAAAAHHH!

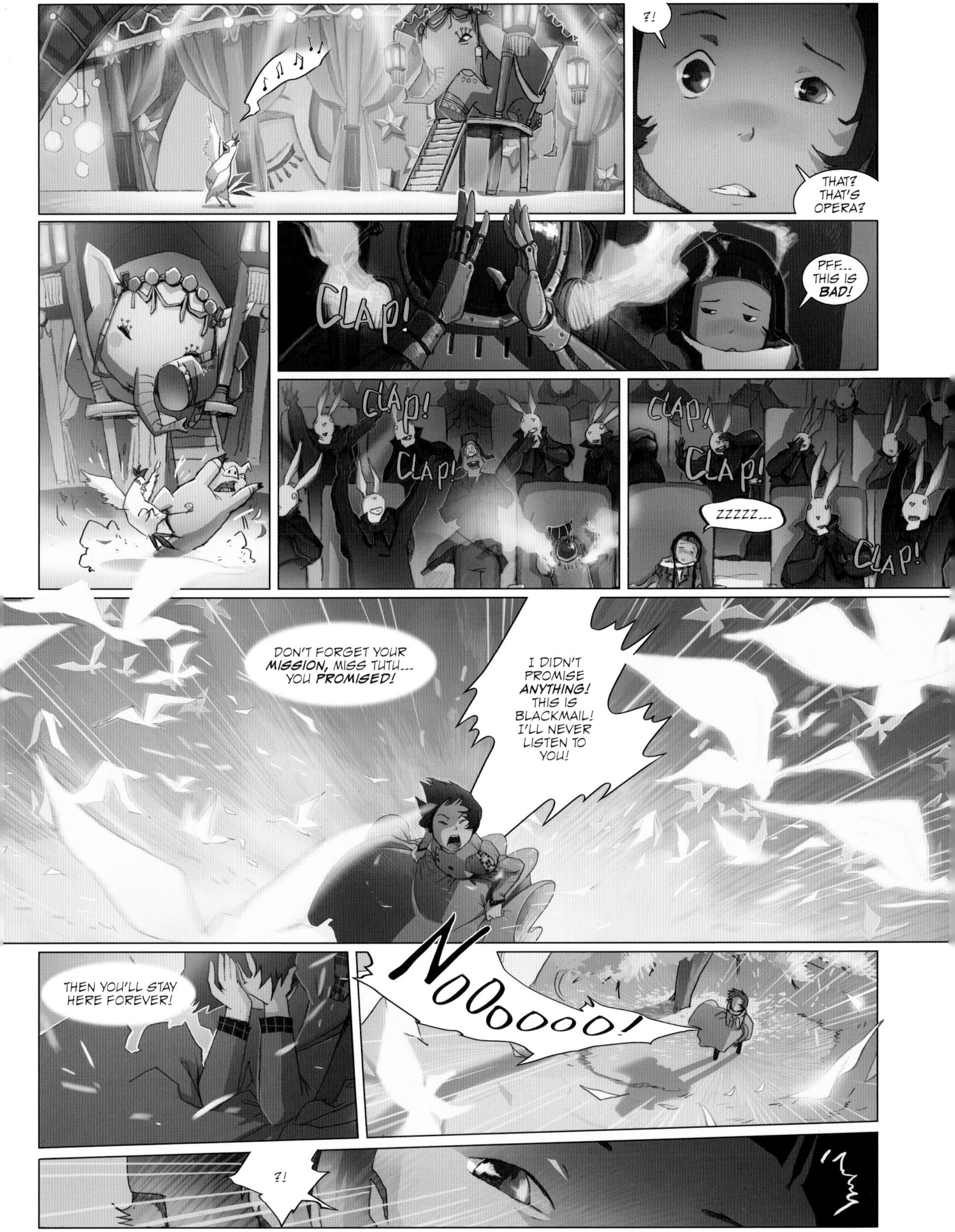
?!
THAT? THAT'S OPERA?
CLAP!
PFF... THIS IS BAD!
CLAP!
CLAP!
CLAP!
CLAP!
ZZZZZ...
CLAP!
DON'T FORGET YOUR MISSION, MISS TUTU... YOU PROMISED!
I DIDN'T PROMISE ANYTHING! THIS IS BLACKMAIL! I'LL NEVER LISTEN TO YOU!
THEN YOU'LL STAY HERE FOREVER!
NOOOOOO!
?!

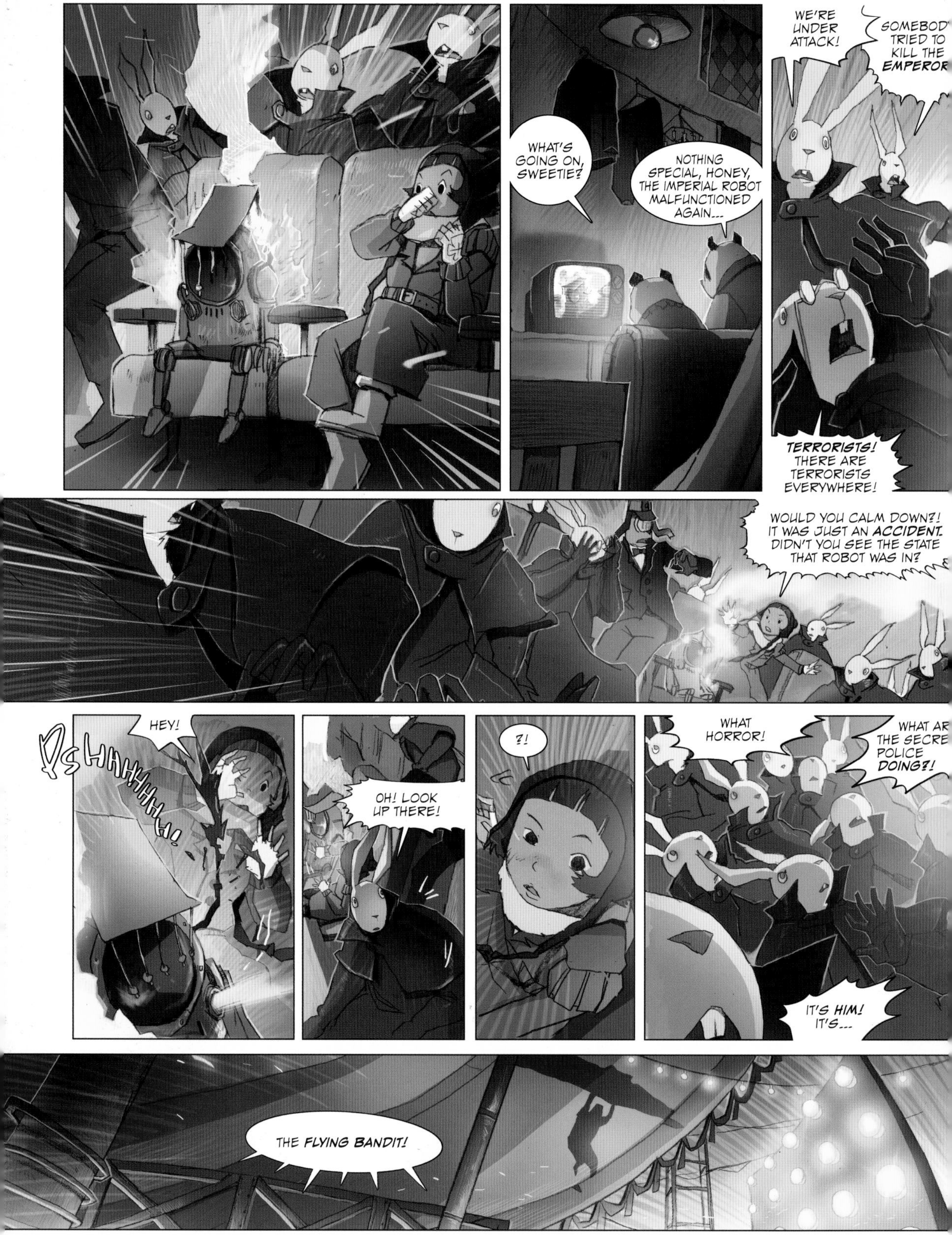
WHAT'S GOING ON, SWEETIE?
NOTHING SPECIAL, HONEY, THE IMPERIAL ROBOT MALFUNCTIONED AGAIN...
WE'RE UNDER ATTACK!
SOMEBOD' TRIED TO KILL THE EMPEROR
TERRORISTS! THERE ARE TERRORISTS EVERYWHERE!
WOULD YOU CALM DOWN?! IT WAS JUST AN ACCIDENT. DIDN'T YOU SEE THE STATE THAT ROBOT WAS IN?
PSHHHHHH!
HEY!
OH! LOOK UP THERE!
?!
WHAT HORROR!
WHAT AR THE SECRE POLICE DOING?!
IT'S HIM! IT'S...
THE FLYING BANDIT!

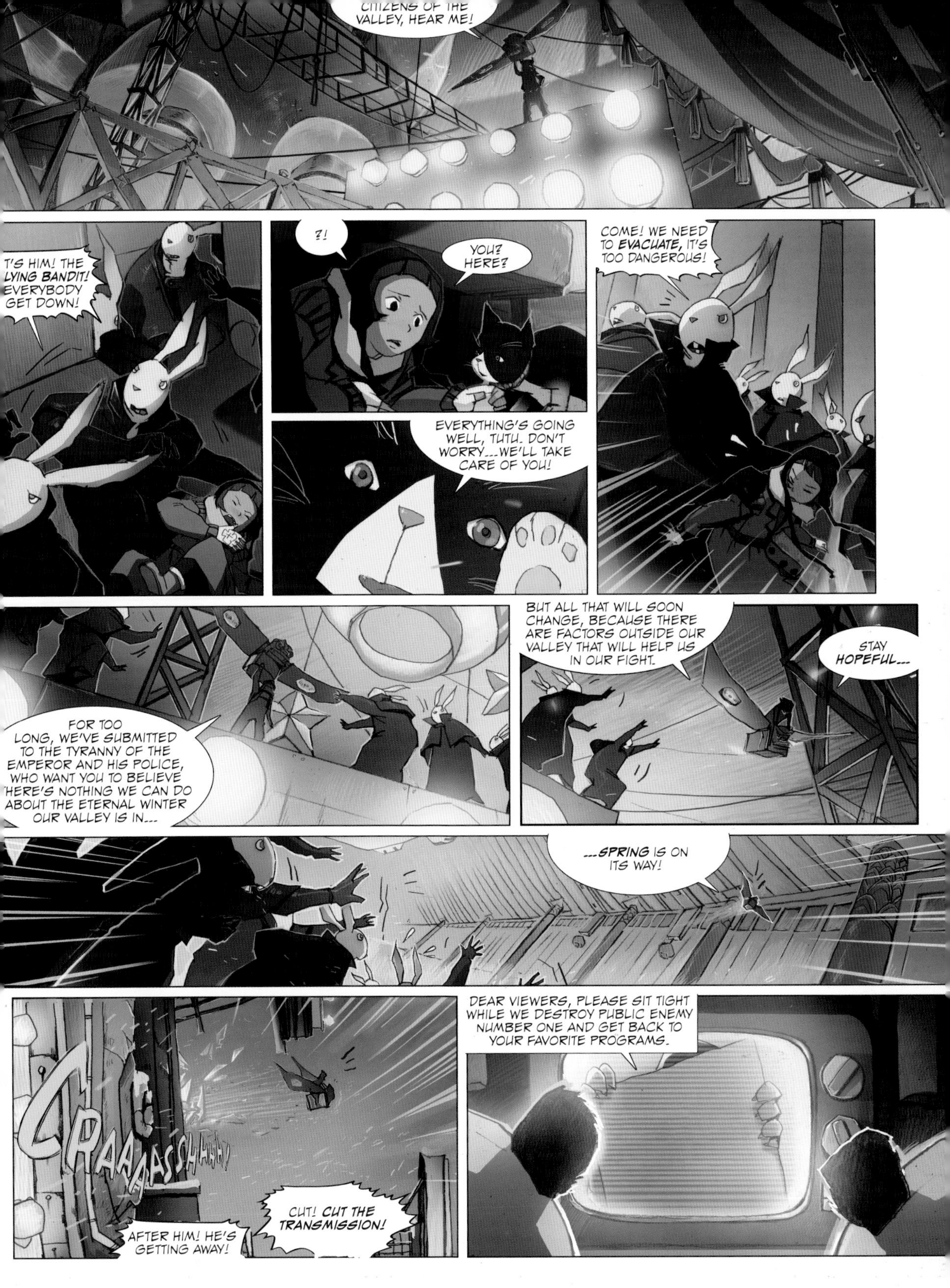

CITIZENS OF THE VALLEY, HEAR ME!
IT'S HIM! THE LYING BANDIT! EVERYBODY GET DOWN!
?!
YOU? HERE?
EVERYTHING'S GOING WELL, TUTU. DON'T WORRY... WE'LL TAKE CARE OF YOU!
COME! WE NEED TO EVACUATE, IT'S TOO DANGEROUS!
FOR TOO LONG, WE'VE SUBMITTED TO THE TYRANNY OF THE EMPEROR AND HIS POLICE, WHO WANT YOU TO BELIEVE THERE'S NOTHING WE CAN DO ABOUT THE ETERNAL WINTER OUR VALLEY IS IN...
BUT ALL THAT WILL SOON CHANGE, BECAUSE THERE ARE FACTORS OUTSIDE OUR VALLEY THAT WILL HELP US IN OUR FIGHT.
STAY HOPEFUL...
...SPRING IS ON ITS WAY!
CRAAAASSHHH!
AFTER HIM! HE'S GETTING AWAY!
CUT! CUT THE TRANSMISSION!
DEAR VIEWERS, PLEASE SIT TIGHT WHILE WE DESTROY PUBLIC ENEMY NUMBER ONE AND GET BACK TO YOUR FAVORITE PROGRAMS.

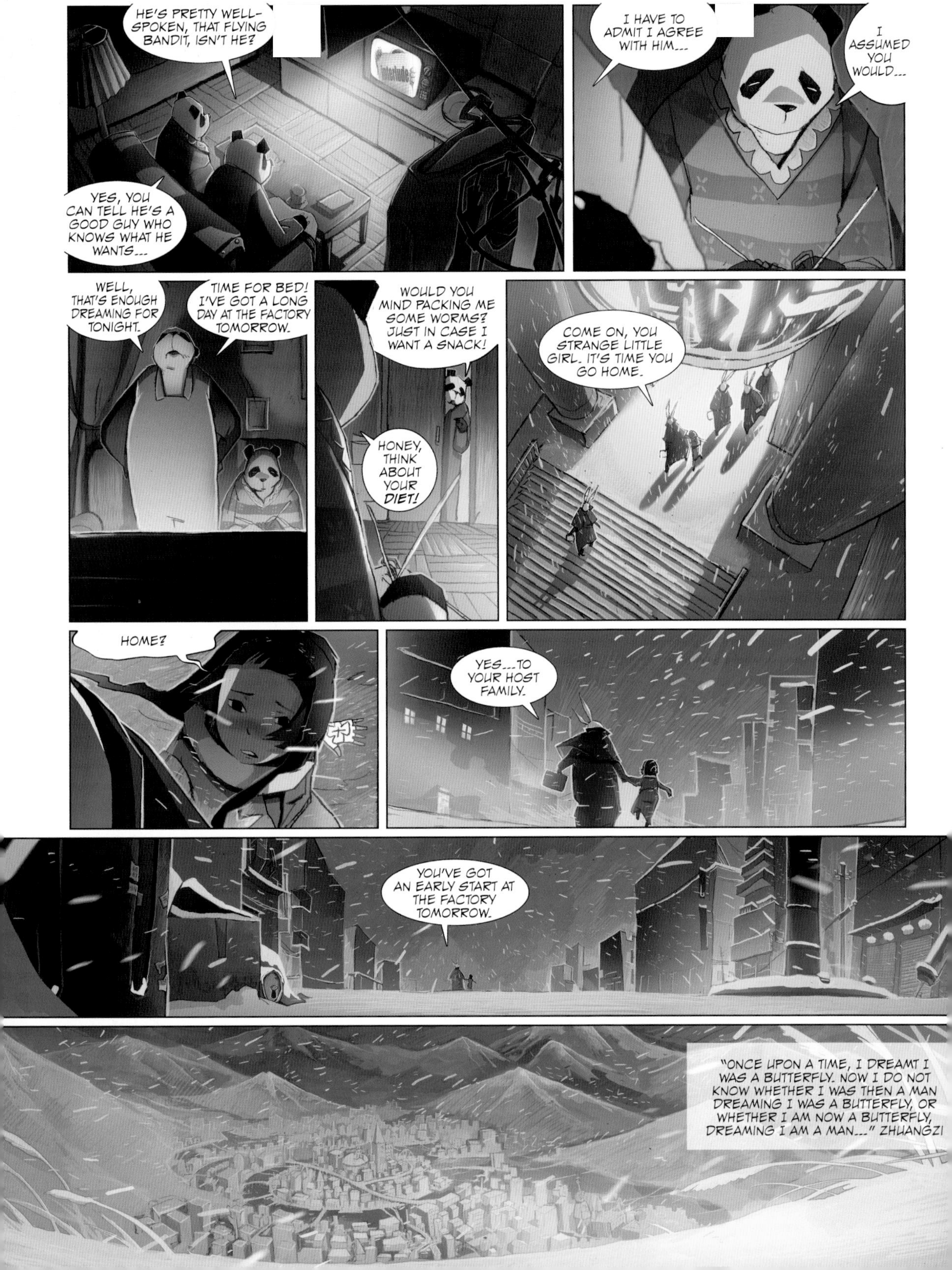
HE'S PRETTY WELL-SPOKEN, THAT FLYING BANDIT, ISN'T HE?
YES, YOU CAN TELL HE'S A GOOD GUY WHO KNOWS WHAT HE WANTS...
I HAVE TO ADMIT I AGREE WITH HIM...
I ASSUMED YOU WOULD...
WELL, THAT'S ENOUGH DREAMING FOR TONIGHT.
TIME FOR BED! I'VE GOT A LONG DAY AT THE FACTORY TOMORROW.
WOULD YOU MIND PACKING ME SOME WORMS? JUST IN CASE I WANT A SNACK!
HONEY, THINK ABOUT YOUR *DIET!*
COME ON, YOU STRANGE LITTLE GIRL. IT'S TIME YOU GO HOME.
HOME?
YES... TO YOUR HOST FAMILY.
YOU'VE GOT AN EARLY START AT THE FACTORY TOMORROW.
"ONCE UPON A TIME, I DREAMT I WAS A BUTTERFLY. NOW I DO NOT KNOW WHETHER I WAS THEN A MAN DREAMING I WAS A BUTTERFLY, OR WHETHER I AM NOW A BUTTERFLY, DREAMING I AM A MAN..." ZHUANGZI

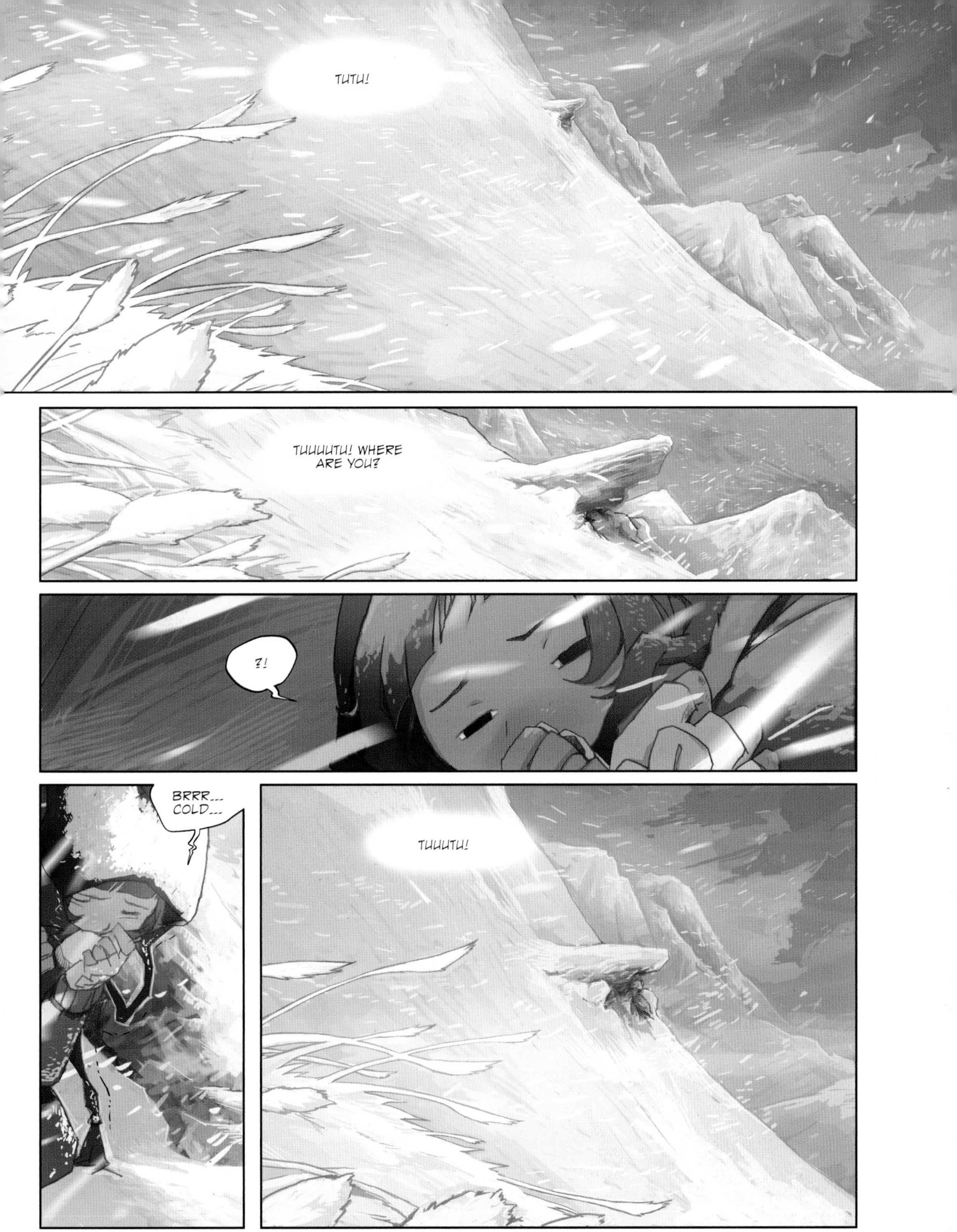
TUTU!
TUUUUTU! WHERE ARE YOU?
?!
BRRR... COLD...
TUUUTU!

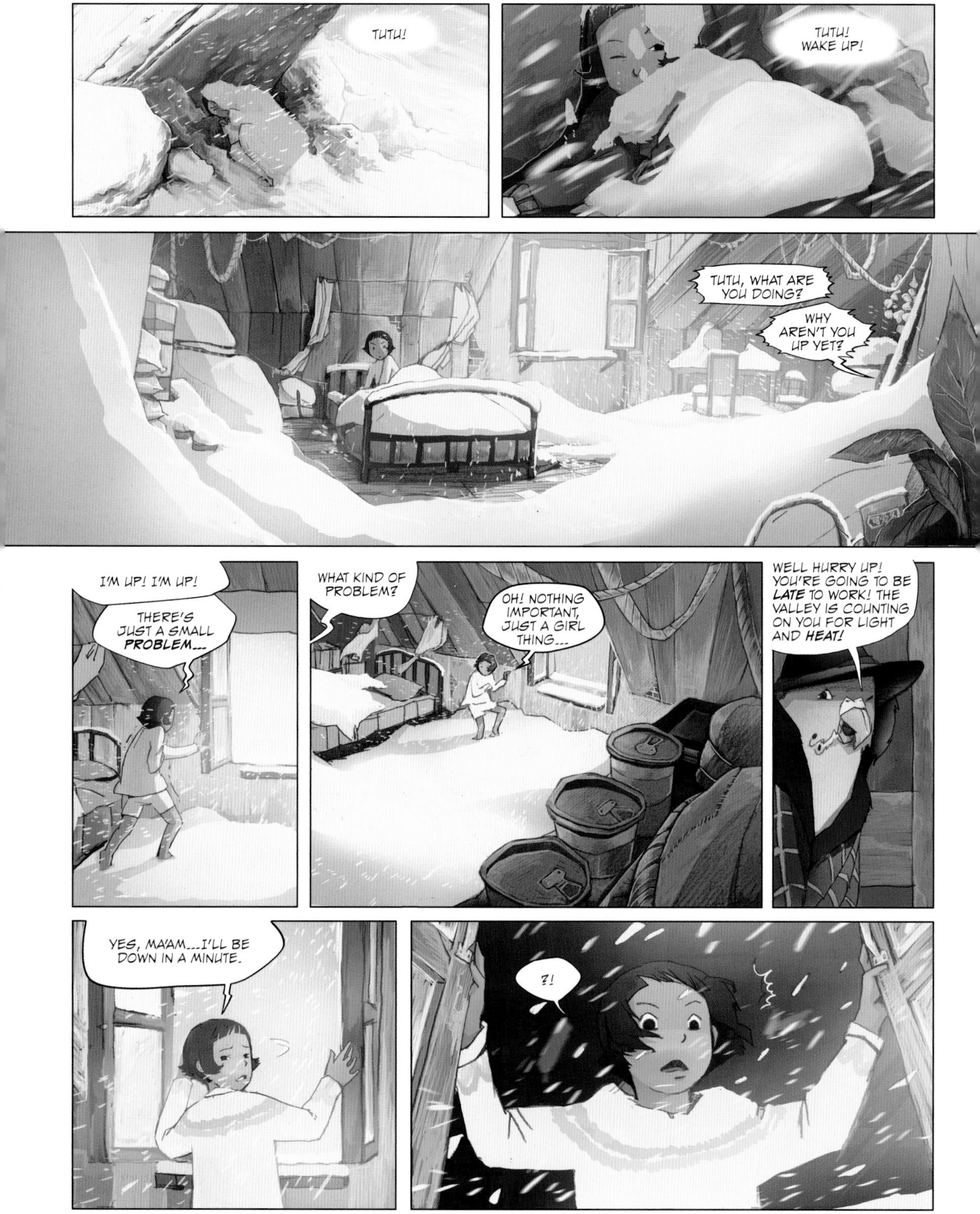
TUTU!
TUTU! WAKE UP!
TUTU, WHAT ARE YOU DOING?
WHY AREN'T YOU UP YET?
I'M UP! I'M UP!
THERE'S JUST A SMALL PROBLEM...
WHAT KIND OF PROBLEM?
OH! NOTHING IMPORTANT, JUST A GIRL THING...
WELL HURRY UP! YOU'RE GOING TO BE LATE TO WORK! THE VALLEY IS COUNTING ON YOU FOR LIGHT AND HEAT!
YES, MA'AM...I'LL BE DOWN IN A MINUTE.
?!

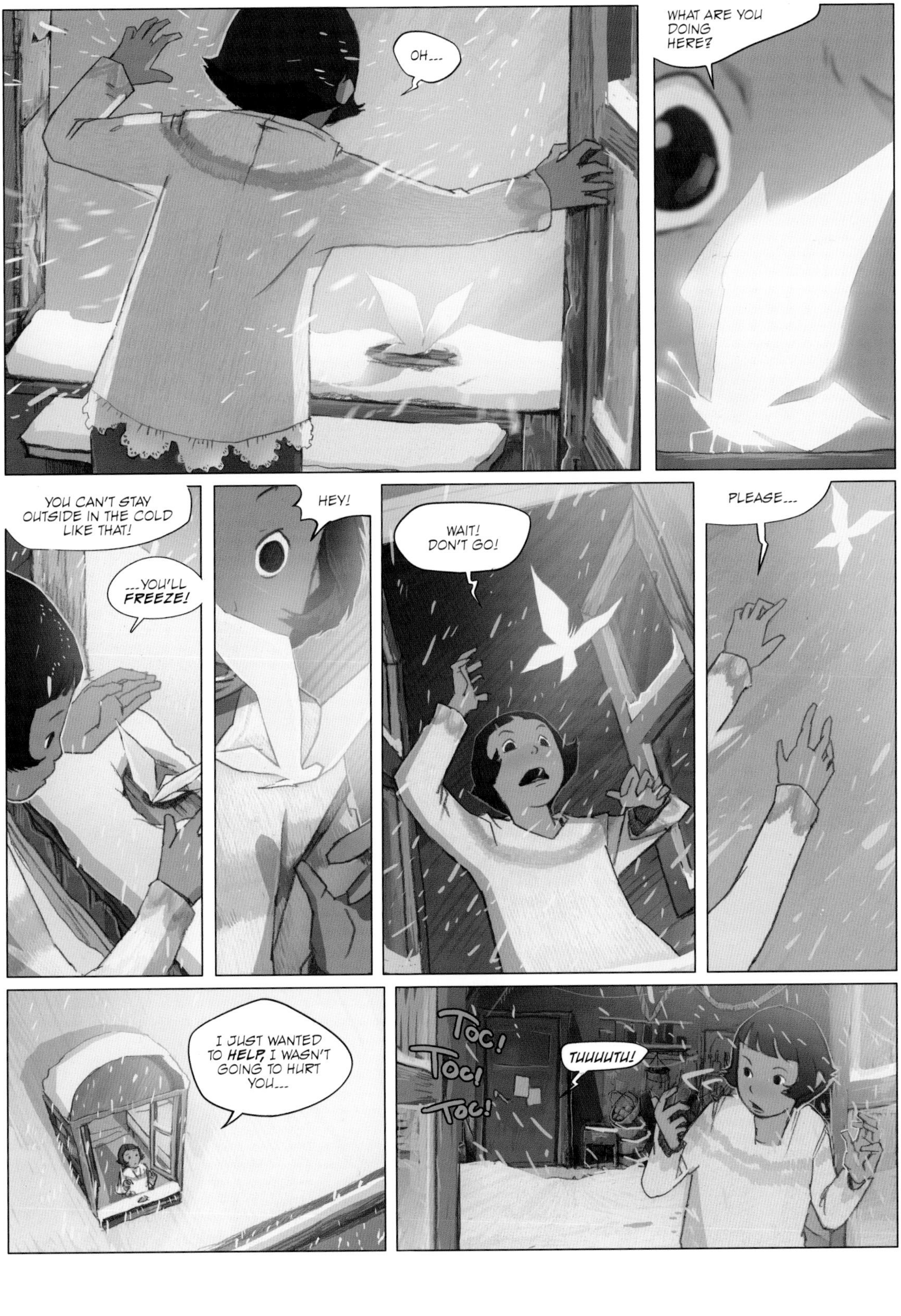
OH...
WHAT ARE YOU DOING HERE?
YOU CAN'T STAY OUTSIDE IN THE COLD LIKE THAT!
...YOU'LL FREEZE!
HEY!
WAIT! DON'T GO!
PLEASE...
I JUST WANTED TO HELP, I WASN'T GOING TO HURT YOU...
TOC! TOC! TOC!
TUUUUTU!

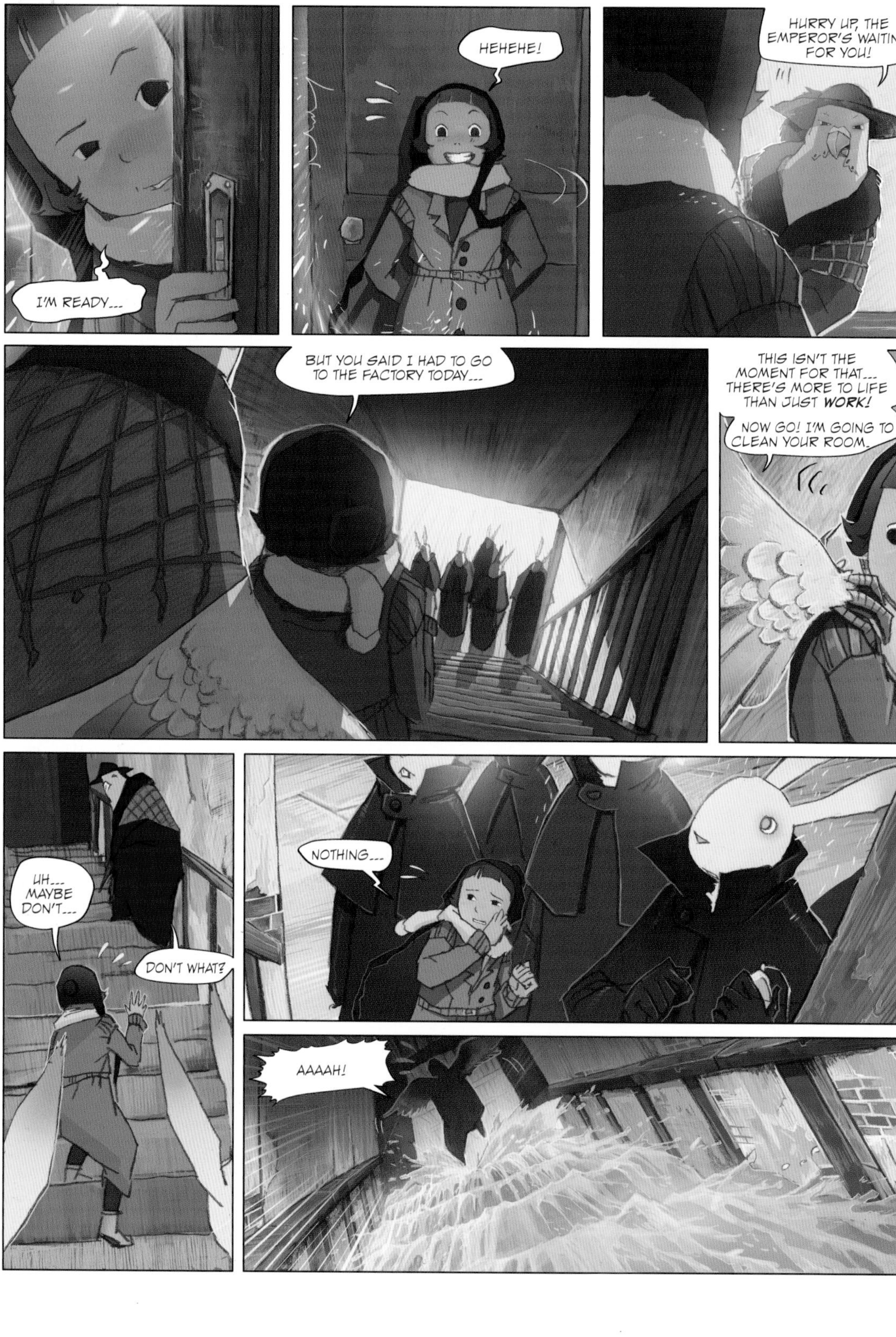
I'M READY...
HEHEHE!
HURRY UP, THE EMPEROR'S WAITING FOR YOU!
BUT YOU SAID I HAD TO GO TO THE FACTORY TODAY...
THIS ISN'T THE MOMENT FOR THAT... THERE'S MORE TO LIFE THAN JUST WORK!
NOW GO! I'M GOING TO CLEAN YOUR ROOM.
UH... MAYBE DON'T...
DON'T WHAT?
NOTHING...
AAAAH!

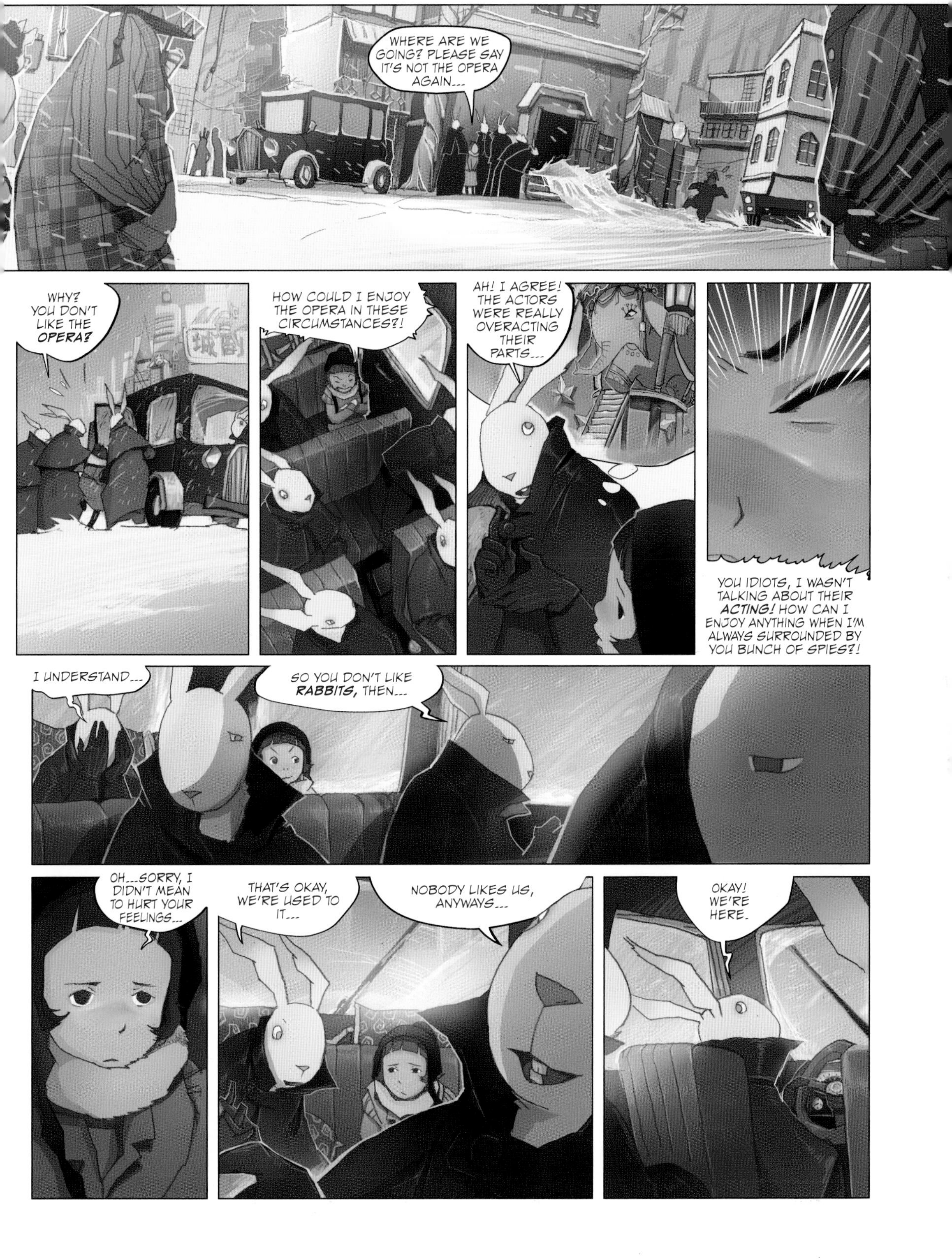
WHERE ARE WE GOING? PLEASE SAY IT'S NOT THE OPERA AGAIN...
WHY? YOU DON'T LIKE THE OPERA?
HOW COULD I ENJOY THE OPERA IN THESE CIRCUMSTANCES?!
AH! I AGREE! THE ACTORS WERE REALLY OVERACTING THEIR PARTS...
YOU IDIOTS, I WASN'T TALKING ABOUT THEIR ACTING! HOW CAN I ENJOY ANYTHING WHEN I'M ALWAYS SURROUNDED BY YOU BUNCH OF SPIES?!
I UNDERSTAND...
SO YOU DON'T LIKE RABBITS, THEN...
OH...SORRY, I DIDN'T MEAN TO HURT YOUR FEELINGS...
THAT'S OKAY, WE'RE USED TO IT...
NOBODY LIKES US, ANYWAYS...
OKAY! WE'RE HERE.

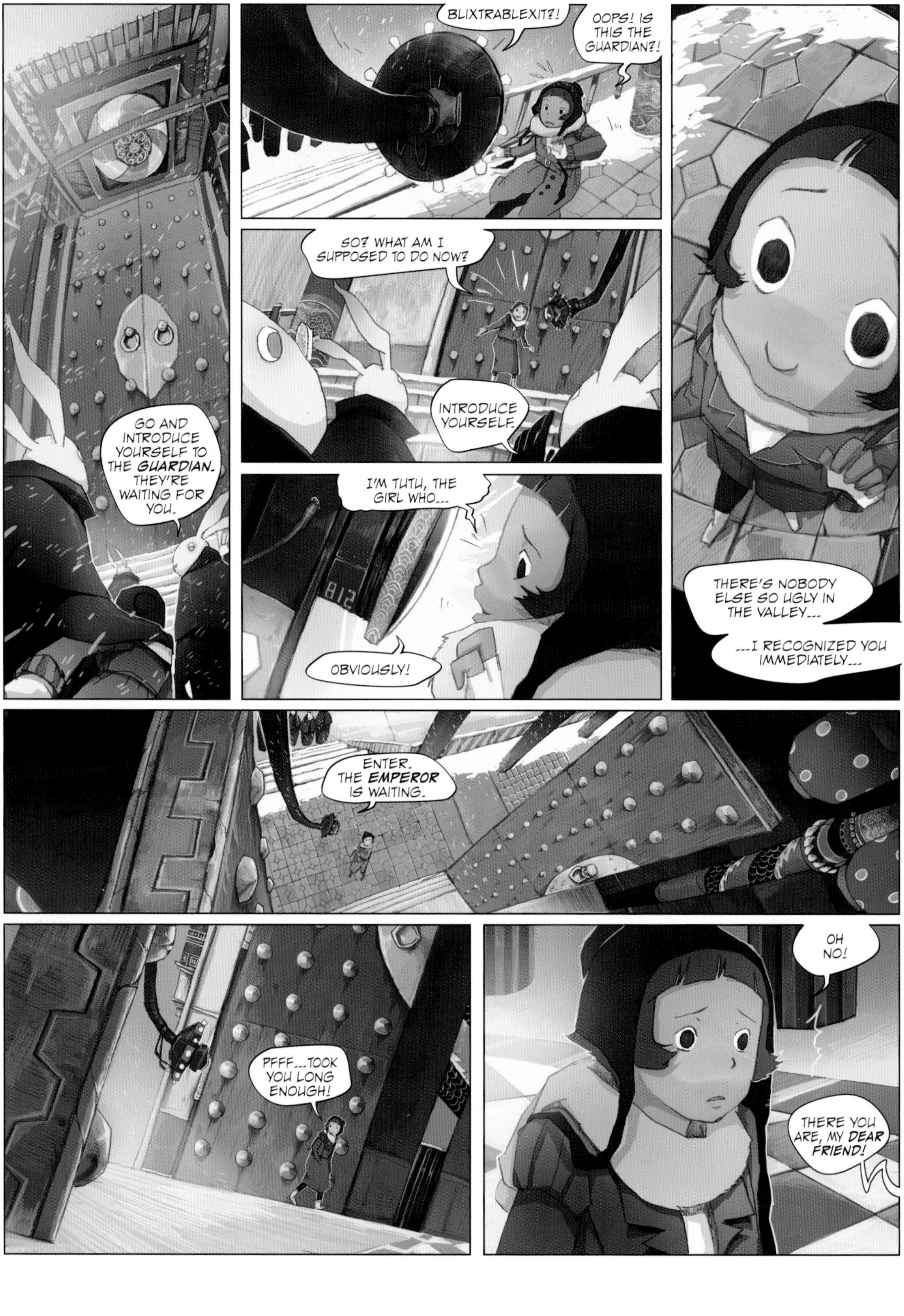
GO AND INTRODUCE YOURSELF TO THE GUARDIAN. THEY'RE WAITING FOR YOU.
BLIXTRABLEXIT?!
OOPS! IS THIS THE GUARDIAN?!
SO? WHAT AM I SUPPOSED TO DO NOW?
INTRODUCE YOURSELF.
I'M TUTU, THE GIRL WHO...
OBVIOUSLY!
THERE'S NOBODY ELSE SO UGLY IN THE VALLEY...
...I RECOGNIZED YOU IMMEDIATELY...
ENTER. THE EMPEROR IS WAITING.
PFFF...TOOK YOU LONG ENOUGH!
OH NO!
THERE YOU ARE, MY DEAR FRIEND!

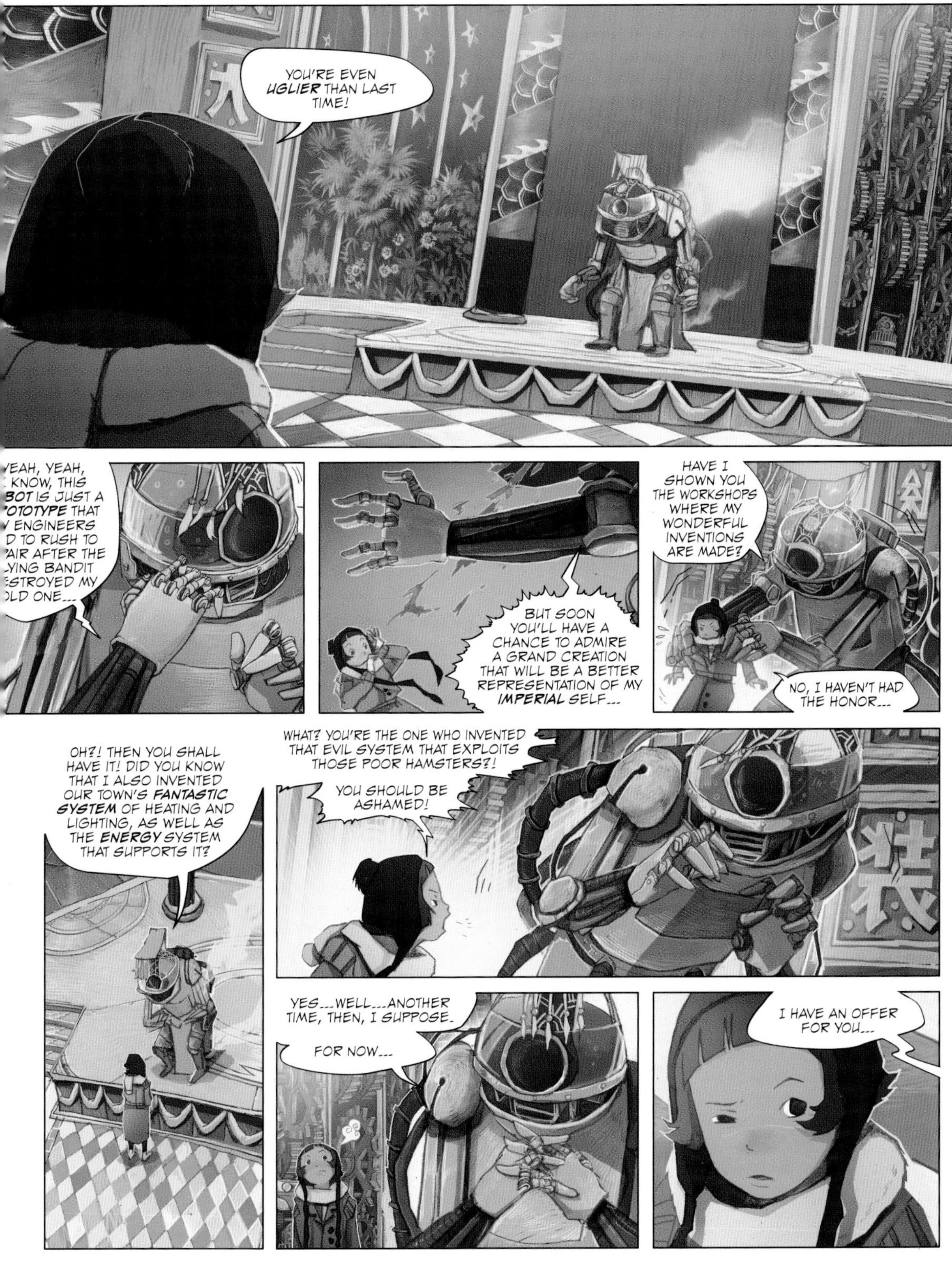

YOU'RE EVEN UGLIER THAN LAST TIME!
EAH, YEAH, KNOW, THIS BOT IS JUST A OTOTYPE THAT ENGINEERS D TO RUSH TO PAIR AFTER THE YING BANDIT ESTROYED MY OLD ONE...
BUT SOON YOU'LL HAVE A CHANCE TO ADMIRE A GRAND CREATION THAT WILL BE A BETTER REPRESENTATION OF MY IMPERIAL SELF...
HAVE I SHOWN YOU THE WORKSHOPS WHERE MY WONDERFUL INVENTIONS ARE MADE?
NO, I HAVEN'T HAD THE HONOR...
OH?! THEN YOU SHALL HAVE IT! DID YOU KNOW THAT I ALSO INVENTED OUR TOWN'S FANTASTIC SYSTEM OF HEATING AND LIGHTING, AS WELL AS THE ENERGY SYSTEM THAT SUPPORTS IT?
WHAT? YOU'RE THE ONE WHO INVENTED THAT EVIL SYSTEM THAT EXPLOITS THOSE POOR HAMSTERS?!
YOU SHOULD BE ASHAMED!
YES... WELL... ANOTHER TIME, THEN, I SUPPOSE.
FOR NOW...
I HAVE AN OFFER FOR YOU...

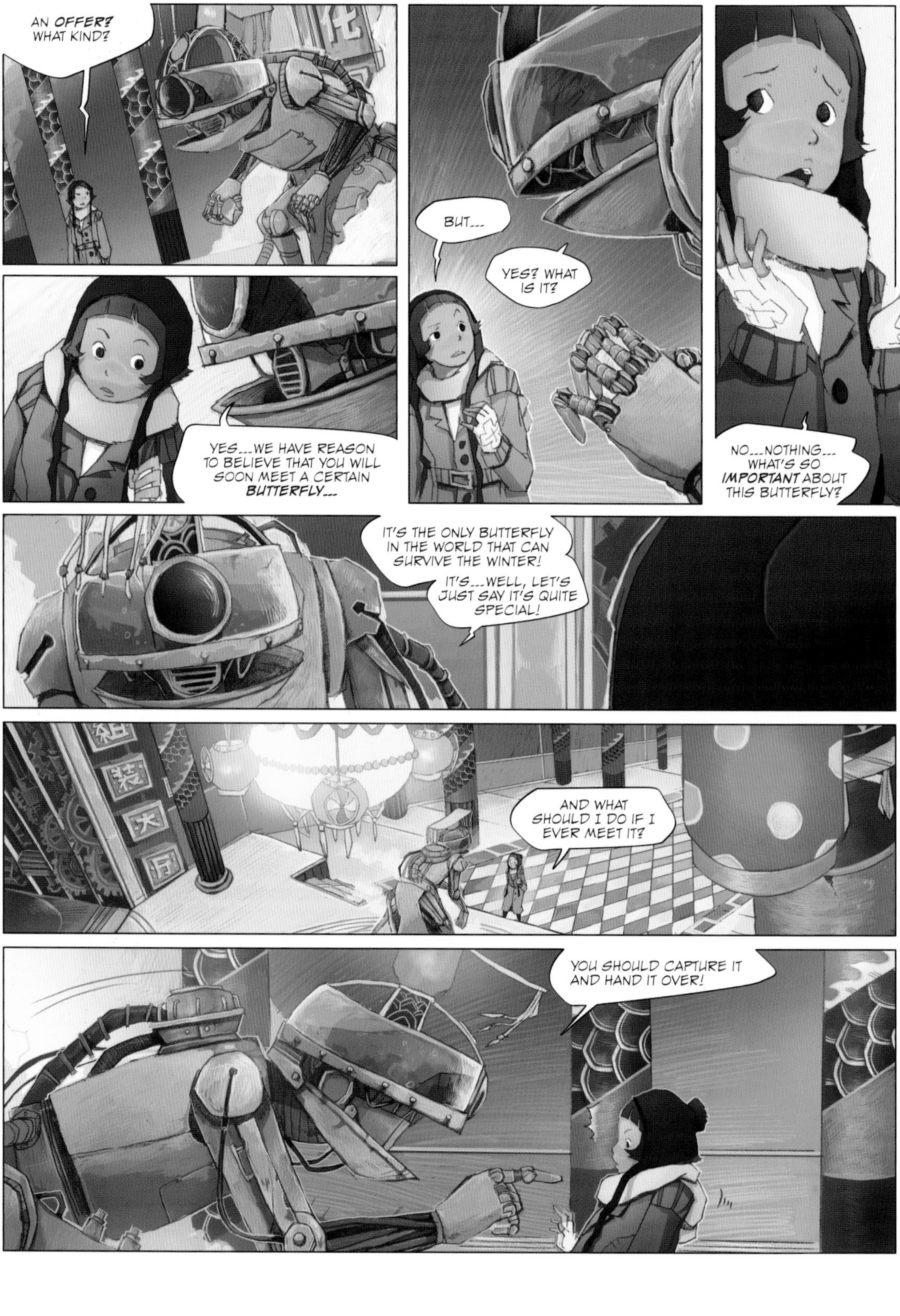
AN OFFER? WHAT KIND?
YES... WE HAVE REASON TO BELIEVE THAT YOU WILL SOON MEET A CERTAIN BUTTERFLY...
BUT...
YES? WHAT IS IT?
NO... NOTHING... WHAT'S SO IMPORTANT ABOUT THIS BUTTERFLY?
IT'S THE ONLY BUTTERFLY IN THE WORLD THAT CAN SURVIVE THE WINTER!
IT'S... WELL, LET'S JUST SAY IT'S QUITE SPECIAL!
AND WHAT SHOULD I DO IF I EVER MEET IT?
YOU SHOULD CAPTURE IT AND HAND IT OVER!

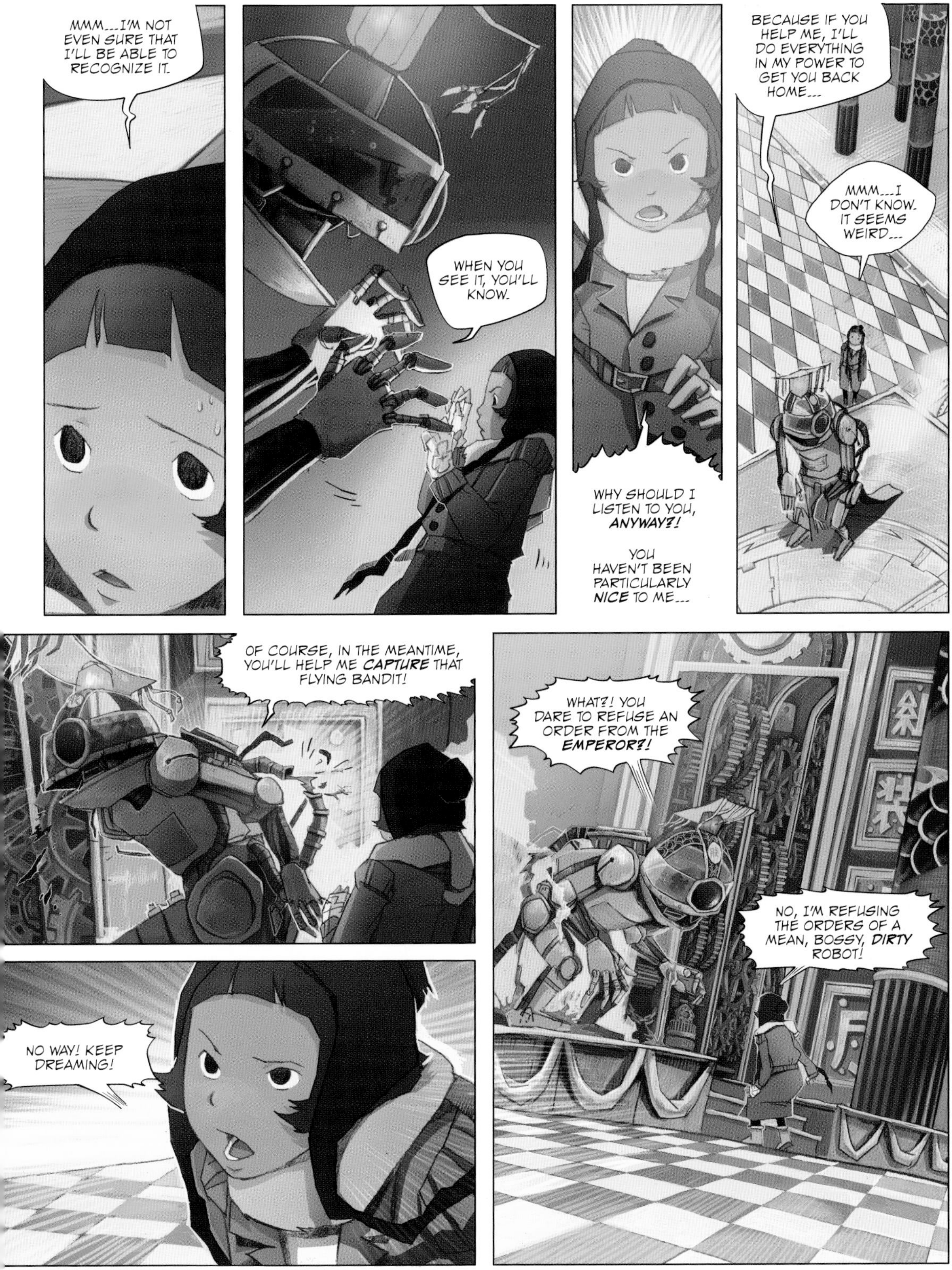
MMM... I'M NOT EVEN SURE THAT I'LL BE ABLE TO RECOGNIZE IT.
WHEN YOU SEE IT, YOU'LL KNOW.
WHY SHOULD I LISTEN TO YOU, ANYWAY?!
YOU HAVEN'T BEEN PARTICULARLY NICE TO ME...
BECAUSE IF YOU HELP ME, I'LL DO EVERYTHING IN MY POWER TO GET YOU BACK HOME...
MMM... I DON'T KNOW. IT SEEMS WEIRD...
OF COURSE, IN THE MEANTIME, YOU'LL HELP ME CAPTURE THAT FLYING BANDIT!
NO WAY! KEEP DREAMING!
WHAT?! YOU DARE TO REFUSE AN ORDER FROM THE EMPEROR?!
NO, I'M REFUSING THE ORDERS OF A MEAN, BOSSY, DIRTY ROBOT!

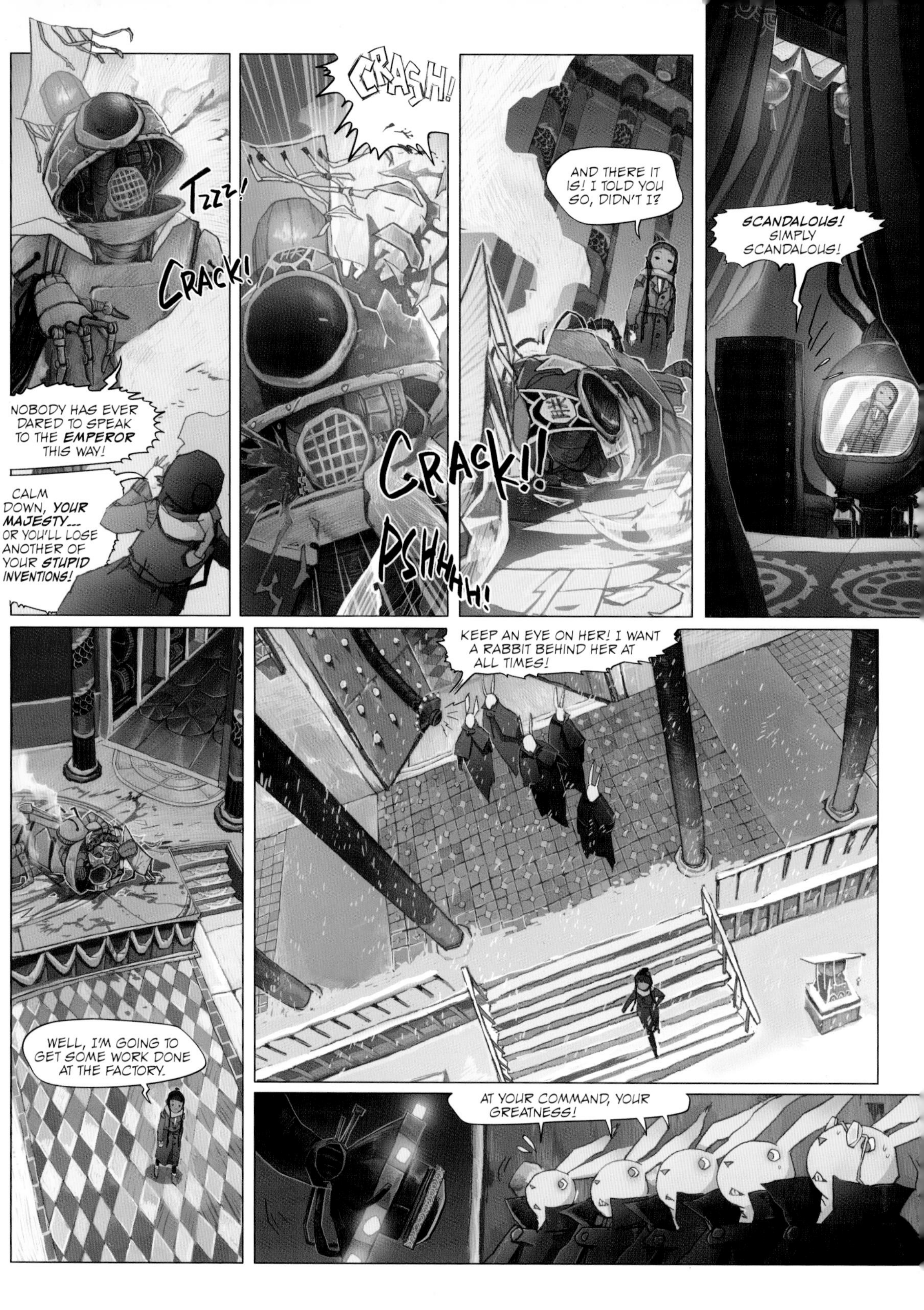
Tzzz!
CRACK!
NOBODY HAS EVER DARED TO SPEAK TO THE EMPEROR THIS WAY!
CALM DOWN, YOUR MAJESTY... OR YOU'LL LOSE ANOTHER OF YOUR STUPID INVENTIONS!
CRASH!
CRACK!!
PSHHHHH!
AND THERE IT IS! I TOLD YOU SO, DIDN'T I?
SCANDALOUS! SIMPLY SCANDALOUS!
WELL, I'M GOING TO GET SOME WORK DONE AT THE FACTORY.
KEEP AN EYE ON HER! I WANT A RABBIT BEHIND HER AT ALL TIMES!
AT YOUR COMMAND, YOUR GREATNESS!

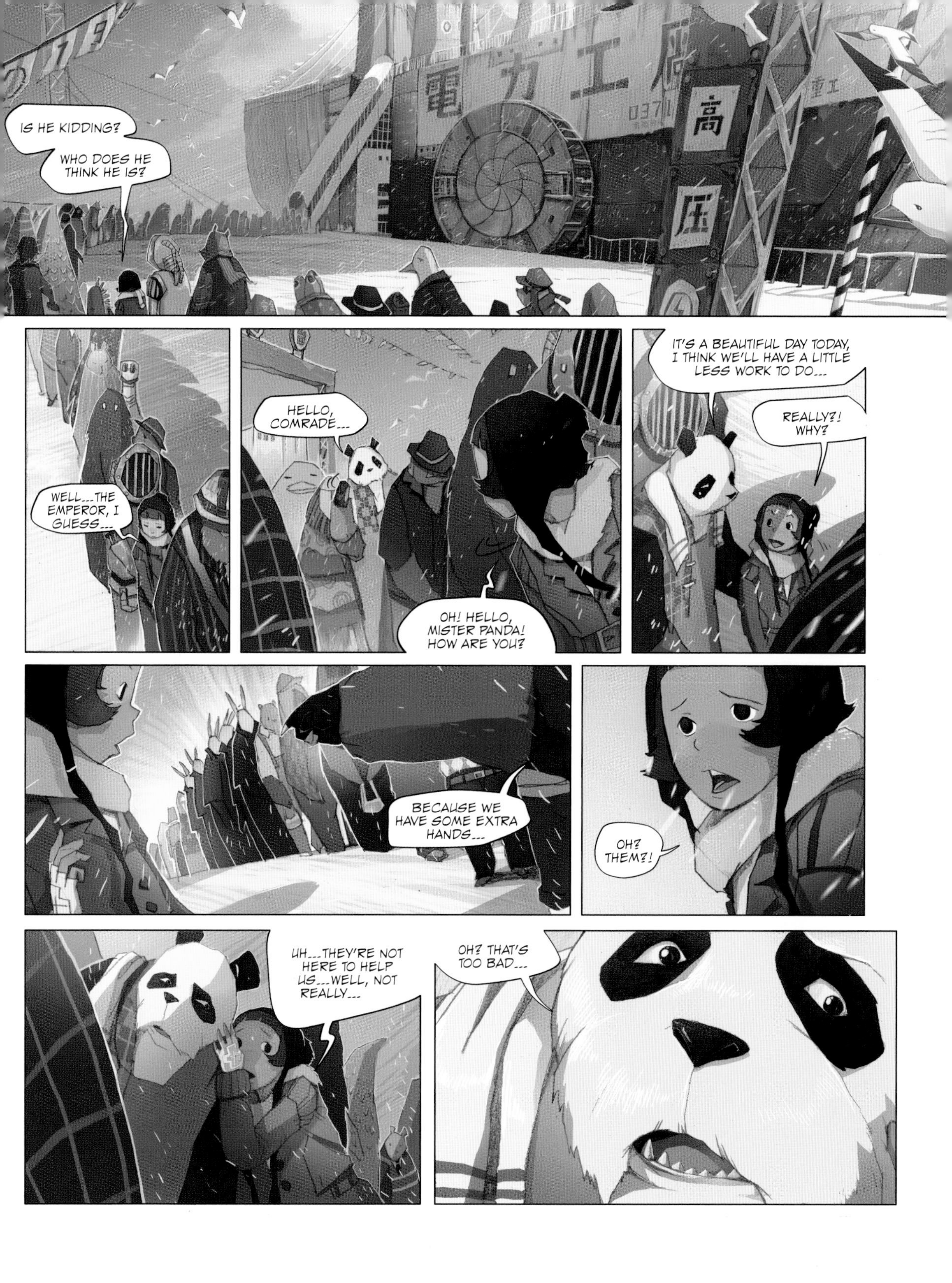
IS HE KIDDING?
WHO DOES HE THINK HE IS?
WELL... THE EMPEROR, I GUESS...
HELLO, COMRADE...
OH! HELLO, MISTER PANDA! HOW ARE YOU?
IT'S A BEAUTIFUL DAY TODAY, I THINK WE'LL HAVE A LITTLE LESS WORK TO DO...
REALLY?! WHY?
BECAUSE WE HAVE SOME EXTRA HANDS...
OH? THEM?!
UH... THEY'RE NOT HERE TO HELP US... WELL, NOT REALLY...
OH? THAT'S TOO BAD...

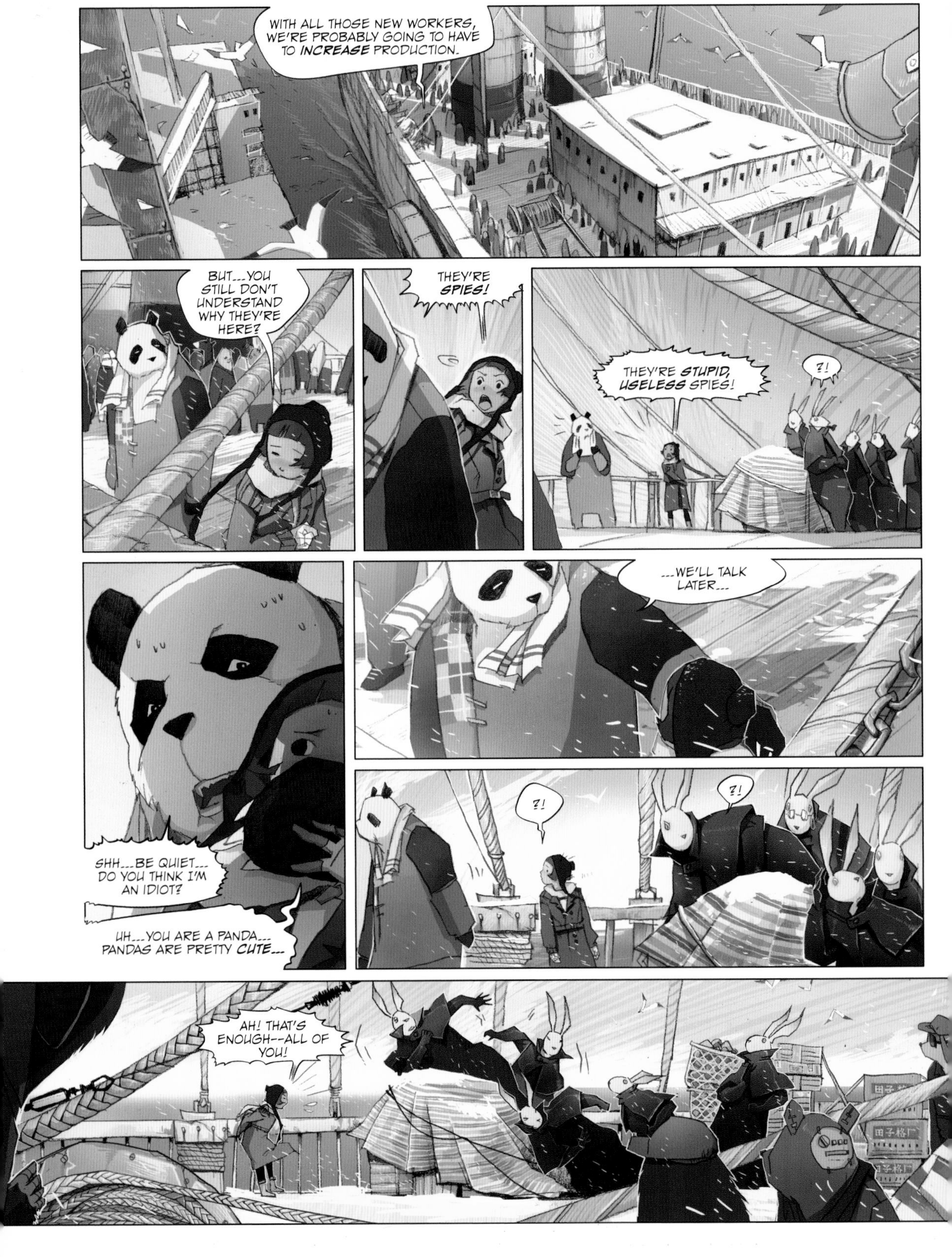
WITH ALL THOSE NEW WORKERS, WE'RE PROBABLY GOING TO HAVE TO INCREASE PRODUCTION.
BUT... YOU STILL DON'T UNDERSTAND WHY THEY'RE HERE?
THEY'RE SPIES!
THEY'RE STUPID, USELESS SPIES!
?!
SHH... BE QUIET... DO YOU THINK I'M AN IDIOT?
UH... YOU ARE A PANDA... PANDAS ARE PRETTY CUTE...
...WE'LL TALK LATER...
?!
?!
AH! THAT'S ENOUGH--ALL OF YOU!

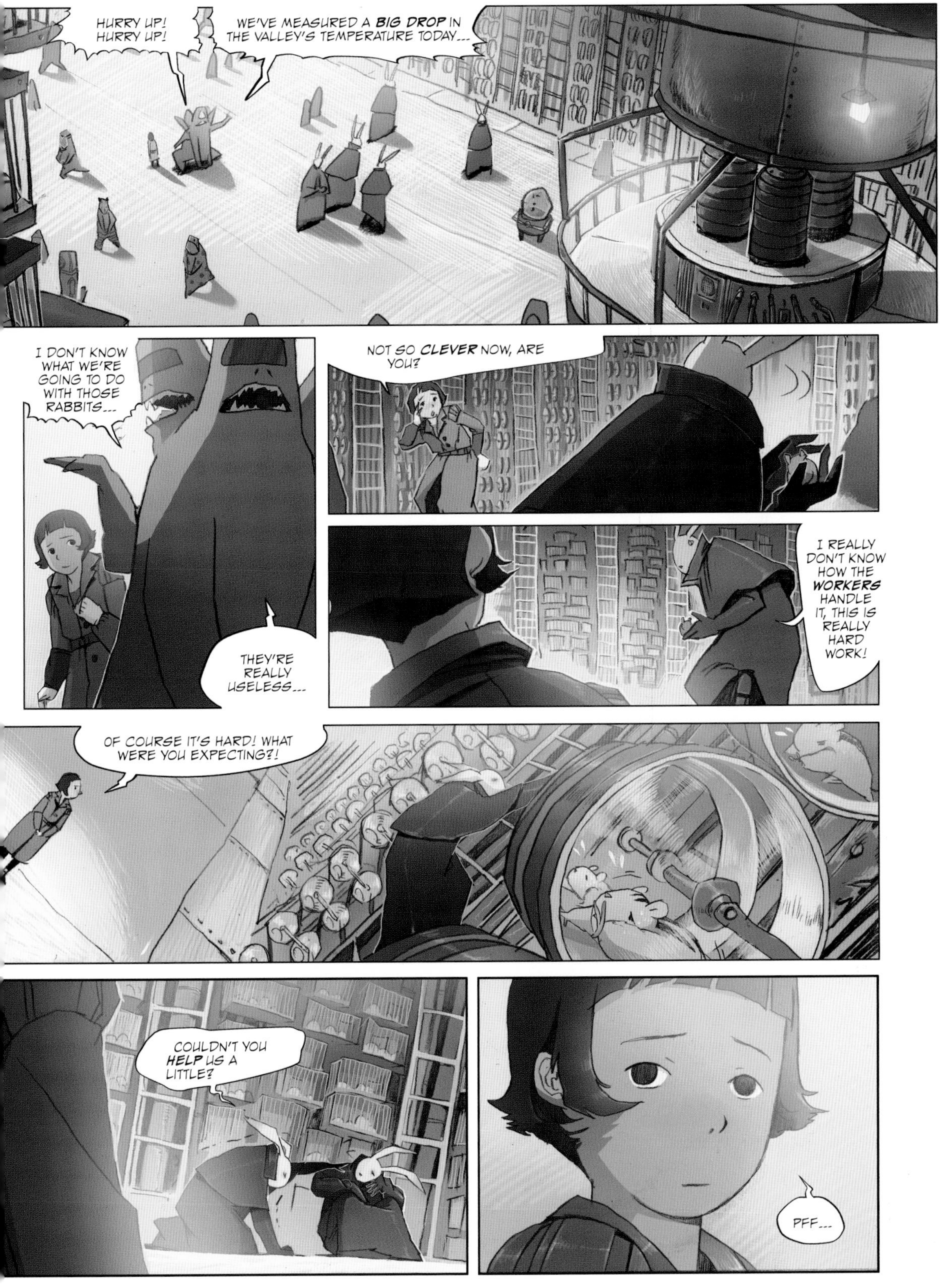
HURRY UP! HURRY UP!
WE'VE MEASURED A BIG DROP IN THE VALLEY'S TEMPERATURE TODAY...
I DON'T KNOW WHAT WE'RE GOING TO DO WITH THOSE RABBITS...
THEY'RE REALLY USELESS...
NOT SO CLEVER NOW, ARE YOU?
I REALLY DON'T KNOW HOW THE WORKERS HANDLE IT, THIS IS REALLY HARD WORK!
OF COURSE IT'S HARD! WHAT WERE YOU EXPECTING?!
COULDN'T YOU HELP US A LITTLE?
PFF...

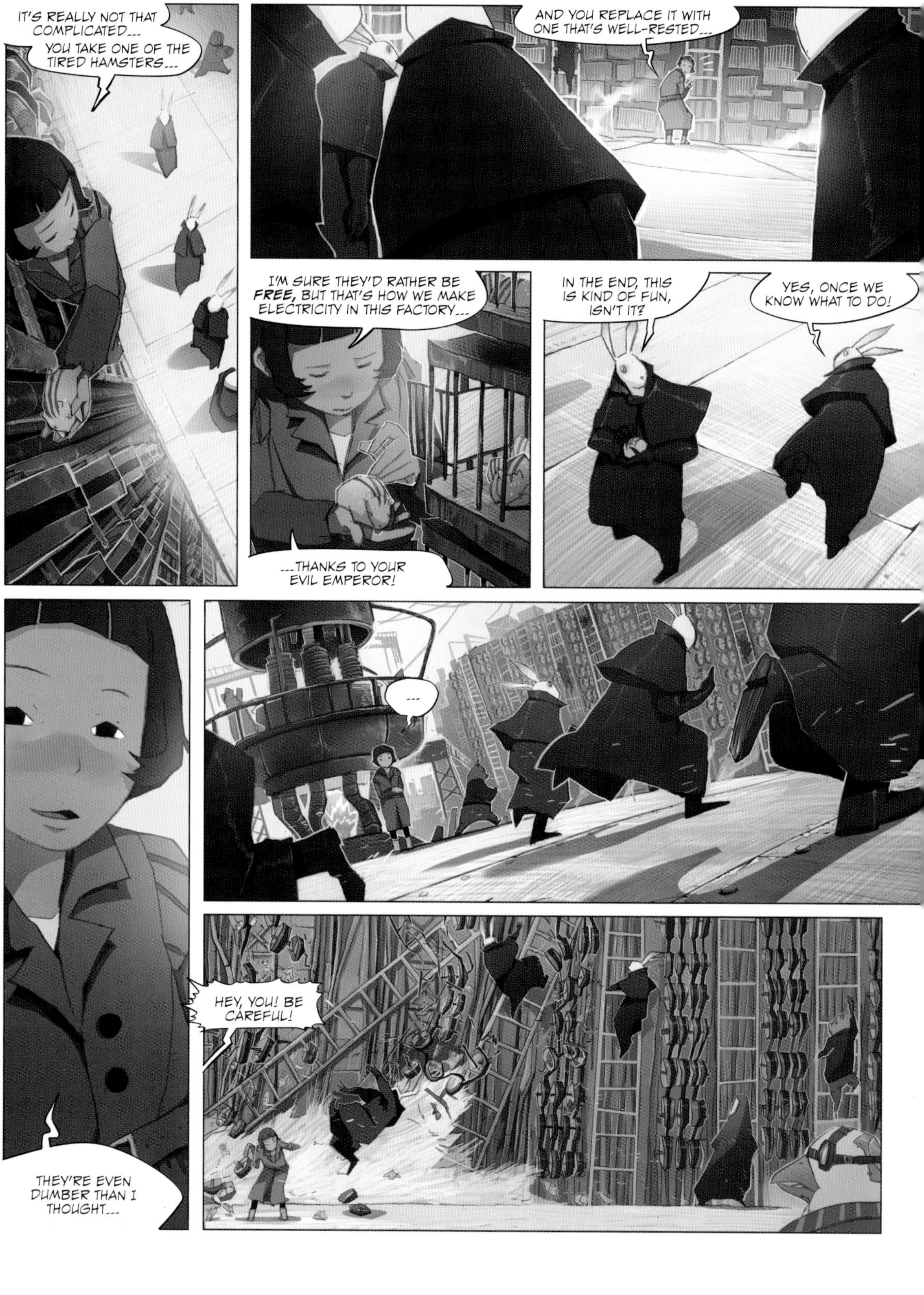
IT'S REALLY NOT THAT COMPLICATED...
YOU TAKE ONE OF THE TIRED HAMSTERS...
AND YOU REPLACE IT WITH ONE THAT'S WELL-RESTED...
I'M SURE THEY'D RATHER BE FREE, BUT THAT'S HOW WE MAKE ELECTRICITY IN THIS FACTORY...
...THANKS TO YOUR EVIL EMPEROR!
IN THE END, THIS IS KIND OF FUN, ISN'T IT?
YES, ONCE WE KNOW WHAT TO DO!
...
HEY, YOU! BE CAREFUL!
THEY'RE EVEN DUMBER THAN I THOUGHT...

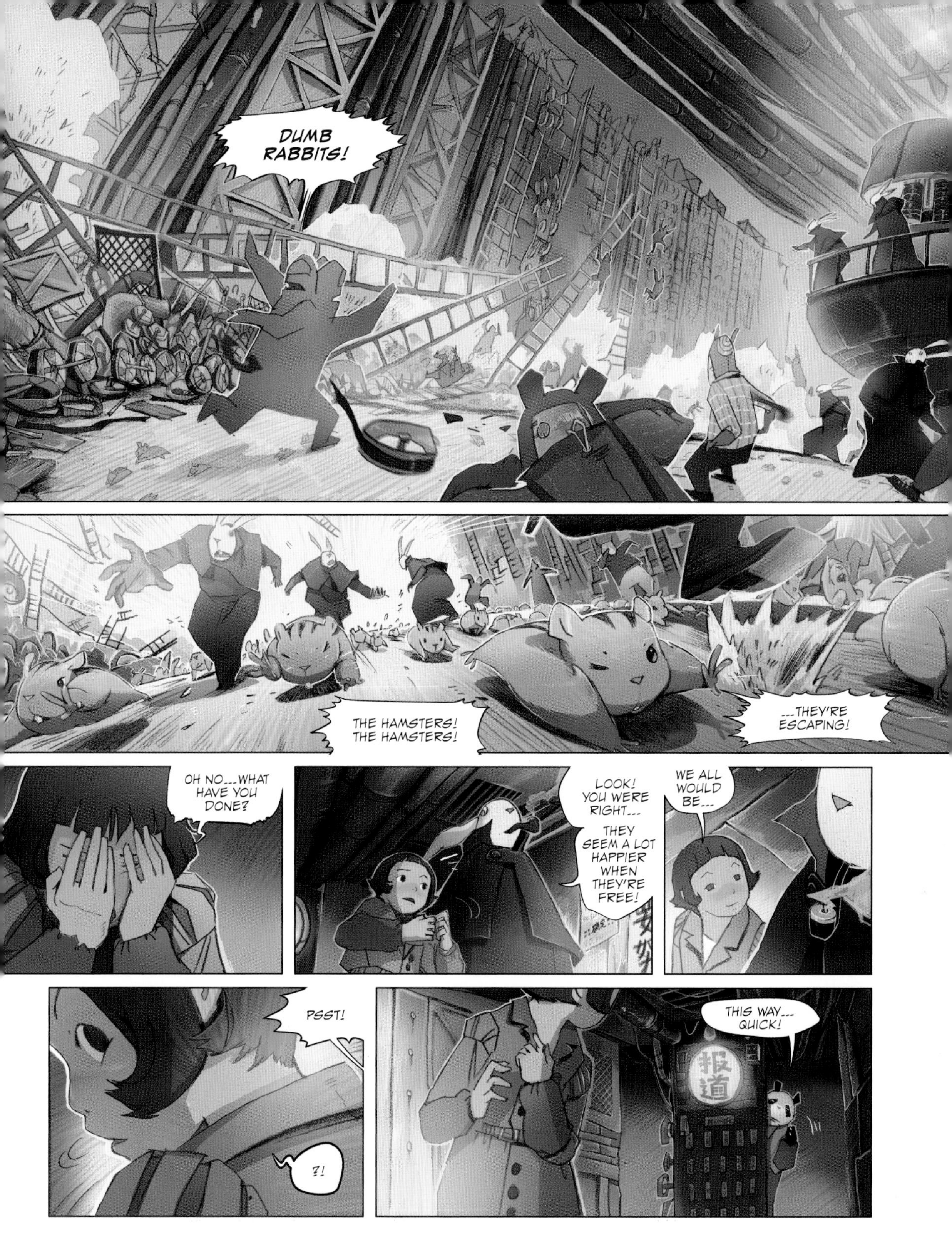
DUMB RABBITS!
THE HAMSTERS! THE HAMSTERS!
...THEY'RE ESCAPING!
OH NO...WHAT HAVE YOU DONE?
LOOK! YOU WERE RIGHT...
THEY SEEM A LOT HAPPIER WHEN THEY'RE FREE!
WE ALL WOULD BE...
PSST!
?!
THIS WAY... QUICK!

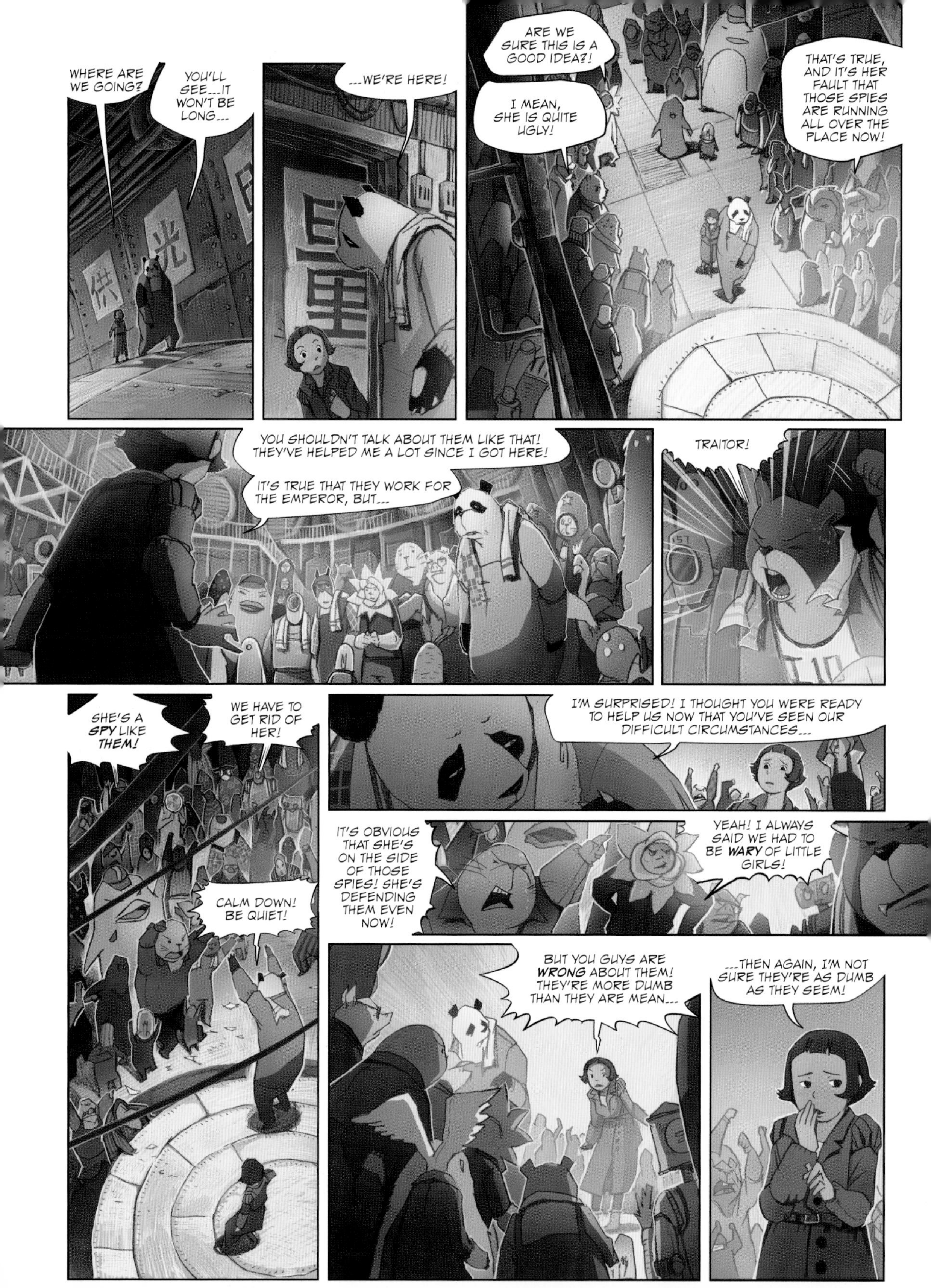

WHERE ARE WE GOING?
YOU'LL SEE...IT WON'T BE LONG...
...WE'RE HERE!
ARE WE SURE THIS IS A GOOD IDEA?!
I MEAN, SHE IS QUITE UGLY!
THAT'S TRUE, AND IT'S HER FAULT THAT THOSE SPIES ARE RUNNING ALL OVER THE PLACE NOW!
YOU SHOULDN'T TALK ABOUT THEM LIKE THAT! THEY'VE HELPED ME A LOT SINCE I GOT HERE!
IT'S TRUE THAT THEY WORK FOR THE EMPEROR, BUT...
TRAITOR!
SHE'S A SPY LIKE THEM!
WE HAVE TO GET RID OF HER!
CALM DOWN! BE QUIET!
I'M SURPRISED! I THOUGHT YOU WERE READY TO HELP US NOW THAT YOU'VE SEEN OUR DIFFICULT CIRCUMSTANCES...
IT'S OBVIOUS THAT SHE'S ON THE SIDE OF THOSE SPIES! SHE'S DEFENDING THEM EVEN NOW!
YEAH! I ALWAYS SAID WE HAD TO BE WARY OF LITTLE GIRLS!
BUT YOU GUYS ARE WRONG ABOUT THEM! THEY'RE MORE DUMB THAN THEY ARE MEAN...
...THEN AGAIN, I'M NOT SURE THEY'RE AS DUMB AS THEY SEEM!

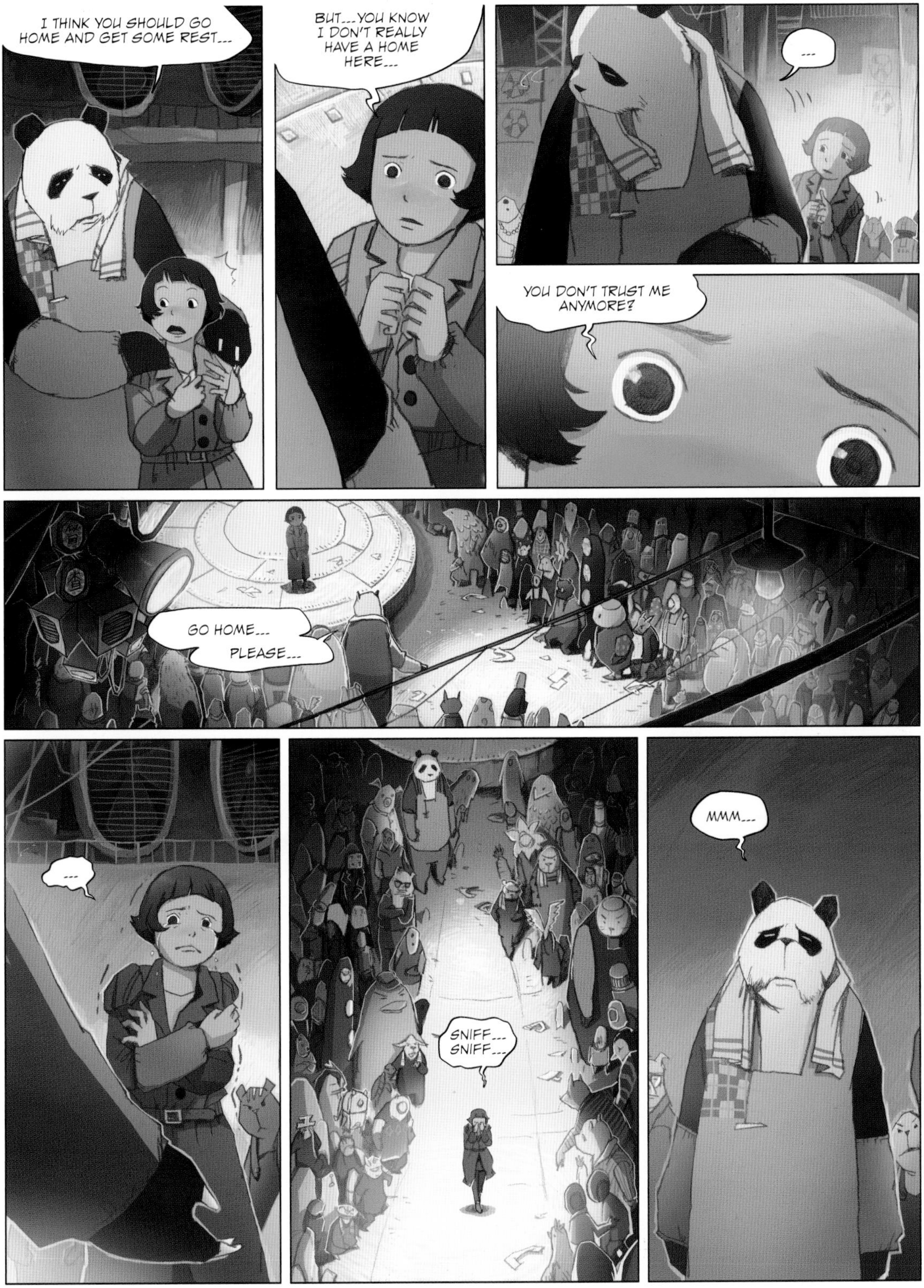
I THINK YOU SHOULD GO HOME AND GET SOME REST...
BUT... YOU KNOW I DON'T REALLY HAVE A HOME HERE...
...
YOU DON'T TRUST ME ANYMORE?
GO HOME...
PLEASE...
...
SNIFF... SNIFF...
MMM...

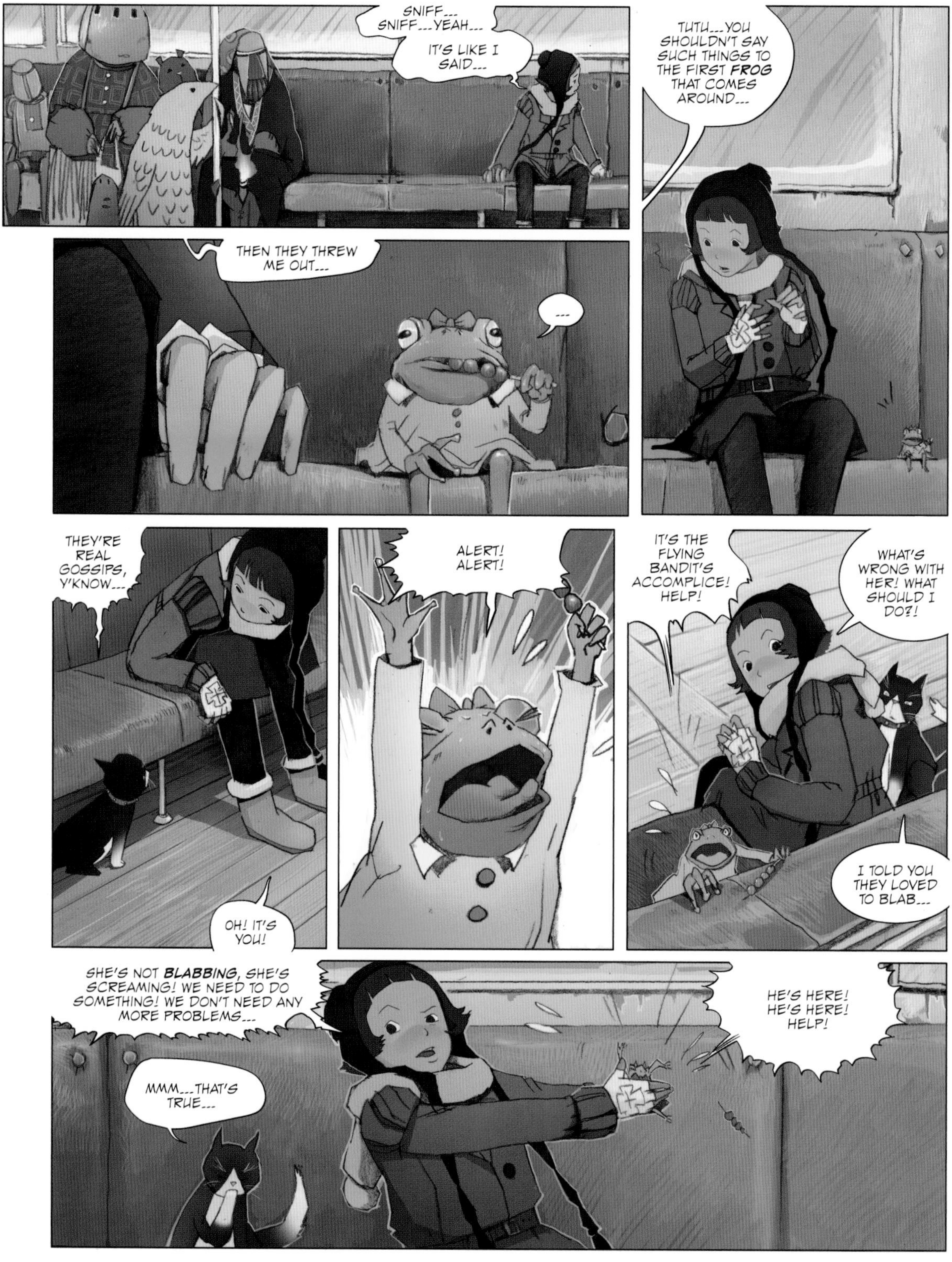

SNIFF... SNIFF... YEAH...
IT'S LIKE I SAID...
TUTU... YOU SHOULDN'T SAY SUCH THINGS TO THE FIRST **FROG** THAT COMES AROUND...
THEN THEY THREW ME OUT...
...
THEY'RE REAL GOSSIPS, Y'KNOW...
OH! IT'S YOU!
ALERT! ALERT!
IT'S THE FLYING BANDIT'S ACCOMPLICE! HELP!
WHAT'S WRONG WITH HER! WHAT SHOULD I DO?!
I TOLD YOU THEY LOVED TO BLAB...
SHE'S NOT **BLABBING**, SHE'S SCREAMING! WE NEED TO DO SOMETHING! WE DON'T NEED ANY MORE PROBLEMS...
HE'S HERE! HE'S HERE! HELP!
MMM... THAT'S TRUE...

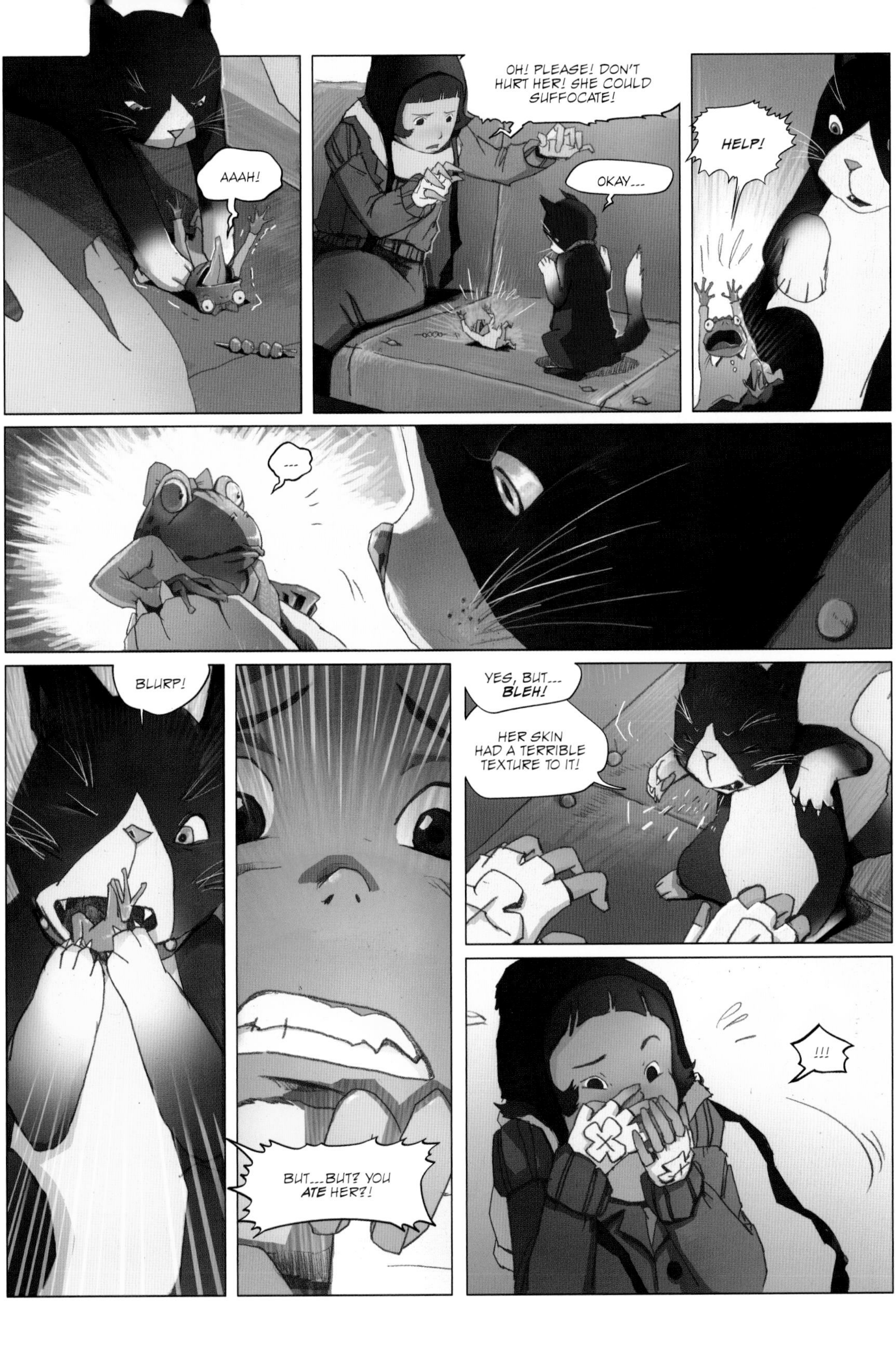
AAAH!
OH! PLEASE! DON'T HURT HER! SHE COULD SUFFOCATE!
OKAY...
HELP!
...
BLURP!
BUT...BUT? YOU ATE HER?!
YES, BUT... BLEH!
HER SKIN HAD A TERRIBLE TEXTURE TO IT!
!!!

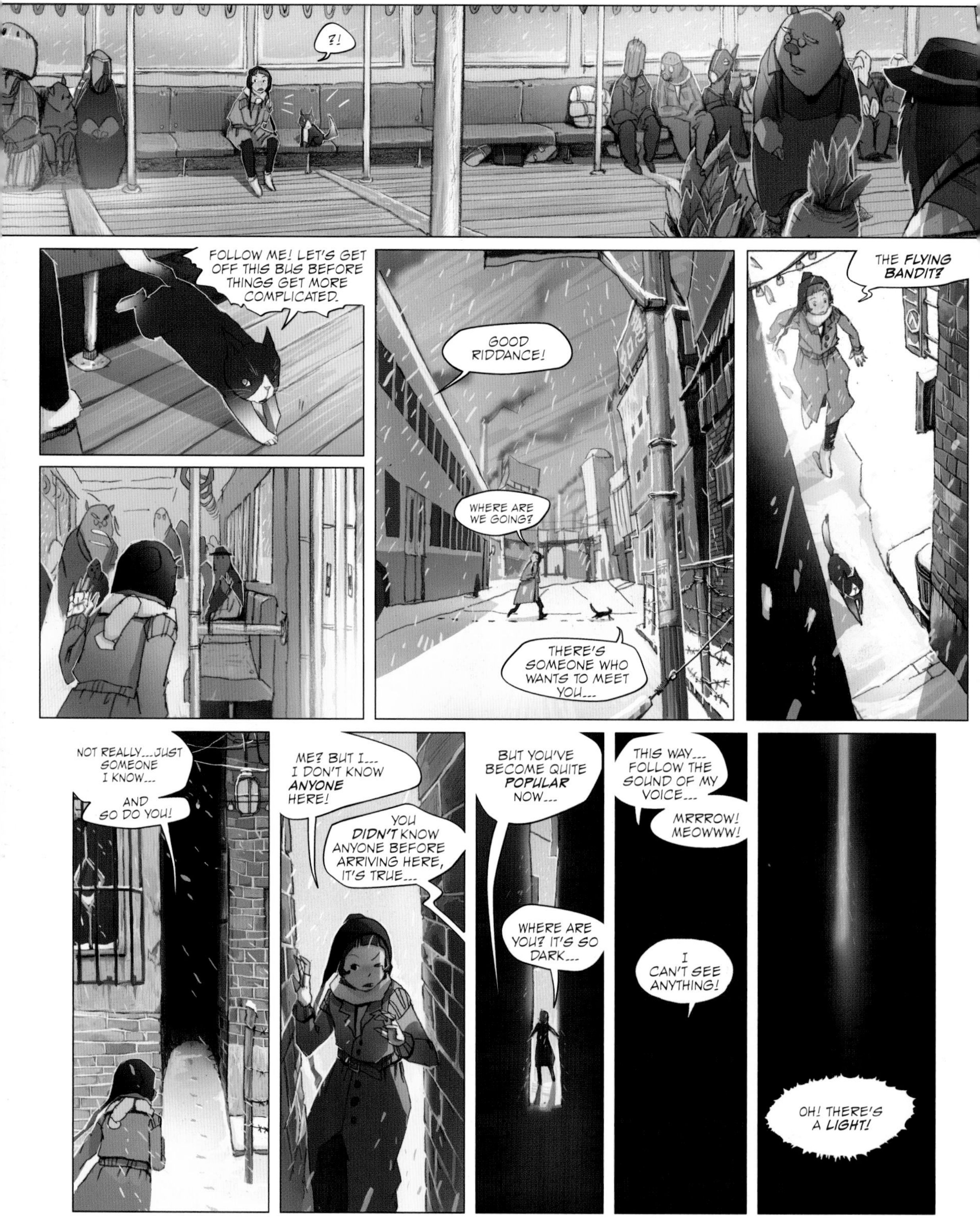
?!
FOLLOW ME! LET'S GET OFF THIS BUS BEFORE THINGS GET MORE COMPLICATED.
GOOD RIDDANCE!
WHERE ARE WE GOING?
THERE'S SOMEONE WHO WANTS TO MEET YOU...
THE FLYING BANDIT?
NOT REALLY... JUST SOMEONE I KNOW...
AND SO DO YOU!
ME? BUT I... I DON'T KNOW ANYONE HERE!
YOU DIDN'T KNOW ANYONE BEFORE ARRIVING HERE, IT'S TRUE...
BUT YOU'VE BECOME QUITE POPULAR NOW...
WHERE ARE YOU? IT'S SO DARK...
THIS WAY... FOLLOW THE SOUND OF MY VOICE...
MRRROW! MEOWWW!
I CAN'T SEE ANYTHING!
OH! THERE'S A LIGHT!

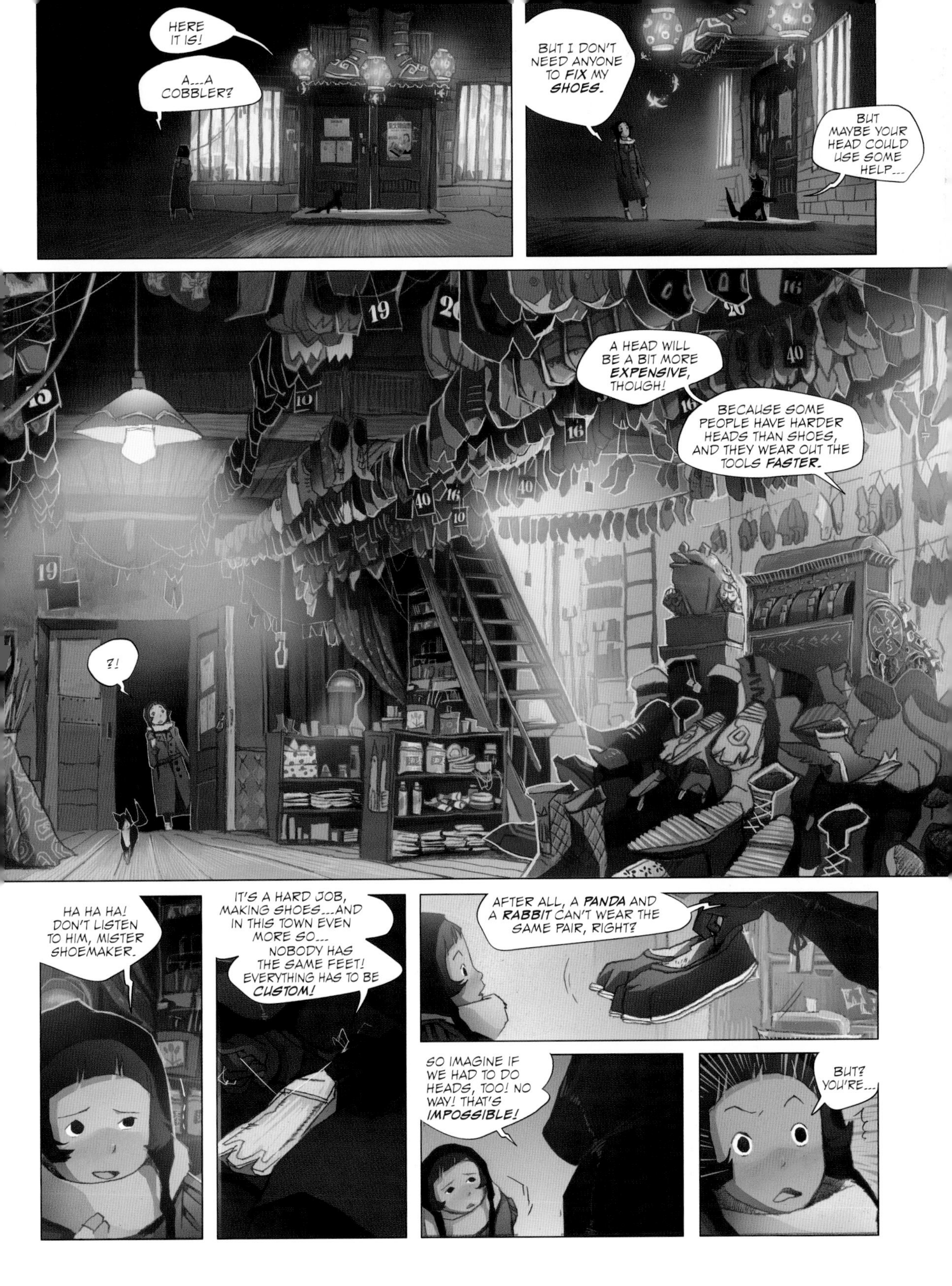
HERE IT IS!
A...A COBBLER?
BUT I DON'T NEED ANYONE TO FIX MY SHOES.
BUT MAYBE YOUR HEAD COULD USE SOME HELP...
A HEAD WILL BE A BIT MORE EXPENSIVE, THOUGH!
BECAUSE SOME PEOPLE HAVE HARDER HEADS THAN SHOES, AND THEY WEAR OUT THE TOOLS FASTER.
?!
HA HA HA! DON'T LISTEN TO HIM, MISTER SHOEMAKER.
IT'S A HARD JOB, MAKING SHOES...AND IN THIS TOWN EVEN MORE SO...
NOBODY HAS THE SAME FEET! EVERYTHING HAS TO BE CUSTOM!
AFTER ALL, A PANDA AND A RABBIT CAN'T WEAR THE SAME PAIR, RIGHT?
SO IMAGINE IF WE HAD TO DO HEADS, TOO! NO WAY! THAT'S IMPOSSIBLE!
BUT? YOU'RE...

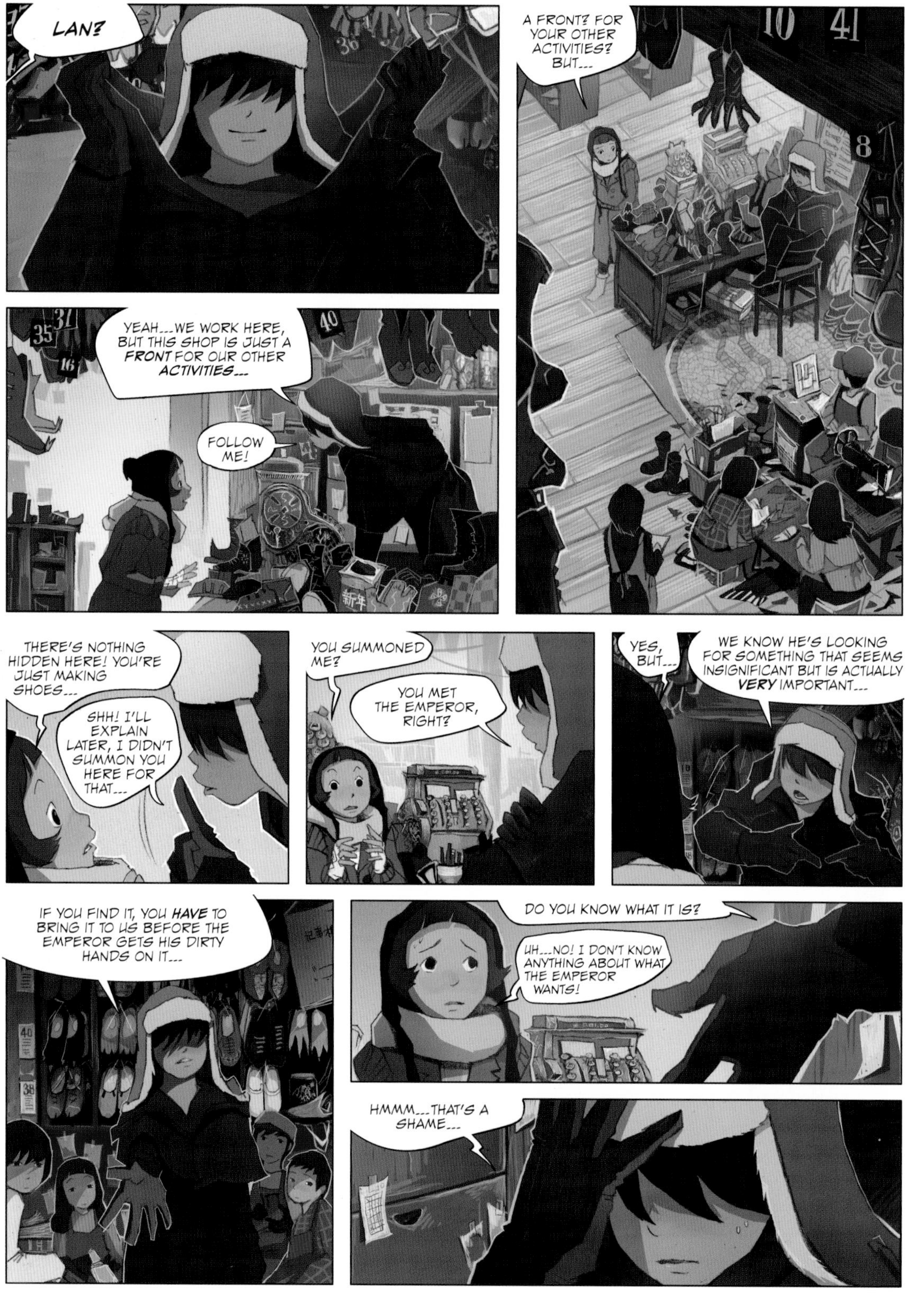
LAN?
A FRONT? FOR YOUR OTHER ACTIVITIES? BUT...
YEAH...WE WORK HERE, BUT THIS SHOP IS JUST A FRONT FOR OUR OTHER ACTIVITIES...
FOLLOW ME!
THERE'S NOTHING HIDDEN HERE! YOU'RE JUST MAKING SHOES...
SHH! I'LL EXPLAIN LATER, I DIDN'T SUMMON YOU HERE FOR THAT...
YOU SUMMONED ME?
YOU MET THE EMPEROR, RIGHT?
YES, BUT...
WE KNOW HE'S LOOKING FOR SOMETHING THAT SEEMS INSIGNIFICANT BUT IS ACTUALLY VERY IMPORTANT...
IF YOU FIND IT, YOU HAVE TO BRING IT TO US BEFORE THE EMPEROR GETS HIS DIRTY HANDS ON IT...
DO YOU KNOW WHAT IT IS?
UH...NO! I DON'T KNOW ANYTHING ABOUT WHAT THE EMPEROR WANTS!
HMMM...THAT'S A SHAME...

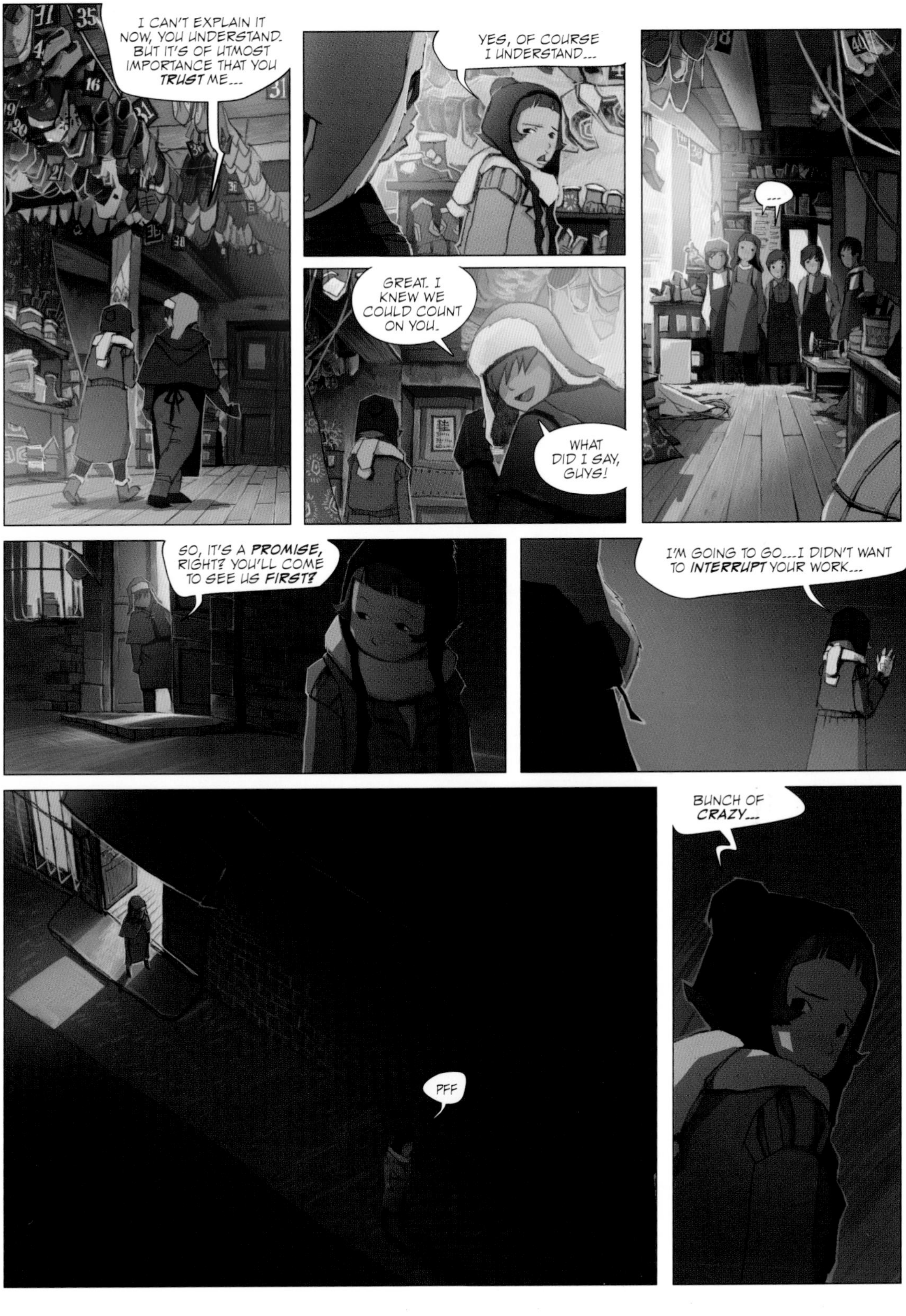
I CAN'T EXPLAIN IT NOW, YOU UNDERSTAND. BUT IT'S OF UTMOST IMPORTANCE THAT YOU TRUST ME...
YES, OF COURSE I UNDERSTAND...
GREAT. I KNEW WE COULD COUNT ON YOU.
WHAT DID I SAY, GUYS!
...
SO, IT'S A PROMISE, RIGHT? YOU'LL COME TO SEE US FIRST?
I'M GOING TO GO... I DIDN'T WANT TO INTERRUPT YOUR WORK...
PFF
BUNCH OF CRAZY...

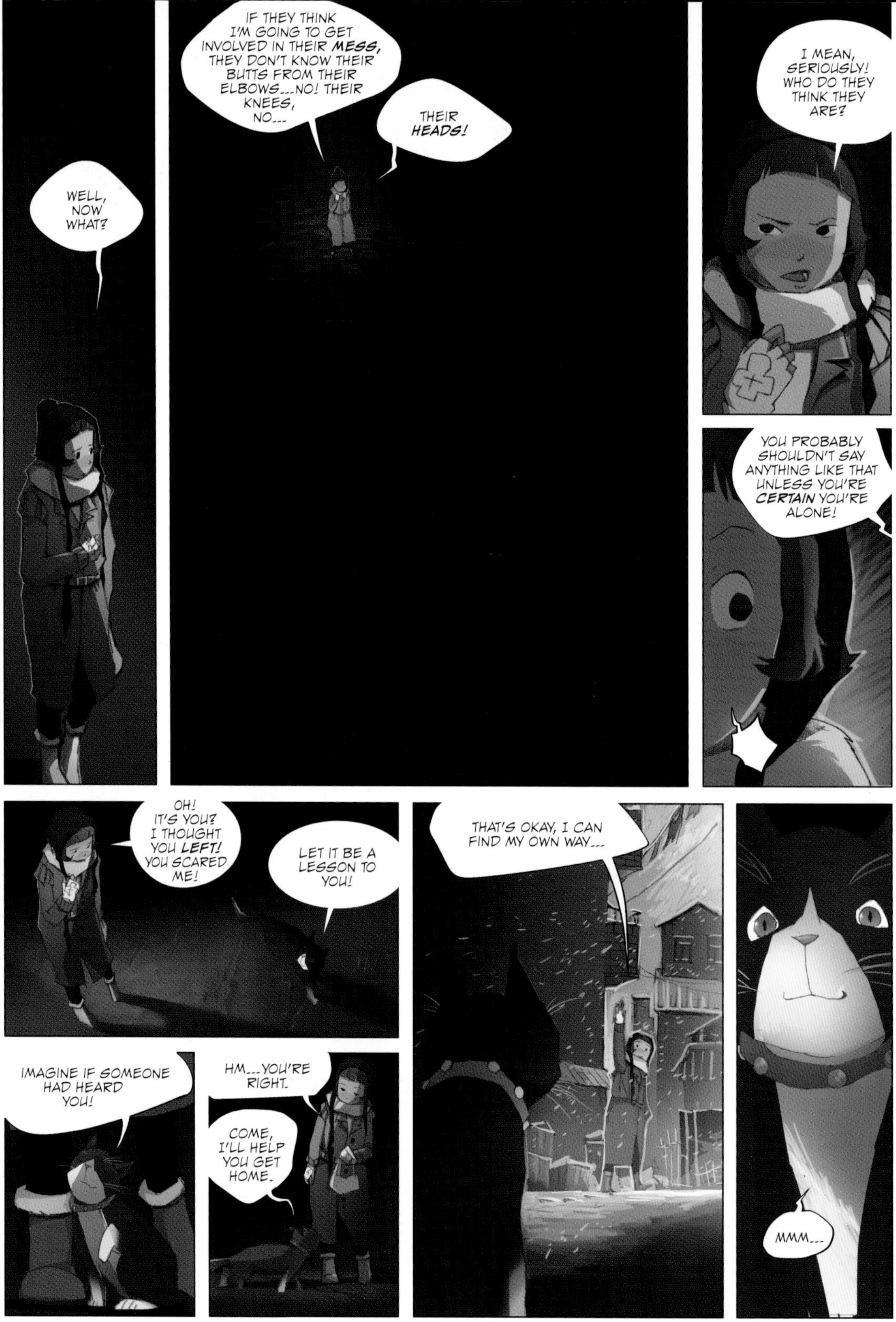
WELL, NOW WHAT?
IF THEY THINK I'M GOING TO GET INVOLVED IN THEIR MESS, THEY DON'T KNOW THEIR BUTTS FROM THEIR ELBOWS...NO! THEIR KNEES, NO...
THEIR HEADS!
I MEAN, SERIOUSLY! WHO DO THEY THINK THEY ARE?
YOU PROBABLY SHOULDN'T SAY ANYTHING LIKE THAT UNLESS YOU'RE CERTAIN YOU'RE ALONE!
OH! IT'S YOU? I THOUGHT YOU LEFT! YOU SCARED ME!
LET IT BE A LESSON TO YOU!
IMAGINE IF SOMEONE HAD HEARD YOU!
HM...YOU'RE RIGHT.
COME, I'LL HELP YOU GET HOME.
THAT'S OKAY, I CAN FIND MY OWN WAY...
MMM...

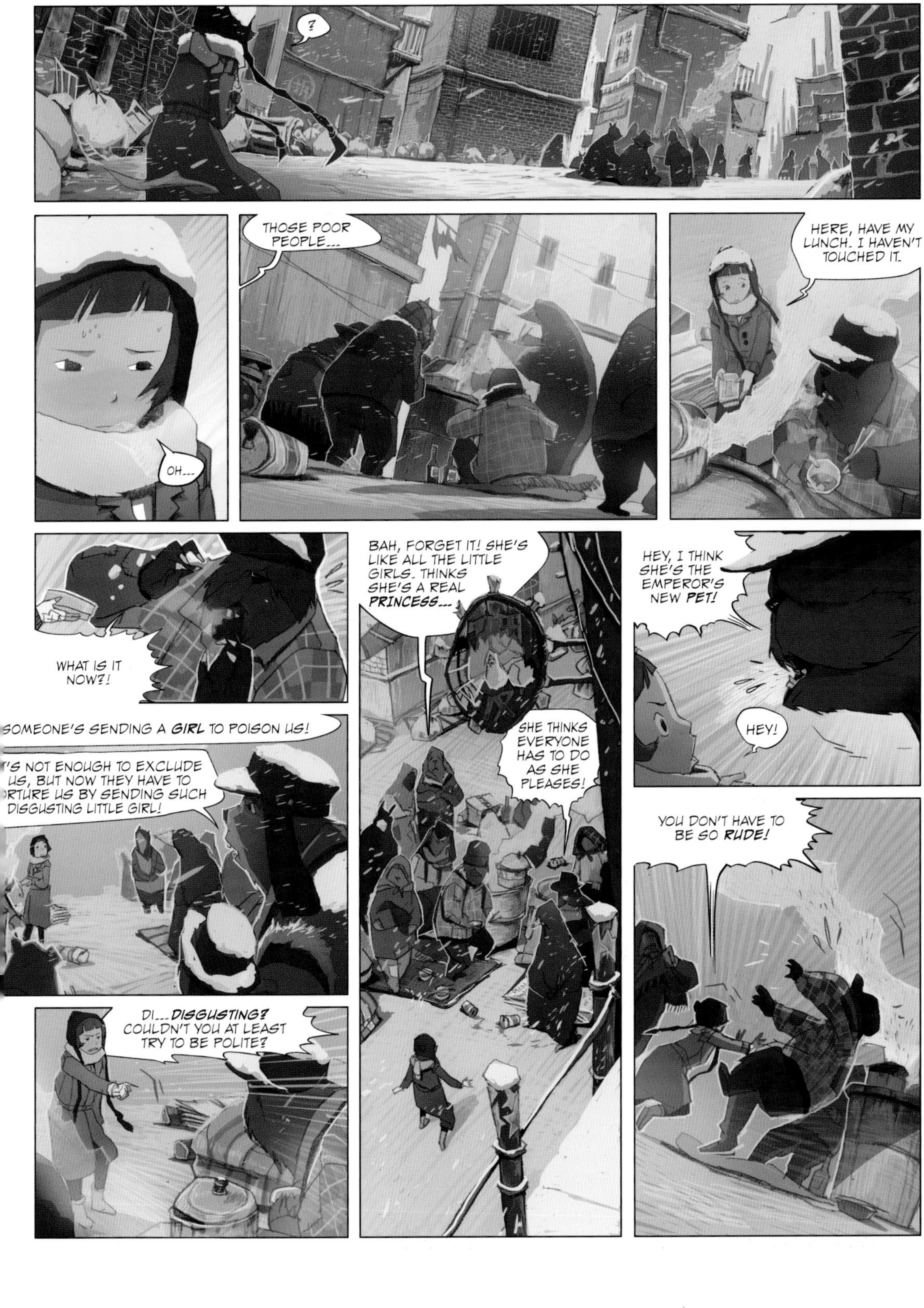
?
OH...
THOSE POOR PEOPLE...
HERE, HAVE MY LUNCH. I HAVEN'T TOUCHED IT.
WHAT IS IT NOW?!
SOMEONE'S SENDING A GIRL TO POISON US!
'S NOT ENOUGH TO EXCLUDE US, BUT NOW THEY HAVE TO RTURE US BY SENDING SUCH DISGUSTING LITTLE GIRL!
DI... DISGUSTING? COULDN'T YOU AT LEAST TRY TO BE POLITE?
BAH, FORGET IT! SHE'S LIKE ALL THE LITTLE GIRLS. THINKS SHE'S A REAL PRINCESS...
SHE THINKS EVERYONE HAS TO DO AS SHE PLEASES!
HEY, I THINK SHE'S THE EMPEROR'S NEW PET!
HEY!
YOU DON'T HAVE TO BE SO RUDE!

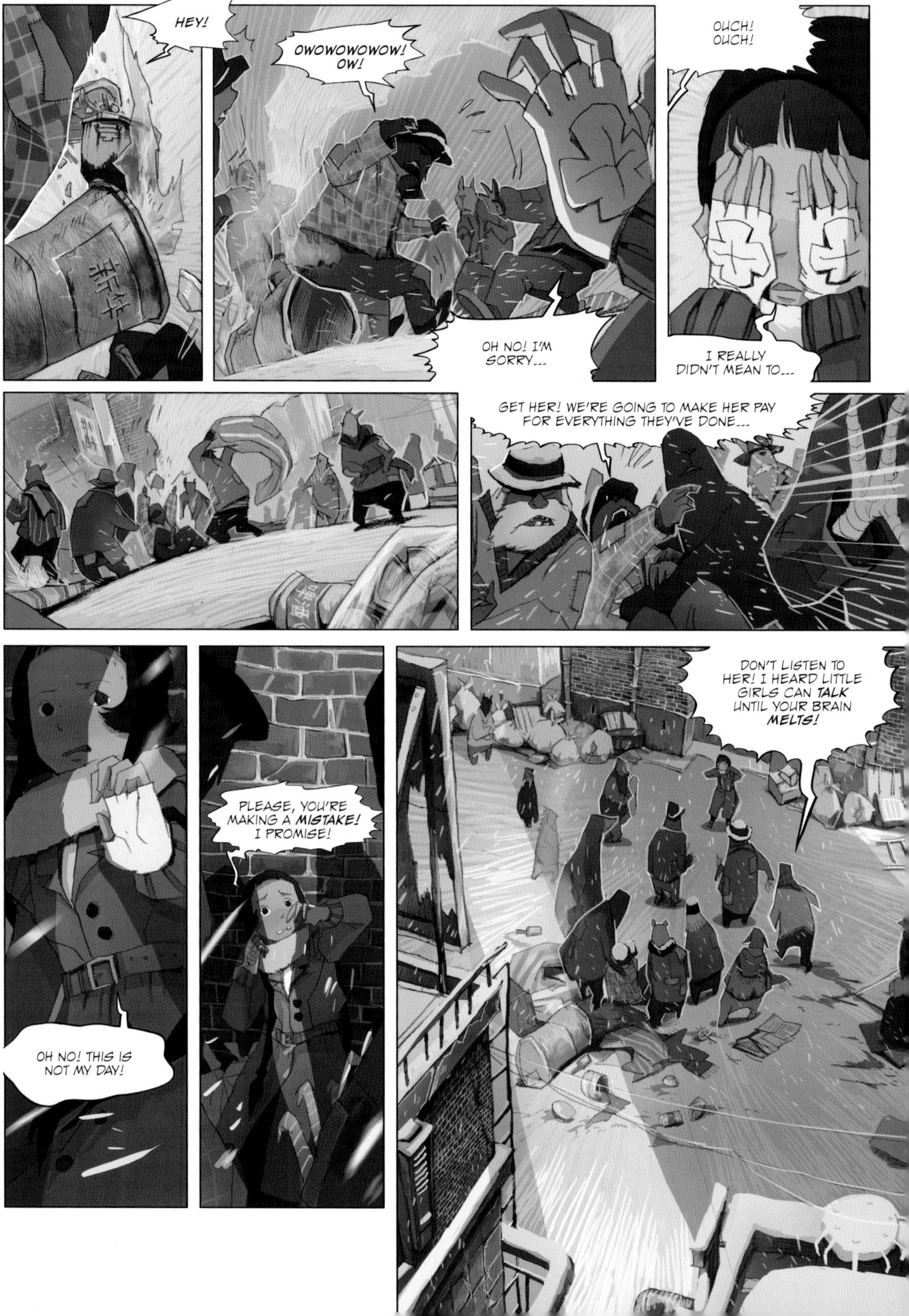
HEY!
OWOWOWOWOW! OW!
OH NO! I'M SORRY...
OUCH! OUCH!
I REALLY DIDN'T MEAN TO...
GET HER! WE'RE GOING TO MAKE HER PAY FOR EVERYTHING THEY'VE DONE...
OH NO! THIS IS NOT MY DAY!
PLEASE, YOU'RE MAKING A MISTAKE! I PROMISE!
DON'T LISTEN TO HER! I HEARD LITTLE GIRLS CAN TALK UNTIL YOUR BRAIN MELTS!

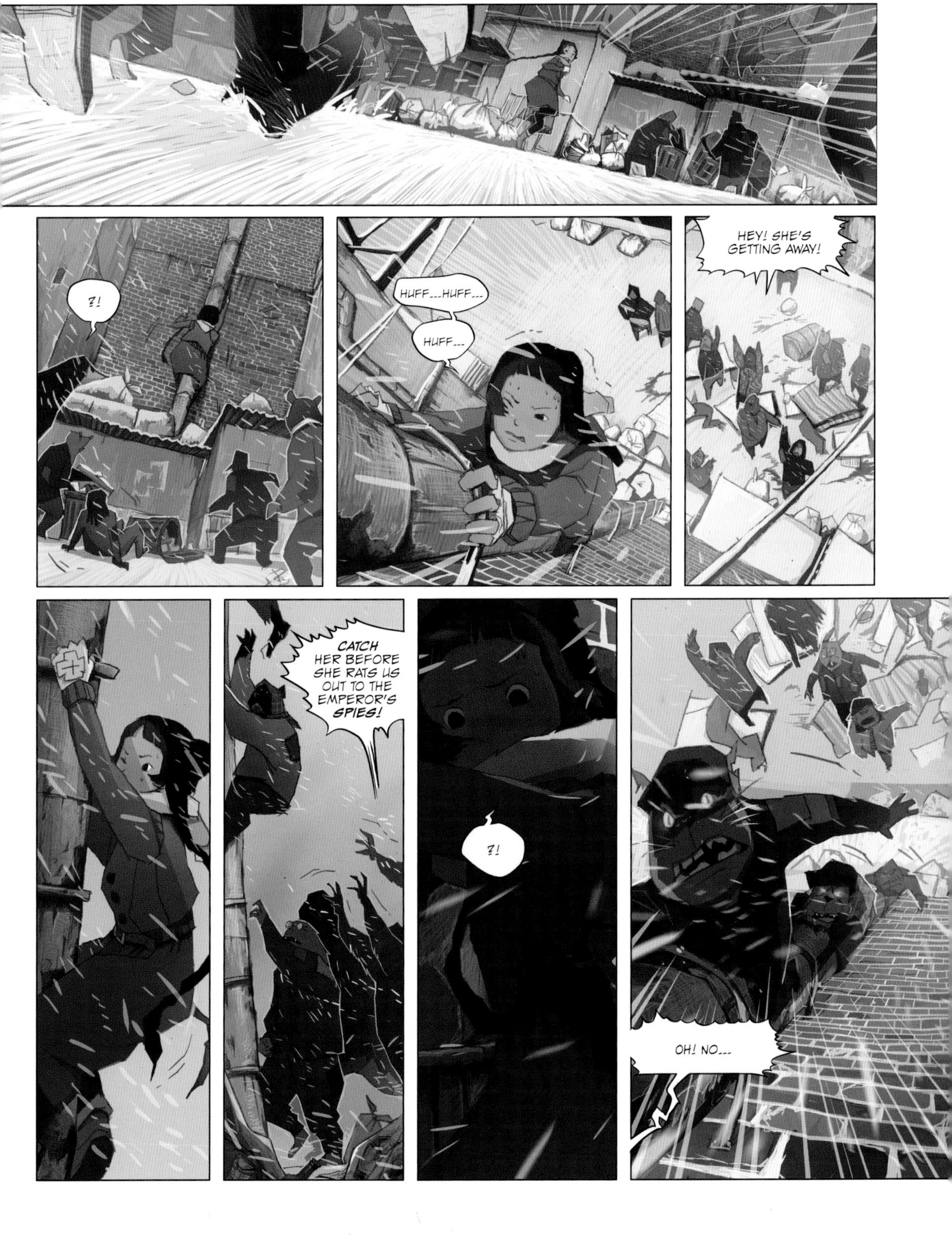
?!
HUFF...HUFF...
HUFF...
HEY! SHE'S GETTING AWAY!
CATCH HER BEFORE SHE RATS US OUT TO THE EMPEROR'S SPIES!
?!
OH! NO...

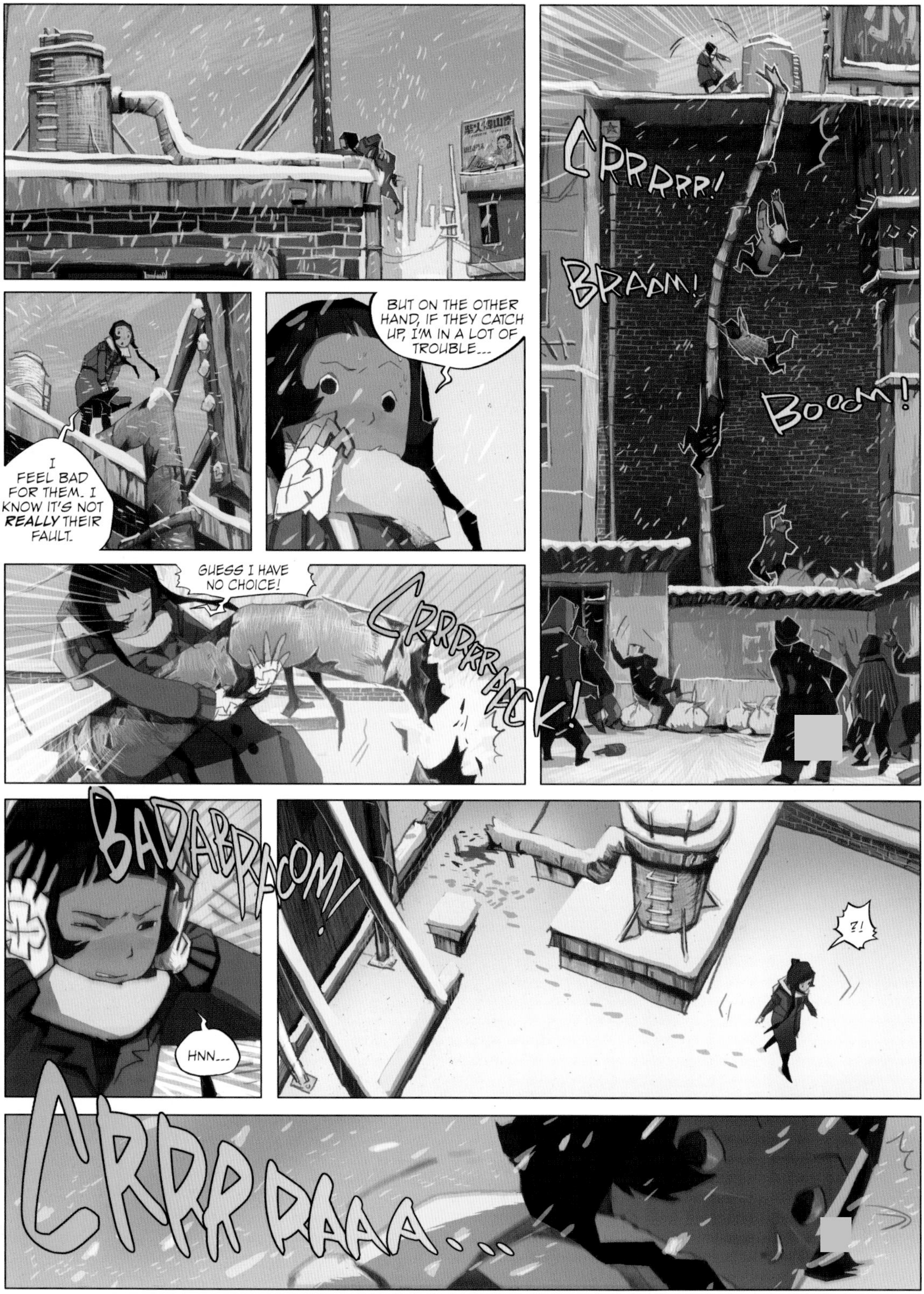

I FEEL BAD FOR THEM. I KNOW IT'S NOT ***REALLY*** THEIR FAULT.
BUT ON THE OTHER HAND, IF THEY CATCH UP, I'M IN A LOT OF TROUBLE...
CRRRRRR!
BRAAM!
BOOOM!
GUESS I HAVE NO CHOICE!
CRRRRRRACK!
BADABRAOOM!
HNN...
?!
CRRRRAAA...

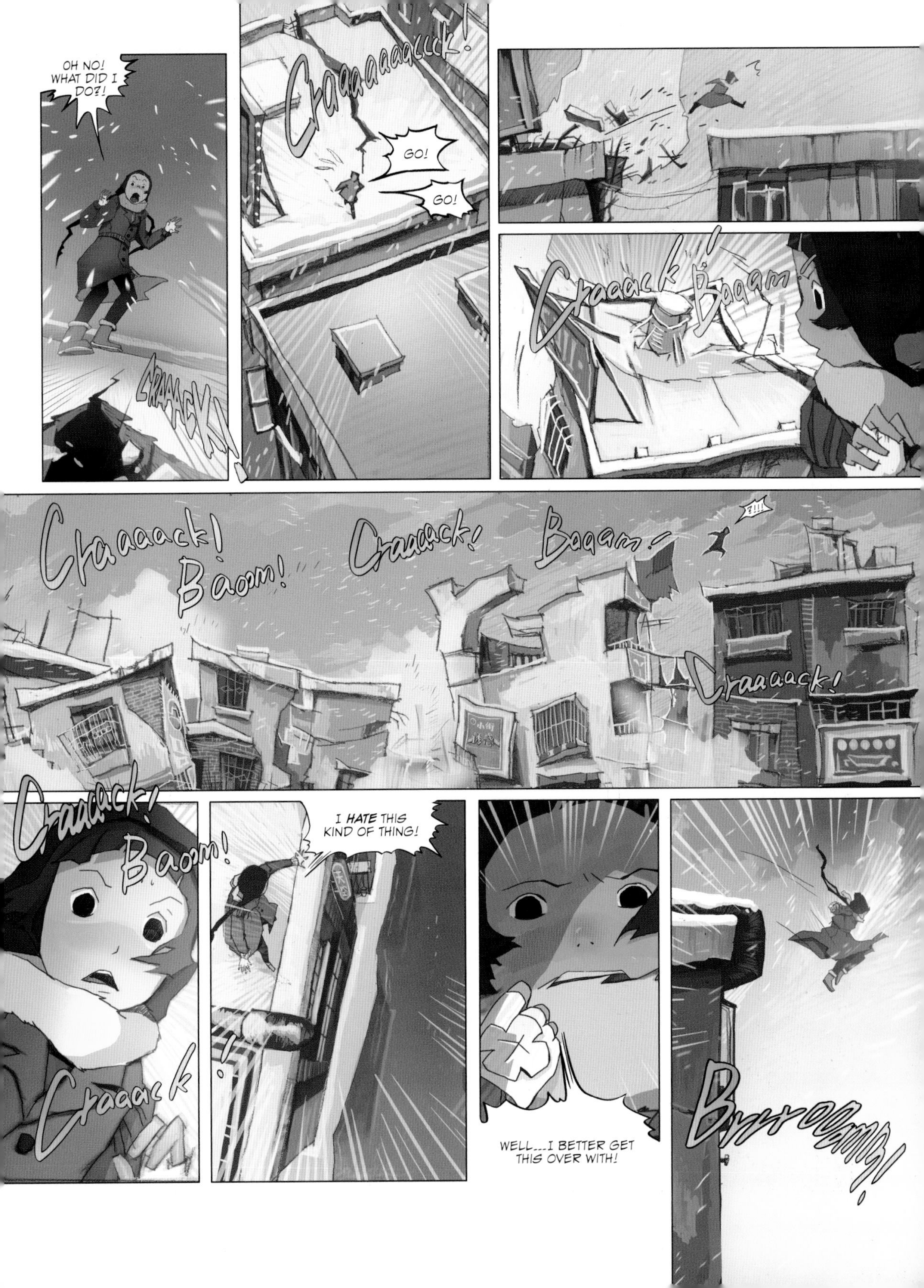
OH NO! WHAT DID I DO?!
CRAAACK!!
Craaaaaaaacck!
GO!
GO!
Craaack Baaam!
Craaaack! Baoom!
Craaack!
Baaam!
Craaaack!
Craaack! Baoom!
Craaack!
I HATE THIS KIND OF THING!
WELL... I BETTER GET THIS OVER WITH!
Brrroooom!

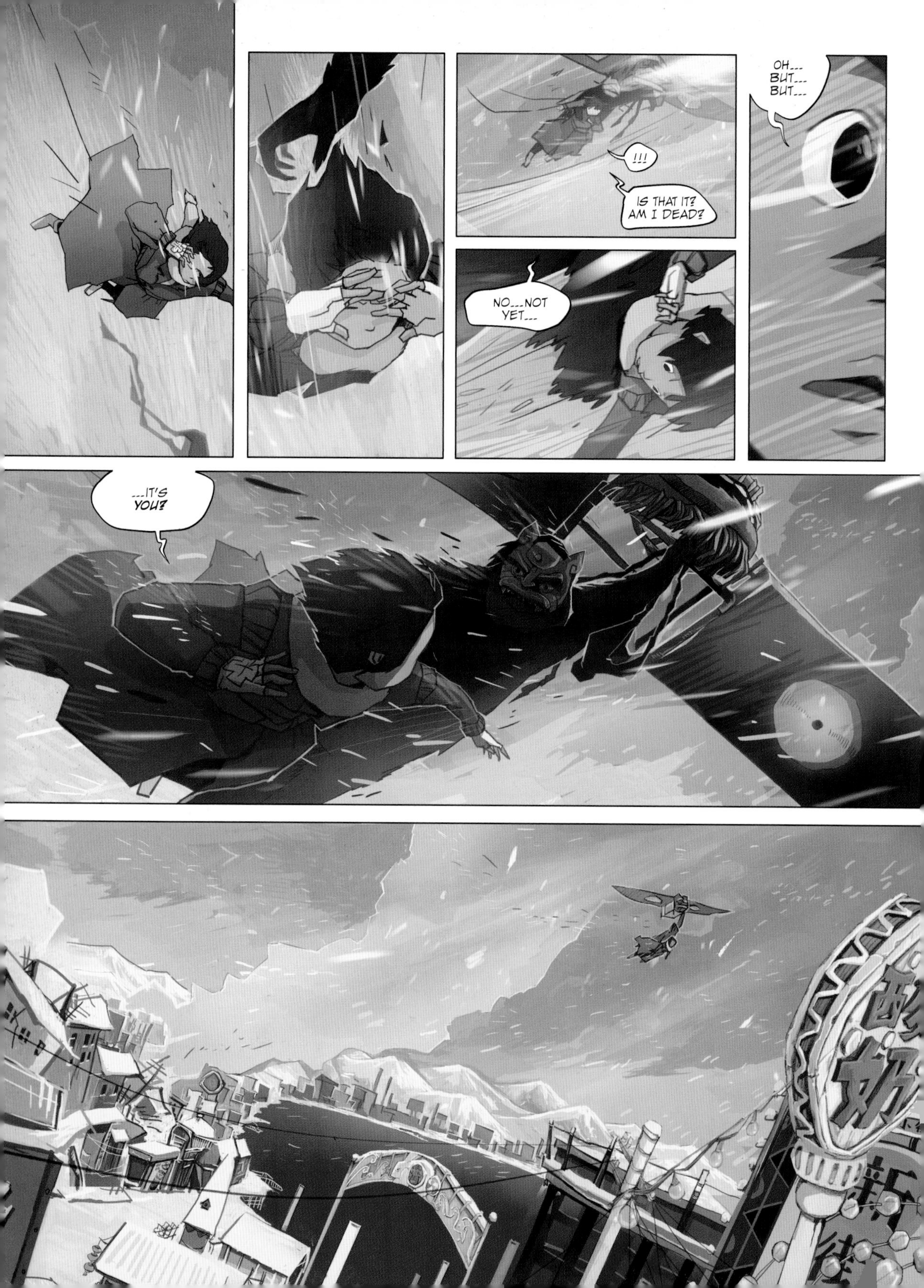
!!!
IS THAT IT? AM I DEAD?
NO... NOT YET...
OH... BUT... BUT...
...IT'S YOU?

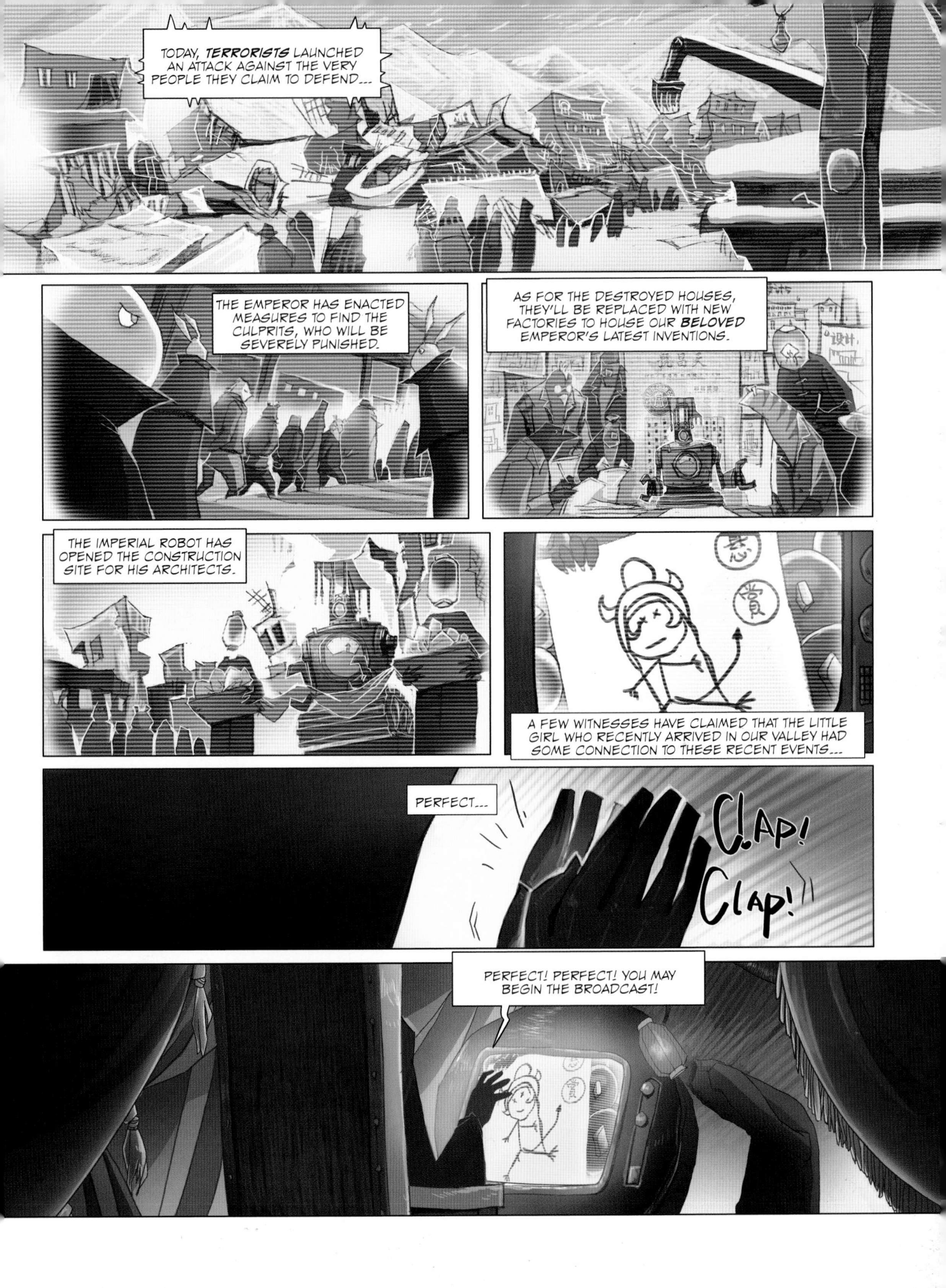
TODAY, TERRORISTS LAUNCHED AN ATTACK AGAINST THE VERY PEOPLE THEY CLAIM TO DEFEND...
THE EMPEROR HAS ENACTED MEASURES TO FIND THE CULPRITS, WHO WILL BE SEVERELY PUNISHED.
AS FOR THE DESTROYED HOUSES, THEY'LL BE REPLACED WITH NEW FACTORIES TO HOUSE OUR BELOVED EMPEROR'S LATEST INVENTIONS.
THE IMPERIAL ROBOT HAS OPENED THE CONSTRUCTION SITE FOR HIS ARCHITECTS.
A FEW WITNESSES HAVE CLAIMED THAT THE LITTLE GIRL WHO RECENTLY ARRIVED IN OUR VALLEY HAD SOME CONNECTION TO THESE RECENT EVENTS...
PERFECT...
CLAP!
CLAP!
PERFECT! PERFECT! YOU MAY BEGIN THE BROADCAST!

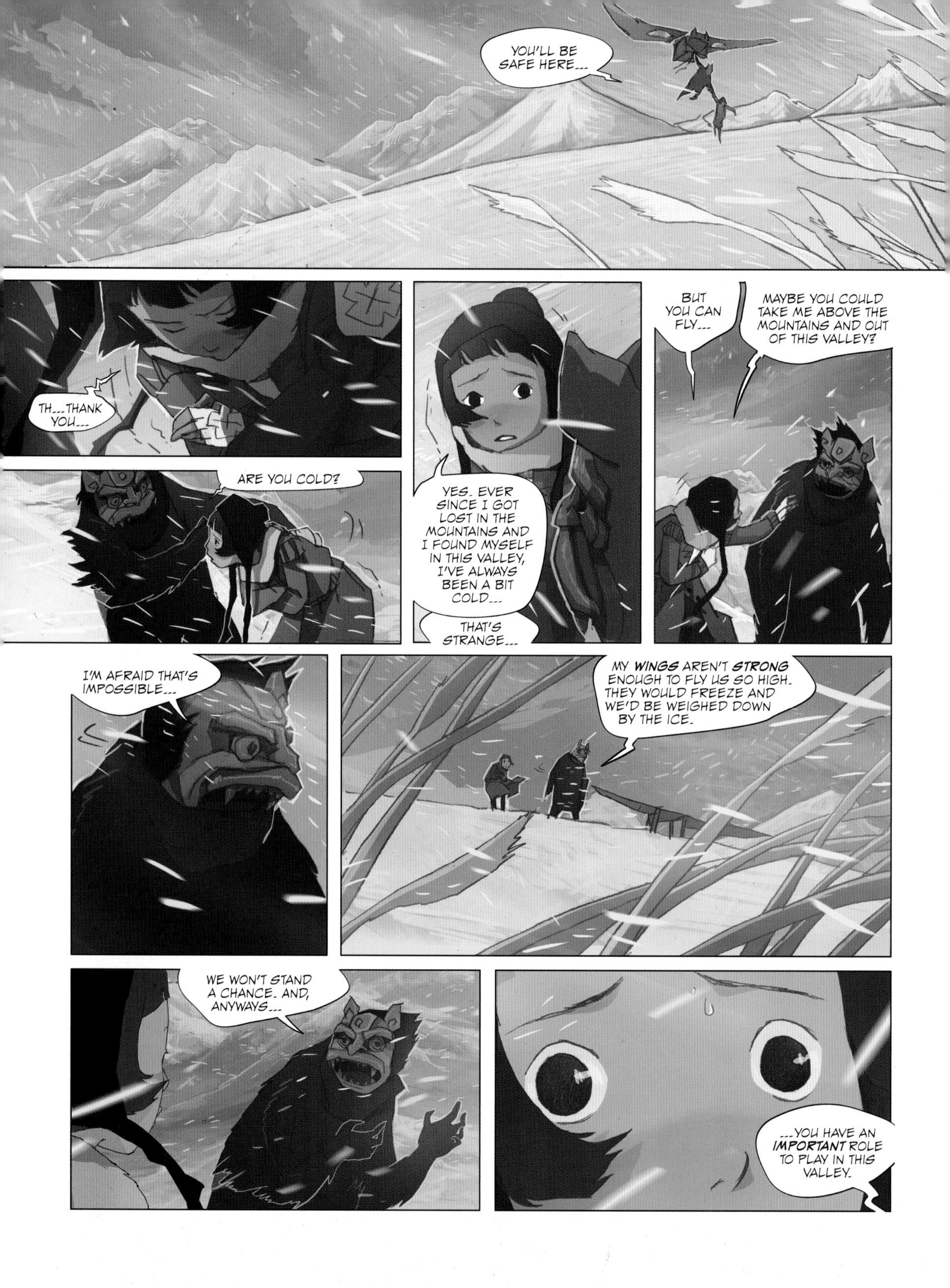
YOU'LL BE SAFE HERE...
TH... THANK YOU...
ARE YOU COLD?
YES. EVER SINCE I GOT LOST IN THE MOUNTAINS AND I FOUND MYSELF IN THIS VALLEY, I'VE ALWAYS BEEN A BIT COLD...
THAT'S STRANGE...
BUT YOU CAN FLY...
MAYBE YOU COULD TAKE ME ABOVE THE MOUNTAINS AND OUT OF THIS VALLEY?
I'M AFRAID THAT'S IMPOSSIBLE...
MY WINGS AREN'T STRONG ENOUGH TO FLY US SO HIGH. THEY WOULD FREEZE AND WE'D BE WEIGHED DOWN BY THE ICE.
WE WON'T STAND A CHANCE. AND, ANYWAYS...
...YOU HAVE AN IMPORTANT ROLE TO PLAY IN THIS VALLEY.

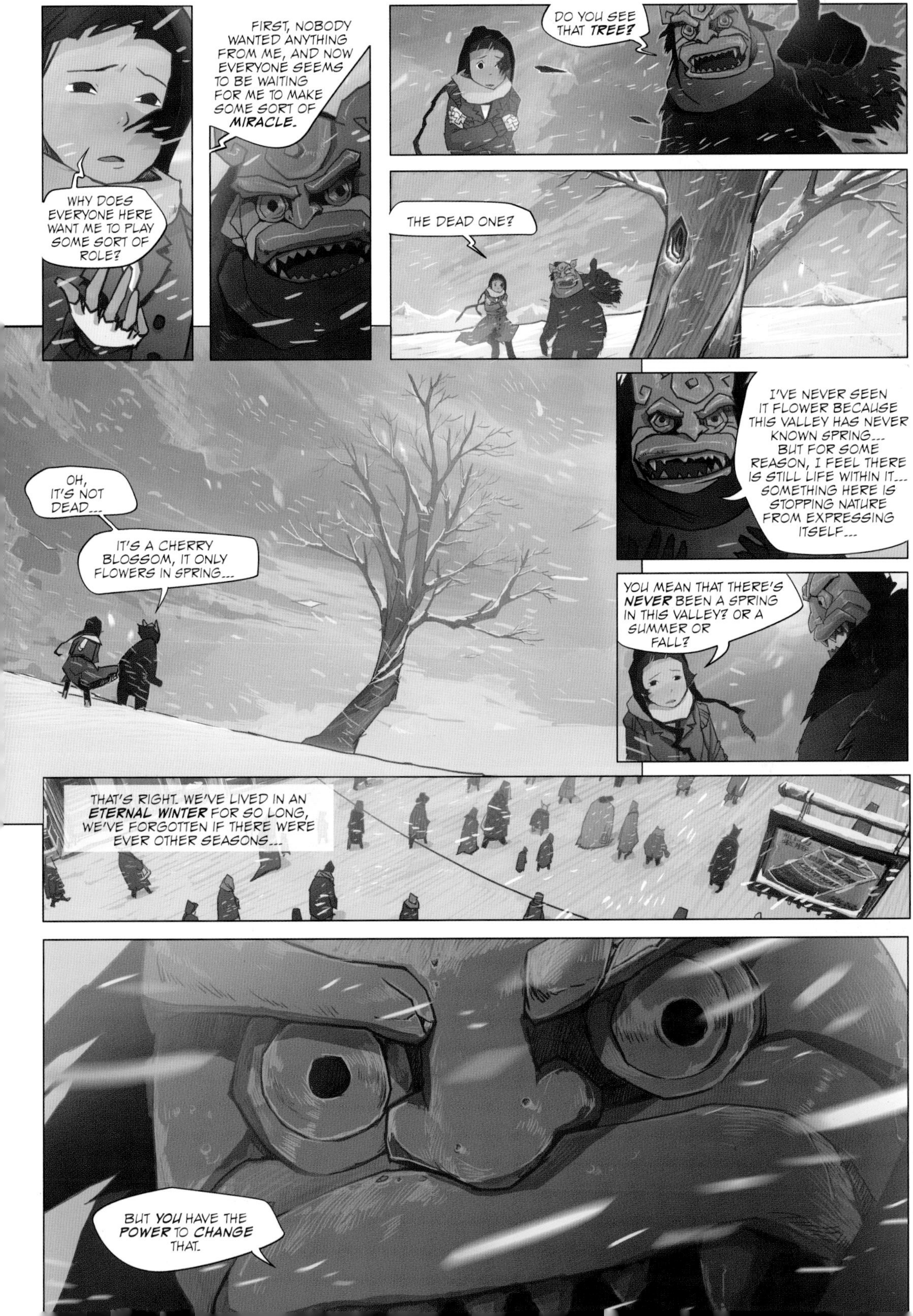
WHY DOES EVERYONE HERE WANT ME TO PLAY SOME SORT OF ROLE?
FIRST, NOBODY WANTED ANYTHING FROM ME, AND NOW EVERYONE SEEMS TO BE WAITING FOR ME TO MAKE SOME SORT OF **MIRACLE**.
DO YOU SEE THAT **TREE?**
THE DEAD ONE?
OH, IT'S NOT DEAD...
IT'S A CHERRY BLOSSOM, IT ONLY FLOWERS IN SPRING...
I'VE NEVER SEEN IT FLOWER BECAUSE THIS VALLEY HAS NEVER KNOWN SPRING... BUT FOR SOME REASON, I FEEL THERE IS STILL LIFE WITHIN IT... SOMETHING HERE IS STOPPING NATURE FROM EXPRESSING ITSELF...
YOU MEAN THAT THERE'S **NEVER** BEEN A SPRING IN THIS VALLEY? OR A SUMMER OR FALL?
THAT'S RIGHT. WE'VE LIVED IN AN **ETERNAL WINTER** FOR SO LONG, WE'VE FORGOTTEN IF THERE WERE EVER OTHER SEASONS...
BUT **YOU** HAVE THE **POWER** TO **CHANGE** THAT.

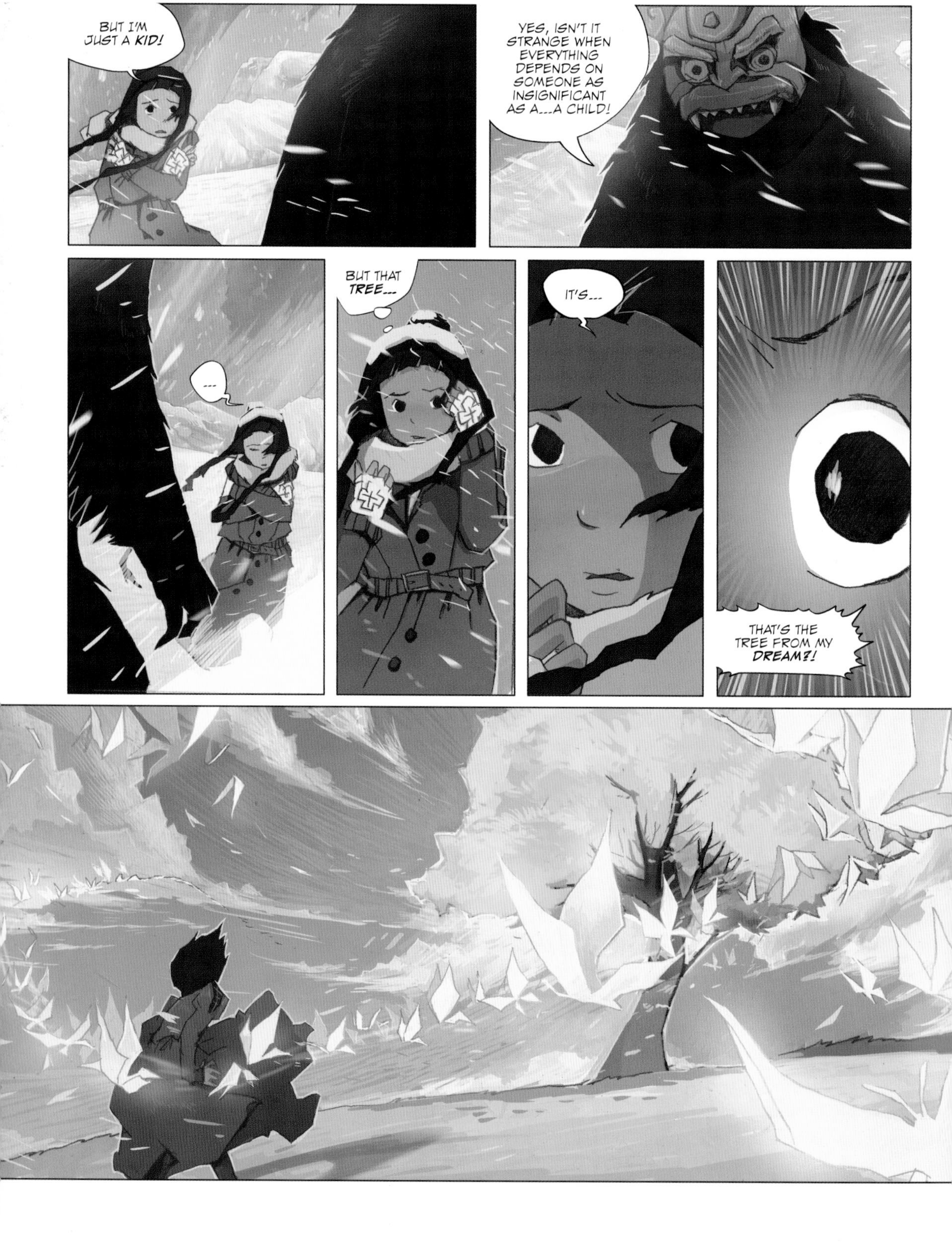
BUT I'M JUST A KID!
YES, ISN'T IT STRANGE WHEN EVERYTHING DEPENDS ON SOMEONE AS INSIGNIFICANT AS A...A CHILD!
...
BUT THAT TREE...
IT'S...
THAT'S THE TREE FROM MY DREAM?!

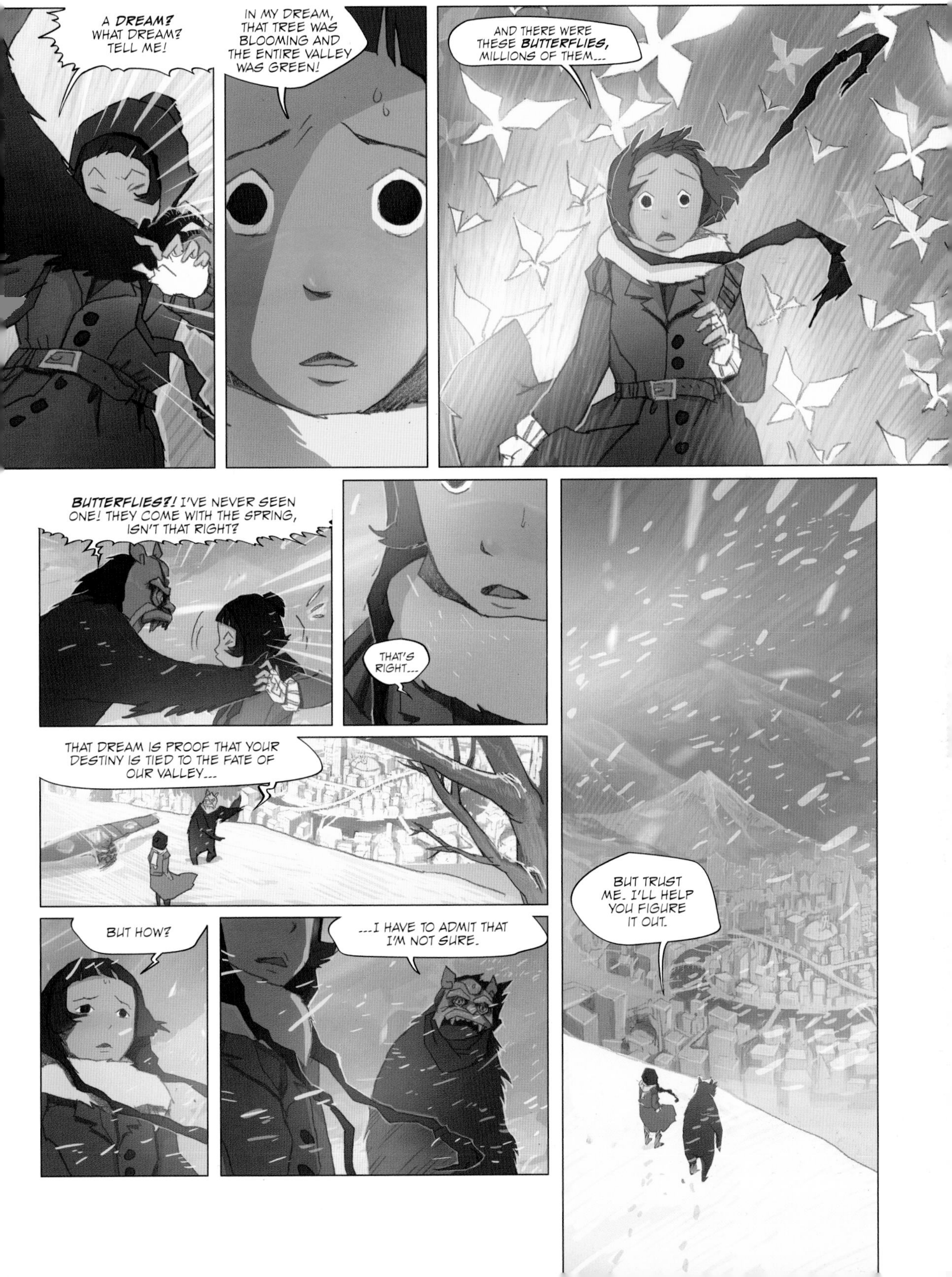

A DREAM? WHAT DREAM? TELL ME!
IN MY DREAM, THAT TREE WAS BLOOMING AND THE ENTIRE VALLEY WAS GREEN!
AND THERE WERE THESE BUTTERFLIES, MILLIONS OF THEM...
BUTTERFLIES?! I'VE NEVER SEEN ONE! THEY COME WITH THE SPRING, ISN'T THAT RIGHT?
THAT'S RIGHT...
THAT DREAM IS PROOF THAT YOUR DESTINY IS TIED TO THE FATE OF OUR VALLEY...
BUT HOW?
...I HAVE TO ADMIT THAT I'M NOT SURE.
BUT TRUST ME. I'LL HELP YOU FIGURE IT OUT.

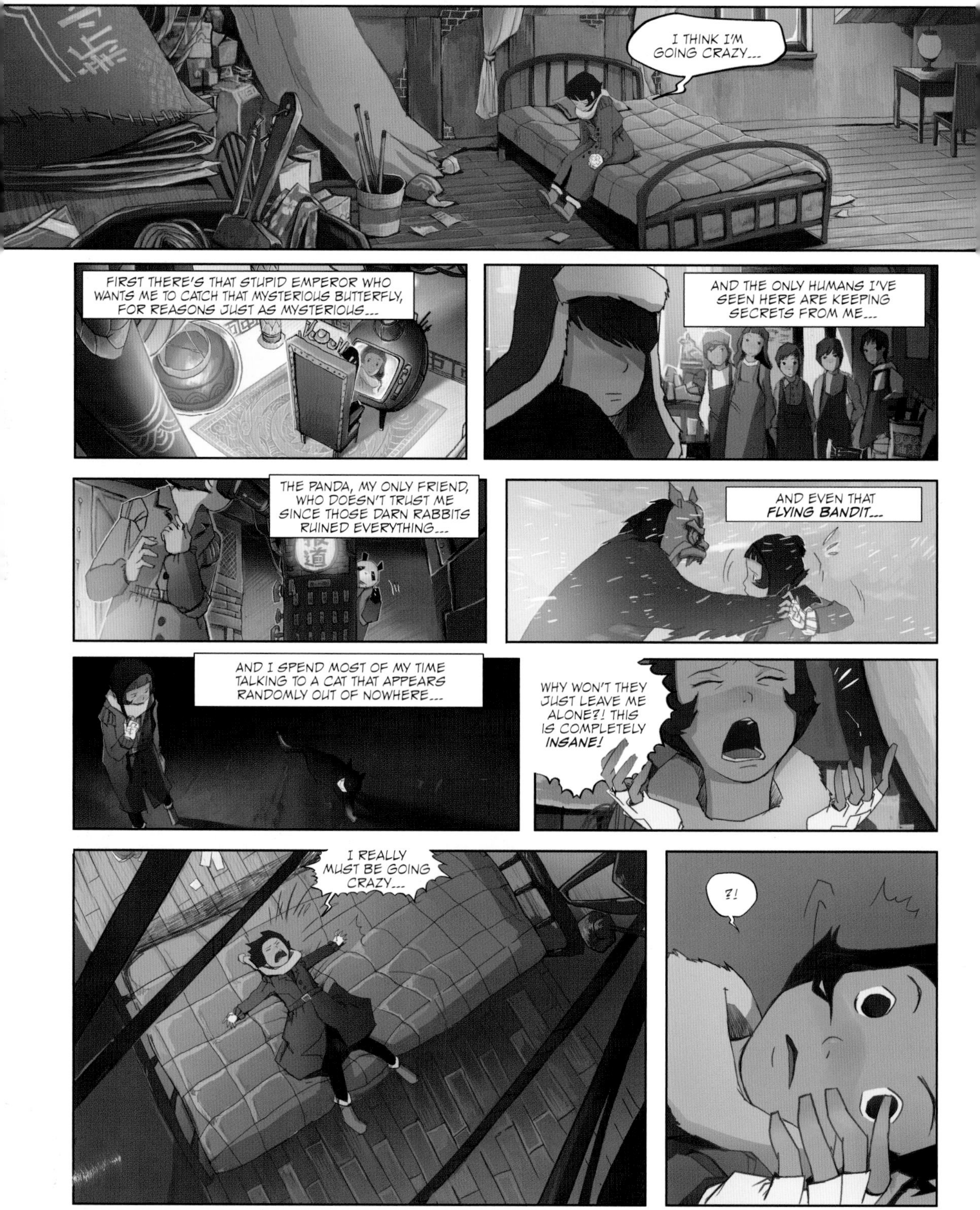
I THINK I'M GOING CRAZY...
FIRST THERE'S THAT STUPID EMPEROR WHO WANTS ME TO CATCH THAT MYSTERIOUS BUTTERFLY, FOR REASONS JUST AS MYSTERIOUS...
AND THE ONLY HUMANS I'VE SEEN HERE ARE KEEPING SECRETS FROM ME...
THE PANDA, MY ONLY FRIEND, WHO DOESN'T TRUST ME SINCE THOSE DARN RABBITS RUINED EVERYTHING...
AND EVEN THAT FLYING BANDIT...
AND I SPEND MOST OF MY TIME TALKING TO A CAT THAT APPEARS RANDOMLY OUT OF NOWHERE...
WHY WON'T THEY JUST LEAVE ME ALONE?! THIS IS COMPLETELY INSANE!
I REALLY MUST BE GOING CRAZY...
?!

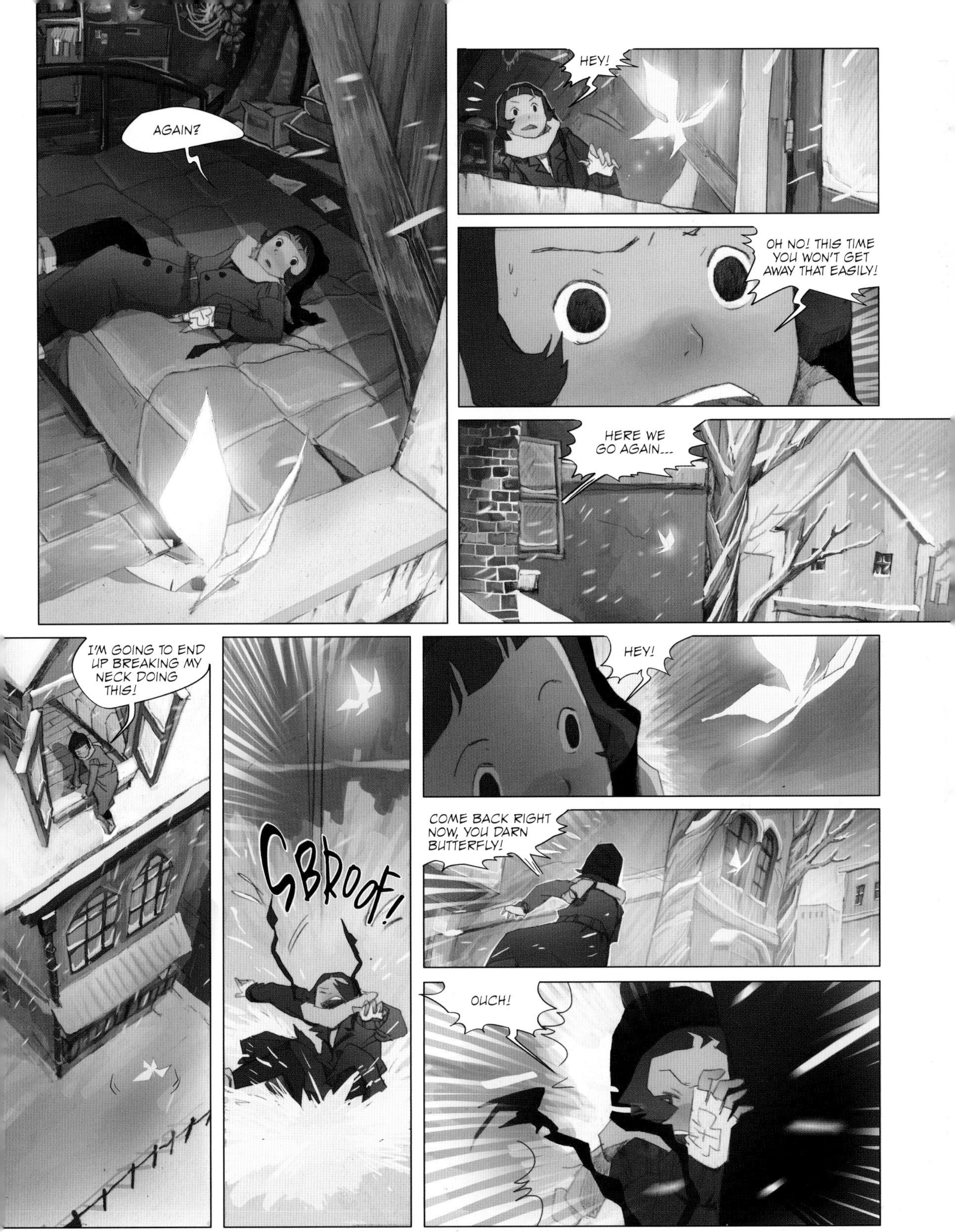

AGAIN?
HEY!
OH NO! THIS TIME YOU WON'T GET AWAY THAT EASILY!
HERE WE GO AGAIN...
I'M GOING TO END UP BREAKING MY NECK DOING THIS!
SBROOF!
HEY!
COME BACK RIGHT NOW, YOU DARN BUTTERFLY!
OUCH!

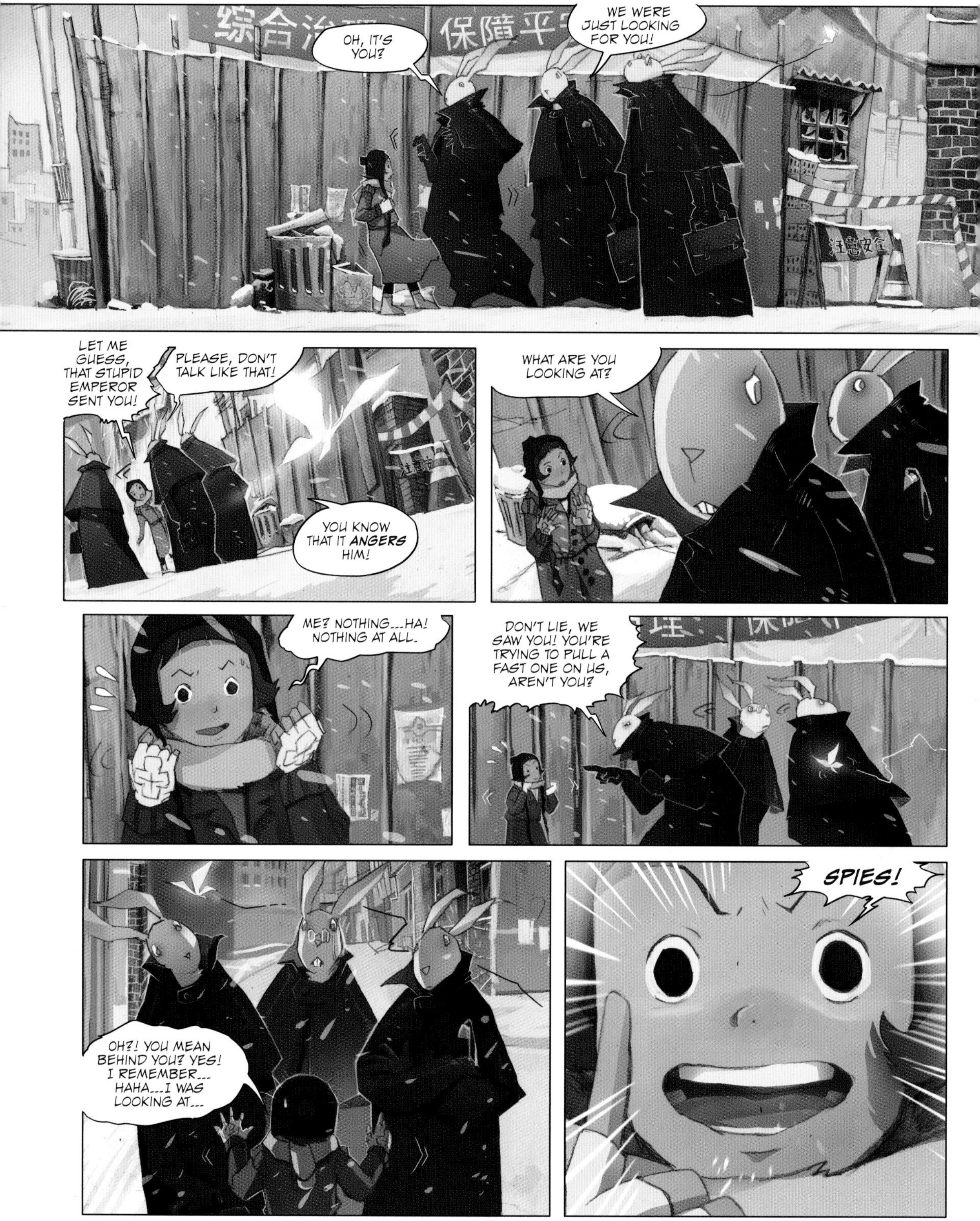

OH, IT'S YOU?
WE WERE JUST LOOKING FOR YOU!
注意安全
LET ME GUESS, THAT STUPID EMPEROR SENT YOU!
PLEASE, DON'T TALK LIKE THAT!
YOU KNOW THAT IT **ANGERS** HIM!
WHAT ARE YOU LOOKING AT?
ME? NOTHING... HA! NOTHING AT ALL.
DON'T LIE, WE SAW YOU! YOU'RE TRYING TO PULL A FAST ONE ON US, AREN'T YOU?
OH?! YOU MEAN BEHIND YOU? YES! I REMEMBER... HAHA... I WAS LOOKING AT...
SPIES!

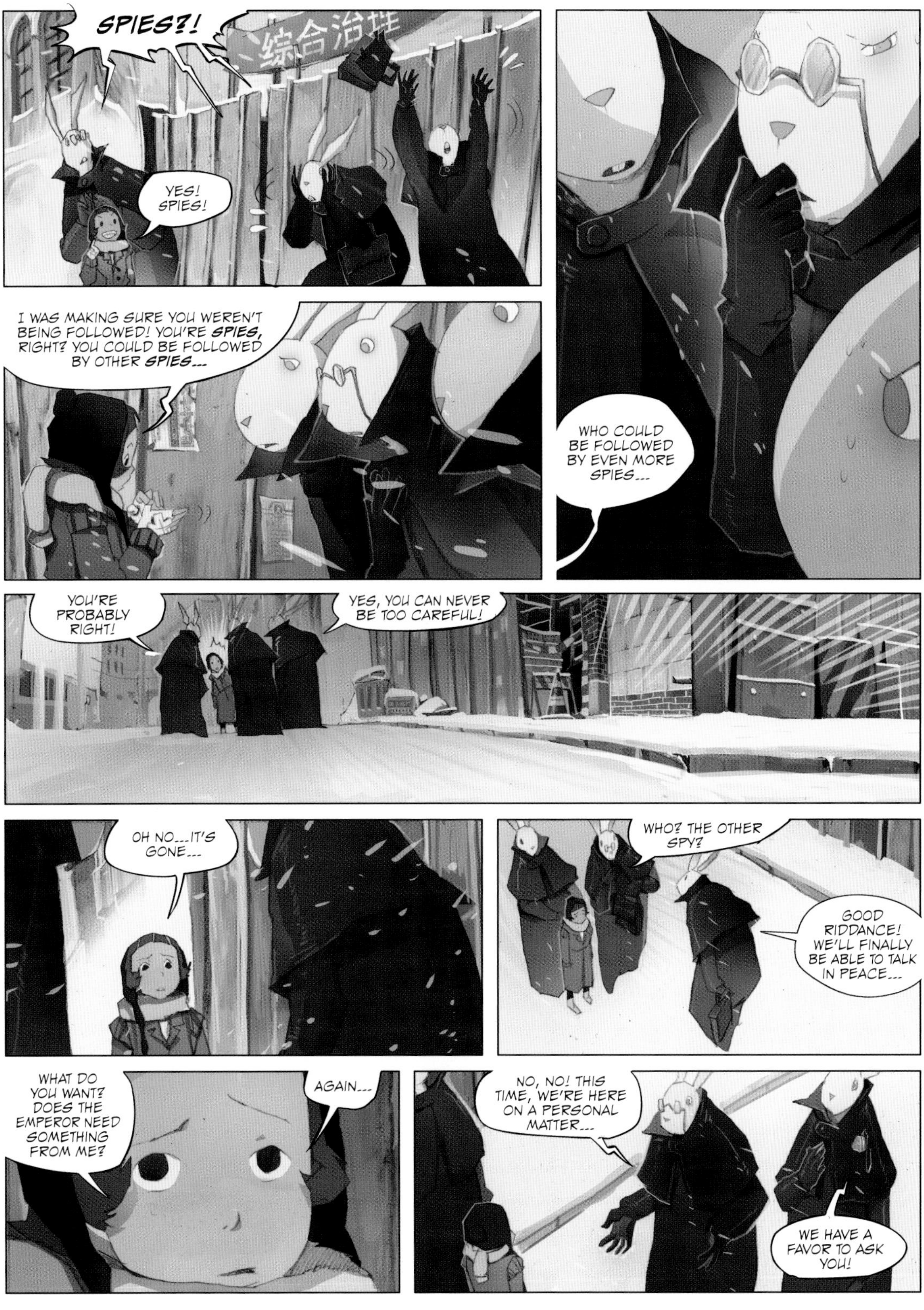
SPIES?!
YES! SPIES!
综合治理
I WAS MAKING SURE YOU WEREN'T BEING FOLLOWED! YOU'RE SPIES, RIGHT? YOU COULD BE FOLLOWED BY OTHER SPIES...
WHO COULD BE FOLLOWED BY EVEN MORE SPIES...
YOU'RE PROBABLY RIGHT!
YES, YOU CAN NEVER BE TOO CAREFUL!
OH NO...IT'S GONE...
WHO? THE OTHER SPY?
GOOD RIDDANCE! WE'LL FINALLY BE ABLE TO TALK IN PEACE...
WHAT DO YOU WANT? DOES THE EMPEROR NEED SOMETHING FROM ME?
AGAIN...
NO, NO! THIS TIME, WE'RE HERE ON A PERSONAL MATTER...
WE HAVE A FAVOR TO ASK YOU!

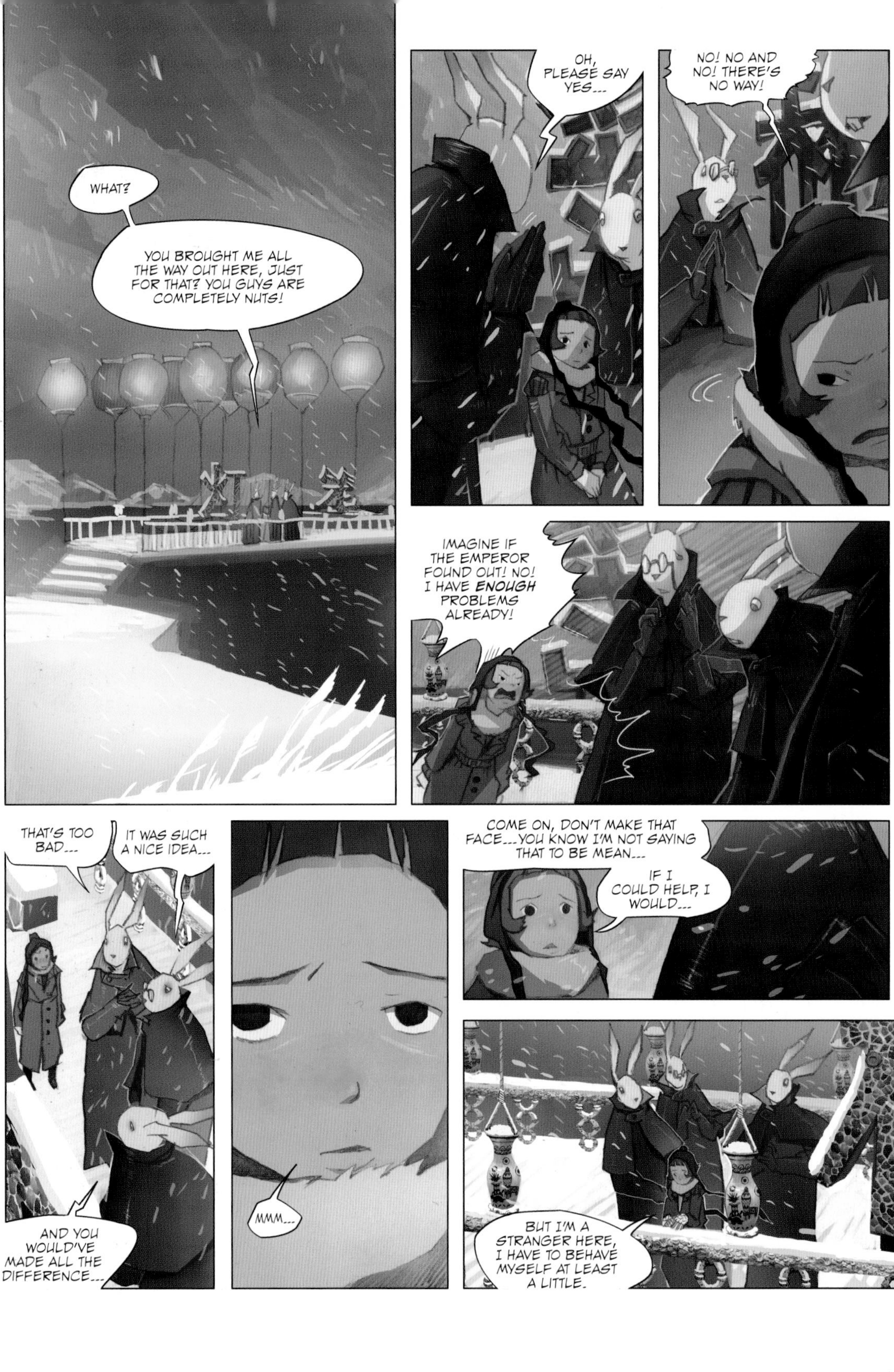
WHAT?
YOU BROUGHT ME ALL THE WAY OUT HERE, JUST FOR THAT? YOU GUYS ARE COMPLETELY NUTS!
OH, PLEASE SAY YES...
NO! NO AND NO! THERE'S NO WAY!
IMAGINE IF THE EMPEROR FOUND OUT! NO! I HAVE ENOUGH PROBLEMS ALREADY!
THAT'S TOO BAD...
IT WAS SUCH A NICE IDEA...
AND YOU WOULD'VE MADE ALL THE DIFFERENCE...
MMM...
COME ON, DON'T MAKE THAT FACE... YOU KNOW I'M NOT SAYING THAT TO BE MEAN...
IF I COULD HELP, I WOULD...
BUT I'M A STRANGER HERE, I HAVE TO BEHAVE MYSELF AT LEAST A LITTLE.

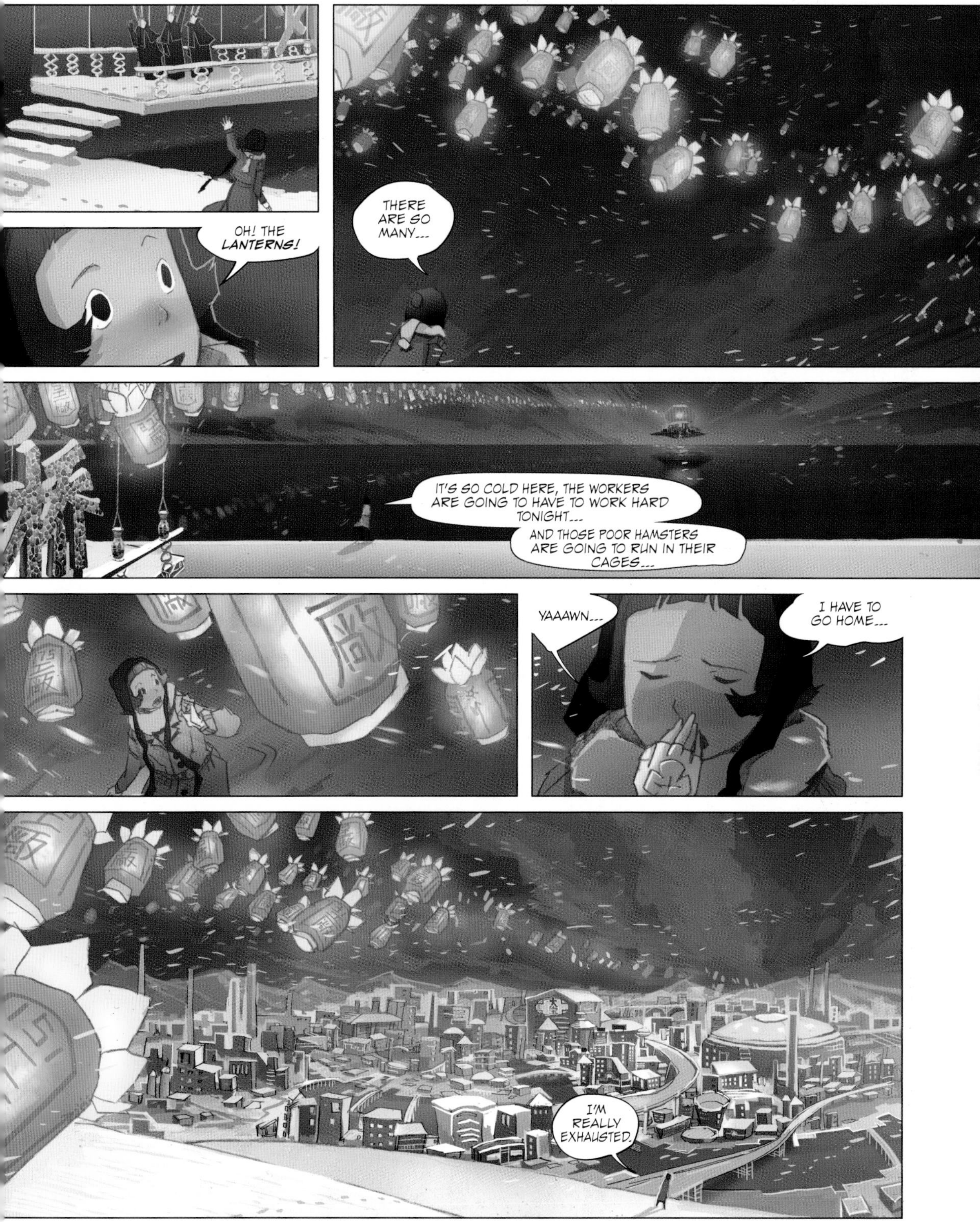
OH! THE LANTERNS!
THERE ARE SO MANY...
IT'S SO COLD HERE, THE WORKERS ARE GOING TO HAVE TO WORK HARD TONIGHT...
AND THOSE POOR HAMSTERS ARE GOING TO RUN IN THEIR CAGES...
YAAAWN...
I HAVE TO GO HOME...
I'M REALLY EXHAUSTED.

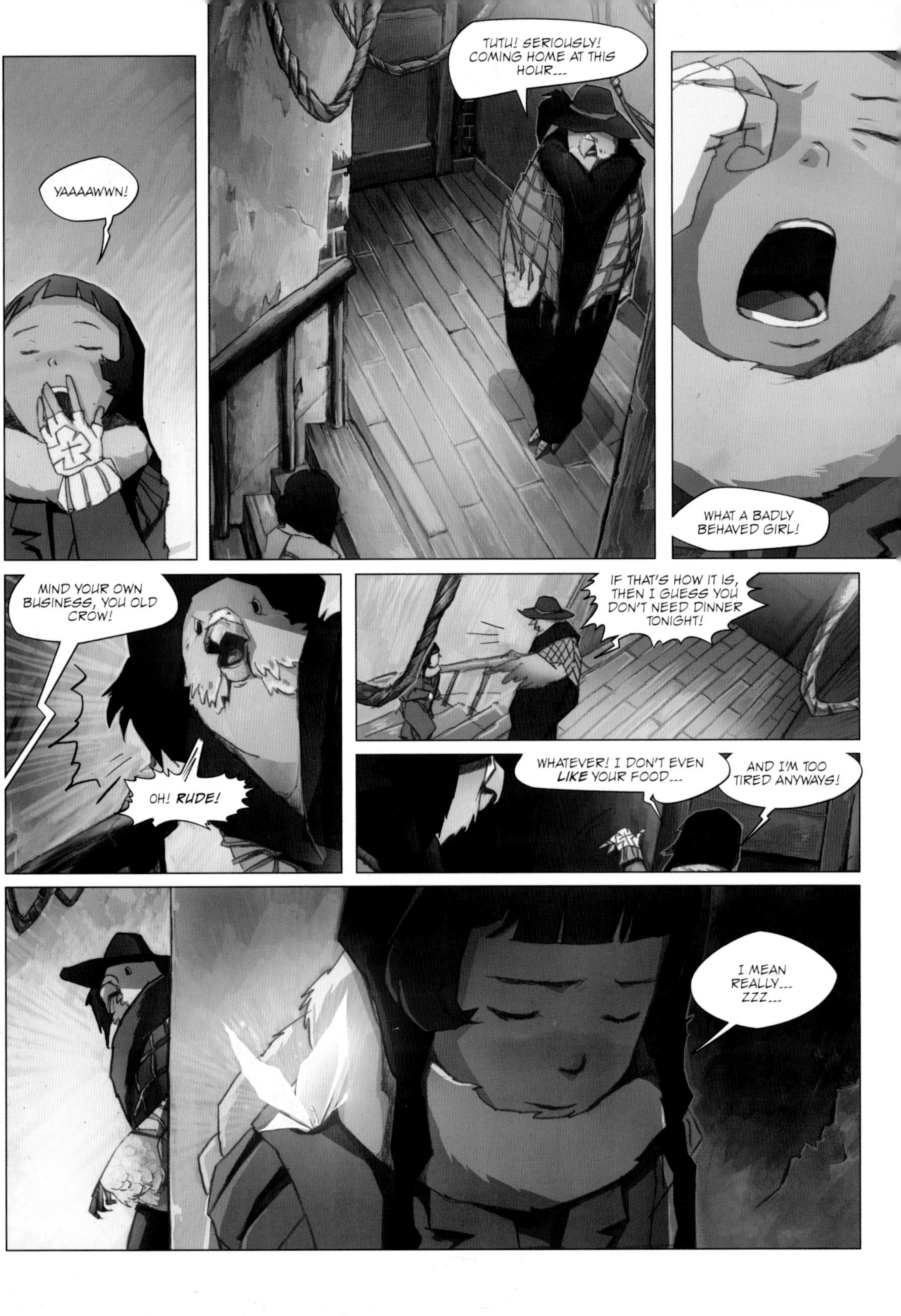
YAAAAWWN!
TUTU! SERIOUSLY! COMING HOME AT THIS HOUR...
WHAT A BADLY BEHAVED GIRL!
MIND YOUR OWN BUSINESS, YOU OLD CROW!
OH! **RUDE!**
IF THAT'S HOW IT IS, THEN I GUESS YOU DON'T NEED DINNER TONIGHT!
WHATEVER! I DON'T EVEN **LIKE** YOUR FOOD...
AND I'M TOO TIRED ANYWAYS!
I MEAN REALLY... ZZZ...

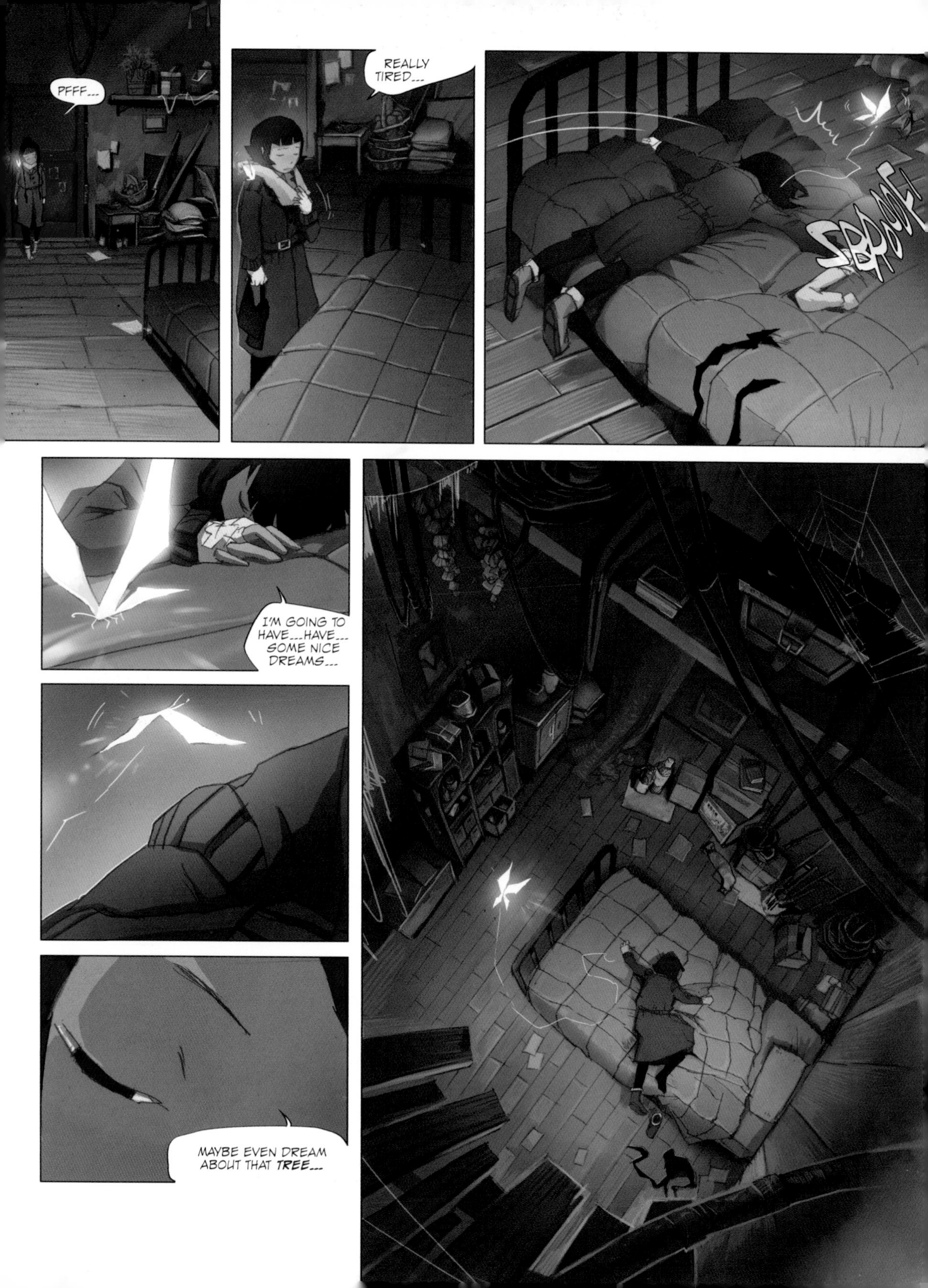
PFFF...
REALLY TIRED...
SBROOF!
I'M GOING TO HAVE...HAVE... SOME NICE DREAMS...
MAYBE EVEN DREAM ABOUT THAT *TREE*...

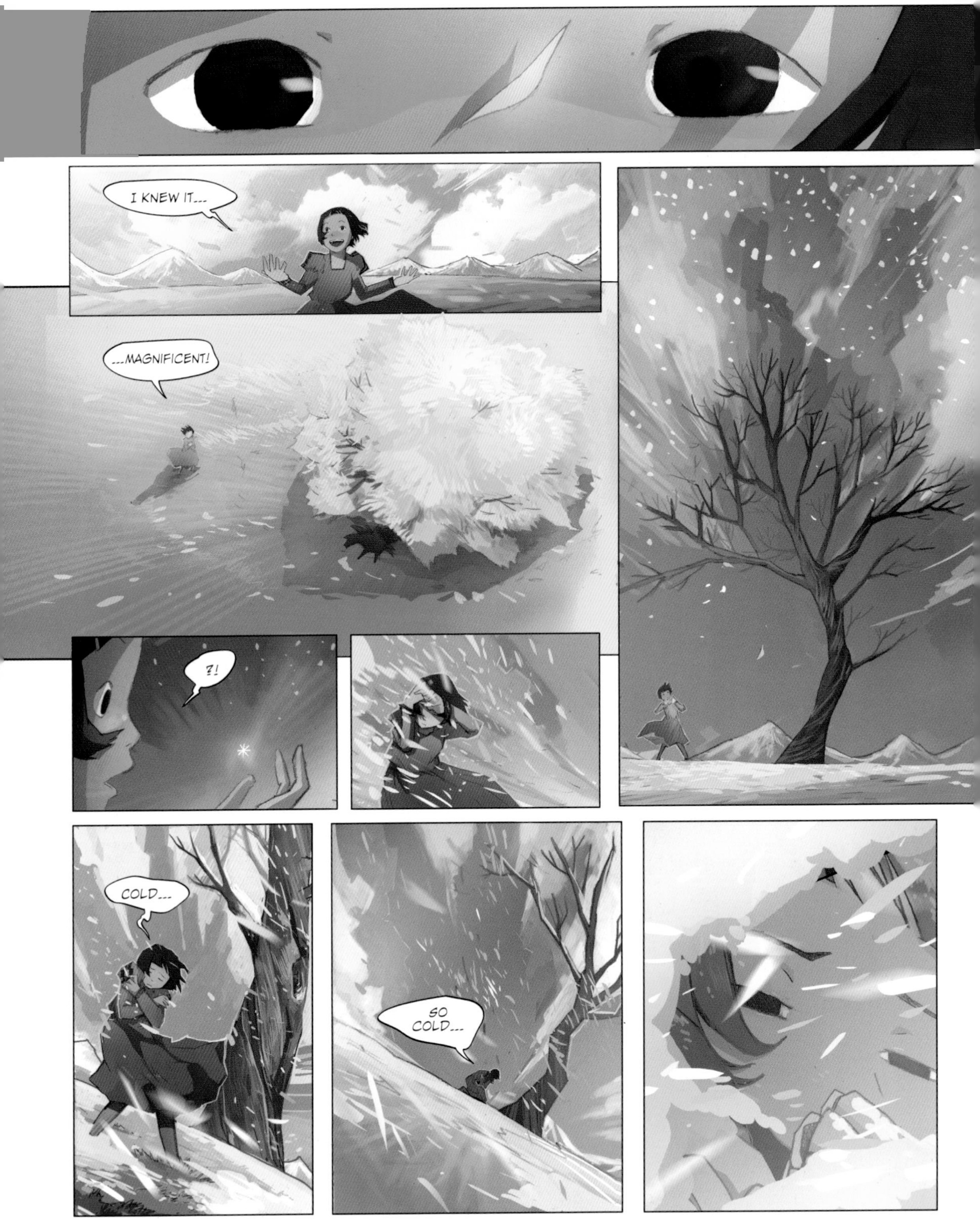
I KNEW IT...
...MAGNIFICENT!
?!
COLD...
SO COLD...

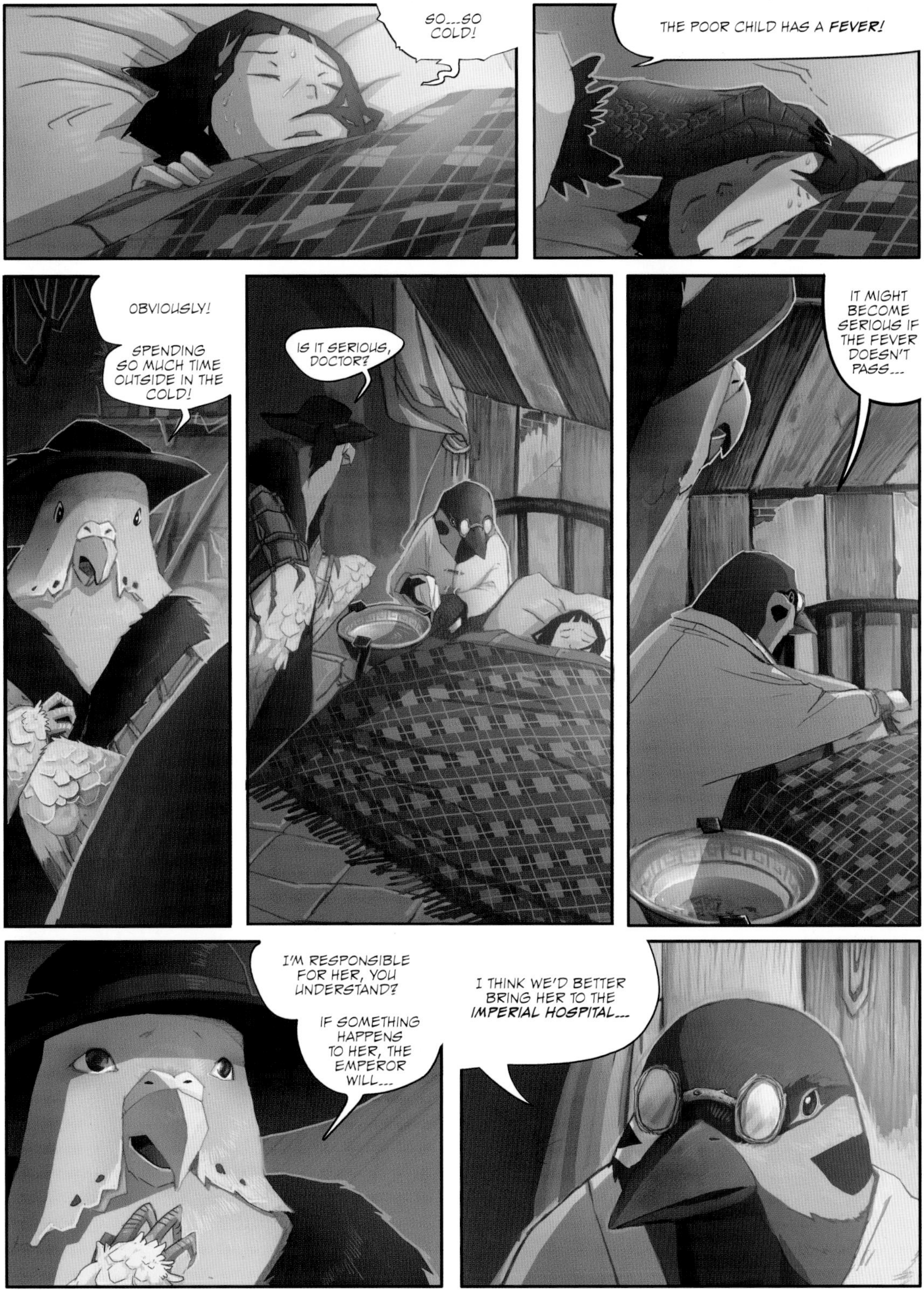
SO... SO COLD!
THE POOR CHILD HAS A FEVER!
OBVIOUSLY!
SPENDING SO MUCH TIME OUTSIDE IN THE COLD!
IS IT SERIOUS, DOCTOR?
IT MIGHT BECOME SERIOUS IF THE FEVER DOESN'T PASS...
I'M RESPONSIBLE FOR HER, YOU UNDERSTAND?
IF SOMETHING HAPPENS TO HER, THE EMPEROR WILL...
I THINK WE'D BETTER BRING HER TO THE IMPERIAL HOSPITAL...

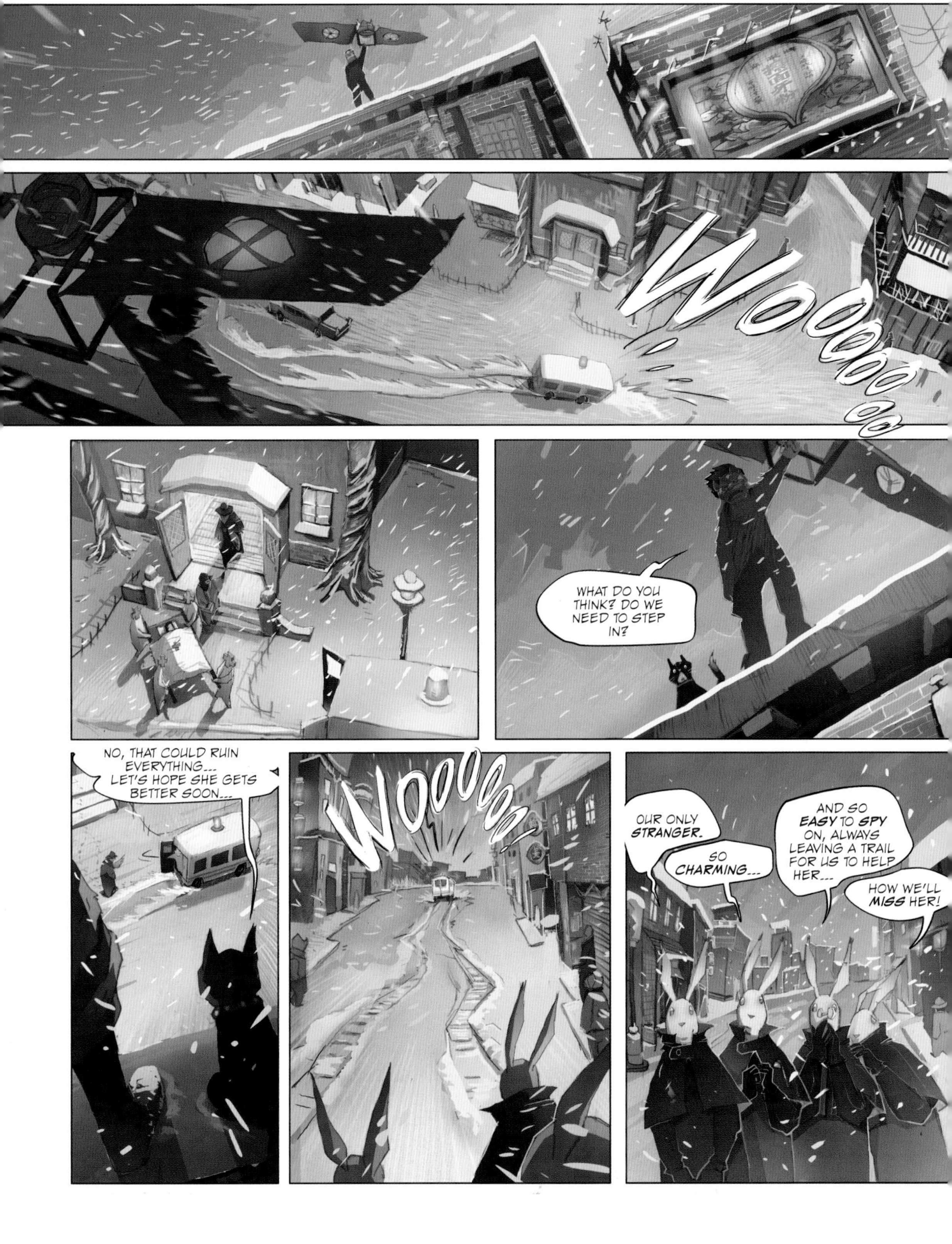
WOOOOOOO
WHAT DO YOU THINK? DO WE NEED TO STEP IN?
NO, THAT COULD RUIN EVERYTHING... LET'S HOPE SHE GETS BETTER SOON...
WOOOOOO!
OUR ONLY STRANGER.
SO CHARMING...
AND SO EASY TO SPY ON, ALWAYS LEAVING A TRAIL FOR US TO HELP HER...
HOW WE'LL MISS HER!

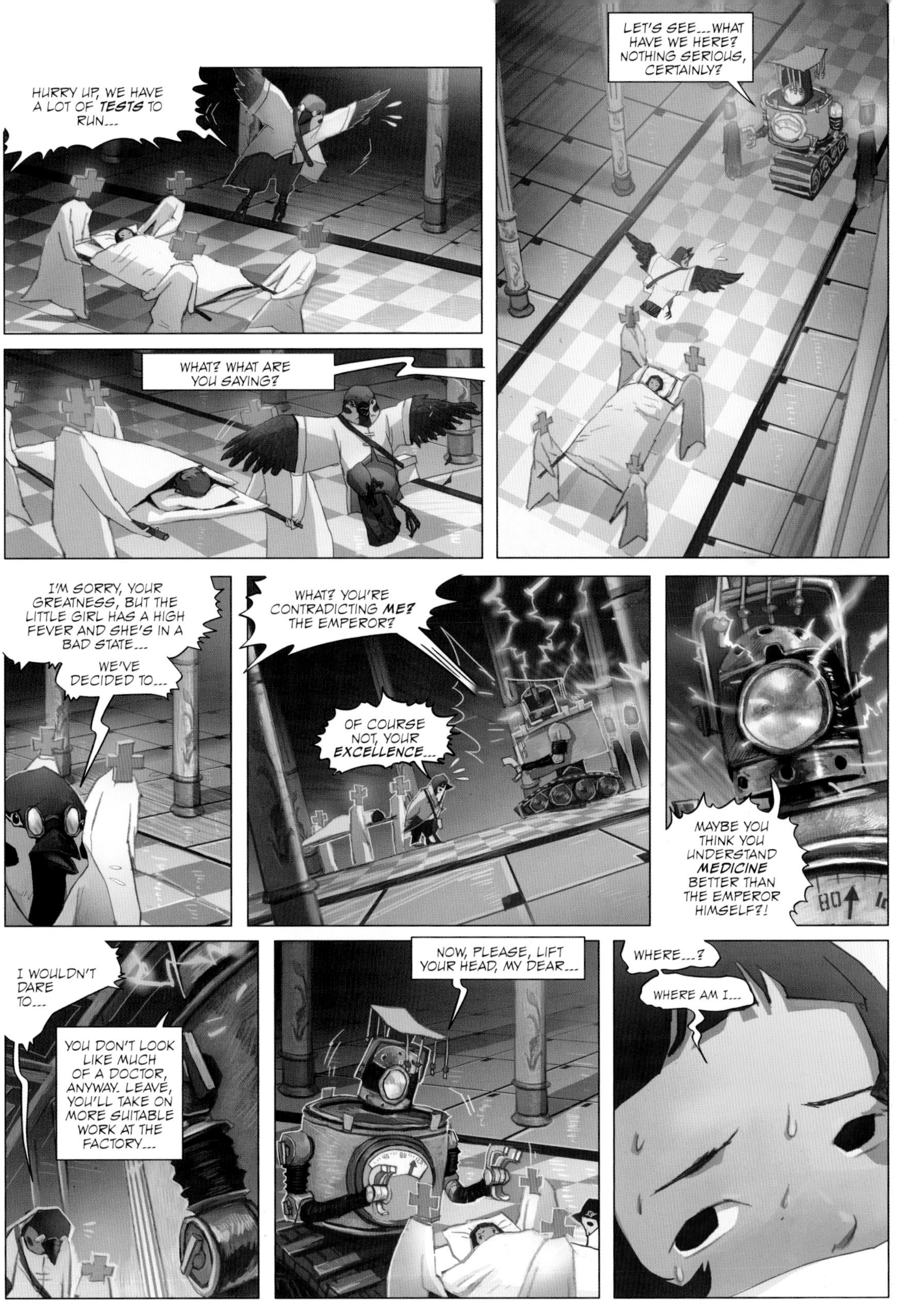
HURRY UP, WE HAVE A LOT OF TESTS TO RUN...
WHAT? WHAT ARE YOU SAYING?
LET'S SEE... WHAT HAVE WE HERE? NOTHING SERIOUS, CERTAINLY?
I'M SORRY, YOUR GREATNESS, BUT THE LITTLE GIRL HAS A HIGH FEVER AND SHE'S IN A BAD STATE...
WE'VE DECIDED TO...
WHAT? YOU'RE CONTRADICTING ME? THE EMPEROR?
OF COURSE NOT, YOUR EXCELLENCE...
MAYBE YOU THINK YOU UNDERSTAND MEDICINE BETTER THAN THE EMPEROR HIMSELF?!
I WOULDN'T DARE TO...
YOU DON'T LOOK LIKE MUCH OF A DOCTOR, ANYWAY. LEAVE, YOU'LL TAKE ON MORE SUITABLE WORK AT THE FACTORY...
NOW, PLEASE, LIFT YOUR HEAD, MY DEAR...
WHERE...?
WHERE AM I...

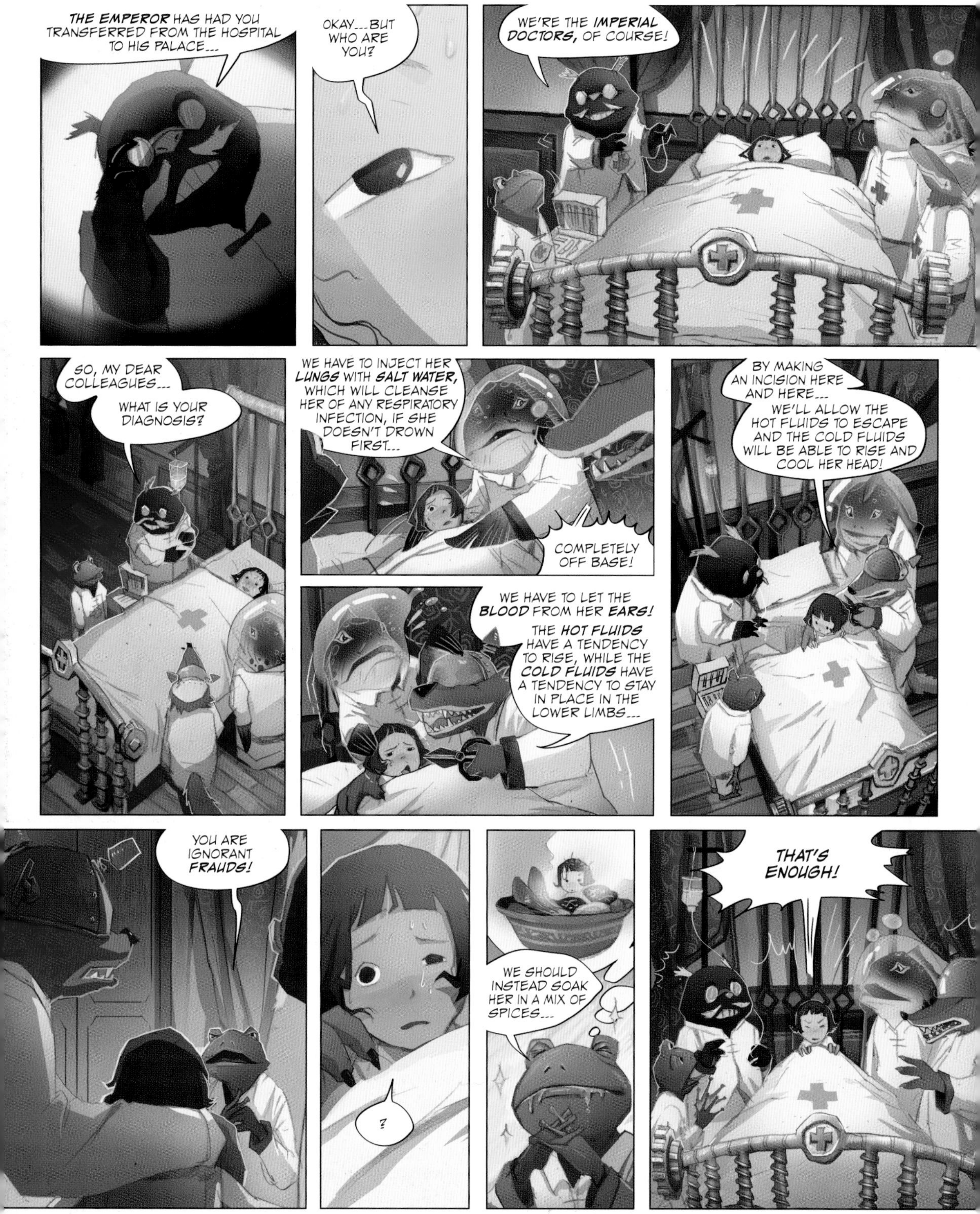
THE EMPEROR HAS HAD YOU TRANSFERRED FROM THE HOSPITAL TO HIS PALACE...
OKAY... BUT WHO ARE YOU?
WE'RE THE IMPERIAL DOCTORS, OF COURSE!
SO, MY DEAR COLLEAGUES...
WHAT IS YOUR DIAGNOSIS?
WE HAVE TO INJECT HER LUNGS WITH SALT WATER, WHICH WILL CLEANSE HER OF ANY RESPIRATORY INFECTION, IF SHE DOESN'T DROWN FIRST...
COMPLETELY OFF BASE!
WE HAVE TO LET THE BLOOD FROM HER EARS!
THE HOT FLUIDS HAVE A TENDENCY TO RISE, WHILE THE COLD FLUIDS HAVE A TENDENCY TO STAY IN PLACE IN THE LOWER LIMBS...
BY MAKING AN INCISION HERE AND HERE...
WE'LL ALLOW THE HOT FLUIDS TO ESCAPE AND THE COLD FLUIDS WILL BE ABLE TO RISE AND COOL HER HEAD!
YOU ARE IGNORANT FRAUDS!
?
WE SHOULD INSTEAD SOAK HER IN A MIX OF SPICES...
THAT'S ENOUGH!

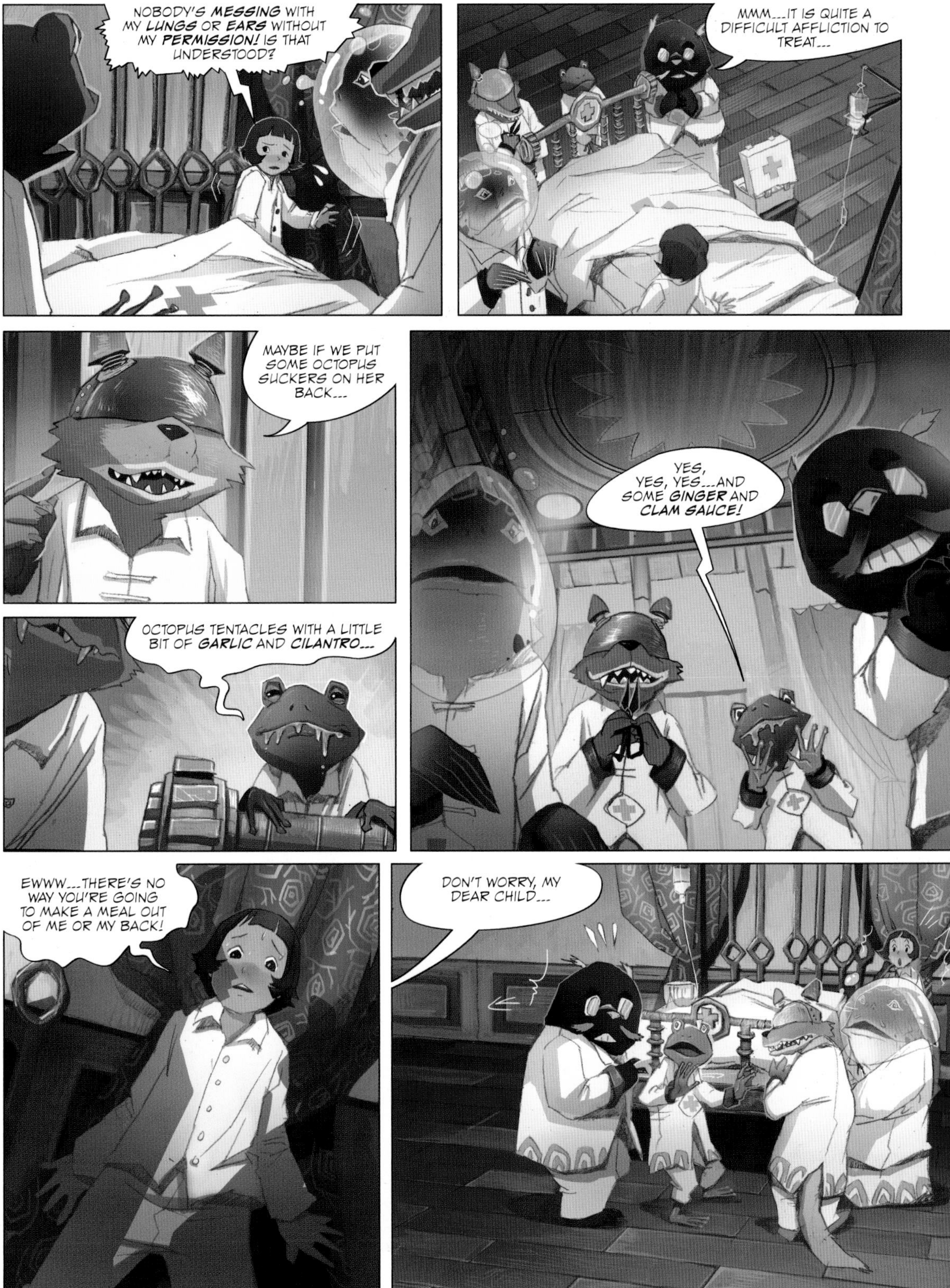
NOBODY'S MESSING WITH MY LUNGS OR EARS WITHOUT MY PERMISSION! IS THAT UNDERSTOOD?
MMM...IT IS QUITE A DIFFICULT AFFLICTION TO TREAT...
MAYBE IF WE PUT SOME OCTOPUS SUCKERS ON HER BACK...
OCTOPUS TENTACLES WITH A LITTLE BIT OF GARLIC AND CILANTRO...
YES, YES, YES...AND SOME GINGER AND CLAM SAUCE!
EWWW...THERE'S NO WAY YOU'RE GOING TO MAKE A MEAL OUT OF ME OR MY BACK!
DON'T WORRY, MY DEAR CHILD...

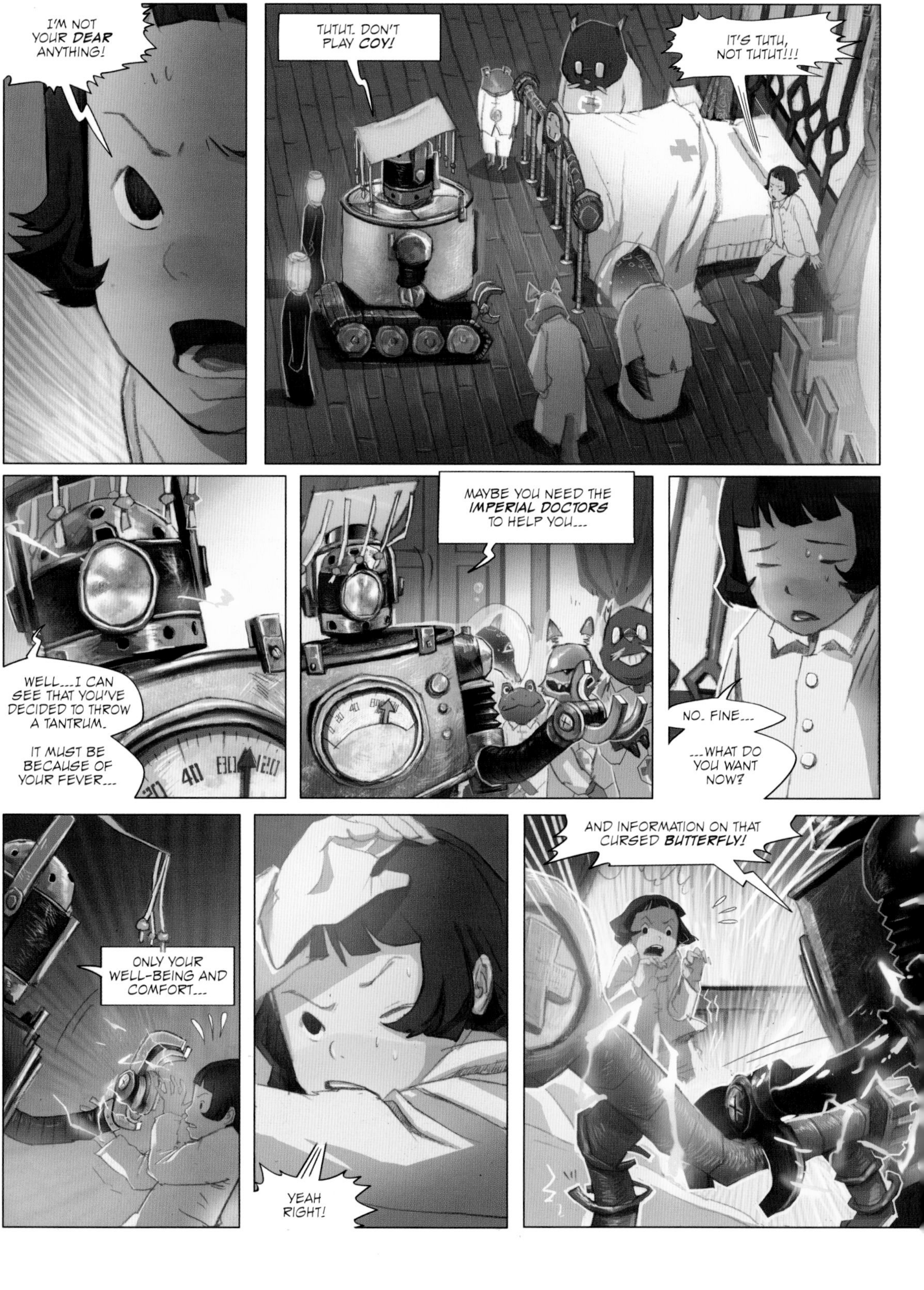
I'M NOT YOUR DEAR ANYTHING!
TUTUT. DON'T PLAY COY!
IT'S TUTU, NOT TUTUT!!!
WELL... I CAN SEE THAT YOU'VE DECIDED TO THROW A TANTRUM.
IT MUST BE BECAUSE OF YOUR FEVER...
MAYBE YOU NEED THE IMPERIAL DOCTORS TO HELP YOU...
NO. FINE...
...WHAT DO YOU WANT NOW?
ONLY YOUR WELL-BEING AND COMFORT...
YEAH RIGHT!
AND INFORMATION ON THAT CURSED BUTTERFLY!

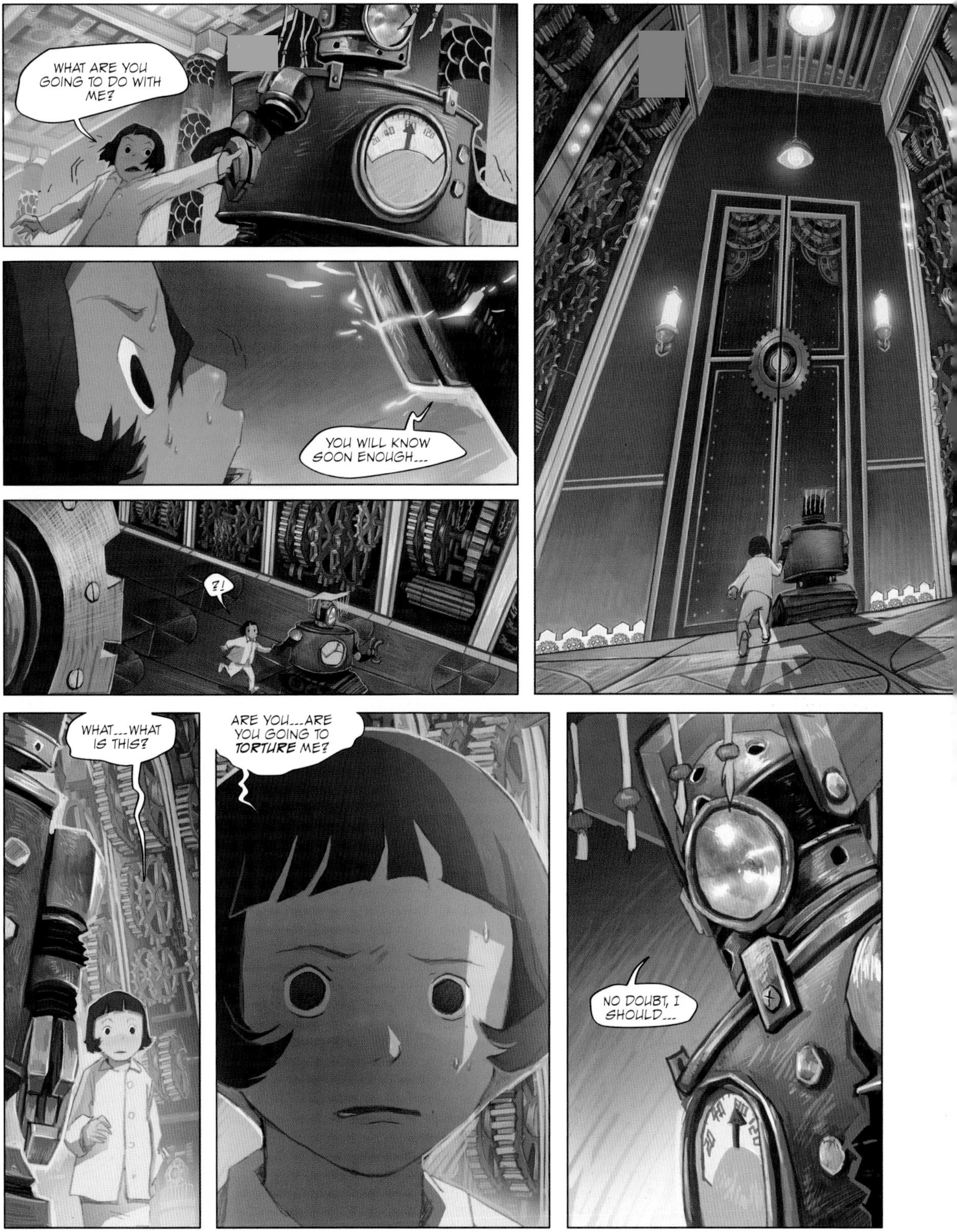
WHAT ARE YOU GOING TO DO WITH ME?
YOU WILL KNOW SOON ENOUGH...
?!
WHAT... WHAT IS THIS?
ARE YOU... ARE YOU GOING TO *TORTURE* ME?
NO DOUBT, I SHOULD...

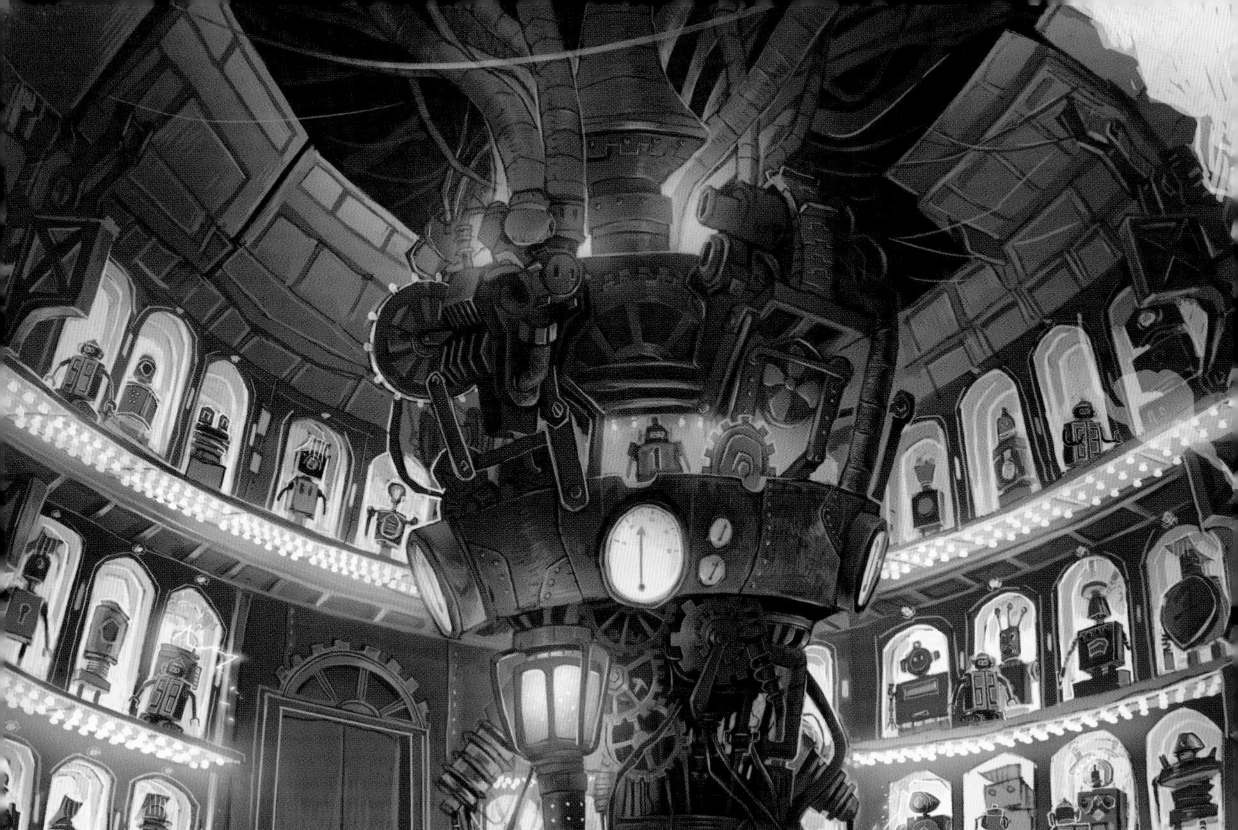
未开启
WOW...

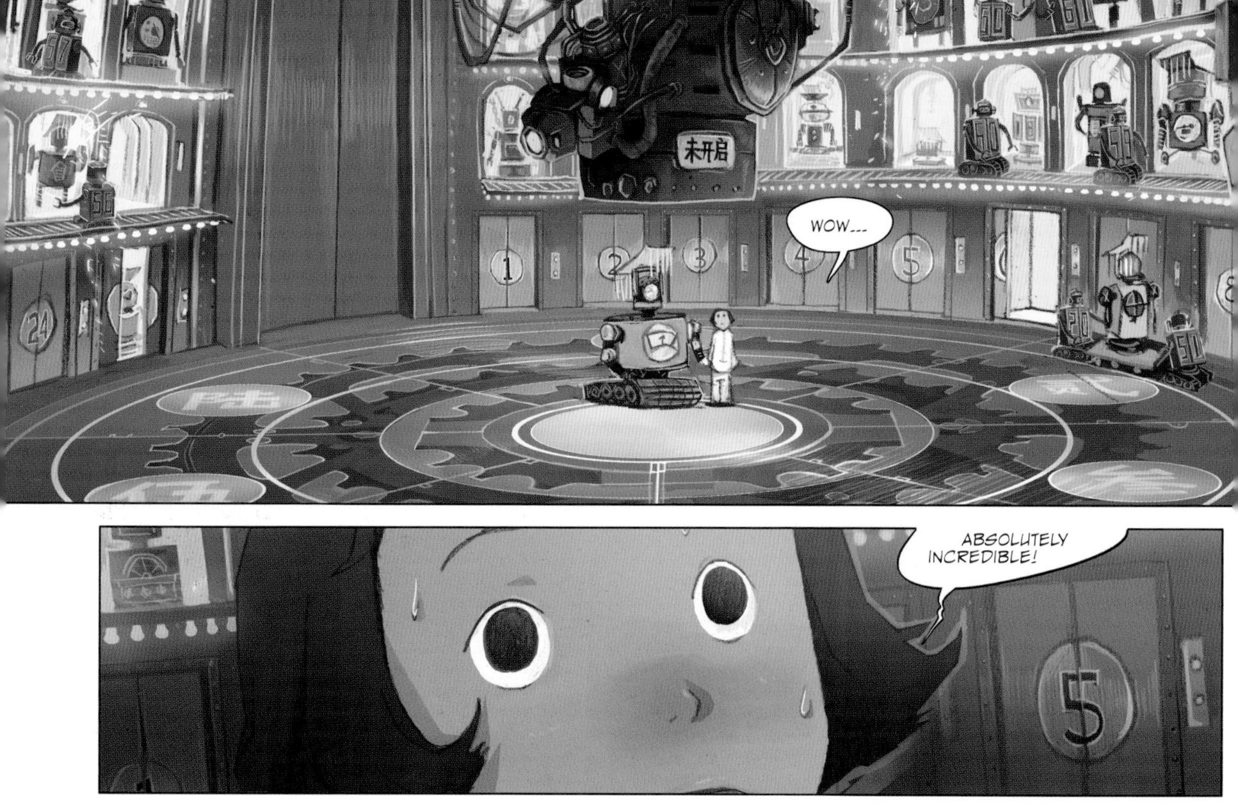
ABSOLUTELY INCREDIBLE!

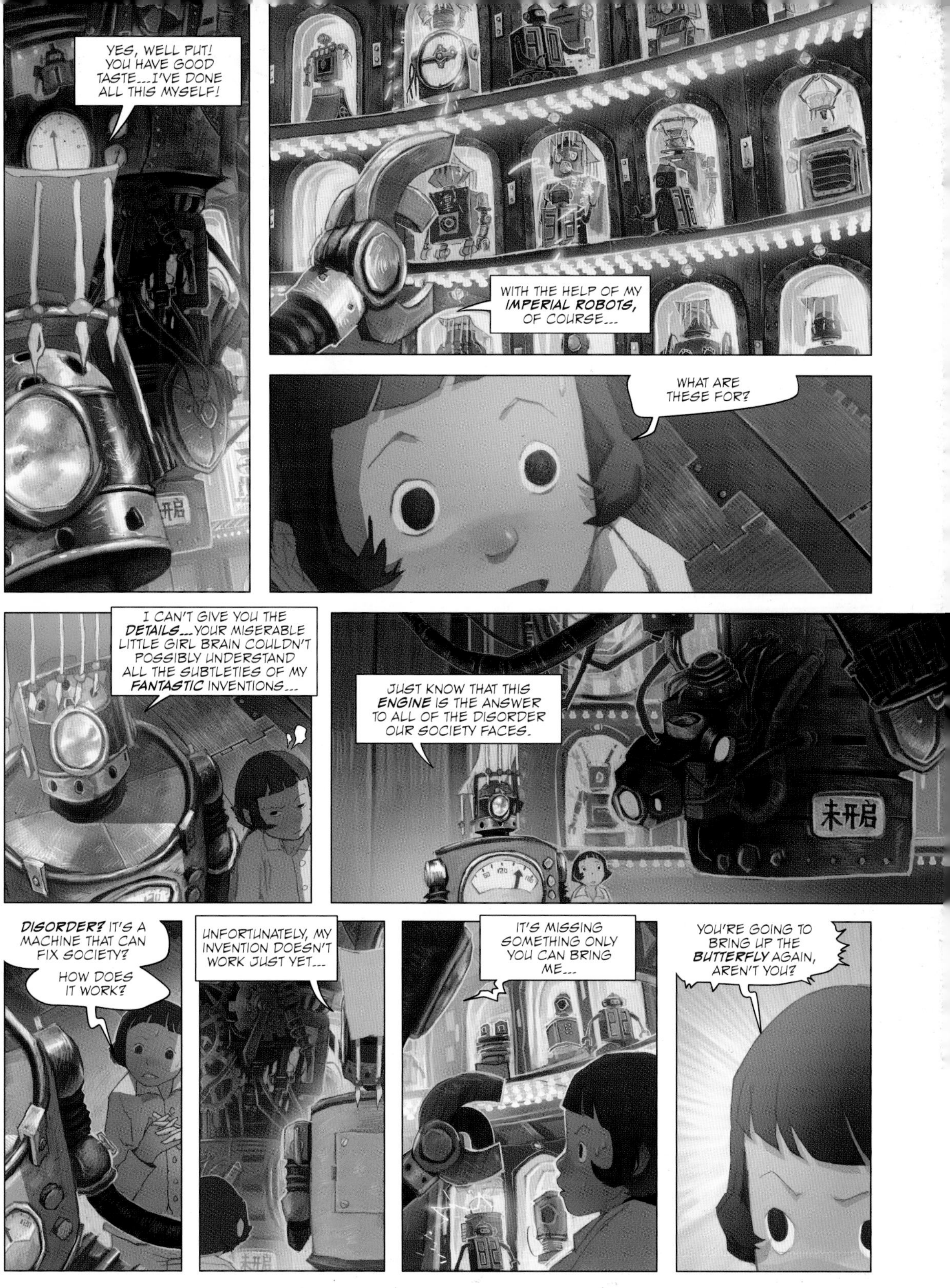
YES, WELL PUT! YOU HAVE GOOD TASTE... I'VE DONE ALL THIS MYSELF!
WITH THE HELP OF MY IMPERIAL ROBOTS, OF COURSE...
WHAT ARE THESE FOR?
I CAN'T GIVE YOU THE DETAILS... YOUR MISERABLE LITTLE GIRL BRAIN COULDN'T POSSIBLY UNDERSTAND ALL THE SUBTLETIES OF MY FANTASTIC INVENTIONS...
JUST KNOW THAT THIS ENGINE IS THE ANSWER TO ALL OF THE DISORDER OUR SOCIETY FACES.
未开启
DISORDER? IT'S A MACHINE THAT CAN FIX SOCIETY?
HOW DOES IT WORK?
UNFORTUNATELY, MY INVENTION DOESN'T WORK JUST YET...
IT'S MISSING SOMETHING ONLY YOU CAN BRING ME...
YOU'RE GOING TO BRING UP THE BUTTERFLY AGAIN, AREN'T YOU?

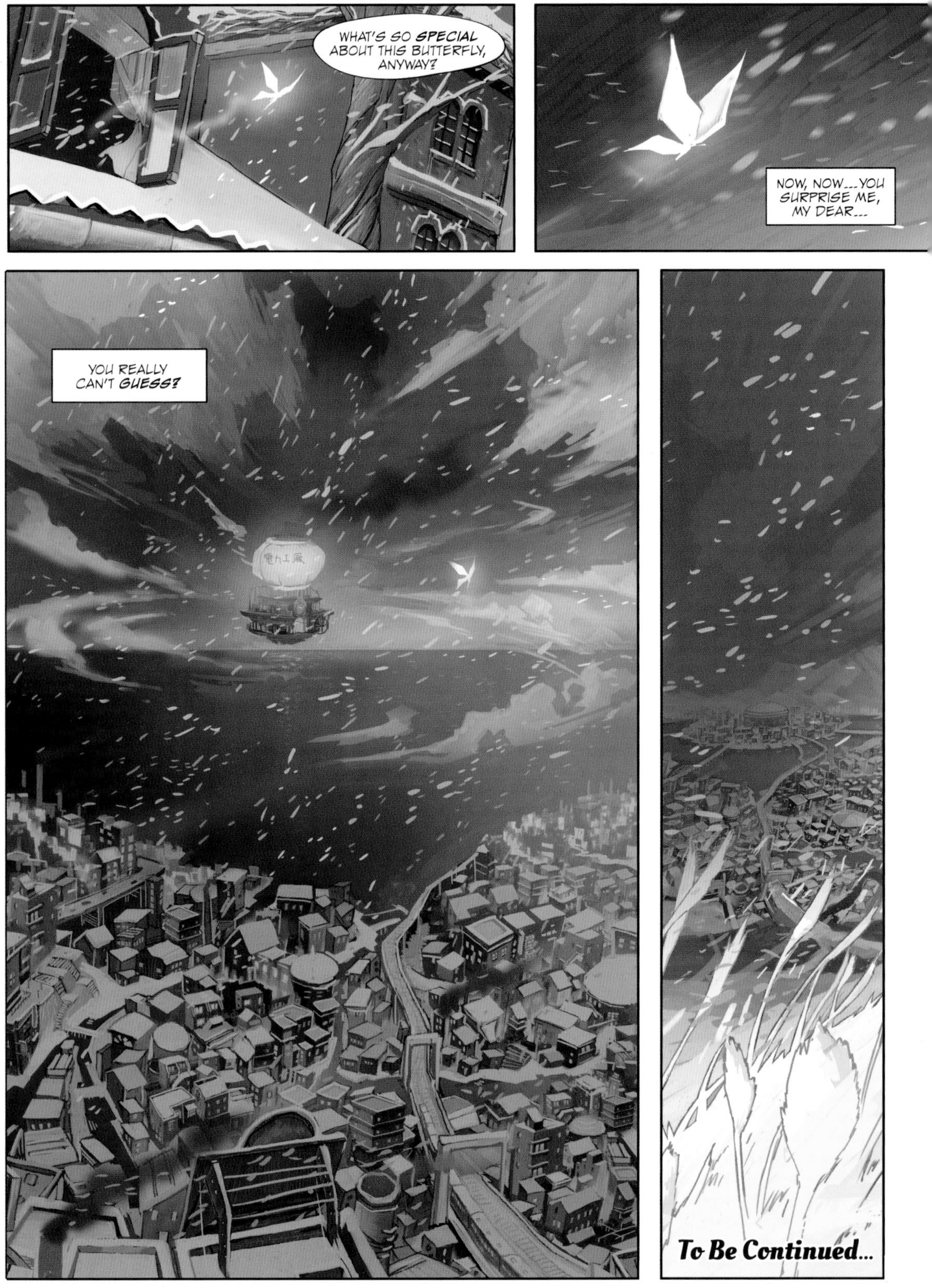
WHAT'S SO **SPECIAL** ABOUT THIS BUTTERFLY, ANYWAY?
NOW, NOW... YOU SURPRISE ME, MY DEAR...
YOU REALLY CAN'T **GUESS?**
To Be Continued...

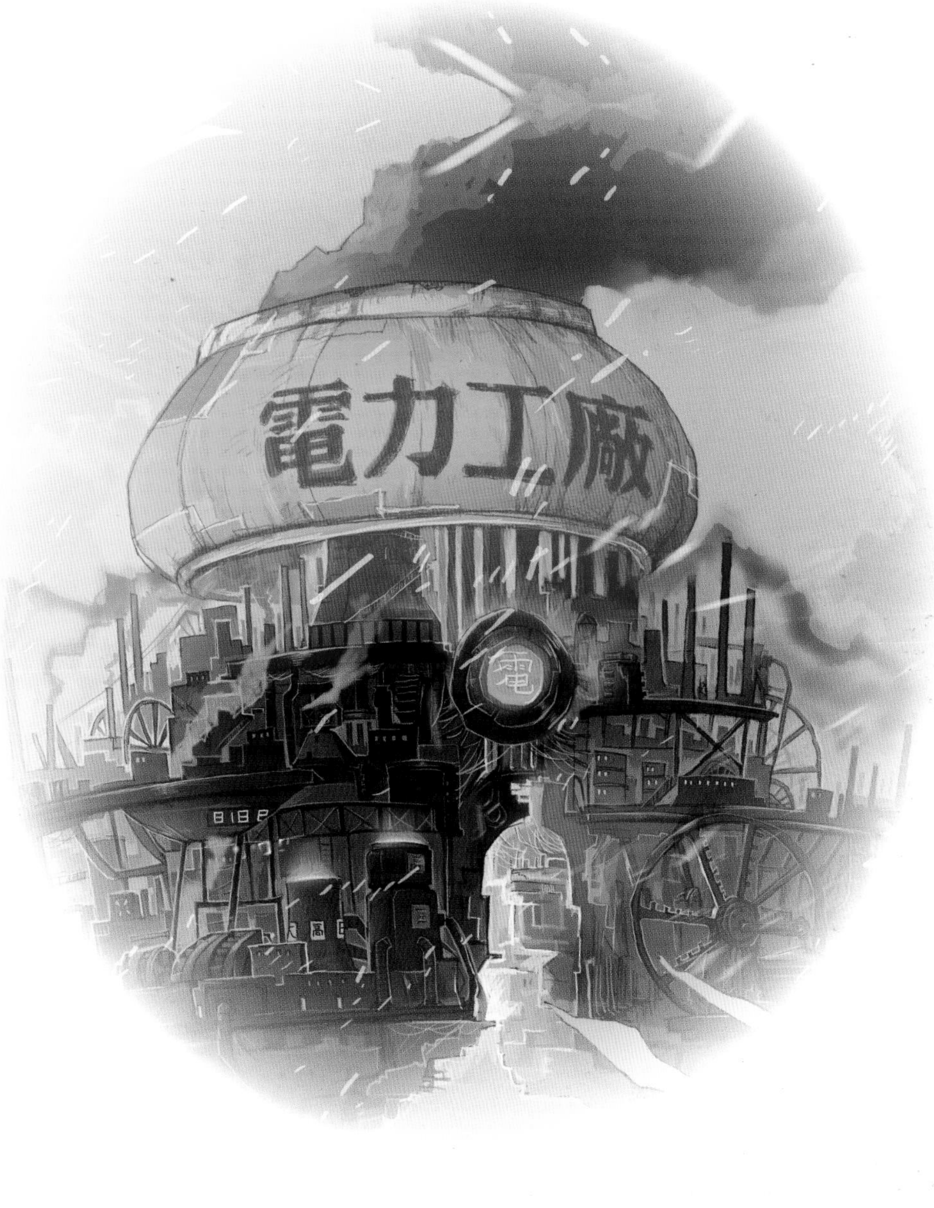
電力工廠
電

Richard Marazano

Richard Marazano is a French cartoonist and writer who studied physics and astrophysics before enrolling at the Fine Arts school in Angoulême. An accomplished comic artist in his own right, he is best known for his writing for other artists. He has written almost thirty books, including the multiple-award-winning series *Cuervos* and *The Chimpanzee Complex*.

Luo Yin

Luo Yin was born in Zhengzhou in the Chinese province of Henan. She graduated from the Beijing Film Academy with a specialization in animation in 2006. She worked as a freelance animator in Beijing for four years. She has also made illustrations for numerous magazines and children's books, including the Chinese and English bilingual children's book, *The Story of Little Penguin* and *Small Glacier*.